BLOODY GENIUS

John Sandford is the pseudonym for the Pulitzer Prize-winning journalist John Camp. He is the author of twenty-nine Prey novels, most recently *Neon Prey*, four Kidd novels, twelve Virgil Flowers novels, and six other books, including three YA novels co-authored with his wife, Michele Cook.

Visit johnsandford.org or find him on Facebook.

ALSO BY JOHN SANDFORD

JOHN SANDFORD
BLOODY GENIUS

**SIMON &
SCHUSTER**

London · New York · Sydney · Toronto · New Delhi

A CBS COMPANY

First published in the United States by G. P. Putnam's Sons, 2019
An imprint of Penguin Random House LLC

First published in Great Britain by Simon & Schuster UK Ltd, 2019
A CBS COMPANY

This paperback edition published 2020

1 3 5 7 9 10 8 6 4 2

Simon & Schuster UK Ltd
1st Floor
222 Gray's Inn Road
London WC1X 8HB

Simon & Schuster Australia, Sydney
Simon & Schuster India, New Delhi

www.simonandschuster.co.uk
www.simonandschuster.com.au
www.simonandschuster.co.in

A CIP catalogue record for this book is available from the British Library

Paperback ISBN: 978-1-4711-8557-1
eBook ISBN: 978-1-4711-8556-4

Printed and bound in Great Britain by CPI Group (UK) Ltd, Croydon, CR0 4YY

BLOODY GENIUS

CHAPTER

ONE

Barthelemy Quill led his companion through the murk and up the library stairs toward his personal study carrel. Though Quill was normally restrained to the point of rigor mortis, she could hear him breathing, quick breaths, excited. They'd been there before, and the woman found the experience both weird and interesting. She was a step behind him, and lower, and she reached out and stroked his thigh.

But at the top of the stairs, Quill put out a hand, pressing it back against her chest, and whispered, "Shh. There's a light."

The library was never entirely dark, not even in the middle of the night, but there'd never before been a moving light. She could see one now, no brighter than an iPhone, dancing like a ghost through the bookshelves.

Not a security guard. It *was* an iPhone, she thought. Not the flashlight, but the much weaker screen light.

Quill moved away from her and closer to the light—he was

wearing gray dress slacks, a gray knit dress shirt, and a black sport coat, so he was basically invisible in the dark. The woman felt a chill crawl up her arms and she stepped sideways into the book stacks. She'd learned well the lesson of trusting her instincts about trouble. She turned a corner on one of the stacks and crouched, listening in the silence.

Then Quill's voice: "Hey! Hey! Where'd you get . . . I'm calling the police! You stay right where you're at."

Then a wet *Whack!* And, after a second, another. *Whack!* The sound was heavy and violent, as if delivered with a crowbar. The whacks were followed by a couple of bumps. And not another word from Quill.

The woman crunched herself up, made herself smaller, opened her mouth wide to silence her breathing, a trick she'd learned in another life while taking singing lessons. Like Quill, she'd dressed in dark clothing, as their entry into the library was unauthorized and possibly illegal. Before this moment, that had added another thrill to their clandestine meetings.

Now . . .

Something terrible had happened, she thought. After the whacks and subsequent bumps, there was a deep silence, as though the iPhone user were listening.

That was followed by shuffling noises, more bumps, a door closed and a locked turned, and then the weak iPhone light reappeared. She never saw the person with the phone but kept her arms over her face and her head down: faces shine in the dark, and eyes are attracted to eyes. She heard light footsteps fading away, risked a look up and saw the iPhone light disappearing around the corner toward the stairs.

The killer was just as stunned. Quill had come out of nowhere, as the killer stood by the open carrel door, laptop in hand. Quill's face had been twisted with anger. He'd shouted, "Hey! Hey!" and something else, then, "I'm calling the police!"

Quill'd turned away, and, without thinking, panicking, the killer had lifted the laptop computer and brought it down on Quill's head.

After the first blow, Quill had said, "Ah!" and gone down, and his forehead had hit the edge of the carrel desk and his head had turned. His gray eyes jerked to the assailant, but had already begun to dim, as he sank to his hands and knees. The killer swung the notebook again and this time Quill went flat on the floor.

The DreamBook Power P87 made an excellent weapon, not because of its Intel Xeon i7 processor, or its 64 gigs of RAM, or its high-definition display, but because it weighed more than twelve pounds and had sharp corners.

By comparison, an Irwin Tools fiberglass-handled general purpose claw hammer, an otherwise excellent weapon, weighs only sixteen ounces, a pound.

When the killer sank the computer into the back of Quill's head, the professor smacked the desk with his forehead, his head turned, and his eyes twisted toward his assailant, and he dropped to his hands and knees like a poleaxed ox, if oxen have hands and knees.

A blow followed, a downward chop like that of a guillotine blade. The later autopsy suggested the first blow had been sufficient enough to kill, if the assailant had been willing to wait a minute. He hadn't.

The second impact certainly finished the job, and Quill lay sprawled across the floor and partially under the carrel desk, leaking both blood and cerebrospinal fluid. Quill never felt much pain, only an awareness of the blows and his beginning to fall. The lights went out, and he dropped into a darkness deeper than any sleep.

The library carrel had been his own personal cubbyhole, renewed semester by semester over the years. Strictly speaking, that shouldn't have been the case, but Quill was rich and handsome and famous for his research into innovative therapies for spinal nerve injuries. So he got by with it. And it had become a go-to place for his late-night sexual assignations, away from all eyes.

The killer had a thousand thoughts raging through his head. Near the top, however, was: Get out! And: DNA! And: Fingerprints!

The library was nearly silent, broken only by the vague clicks and hums of any building at night with heaters and fans. The killer stood listening, then looked down at the body, licked his lips once, thinking. The laptop came with a soft plastic cover. He used it to wrap one of his hands and then dragged Quill's leg from the doorway into the carrel, where, with the door closed, the body couldn't be easily seen through the narrow translucent window.

His heart was pumping hard, he was breathing like a steam engine. He tried to calm himself, took a moment, stepped on something. The fob to Quill's BMW lay on the floor where he'd dropped it, along with his cell phone. The killer picked up the cell, the keys, and the murder weapon, took another moment to listen. As expected, the library was empty and dead silent: it closed at six o'clock, and he'd murdered Quill at the stroke of midnight.

The killer left the carrel at three minutes after midnight, pulled his black ball cap farther down over his eyes and tilted his head down to defeat any cameras. He locked the carrel door and started toward the stairs. The hair on the back of his neck suddenly bristled, like from the chill you'd get walking past a cemetery. He stopped. Was he alone? He listened, heard nothing. He walked slowly and quietly down the stairs to the first floor, creeping through it on his soft-soled running shoes, and out the door.

The river was right there. He went to the walkway running alongside it, stopped under a light to separate the professor's keys from their fob and threw the fob in the river. The keys went in his pocket; he might find a use for them.

He continued across a bridge to the other side, saw no one. He stopped to put the computer and its soft cover in his backpack. The cell phone went into a "Mission Darkness" Faraday bag with a see-through window, along with his own. Quill had begun making a call to 911 when he was killed, so the killer had access to the phone's operation and could keep it working with the occasional poke.

Back inside the library, Quill's companion waited, frozen in place, for what seemed like hours—maybe ten minutes. After the iPhone light disappeared, she had not heard another thing.

Taking a chance, she dug silently in her purse and found the switchblade she'd purchased in Iowa, where they were legal, as personal protection. She wrapped the knife in the tail of her jacket and pushed the button that popped open the razor-sharp four-and-seven-eighths-inch serrated blade, the mechanical un-latching muffled by the cloth.

She listened for another moment, then crawled down the aisle between the book stacks, got to her knees, then to her feet, and slipped over to the carrel. The door had a small, vertical-slit window, but with translucent glass.

She muttered, "Shit," and waited, and waited, listening, tried the door, but it was locked. She turned on her iPhone's flashlight and directed it down through the window but couldn't see anything at all through the cloudy pane. Nothing was moving inside.

Quill, she thought, might be dead. He was probably badly hurt, at the least. She should call the police; but she wasn't the type.

The thought held her for a moment. She didn't owe Quill. He'd brought her into this. If he was still alive, and survived, she could tell him that she ran away and never knew that he'd been hurt.

The decision made, she turned off the light and slipped through the library, her lips moving in a prayer that wasn't a prayer, because she didn't know any, but simply a *Please! Please! Please!* addressed to any god who might be tuned in. She made it down the stairs and out into the river air, the Mississippi curling away beneath the bridge with anything but innocence: it had seen more murders than any single man or woman ever would.

A half block from the library, the woman folded the knife but kept it in her hand, her thumb on the spring release. On the far side of the bridge, she was swallowed up by the night.

Because he was murdered on a Friday night and had no firm ap-pointments over the weekend, and missed only one day at the lab, Quill's body wasn't found until Tuesday, when an untoward odor began leaking under the carrel's locked door.

Definitely not coffee.

Inquiries were made, a second key was found, the door was opened, the cops were called.

Quill had lived alone since his third wife moved out. Neither of his first two wives, nor his estranged third, made any secret of the fact that they thoroughly disliked him.

A two-week investigation produced baffled cops. The cops didn't think they were baffled—not yet, anyway—but the *Star Tribune* and local television stations agreed that they were. And who do you believe, the cops or the mainstream media?

When no suspect had been produced after two weeks, Quill's well-connected sister, co-heir to their father's wildly successful company, Quill Micro-Sprockets, called her old friend and a major political donee, the governor of Minnesota.

The governor called the commissioner of the Department of Public Safety; the commissioner called the director of the Bureau of Criminal Apprehension; the BCA director called one of his supervisory agents; the supervisory agent, after a comprehensive course of vulgarity, obscenity, and profanity, made a call of his own.

At the end of the daisy chain was a Flowers.

CHAPTER

TWO

Virgil Flowers walked out of a café in Blue Earth, Minnesota, slightly bilious after a dinner of brown slices of beef and brown gravy over brown potatoes and dead green beans, coconut cream pie on the side, with a pointless Diet Coke. He had to quit all that; he knew it, but hadn't yet done it. He burped and the burp tasted . . . brown.

He'd taken three steps out the door before he noticed a motley group of twenty people standing in the parking lot, staring up at the sky to the south. When he turned to look, he saw the UFO.

There was no question about it, really.

The alien craft was obviously far away, but still appeared to be more than half the size of a full moon. It was motionless, hovering over the countryside like a polished dime, brilliantly lit, alternating gold and white light, almost as bright as the setting sun, and hard to look at without squinting.

A man dressed like a farmer, in mud-spattered jeans and muddier gum boots, said wisely, "It only *appears* to be motionless. It's probably a jumbo jet headed into the Twin Cities, flying low and right toward us. The sun's hitting it at just the right angle, and we're getting a reflection."

A pale woman with orange-blond dreadlocks, and the voice of a high school teacher, said, "No, it's not a jet. It's not moving. Line it up with that phone pole and you see it's not moving."

Virgil and the farmer edged sideways to line the UFO up with the telephone pole, and the woman was right; the UFO wasn't moving. The farmer exhaled heavily, and said, "Okay. I got nothin'."

More people were coming out of the café, attracted by the crowd in the parking lot.

A man in a plaid sport jacket said, "This could be the start of something big."

"Like an invasion," the dreadlocks lady said. She mimed a shudder. "Like in *Cloverfield*. You don't know exactly what it is, but it's coming and it's bad."

"Wouldn't they invade Washington or someplace like that?" a thin man asked. "Why would they invade Iowa?"

A jocko-looking guy said, "Not because they're recruiting for a pro football team," and he and a jocko friend, who was wearing a red University of Minnesota jacket, exchanged high fives.

Somebody said, "I left my camera at home. Wouldn't you know it? Probably see Bigfoot on the way back."

A short, fat mail carrier: "I saw a show where the aliens completely wasted LA, but it turned out everything was being controlled from one central bunker, and when the Army hit that, all the aliens' tanks and shit quit working."

"*Independence Day*," somebody said. "Where they nuked the mother ship, and then the fighters could get through the force fields?"

"No, I saw that one, too, but this was a different movie," the letter carrier said. "Ground troops in LA. Got the aliens with a bazooka or something."

A young man with black-rimmed glasses and slicked-back dark hair said, with the voice of authority, "*Battle: Los Angeles*. Thirty-five percent on the Tomatometer. The ground squad lit them up with a laser indicator so American fighters could target the alien HQ. Or maybe they called in the artillery, I don't precisely recall."

A young woman in a jewel-blue nylon letter jacket that matched her eyes said, "I hope they don't get us pregnant with those monster things like in *Aliens*. You know, that ate their way out of your womb when they hatched."

"I don't think that was *Aliens*," the authoritative young man said. "But just in case, maybe you oughta get a lotta good lovin' before they arrive."

Jewel Blue, the voice of scorn: "Dream on, Poindexter."

Virgil scratched his chin, momentarily at a loss. He was a tall, thin, blue-eyed man, with blond hair curling well down over his ears. He was wearing a canvas sport coat over a "Moon Taxi" T-shirt and jeans, with cowboy boots and a blue ball cap. As an official law enforcement officer of the state of Minnesota—L'Étoile du Nord—he thought he should do something about an alien invasion but didn't know exactly what. Call it in maybe?

He watched the thing for another moment, the flickering light, then walked over to his truck and dug out a pair of Canon 10-power image-stabilizing binoculars for a closer look. He saw a teardrop-shaped research balloon, several stories high, probably made of translucent polyethylene film. The low-angle sunlight was refracting through it. Most likely flown out of Iowa State University in Ames, he thought, which was more or less directly to the south.

"What do you see?" asked the woman with the dreadlocks.

"Weather balloon," Virgil said.

"That's what they always call it. A weather balloon. Next thing you know, you got an alien probe up your ass," somebody said.

Virgil passed the binoculars around, and they all looked. And then they all went home, disappointed. A UFO invasion would have been a hell of a lot more interesting than Spam 'n' Eggs for dinner. He took the binoculars back to his truck, noticed that he hadn't pulled the plug out of the boat, pulled it, and water started running down into the parking lot.

On his way out of Blue Earth, Virgil saw more groups of people standing in parking lots, watching the UFO. If he wasn't careful, he could wind up investigating a balloon.

Jon Duncan, a supervising agent at the Minnesota Bureau of Criminal Apprehension, called as Virgil crossed I-90, heading north on Highway 169. "We need you to investigate a murder."

"Where at?"

"University of Minnesota," Duncan said.

"What happened?" Virgil asked. "And why me?"

"A professor got murdered. Head bashed in," Duncan said.

"Again?"

"What?"

"A professor got murdered there two weeks ago," Virgil said. "Is this another one?"

"No, no. Same one," Duncan said. "Minneapolis Homicide is

working it, but they got nothing. Turns out the professor was the brother of this rich woman—Boopsie, or Bunny, or Biffy, something like that, last name Quill—who gave a lot of money to the governor's campaign. And you know what the governor thinks of you . . ."

"Ah, Jesus, I hate that guy," Virgil said. "Why doesn't he leave me alone?"

"Because you're good at doing favors for people like him and he's good at doing favors for rich people," Duncan said. "You brought it on yourself, with that school board thing."

With Virgil investigating, the state attorney general (at the time) had managed to send most of a school board to prison for murder; the attorney general, who'd actually done nothing but look good on TV, had taken full credit for the investigation and subsequent prosecution and was now the governor. He did have broad shoulders, a baritone voice, and extra-white teeth.

"You know it'll piss off the Minneapolis cops," Virgil said.

"Does that bother you?"

Virgil said, "Well, yeah, it does, as a matter of fact."

"Huh. Too bad. Doesn't bother me at all, since I won't be there," Duncan said. "Anyway, I have a name for you: Margaret Trane. A sergeant with Minneapolis Homicide. Known as Maggie. She's leading the investigation, coordinating with the campus cops."

"Don't know her," Virgil said. "She any good?"

"Can't say," Duncan said. "I judge women by their looks and the size of their breasts, not whether they're competent detectives." After a moment of empty air, Duncan blurted, "For Christ's sakes, don't tell anybody I said that. I mean, I was joking, okay? Big joke. Maybe a little insensitive . . ."

"I'm not recording you," Virgil said.

"Yeah, but somebody might be, you never know," Duncan said. Virgil could imagine him looking over his shoulder. "We have the most amazing surveillance stuff now, right here at BCA. I've been messing with it all week. Anyway, get your ass up here tomorrow. The governor would like to see this solved by the end of the week."

"It's already Thursday," Virgil said.

"Better get moving, then," Duncan said.

Virgil didn't want to go to the Twin Cities to mess around in a Minneapolis murder investigation. The cops there handled more murders in a year than the BCA did. And they were good at it.

Virgil tried to tap-dance. "You know, I'm supposed to be working that thing in Fulda . . . There are some pretty influential religious groups—"

Duncan interrupted. "Are you towing a boat?"

"A boat?" Virgil could see the Ranger Angler, riding high and still damp, in the rearview mirror.

"Don't bullshit me, Virgie. That thing in Fulda is weird, but it's basically chasing chickens. And you're towing your boat, which means you don't care about Fulda any more than I do. Get your ass to Minneapolis. I got you a room at the Graduate, by the U. It's your dream hotel—it's got a beer joint, a Starbucks, and, the pièce de résistance, an Applebee's. Mmm-mmm."

"Does sound good," Virgil admitted.

"The kind of place I'd stay. Any questions?"

"All kinds of them, but you won't have the answers," Virgil said. "Talk to Trane before I get up there so she'll know I'm coming and it's not my fault."

"I can do that," Duncan said. "I'll blame it on the governor. Anything else I should know?"

"There's a UFO hovering over Iowa, due south of Blue Earth," Virgil said.

"I wouldn't be surprised," Duncan said. "So, I'll email the media coverage of this killing. You'll have it before you get home."

"I'll be home in about five minutes."

"No you won't—you just crossed I-90 heading north. We got a new toy, and I'm tracking your cell phone. Have been ever since you pulled your goddamn boat off the goddamn Mississippi."

The Fulda incident.

A minister with the Universal Life Church—"Get Ordained Today!"—had married six people, three men and three women, to one another as a group, and they'd sent a nude photo off to *The New York Times*, which of course had published it on their "Vows" page, with the appropriate black rectangles covering the naughty bits, along with a narrative about the ceremony.

"We believe there should be no barrier whatsoever to personal sexual expression, in whatever combination the voluntary participants feel to be genuinely authentic," blah, blah, blah.

If the group wedding had actually taken place, it violated Minnesota law. Various conservative ministerial associations had demanded action. Action required investigation to make sure that nobody in officialdom was getting his or her weenie pulled.

Virgil was the designated hitter, but when he got the assignment, his eyes had rolled so far up into his head that he could see his scalp. He had not yet begun to investigate, despite increasing pressure. When asked why, by an attractive, if somewhat hefty,

Rochester television reporter with whom he was sharing a bag of donuts in the Mankato Dunkin' Donuts, he'd unwisely replied, "I had to wash my hair."

He took the opportunity to negotiate with Jon Duncan. "If I investigate up in Minneapolis, I won't have time for Fulda."

"I understand that. If you're out of pocket, I'll pass the word to our new attorney general and get him to send one of his own dimwitted investigators out there."

"Man, you're developing the righteous bureaucratic chops," Virgil said, impressed.

"I am, it's true," Duncan said. He'd once been a competent investigator. "I'll call Trane and tell her you'll be there by noon tomorrow."

Virgil pulled into the farm an hour later, backed the boat into the barn next to the new used compact John Deere tractor they'd bought the previous autumn. They'd rigged it for plowing snow, as well as general farm utility use, and a good thing, too. The past winter had started off easy, but turned ugly in late January and stayed that way. By early March, they'd had a snowdrift in the side yard that reached up to the lowest wire on the clothesline. Then came April and thundersnow. Now, in early September, the snow was gone, barely, and the tractor was hooked up to an aging hay baler.

The farm belonged to Virgil's pregnant girlfriend, Frankie, who was expecting twins sometime in the next couple of months. An ultrasound said they were getting one of each. Frankie, her blond hair done in a pigtail, waddled across the barnyard to meet him.

"Catch anything good?"

"Walleyes. Johnson Johnson's going to clean and freeze them; we'll have a fish fry the next time we go over."

"Good. Listen, Rolf is baling tomorrow—it looks like it could rain Monday, so we got to get it in," she said, squinting up into the UFO-free sky.

She was talking about hay, which was already cut and laying in windrows in the alfalfa field. Rolf was the oldest of her five sons.

"Aw, jeez, honey, Jon Duncan called—"

Fists on her hips. "You're trying to slide out of it *again*?"

"Hey, c'mon, it's work. That professor who got killed up in Minneapolis. Jon wants me up there by noon tomorrow . . ." He was tap-dancing like crazy.

"If you leave here at ten o'clock, you'll get there in plenty of time. And if you get up at five, you could throw for four hours before you have to clean up."

"Five o'clock? Mother of God, Frankie . . ."

"Well, I can't do it. Goodyear called and offered me a hundred dollars to paint their logo on my stomach." She *was* blimp-like. She'd started out short, slender, and busty but now sometimes seemed to Virgil to be wider than she was tall.

"Ah, well. Another couple of months, babe."

She rubbed her stomach. "I don't know. I've been through this a few times and I think it could be sooner. Hope so. This is getting to be a load."

Virgil rolled out the driveway the next morning at ten-fifteen, having kissed both Frankie and his yellow dog, Honus, good-bye. He took two days' worth of clothes, figuring he wouldn't be working on Sunday and would be back home. On the way out the door, Frankie called, "You wanna know what was the last thing Honus licked before he kissed you good-bye?"

Well, no, he didn't, but he wiped his mouth on the back of his hand, thinking, Probably his balls. I hope his balls.

Though the morning had been cool, Virgil's aching arms and neck were covered with thin red scratches from the bales of dried alfalfa he'd been throwing; it would have been much worse if it'd been hot and he'd had to work in a T-shirt. They still hadn't gotten in more than half the field, but Frankie's second- and third-oldest boys, Tall Bear and Moses, would be throwing that afternoon.

Virgil liked all the aspects of living on a farm, except for the farm-work. His parents always had a garden, and the teenage Virgil was expected to put in time picking and pulling and shucking, not because they needed the food, but because it was *good for him*. Later, as a teenager, he'd detassled corn in the summer to make money.

He hated it all. He was a rocker, not a horticulturalist.

Frankie kept an oversized vegetable garden—potatoes, toma-toes, sweet corn, squash, cucumbers, radishes, carrots, green beans, like that—out behind the barn in what had been, decades earlier, a pigsty. A variety of annual flower and herb beds sprawled along the driveway and the front of the house, and all had to be prepped, planted, watered, and harvested.

A month earlier, Virgil had yanked a stunted orange, dirt-smelling carrot out of the ground, had flicked an earthworm off it, and said, "All of that fuckin' work for this? Are you kiddin' me?"

Frankie'd laughed. She'd thought he was joking. He wasn't.

And she had that clothesline in the side yard, left over from the seventeenth century or something. She had a perfectly good clothes dryer, but she made Virgil tote the wet bedsheets and blankets out to the line in the summer because, she said, they smelled like sunshine when they were dry. Virgil had to admit she was right about that.

But carrots? You could get a perfectly good bag of peeled carrots at the supermarket for, what, a couple of bucks?

And that was more carrots than he'd eat in a month . . .

He cut 169 at St. Peter, headed north, rolled past the farm fields and suburbs and then up the interstate highway, I-35W, toward the glass towers of downtown Minneapolis, Dave Alvin and Jimmie Dale Gilmore on the satellite radio singing "Downey to Lubbock." If he could play guitar like Alvin, or the harp like Gilmore, he'd now be famous in Texas, Virgil thought. Part of Texas anyway. Okay, maybe only in Cut and Shoot, but somewhere in Texas.

He parked outside the Minneapolis City Hall in one of the spots reserved for cops, put a BCA card on the dashboard, sighed, and went inside.

The Minneapolis City Hall was not a pretty place, inside or out, and was the most barren public building Virgil had ever been in. Narrow, empty hallways were punctured by closed doors that rarely seemed to open at all. Hard benches that resembled church pews were spotted along the hallways, but he'd never seen anyone sitting on one. Strange things were undoubtedly happening behind all those doors, but he couldn't imagine what they might be.

———————

Minneapolis Homicide was part of a broader department that included other violent-crime units. Entry was through a tiny, dark anteroom, where a young woman sat behind a window through which she could check visitors. She looked at Virgil's ID, said, "Let me get somebody."

The door to the interior popped open a minute later, and a balding cop with a smile and a coffee cup said, "C'mon . . . I'm gonna want to listen to this."

Virgil said, "Aw, man . . ."

The office consisted of an L-shaped room, its two long, narrow wings wrapping around the corner of an exterior wall of the building. Working cubicles were backed up against the wall, each with two desks on opposite sides. Large windows let light into the space.

The cubicles were not overly tidy; sport coats and jackets were hung over partition walls and paper was everywhere. The cop led Virgil down the hall past a half dozen cubicles, most empty, others with cops looking at computers. He stopped halfway down the left wing of the office, pointed at a cubicle two down from where they were standing, and half whispered, "She's in there," as if she were a dragon.

Margaret Trane was a sturdy, fortyish cop with twenty years on the force. She had short brown hair, brown eyes, and was dressed in blue nylon slacks with leg pockets, a white shirt, and a blue jacket. Virgil peeked into her cubicle, where she was peering nearsightedly at a computer screen. She became aware of his presence, turned, frowned, checked his cowboy boots and T-shirt, and asked, "Yes?"

"Okay. I'm Virgil Flowers . . . I was—"

"I know who you are, Flowers," she snapped, leaning back in her chair, not bothering to hide her anger. "What do you want from me?"

"A little less hostility would help," Virgil said. "I don't want to be here any more than you want me here. If I can figure a way to get out of this job, I'll be gone."

"You're pals with the governor."

"No. I don't like the governor. He's a weasel," Virgil said. "I once did something that helped him get elected—"

"I know about the school board thing," Trane said. Her voice was still cold, her eyes as frosty as her voice, and skeptical. "What do you want?"

Virgil shrugged. "Here I am. I thought if I could review what you've already done—"

"Everything we've done so far has been useless, so there's not much point," she said.

Virgil took a breath. "Look. I can start all over, by myself, get everybody confused about who's doing what, and you won't see me again. Be a big waste of my time, probably irritate the hell out of a lot of people, including you, but I can do it. Or, I could look at your reports and start from there."

She opened her mouth to reply, but before she got a word out, a man who'd walked up behind Virgil said, "Margaret, could I speak to you for a moment?"

Trane said, "I'm—"

"I know what you're doing, Margaret. Step in here." He pointed to an interview room across the hall. "Right now."

The man was tall, thin, balding, and black; he wore rumpled gray suit pants, a white shirt, and gold-rimmed glasses. He had an empty holster on one hip. He was a cop who could have done advertisements for an accounting firm. He nodded at Virgil as Trane got up and brushed by him into the interview room. He said, "We'll be just a moment," and closed the door.

The cop who'd pointed out Trane had been eavesdropping from the next cubicle. He stepped out with a grin, and said, "That's Lieutenant Knox. Nothing like getting off on the right foot, huh? Trane's now getting her ass handed to her by the lieutenant, which will make her even happier than she already is."

Virgil said, "I can understand why she's pissed. I would be, too, in her shoes."

"Yeah, but here you are, a cowboy with actual cowboy boots, likely with horse manure on the insteps, and wearing a band shirt, so you probably enjoy standing around on street corners bullshitting with people. Maggie, on the other hand, does not do bullshit. At all."

"What's wrong with my shirt?" Virgil was wearing a vintage Otis Taylor "Trance Blues" T-shirt available only on select internet sites.

"It's not that often that you see a cop wearing one, unless maybe he's undercover," the cop said.

"I'm trying to elevate fashion standards among law enforcement personnel," Virgil said. "So . . . Trane . . . She smart?"

"Yeah, she's smart. Smart as she is, the *Star Tribune* says she's baffled. What pisses her off is, she actually *is*. Baffled. She's got no clue of what happened over at the U. No suspects, no prints, no

DNA, no murder weapon, no time of death even. She doesn't even know for sure why the dead guy was where he was. Or how he got there."

The door to the interview room opened, and Trane scooted out, almost as if she'd been kicked in the ass. She scowled at Virgil as Lieutenant Knox disappeared down the hall, pointed at an empty desk, and said, "That desk belongs to a guy on vacation. You can use it until he gets back. He'll be back in two weeks, but a highly qualified investigator like yourself probably won't need more time than that. All the drawers are locked, but you can use the computer. I'll open my files for you. Let me know when you're done and I'll close them."

Virgil said, "I appreciate it. While you're doing that, if you could point me to a men's room . . ."

"I'll show you," the other cop said. "I'll walk you across the street to the cafeteria, give you the lay of the land." To Trane he said, "We'll be a few minutes. You should go lie down in the ladies' room and put a cool, damp hankie on your forehead."

"Fuck you," Trane said, but not in the mean voice she'd used on Virgil. She was already settling back in front of her computer.

Virgil had been to the Minneapolis cop shop a few times, but the man, whose name was Ansel Neumann and who was a detective sergeant, gave him the full two-dollar tour. They wound up in a cafeteria in the government building across the street from City Hall. The two buildings were connected by an underground tunnel, the government center tall and now, after a few decades of being modern, a little shabby; the City Hall was old and squat and ugly, with dim, empty hallways with ranks of closed doors and stone floors that kicked echoes out from your feet when you walked across them.

They ordered some kind of pie, which was yellow and might have been custard, or possibly banana, and Neumann briefed Virgil on the computer system, and what he could expect in Trane's files, as well as a review of what the media was doing.

"They've been all over Trane's ass—a Channel Three crew ambushed her out at her house during dinner and they spent some time yelling at each other. She's got a problem."

"Why take it out on me? I understand not wanting an outsider, but . . ."

Neumann: "Because it suggests she can't handle the case?"

"I'm not doing that."

"No, but guess what happens when the governor's fair-haired boy shows up here and the case gets solved? Who gets the credit? Who's the village idiot? Trane figures she's going to wind up sitting in the corner with a pointy hat on her head."

"Ah, shit."

When Virgil and Neumann got back to the Homicide office, another cop had shown up and was eating a tuna salad sandwich at the desk on the other side of the cubicle wall from Trane. Trane was again nearsightedly peering at her computer screen. Virgil said, "Margaret?"

"What?"

He tipped his head toward the interview room. "Step in here for a minute. We need to talk."

She launched herself from her chair, followed Virgil into the room, closed the door, and crossed her arms. "What?"

Virgil held up his hands in a placating gesture. "I don't think you need my help. I'm not here voluntarily. I'd be pissed if I were in your shoes, and I told Ansel that. I understand. But we're stuck with it. If we figure this thing out, I'll disappear. Nobody from the media will ever hear my name. And if anybody asks me, I'll tell them you ran the show. Because, honest to God, I don't need this."

She unfolded her arms. "It's just . . . insulting, you know?"

"I know how you feel about it. You know Lucas Davenport, right? You must have overlapped." Davenport had been a Minneapolis Homicide cop before he'd gone on to the BCA, and then to the U.S. Marshals Service.

"Yeah, he's a friend," she said.

"He's a friend of mine, too. We're almost best friends, in an odd way," Virgil said. "Give him a call. See what he thinks."

She agreed, if still a bit grudgingly. "Okay. Let me open the files for you. And I *will* give Lucas a ring."

CHAPTER

THREE

Virgil spent the afternoon reviewing Trane's work; the room was cool and damp and smelled like paper and floor wax. He got up a few times, to walk and think, wandering over to the government building. A few people stopped to peer into the office, checking the guy with the blues T-shirt.

Trane asked, "How are you doing?" a couple of times, and he said, "Good. You're a good reporter," and she was, and she went away, possibly mollified, possibly to pee.

Her reports were chronological, rather than ordered by subject matter, so Virgil made notes on a yellow legal pad, organized by subject.

There was one picture of the murder victim, Professor Barthelemy Quill, when he was alive, an informal portrait in his laboratory that looked like it might have been taken by a newspaper reporter—it had a newsy look.

Judging from a door behind Quill's shoulder, he was a tall man, over six feet. He had neatly trimmed hair—originally light brown or blond, now shot through with gray—and a full head of it. The short hair framed a sober oval face punctuated with thin blond eyebrows and sharp blue-gray eyes that said "I went to a private boys' school and then off to the Ivy League"—the face of a high-level federal prosecutor or Naval officer.

The file also included a couple of dozen digital prints of the body as it was found, as well as close-ups of the entire carrel and the area around it.

The blood from the head wound appeared black against the fair hair both at the site and where it trickled down Quill's skull and left a stain on the stone-tiled floor beneath his chin. He was wearing gray slacks, a gray shirt, and a black sport coat. The ensemble lent him the aspect of a vampire, especially since his lips were pulled back in a death grimace, revealing a long eyetooth.

Trane had interviewed more than fifty persons who'd known Quill, including his estranged current wife, two ex-wives, two ex-lovers, all the lab employees, colleagues at the university and the neighbors, and a group of academics with whom he was feuding. She'd extracted from them narratives of their relationships to the dead man and accountings of their whereabouts on Friday and Saturday.

The academic feud had taken quite a bit of Trane's time: she'd conducted interviews with both Quill supporters and Quill haters, and there had been some violence involved.

Trane had had trouble determining the victim's exact time of death because he'd been known to take solitary walks around campus. Quill left his lab, alone, at one o'clock Friday afternoon, and hadn't returned. He hadn't shown up on Monday, either, which was unusual but not unprecedented. His laboratory director had tried to call him twice on Monday, but Quill's phone had apparently been turned off. That also was not unusual—famously, he hated being interrupted "by any idiot who can poke a number into a keypad."

Because Trane hadn't a time of death—the medical examiner pegged it as being between Friday evening and noon Saturday— she'd been unable to eliminate alibis of the people closest to Quill or those who'd been involved with Quill in the feud, a vicious campus controversy concerning the relationship of medicine to culture.

Quill had an office and lab in Moos Tower, a research center on campus. He would spend mornings there, arriving around eight o'clock after a stop at a Starbucks, where he picked up coffee and a slice of banana or pumpkin bread, which he ate at his desk.

The next few hours were spent conferring with his senior lab assistants and reviewing ongoing work. In the afternoons, he often left the lab to walk and think, sometimes returning to work on into the evening on scientific papers. The lab's work had been published in all the major medical journals concerned with spinal injuries.

Trane noted that Quill's assistants called him either Barth— not Bart—or Dr. Quill. He had a medical degree, but had never used it to practice; he also had a Ph.D. in biomedicine and had done advanced work in biorobotics.

After leaving the lab on Friday, Quill had met with a professor of microsurgery and a professor of radiology at the university medical center. That meeting had lasted until about three o'clock.

He'd been sighted by two medical students at Coffman Memorial Union around three o'clock, at the coffee bar; and may have been sighted by two neighbors, walking near his home, around five o'clock, but that was uncertain.

According to Trane's reports, Quill lived alone in a large red-brick house on East River Parkway, within long walking distance of his lab. In good weather, he often walked, and occasionally biked, to the university. If he'd actually been spotted by the neighbors, that was the last time he'd been seen alive by any witnesses Trane had been able to locate.

Quill's estranged wife lived in a condo, owned by Quill, east of the university. At the time of his death, they were negotiating the terms of a divorce. There was a severe prenuptial agreement. Interestingly, the estranged wife would get little of Quill's money, and no alimony at all, if they divorced while he was alive, but would inherit a substantial fortune if he "predeceased" her.

Virgil said, "Huh," but noted that the wife had an ironclad alibi—she was also an academic and had been in Cleveland attending a conference on the structure of natural languages. That didn't mean she couldn't have had an accomplice to do the killing.

The will—actually, a revocable trust—dictated precisely what would happen with Quill's estate when he died. Other than his estranged wife, nobody would get more or less if Quill were killed yesterday or thirty years later; but most would get it sooner if he were killed yesterday.

His daughter was an exception. Under the terms of the trust, she was to be paid sixty thousand dollars a year until she was thirty, the money intended to cover her education. After age thirty, she wouldn't get another nickel—ever. Since she was already getting the payments from the trust, it made no financial difference to her when or whether Quill died.

Trane had gone to Verizon, Quill's phone service provider, and had extracted a record of where the phone had been. The phone had been turned off around six o'clock on Friday night, but Verizon's automated system had continued to track it until midnight. Quill had been around his house and neighborhood until about nine-thirty, when he'd driven to an area known as Dinkytown. He'd left his car in a private parking lot and never gone back to it.

After leaving the car, he'd wandered around on foot, with no protracted stops. Then the phone traced a walk across the campus and then across a footbridge over the Mississippi.

At midnight, the phone had been turned back on, in the library—but then, ten minutes later, again outside the library, it had disappeared altogether. At six o'clock the next morning, it popped up again, on the footbridge between the east and west banks of the river. A Google search had been made of Starbucks, perhaps to check opening times. The phone then was carried to the library, which didn't open until eight, had been turned off again there, was tracked for a few more minutes, then disappeared again. It hadn't yet reappeared on Verizon's records. Or been found.

"You're telling me that he was killed Saturday morning,

before the library opened. He must've had a key to an outside door to get up to his carrel," Virgil said to Trane.

She turned from her computer. "He had a key, no question about that," Trane said. "We don't know who gave it to him. Of course, it's possible that somebody with a key let him in. I talked to an assistant at the library, who said she saw him once very shortly after the library opened coming out of his carrel. Not to say that he couldn't have been waiting outside and got in the minute it opened, but she had the impression that he might have slept in the library. Doesn't know for sure. I originally thought he must've been killed after six-fifteen, the last time we can locate his phone, but now . . ."

She pressed a hand to the side of her face, thinking about it, and Virgil asked, "What?"

"I keep reminding myself, I know where the cell phone was," Trane said. "I'm not a hundred percent sure where Quill was— that he was with the phone. The cell wasn't with the body, and neither were the computer nor his keys. We know he kept his house and office keys on his car fob. He was driving a BMW that night—the BMW that we found in the parking lot."

"If Verizon can track phones when they're turned off—"

"They can, if the battery isn't pulled."

"—then what happened when it disappeared? He took the battery out?"

"That would be one way, but there are a couple of others. You can buy cases that shield phones from electromagnetic radiation. Maybe he had one."

"Or the killer did," Virgil said.

"Yup—or the killer did. It's possible he was killed at midnight, and the subsequent tracks were the killer's. It's also possible that

Quill had a phone shield case. Met somebody at the library, dropped his phone in the case so he couldn't be tracked, spent the night somewhere—maybe with a woman?—then went back to the library the next morning and was killed there. None of his lab associates ever saw such a case. If he was deliberately blocking his phone at times, he might have kept it a secret. The Verizon records don't show any previous instances, though."

"Then if the phone was shielded, it was most likely the killer who did it," Virgil said.

"You could make that argument. If that's right, Quill was mostly likely killed at midnight. But then the killer would have to have had Quill's access code, because it popped up again the next morning."

"All this only applies if Quill's phone had a keypad code. Or maybe a fingerprint code . . ."

"He did have a code and he kept it secret," Trane said. "We know that from his wives . . . And he hadn't changed phones since the second divorce."

"If he kept it secret from his wives, is it possible he was having affairs?" Virgil asked. "Patronizing hookers?"

"It's possible, and I've already asked that question," Trane said. "Nobody knows of such a history. He apparently was sexually straight, his wives agreed that he was always sexually active, and even a little rough, but he wasn't driven by sex. He was driven by his research."

"Rough? How rough?" Virgil asked. "Violent?"

She shook her head. "Nothing like that. Muscly. He manipulated them enough that they sometimes had bruises, but none of them said they didn't like it."

"He was a strong guy, then?"

"Not a bodybuilder or a weight lifter, but three times a week at the gym, doing a full circuit, working hard at it. He owned a Peloton bike, it's at his house, and Peloton records show he worked out almost every day, for exactly half an hour, but heavily. He was in good shape. No, he was in great shape."

"Yet no signs that he resisted the killer?"

"The killer hit him from behind," Trane said. "He never saw it coming."

The murder weapon was unknown. People who'd spoken to Quill at his library carrel said Quill kept a large and powerful laptop computer there. The computer was missing, but Trane had learned from credit card records that Quill had spent more than twelve thousand dollars on a high-end laptop, a DreamBook Power P87, the year before.

She'd found a similar computer, with an identical case, and the medical examiner had confirmed that a corner of it could have done the damage to Quill's skull, but Trane didn't have the actual laptop, so that was also uncertain.

Virgil asked Trane, "Is it possible that there was something on his computer or phone that somebody was desperate to get?"

She shrugged. "Who knows? I've asked the question, and nobody can think of what it might be. He was a research scientist, but not a loner. There are extensive notes on everything done in the lab. This laptop . . . We know Quill wasn't a gamer, he didn't play video games. This thing had fast processors and a lot of storage, and would work well with virtual reality. His top assistant said you might use it to display and manipulate MRI images, yet he didn't know why Quill would try to hide that, what he'd be doing with it in a study carrel. They have plenty of computer power in the lab. Still . . . he had a huge amount of power there. He must've been using it for something."

"Maybe he screwed something up, with a patient, and wanted to keep the images where only he could see them."

"That had occurred to me, too. While there is a lawsuit involving one of his patients, a suicide, I don't see anything there. Virgil, this is something I've been struggling with, thinking he might have a secret life of some kind—but all of his work is very public. I mean, it's all done as a team. When surgery is involved, he doesn't do it, a team of surgeons does. I cannot, for the life of me, find anything in his professional life that he'd want to hide."

"Okay."

"One other thing: that computer is fairly rare. I've been watching the local Craigslist and eBay and Googling laptops for sale, and it hasn't shown up on any of that. It could be in the river."

Virgil finished taking notes at three o'clock. Trane had been coming and going while he worked, and when he kicked back from the computer, she was coming through the doorway with a paper cup full of coffee.

"Finished?"

"Not really. I need to think about it all. You get any . . . vibrations . . . from anyone?"

"I got vibrations from a lot of people. Quill was highly respected, but not much liked," Trane said. "A couple of people hinted that he wasn't particularly generous with giving others credit for scientific papers. That's a big deal for young job-hunting scientists. His ex-wives didn't like him, either. I asked them why and they said he was arrogant, cold, mean. Everything but violent. He had a child with his first wife, a daughter, who also didn't like him much, although he supported her and his first wife quite adequately for more than twenty years until his death. His daughter goes to St. Thomas. She's pretty much a slacker . . . a C to B student, though her mother says she's bright enough. She doesn't want to work, that's all. Doesn't want to work—ever."

"Does she inherit anything? Outside that trust?"

"Nope. She gets a trust fund payout until she's thirty, enough to pay college tuition through to a Ph.D., if that's what she wants, and to live in a decent apartment and eat. Then it ends. She gets nothing more in the will. Of course, if he'd lived, he could have changed that."

"How old is she now?" Virgil asked.

"Nineteen. I interviewed her. She wasn't too upset about him getting killed," Trane said. "He wasn't present as a father—only his money was. I gotta say, my impression was that she's way too lazy to actually kill somebody. And she's got a solid alibi for the whole time span when Quill was killed."

"Quill, on some level, seems to have been successful with women? Maybe girlfriends? Jealousy?"

"Not finding it. Hasn't dated recently, as far as I've been able to determine, but . . . maybe. I'm still looking. Nobody's come forward. His wife and his exes say he was incredibly smart, which was why they were attracted . . . And, of course, he had family money. Quite a bit of it. Money's often attractive in a man."

"I wouldn't know. I've had to rely on my good looks and personal charm," Virgil said.

She gave him the stink eye, unsure whether he was joking or not, and Virgil said, "You've got to get used to my sense of humor."

She said, "I talked to Lucas. He said you weren't a terrible guy. Most of the time.. Nothing like Hitler anyway. I was supposed to remind you to keep your hands off his daughter."

"That's a Davenport joke," Virgil said.

"I got the impression that it was ninety percent joke and ten percent death threat," Trane said.

"Yeah, that's about right," Virgil said. "So. In five hundred words or less, tell me what you've figured out."

"Won't take five hundred words. He was killed in the carrel. He must've trusted the killer because he'd turned his back to him in a close space—the killer almost had to be inside the carrel with him. If it was a him. It might not have been because the carrel would be crowded with two men in it. If the killer is a her, she's strong. I've tried lifting a similar laptop over my head quickly and then swinging it down hard enough to kill. I can do it, but twelve pounds, overhead, chopping down, accelerating, doing it fast enough that Quill wouldn't see it coming . . . It's harder than you'd think."

"Okay."

"The autopsy gave me nothing more than the cause of death. He had no alcohol or any trace of drugs in his system. Nothing under the fingernails or on his clothes—and no reason there should be, he obviously didn't resist—and no DNA."

"Okay." Virgil scrolled down the computer screen, tapped the screen. "You've got all these NCIC files on a guy named Boyd Nash. What's that about?"

"Nash is a . . . I guess a scientist would say he's a dirtbag. I don't understand all the details, but he's some kind of scientific predator and he had some contact with Quill."

"Predator?"

"Yeah. He looks for new research that he can get some details on, then he goes to this law firm that cooperates with him . . . Conspires with him, I'd say . . . Anyway, give me some rope here because I don't entirely understand it . . . They find a graduate student or low-level technician who knows something about the field that the research involves and they write up a description of the work and then they file for a patent. When the original company or laboratory tries to use their own research, the law firm files for a patent violation. It's technical and complicated enough that the courts don't usually understand what's going on. Sometimes Nash wins, sometimes he loses, but if he wins, he can get a substantial settlement because fighting the court's judgment can cost more than the settlement. The law firm gets a third, of course, but Nash can still get out with tens of thousands of dollars."

"In other words, he steals research, pretends it's his, or belongs to somebody he's working with, and uses a court decision to extort a settlement from the good guys."

"That's about it," Trane said.

"You eliminated Nash as a suspect?"

"Not completely, but there seemed to be better leads," Trane said. "The night that Quill disappeared, Nash was in Rochester. He checked into the DoubleTree hotel for a convention . . . It's in the notes, something like the American Institute for Medical Technology. I talked to him, he gave me names of people he spoke to there, both that night and on Saturday, and on Sunday, when the convention ended. I called those people and it all checked out. He had American Express receipts for the hotel for both nights, Friday and Saturday."

"It's only about an hour and a half each way. He could have been down there until ten o'clock . . ."

"I know. I worked through all that," Trane said. "It seems unlikely—it's the kind of convention he'd go to, for the contacts he needs, and why would he think he'd need an elaborate alibi? He couldn't have known Quill would be at the library at midnight. And how would he have gotten in the library? Lot of moving parts there."

"All right. Now, tell me about this big feud that Quill was involved in."

"Oh my God," Trane said. "You ever get in one of those situations where somebody's yelling at you and you feel like your sinuses are getting jammed up by the sheer bullshit?"

"All the time. That's my life story," Virgil said. "What's going on?"

A woman named Katherine Green, Trane said, a newly tenured professor in the university's Department of Cultural Science, had written a well-received book entitled *Cultural Medicine*, which argued that medicine which worked well in the West might not work so well in other cultures, or what she called microcultures.

In a particularly controversial passage, she'd suggested that families in Marin County, California, and Clark County, Washington, had developed their own microcultures that rejected the

Western imperative of childhood vaccination. The Marin and Clark microcultures' emphasis on a naturally robust lifestyle would likely prove as effective as vaccination, Green said, possibly more so.

"That started people screaming," Trane said. "Because it seemed to offer support for the anti-vaccination movement, which mostly consists of uncertified crazies."

The book made it onto *The New York Times*'s bestseller list, and Green, after making a three-week tour in support of sales, returned to home ground at the university, where she was invited to give a lecture at the Coffman Memorial Union.

"I've seen a video," Trane said. "About halfway through, several people started booing. That started a bunch of arguments, and people in the audience started pushing one another around. There were a couple of campus cops there and they got everybody back in their seats, and Green managed to finish the lecture.

"Then Quill got up and said her book was ignorant, unscholarly, uninformed, and a bunch of other stuff. Green has a reputation herself—she likes to fight. It seems like she lives for controversy. She called him rude, culturally illiterate, a racist, and a few other things, and he called her a silly twat. Yelled it, actually," Trane said. "That set things off again, and they had to call more cops because it got out of hand—a small riot. A graduate student got hauled off to jail and was charged with assault because he hit another guy with a chair."

"Did it break like they do on TV?" Virgil asked.

"No," Trane said, a trifle impatiently. "Anyway, Green tried to get Quill fired for sexism, filed against him with the Title IX committee—the word 'twat.' Quill insisted that he'd called her a silly twit, not twat. He was lying because he did call her a twat. It was plain as day on the video, but there was no way the U was going to fire or even censure Quill. He was way too important."

A week or so after Green's lecture, Quill and three professors from the medical school held an open seminar at the Mayo Auditorium to discuss the wrong-headedness of Green's book and to question the very existence of the Department of Cultural Science, which, according to flyers posted in the medical school, advocated "Witchcraft vs. Medicine."

"Well, you can guess what happened. Green showed up with staff and students from Cultural Science, and they had another riot on their hands," Trane said. "It's been pretty much open warfare since then. Quill proposed eliminating the Cultural Science Department entirely—it's hard to get rid of tenured professors, but if their department is abolished, well, they don't have jobs."

"Then everybody in Cultural Science is a suspect."

"Yeah," Trane said, "That would be eighteen faculty and graduate assistants and support staff, and a large but unknown number of students."

"Sounds like you've come down on Quill's side of this thing," Virgil ventured. "You know, intellectually."

"Of course I have," Trane said. "I wouldn't say it on television, but the Green people, the Cultural Science people, are a bunch of Froot Loops."

Virgil leaned back in his chair, put his boots up on the desk, and said, "I don't know. I feel the great karmic twang might favor Greenites. I'll start there, find this Katherine Green."

Trane rubbed her face with both hands. "Karmic twang? Oh my God, he said 'karmic twang.' You could probably go undercover with Cultural Science. They'd love that T-shirt."

From the other side of the cubicle wall the cop, who'd by now finished his tuna fish sandwich, said, "I thought he said 'karmic wang.'"

Trane said, "Shut up," then said to Virgil, "I'll get you a phone number."

"I'd like to go through Quill's house this evening, if it's not sealed up," Virgil said.

"I've got the key, I can meet you there after dinner . . . like, seven o'clock?"

"That's good."

Tuna Fish said, "You oughta tell Karmic Wang that Green is quite the hottie."

Trane again said, "Shut up," and to Virgil said, "I guess she is, but that's irrelevant."

Tuna Fish said, "No, it's not. The hottest sex is always between two people who don't like each other. That's why feminists date drug dealers or drummers at some point in their lives. In your situation, you got the handsome, brilliant, rich, and probably horny divorcing professor on one side and the best-selling academic, unmarried hottie on the other. Did you even look at her boobies? Think there might be sparks?"

"Thank you, Dr. Freud."

"You're welcome. It's better than anything you've come up with," Tuna Fish said.

Virgil: "Give me the number for Green."

Trane gave him the number, and asked, "How are we going to do this? You and me?"

"How about if I work it as kind of, like, an assistant or intern," Virgil suggested. "On my own, because there's no point in both of us standing around looking at the same guy. You do your thing,

I do mine, and we meet every morning and again every night until we get the killer."

"I'm happy you're so . . . sanguine . . . about getting him. We had a fifty percent clearance rate on murders last year. If we don't do better, Knox's going to be the new lieutenant guarding the landfill. I'll be the sergeant in charge of the sloppy diaper dump."

"Aw, we'll get him," Virgil said. "If we don't, I've got an extra pair of barn boots I can give you. You know, for the diapers."

FOUR

Virgil called Green, who rejected the call. He called again, was rejected again. The third time a woman answered, a low-pitched growl. "What? Who is this?"

Virgil introduced himself, and Green said, "I've spoken to the police several times, Margaret Trane—"

"Yes, but I've been appointed to be Sergeant Trane's assistant on the case and she suggested I start by talking with you," Virgil said. Trane rolled her eyes. "I need to get a feel for all the various . . . personalities . . . who knew Dr. Quill."

"I didn't know Quill, I only knew who he was. And I certainly didn't murder him, though I should have for calling me a twat. I think it would have been ruled justifiable homicide."

"Still . . ."

She agreed to meet him at four-thirty, at her office in the Hum-phrey Center. When Virgil got off the call, he and Trane talked about the case for another ten minutes, then he asked her for a few of her business cards to give to interviewees. She said, "Take a whole stack," and pushed them across her desk.

Back on the street, Virgil drove across the Mississippi to check into his hotel, which indeed did have an Applebee's, a Starbucks, and a beer joint. The room was small and decorated in tints of sage, which made him look sickly pale in the bathroom mirror, but was nothing to complain about after years of Motel 6's. He dumped his bag. went back down to the street, got his car, drove back across the river to the Humphrey Center, a boring brick bunker that any SS dead-ender might have approved of.

Hubert Humphrey, the former vice president and onetime Democratic presidential candidate, had a lot of stuff named after him around the Twin Cities, including an airport, a domed stadium—later torn down—and the building where Virgil was parking.

Minnesota, for some unknown reason, had chosen the thirteen-lined ground squirrel as its mascot, although they called it a golden gopher, and, in a stroke of literary brilliance, had named it Goldy Gopher. The university's colors were red and gold, and red was splashed everywhere on buildings, including the Humphrey Center.

The center housed the Humphrey School of Public Affairs and both the Cultural Science and Anthropology departments, all of which had gopher-red carpets. Above the atrium were hung the flags of all the nations of the world, Virgil thought as he walked in, though he didn't count them.

Green's office was on the third floor, and Virgil took the stairs, cruised by the Cultural Science office once, checked a bulletin board in the hallway, saw nothing of interest except for a home-made "Pretty Kittens" poster with pull-off phone number tabs and with a photograph of two attractive, decidedly non-collegiate-looking blondes holding kitties in their laps. Virgil spent a moment considering the ambiguity of the poster, then ambled back to the office, a few minutes early for the appointment.

The bird-like, gum-chewing secretary gave him a puzzled look: he didn't fit into any of the niches with which she was familiar. "Yes?"

"I'm Virgil Flowers, BCA agent. I have an appointment to speak with Professor Green at four-thirty."

"Really? Where's your gun? You don't look like a police officer," she said. She gave her gum a few rapid chews with a snap at the end for emphasis.

"My gun's locked in my truck. I don't usually carry it," Virgil said.

"Really? Is that a new trend with police officers?"

"I'm trying to start one. Anyway, when I need to kill someone, I use a shotgun," Virgil said. "They're awkward to carry in offices."

"Oh . . . Okay . . . Well, that makes sense . . . I guess," she said. "We were expecting you. Let me check that Dr. Green is off the phone."

She turned away, made a call, mumbled for a moment, hung up, and said, "This way."

Virgil followed her to a modest office done in blond wood with a blond wooden desk and gopher-red carpet and a blond occupant. A large built-in bookcase dominated an interior wall and was stuffed with academic awards, appreciation plaques, ethnic pottery, and doodads. A vase of pale yellow silk flowers sat on a windowsill, which looked out over an atrium.

As Tuna Fish had said, Green was a hottie, one of those attractive, smart, professional women with wire-rimmed glasses and a nice haircut and tidy breasts under a pale blue blouse who'd look great with her head on a pillow and her legs wrapped around his neck, in Virgil's humble opinion. He didn't mention his opinion but looked steadily into her eyes and extended a hand to be shaken, which she did.

She pointed at the visitor's chair, sat down herself, and asked, "Have you really killed someone with your shotgun?"

"Yes," Virgil said. "He was trying to kill me at the time. I tried to talk him out of it, but he was recalcitrant and continued trying to kill me. So, I shot him. I feel bad about it. But not too bad. The memory isn't incapacitating or anything."

"That would be an interesting study . . . people who have killed other people and how they feel about it," Green said. "Has modern American gun society so deadened our reactions to killing that we don't even experience an emotional toll when we ourselves kill someone? A longitudinal study, going back after a month, six months, a year, two years, and so on, would be interesting. Does the memory fade? Does the shooter avoid negative psychological consequences because of cultural conditioning through social media? How do American reactions to killing compare with non-gun societies? England, perhaps. Or Denmark."

Virgil crossed his legs, settling into his chair, and said, "I personally know several guys—actually, I know a woman as well—who've killed other people and their reactions are all over the place. Some of them, it doesn't seem to affect, but others are screwed up about it. Still others seem screwed up, but only to the

extent that it gets them time off or disability pay or job prefer-
ences."

"Interesting," she said. She made a note on a desk pad. "Now,
what can I do for you? On this Quill murder? I've told the police—"

Virgil held up a hand. "I know, I read Sergeant Trane's account
of your testimony. I just wanted to push it around the plate."

"I don't believe I've encountered that idiom before, 'push it
around the plate,'" Green said. She scribbled another note. "Where'd
you hear it?"

"My mother used it," Virgil said. "So. What was your personal
relationship to Dr. Quill?"

She recoiled. "None. I never . . . Are you suggesting—"

"No, no, no." Virgil smiled. "I'm not talking about sex, heaven
forbid. I'm asking if you talked, outside of these conflicts you had
recently, about the t-word thing?"

"'T-word'? You mean 'twat'?'"

"Yes. Did you talk—"

"I don't believe I ever said a word to him in my entire life before he came to my lecture and began yelling at me," Green said.
"Then I went to his seminar, and, well, we didn't actually speak,
we shouted at each other."

"And you didn't kill him?"

"Of course not! I mean—"

"I had to ask," Virgil said, holding up his hands, flashing another smile. "How about other people from Cultural Science? Is
there anyone involved with your department that you might
think capable of murder? Even if the murder was impulsive, as
opposed to planned?"

She stared at him for a moment, then said, "I suppose you do
have to ask." She turned away, looking out a window at the brick

wall of another building, then turned back and said, "Do you know about Clete?"

"Clete? Was he the guy charged with assault after your speech?"

"Yes. Clete May. He has what I'd call a machismo thing—sometimes a problem, sometimes not. That can be quite useful when doing cultural research. You know, he's happy to carry heavy things for us women, pick up the check more often than he has to, possibly defend us in the more misogynistic cultures. That kind of thing. He also has a tendency to lean into our female students and staff."

"'Lean into'? You mean 'grab'? 'Pressure'? 'Assault'?" Virgil asked.

"No, I meant what I said: lean. He leans into them. He moves into their spaces, whether he's welcome or not. Somehow, I feel that you might be familiar with the concept."

"I would never lean into anyone's space if I weren't welcome," Virgil said.

"How can you tell without trying?" Green asked.

"You'd have to be a moron not to know," Virgil said.

"Really?"

"Yes."

"Interesting. Differing levels of empathy among males. Does it begin in childhood? Is a dominant mother involved?" She made another note, then asked, "Would you consider your mother to hold the dominant role in your kinship group?"

"Who?"

"Your nuclear family?"

"Well, I never thought about it. Now that you ask, no, not especially. We were all pretty equal."

"Interesting," she said. "Did your family group hold any extensive moral attitudes?"

Virgil shrugged. "My father's a Lutheran minister. I went to church every Sunday and Wednesday night until I was eighteen."

"Interesting," she said, and she made another note.

Virgil tried to regain control of the interview. "This Clete May. Do you think—"

"He might be capable of violence, but he's not a stupid person, a thug, by any means. I know that he's studied martial arts, but also that he's deeply interested in Zen Buddhism. He makes friends easily enough, yet I sense a certain . . . calculation . . . in all of it. I've heard him talk about fighting—street fighting—but I'm not sure he's done it, but he sure talks about it. Maybe he gets it from movies, I don't know."

"I'll speak to him," Virgil said. "You won't come into it."

"I appreciate that," Green said. "There's another man, Terry Foster, who served in the military in the Middle East. He's quite mild-mannered. I've never seen anything that would suggest that he could become violent, but I've been told that he was wounded in action over there. I've never heard him speak about it and I never asked."

Virgil noted the names, and Green said he could get contact information from the secretary. He pushed her on her relationship with Quill, and if she was telling the truth, there was nothing there but an academic conflict.

"Quill was trying to get your department abolished. If that happened, who'd be hurt worst?"

"Well, me," she said. "I'm the head of the department. If the university abolished the department, I might be able to move to Anthropology, but it would certainly be a step backwards. Most of the students could probably transfer their credits there, but we have two Ph.D. candidates who'd be badly damaged by such a thing. They are deep into their thesis work and might have to start over."

Virgil took their names. They were both women, and Virgil said, "Women are less inclined to this kind of violence. A heavy physical attack. When women kill, it's usually a last resort to fend off what they see as a life-threatening situation. They use a gun or a knife, but they don't bludgeon somebody, because they recognize that men are larger and stronger. If they feel desperate and cornered, they go for a real kill, with a real weapon. And they're often older than student age. Not always, but usually."

"Then you think the killer is male?"

"Oh, probably. Not a sure thing, but probably," Virgil said. "Women do bludgeon people to death, but it's usually a child. Usually their own."

Green winced, then asked, "Anything else?"

Virgil shook his head. "No, not at the moment. I might come back to consult with you if anything suggests that one of your students or staff was involved . . ."

She smiled for the first time, but her smile reminded Virgil of Lucas Davenport's smile, which could turn predatory and even downright mean. "Do that."

In the outer office, Virgil got contact information for the people mentioned by Green. He asked the secretary, "The Wilson Library is around here, isn't it? I went to school here, but it was quite a while ago."

"It's right next door," she said. "You gonna go look at the murder scene?"

"I guess," Virgil said, "since I'm right here."

The secretary dropped her voice. "It was pretty gory. The blood soaked into the floor, and I'm told there's no way to get the stain out. They'll probably cover it with carpet, but it'll be there forever."

"That would be a little grim for the next occupant of the room," Virgil allowed.

The secretary shivered. "I wouldn't take it." She leaned forward in her chair to look down the hall to Green's office, then sat upright again and asked, quietly, "If I tell you something, would you promise not to tell anyone?"

"Sure, unless it's awful and illegal."

"It's not, though some people"—she tilted her head toward Green's office—"would probably think so. Things are so dangerous in the world now that my husband made me get a carry permit. I have a Sig 938 and a carry purse. If I get attacked, somebody's gonna get three Speer Gold Dots right in the breadbasket." She snapped her gum.

"Be careful," Virgil said. "Really, really careful."

"I am careful," she said solemnly.

Virgil moved closer, and asked, "You think Professor Green is clear on this thing, right?"

"Oh, sure. She likes to create a lot of commotion, but she wouldn't hurt anyone."

"Do you think that there are any males—you know, who have attachments to her or fantasies about her—who might be thinking they're protecting her? By killing Quill?"

"In the department?" She thought for a moment. "People will tell you Clete May, but he's a big cream puff. No, I can't think of anybody."

Virgil left the truck where it was and walked around to the Wilson Library. The director, who looked like a library lady should, with horn-rimmed glasses and a doughy oval face, reacted as Green's secretary had. "You're sure you're a police officer?"

"I wouldn't want you to worry about it, so"—Virgil dug Trane's card out of his ID case and handed it to her—"call Sergeant Trane and ask."

"No, no . . ."

"If you don't, you'll worry about it," Virgil said.

She called Margaret Trane, identified herself, asked the question, smiled, said, "Yes, he is wearing an Otis Taylor T-shirt. I think he looks quite handsome in it." She listened some more, then exclaimed, "Shut up! Three times?" She looked at Virgil, reevaluating. "He doesn't look old enough."

When she got off the phone, she led him up a flight of steps to Quill's carrel, which was on an outer wall, behind deep stacks of floor to ceiling bookcases. The carrel had crime scene tape across the door. Virgil pulled the tape loose and unlocked the door with a key he'd gotten from Trane.

As he stepped inside, the library lady asked, "You've really been married and divorced three times already?"

"Yes, but I was only fourteen the first time, so nobody expected that one to last," Virgil said.

The library lady said, "Oh," and vanished, and Virgil smothered the impulse to run after her and tell her he was joking. So much for his awkward sense of humor.

The carrel was a small room, narrow, maybe ten feet long. There was indeed the shadow of a stain on the tile floor, no doubt Quill's blood. Traces of black fingerprint powder were everywhere. He tried to avoid it as best he could. The stuff was like slime mold: it would stick to anything and spread like chicken pox.

The carrel had a built-in desk, with a shelf above it, and an expensive-looking leather office chair. A half dozen heavy-looking texts rested in the bookcase, all of which looked as though they'd been roughly handled by investigators. A rolled-up yoga mat sat behind the books on the shelf. The silver metal wastebasket was empty.

The place smelled like . . . nothing. Not smoke, not sweat, not even like the cleaner that would have been used to get rid of the blood. Not much to see, with plenty of room to swing a laptop— if a laptop, in fact, had been used to murder.

He was about to leave when he noticed the yoga mat again. He reached over the chair, pushed a couple of books aside, and took it down off the shelf. It was a thicker than normal mat made of a soft, nubby light blue plastic. Why would anyone be doing yoga in such a confined space and often enough to bring a mat?

He thought about that for a moment and flashed back to his junior year: a hasty relationship with a young woman named what? Jean? Under a library table on the third floor, just before closing. Was it Jean? His mind was going, he thought.

He unrolled the mat on the floor, got down on his knees. As he did, the library lady returned, opened the carrel door, gasped, and said, "Oh, I'm so sorry! Are you praying?"

"No. I'm looking at Dr. Quill's yoga mat," Virgil said. "If you could step back, you're in my light."

She stepped back, and he scanned the mat from one end to the other, flipped it over, did the same thing with the back. Halfway down, he stopped, squinted. The library lady was peering over his shoulder. Virgil stood up, stepped back, and said, pointing, "I want you to get down and look right there." He took a pencil from his pocket, bent over, and laid it on the mat.

"Well . . ." She got down on her knees anyway, looked where the pencil tip pointed, and after a moment said, "Oh."

"You think that's an eyelash?" Virgil asked.

"No, I—"

"Mustache hair?"

"No, I—"

"What, then?"

"I think it might be a . . . You know . . ."

"Dr. Quill was blond. Do you think his pubic hair would be that color? Dark brown, almost black?"

"Well, I don't—"

"Neither do I," Virgil said. He got on his phone to Trane. "There's a yoga mat in Trane's carrel."

"Yes, I saw it," she said.

"Did you unroll it?"

"Yes, just to make sure nothing was rolled up inside. Why?"

"I unrolled it and found what a pubic hair expert here at the library thinks just might be one. In her preliminary opinion, she doesn't think it came from Dr. Quill since he's a blond and this hair is not."

"Shit! Shit! We missed it," Trane said. "I knew you were gonna be trouble, Flowers. I'll call the lab, see how closely they scanned the mat. If they really missed it, I'll get somebody over there to collect it."

"Okay. Tell the lab guys to bring new crime scene tape. I'll wait until they get here."

"Shit! Shit! Listen, I'm coming, too. I'll be there in fifteen minutes."

When Virgil got off the phone, the library lady said, "I'm not a . . . hair . . . expert . . ."

"I must have misunderstood," Virgil said.

Virgil left the yoga mat unrolled on the floor, stepped out of the carrel, and closed the door as the library lady hurried away, glancing back over her shoulder only once. As Virgil was picking up the clump of crime scene tape, two uniformed campus cops walked past the far end of the book stacks, hesitated when they saw Virgil at the carrel door with the tangle of tape. They walked over, and the older one asked, "What were you doing here, sir?"

Virgil said, "I'm with the BCA. I'm working with Margaret Trane on the murder of Dr. Quill."

He slipped his ID out of his jacket pocket and handed it to the ranking cop, a sergeant. The cop glanced at it and handed it back. "Figure out anything?"

"Couple of things. Like, maybe I ought to be wearing a shirt and tie. Nobody seems to believe I'm a cop. Anyway, Margaret's on her way over right now, to take another look at the carrel."

"Kinda stuck?"

"Ah, we'll get there," Virgil said. "What's up with you guys? Anything to do with Quill?"

"Nah. You know the Andersen Library, across the street?" the sergeant asked.

"They were building it when I was a student here. I was never inside."

"Well, it's where they keep the rare book collections and other valuable stuff. Most of it's underground. Anyway, they're missing maps. At least several. They're doing an inventory now, but there are a hell of a lot of maps. We were looking at the cleaning staff because they've got keys to most things and could probably get keys to everything if they set their minds to it. One of the janitors told us he thought he saw a woman over there, well after hours, who actually works over here. She used to work over there. She denies it, said she never goes over there anymore except during the day. She does know the janitor by sight. She says she sees him over here, late in the day, out back. She says he's toking up before he goes to work. So, you know, stoned, confused, familiar with her face . . ."

He shrugged.

Virgil asked, "How much are the maps worth?"

"Several thousand dollars each, maybe more . . . The library hasn't tried to market them, so they don't know for sure. The thing is, the missing ones are all old European maps and would probably get the biggest bucks if they were sold in Germany or France. And if they're sold there, through a private dealer, we'd never hear about it."

"The woman here . . . What's her name?"

"Genevieve O'Hara. First name is pronounced the French way: *Jzhan-vee-EHV.*"

"And what do you think?"

"Well, the janitor wasn't sure that it was her he saw. If he was stoned . . . and knew her face . . . that's a problem. Whoever took the maps knew what they were doing—they're valuable, but not the most valuable; they weren't often referenced; and they're not so uncommon that their sale would get special attention. So there's all that."

"Huh. Is this woman French?"

"No. Not Irish, either. Born right here in Minnesota."

They were still talking about the map thefts and the Quill murder when Trane came up the stairs, looking harassed. She blew a stray hank of hair from her face, and said, "Okay, let's see it."

The two campus cops followed them to Quill's carrel. Virgil unlocked the door, and said, "The pencil point is an inch away from it."

"What is it?" the shorter of the two cops asked.

Trane didn't answer. She got down on her knees, pushed her glasses back on her nose, looked, and said, "Okay."

She stood up, and said, "Lock the door."

Virgil did, and said, "We've got to go somewhere and talk about it."

"There are a couple of study rooms here . . ."

The campus cops would have been happy to hear their conversation, but Virgil waved them off with a cheerful "See you later, guys" as he followed Trane to an empty room.

"Crime Scene ought to be here pretty quick, given what I told them and how their asses are now up around their ears," Trane said. "If Quill was screwing somebody in there, it'd have to be after hours. And we know he was there after hours."

"You had no hint that he was dating anybody?"

"Haven't been able to find anyone," she said. "There've been two weeks of publicity, and nobody's come forward. Why would he be nailing somebody in the library? His house is a five-minute drive from here."

"There's something else," Virgil said, and Trane's eyebrows went up.

He told her about the campus cops investigating the maps theft and that a woman who worked in the library, apparently on the next floor up, had been questioned.

"A janitor, who may have been stoned at the time, thought he saw the woman over there late at night. In the map collection," Virgil said. "She used to work there and might have had keys for both buildings. Suppose he spooked her and she wanted to get out of sight, so she came over here . . ."

". . . and ran into Quill. But would she kill him? If she's a librarian, wouldn't she make an excuse and then ask him what the heck he was doing there?"

"That sounds reasonable, depending on how spooked she was. Whoever took the maps took at least thousands of dollars' worth. From what those cops told me, they could be missing even more."

"We need to dig into this," Trane said.

"I'll tell you what, Margaret, I think *you* need to dig into it. I've talked to two campus cops and a librarian here, and a secretary over at the Humphrey Center, and there have been all kinds of people walking around here since I reopened the carrel—so word could get out that some new guy is investigating. It'd be better for all of us if you were running this part of it."

"You're right," Trane said, looking around. A student seemed to be watching them through the study room window. "I'll take it. Thank you. What are you going to do?"

"I'm going to give you the name of the woman the cops talked to . . ."

"I'll check her hair color, too . . ." Trane said.

Virgil: "Yeah, do that, although—"

"I know. Would Quill be screwing a map thief? And why? That doesn't sound right. But if that's a pubic hair, it didn't drift down from heaven."

"We don't know how long it's been there," Virgil said. "He might have been having an affair, bringing someone here, before he and his last wife broke up."

"I don't think so." Trane shook her head. "He was an aristo-cratic kind of guy. If he was sleeping with someone, an equal, it would have been in a hotel. Someplace with a handy bathroom. It wouldn't have been like this . . . in a library . . . on a yoga mat . . . after hours."

"Margaret, there's a pubic hair on the yoga mat and it ain't his. There's a bathroom fifty feet from here."

"I'll figure it out," she said. She chewed on her lower lip, then said, "What if it was somebody young who he wouldn't want to be seen in public with? A student?"

"Could be. But if he was the aristocratic sort, he might not care as long as she wasn't thirteen or something."

"Yeah . . . Okay . . . Now, what are you going to do?"

"I was going to meet you over at his house. That was next. Give me the key, come over when you're done here. I'll be a while."

She nodded. "Be aware that his house has been lived in by several different women—his mother, for one, at least for a while before she died, plus three wives, and probably a couple of girl-friends. It's full of about eighty years' worth of family junk, including a stuffed pelican and several stuffed fish. We went through it all. Maybe you'll find something. But I won't be holding my breath."

CHAPTER

FIVE

One of the things that Virgil liked best about the farm was the way it smelled. They had no animals, other than the dog and a chicken that had apparently escaped from a neighboring hen-house, so they didn't have a barnyard stench. They did have fresh-cut hay, one of the best odors in the world, and hot summer flowers, which smelled as good as the hay. In Virgil's opinion, August and September on the rural back roads of Minnesota made one of the prettiest landscapes imaginable, the roadside weeds and grasses and flowers going gold with the approaching autumn . . .

Not so much in the city, though. He walked out to his truck through the smell of asphalt and motor exhaust and what always struck him as spoiled Juicy Fruit gum and rotting bananas.

That changed as he crossed the river again, giving him a shot of dead carp and river weeds. He followed his GPS downstream to Quill's redbrick mansion on the bluff above the Mississippi. Quill had lived in one of the best spots in the Cities, he thought, green with overhanging trees, and quiet, pleasant streets, with the river right there.

But it wasn't the farm.

Quill's house was two stories high, plus an attic, under a complicated roof, and a basement. A detached three-car garage had a storage room above the parking pad. Both house and garage were built of deep red brick pierced by white-framed windows. Trane had told Virgil to park by the garage. Both its access door and the house could be unlocked with the same high-security digital key; and inside each door was an alarm keypad, security code 388783873.

When Trane gave him the code, Virgil said he'd never seen a nine-digit one. He wondered if the repetition of 3, 8, and 7 had some meaning, but Trane said one of Quill's wives told her that Quill used a random-number generator to create his codes. "Besides, how could the numbers have anything to do with our problem?"

"Maybe he had a security situation?" Virgil said.

"Uh, weak."

Virgil parked, looked through the garage window, saw two cars inside, used the key, and punched the alarm deactivation code into the pad. As he did, a clutch of sparrows flew overhead, their wings whirring in the stolid interior air. They disappeared through a hatch to the loft above.

The closest of the cars was an unlocked black Mercedes-Benz SUV, and, on the other side of it, was a silver BMW Z8. The third parking space was empty: the second BMW had been towed away to a police impound lot as possible evidence.

Virgil got vinyl gloves from his truck, went through both cars, and found nothing at all—it appeared that both had been cleaned out, probably by a Crime Scene crew. He climbed the ladder that led to the loft, stuck his head through the hatch, and saw a jumble of old furniture and worn carpets spotted with sparrow droppings. He couldn't imagine that any of it could have any bearing on an attack at the university library, so he went back out and locked the garage.

The house was surrounded by a wrought-iron fence lined with annual flowers, which also edged the cracked concrete sidewalk between the garage and the back door of the house. Instead of going in the door, he walked around the house, looking it over. At the front door, he peered through its window, saw nothing in particular, turned the key, and stepped inside.

The door opened into a generous reception area, the dark oak floor mostly covered with a red-and-blue oriental carpet. A circular staircase wound around and up to a balcony overhead, looking down at the door. A central hallway separated a living room from a library/music room.

The living room was arranged for entertaining, with three couches around a center carpet, a sideboard for drinks and food; a mahogany grandfather clock stood in a corner, its hands stopped at four forty-four because its winder had been murdered. The library had a wall of books interspersed with a variety of keepsakes, including a collection of chipped Hummels that appeared to be very old and a shelf of aging stereo equipment, including a turntable, with speakers on shelves at opposite ends of the bookcase.

A walnut-cased Steinway baby grand sat in one corner, a stack of sheet music on it. He looked at the music for a moment. Half classical, in the full piano forms—somebody was a good pianist—and half romantic stuff from the swing era pre–World War II—Cole Porter, George Gershwin, like that. Irving Berlin's "Blue Skies" was open on the music stand.

Farther back down the hall was a formal dining room with a rectangular walnut table and ten matching bentwood chairs, and, on the other side of the hall, a breakfast room with a table and two chairs and a door leading to the kitchen. A powder room was built in near the kitchen.

The house was silent as a coffin.

Virgil took the stairs, found Quill's bedroom, plus a home office with more books, three more bedrooms, and a door leading up to the attic. The bathroom was expansive and modern.

A rich guy for sure. Everything was notably tidy except the home office, which had the look of a working space, with papers and books and journals and pens and transparent highlighters spread around all the flat surfaces. Everything else in the house had the feel of professional maintenance: a maid, at least, and possibly a gardener.

Virgil worked his way slowly through the entire house with the exception of the cellar and the attic, which he checked briefly and then dismissed. Again, he couldn't imagine how either might factor in a murder that had taken place a mile away. He was looking for words—in letters, texts, or printouts—or personal possessions that weren't Quill's. Something that would suggest or reveal an inimical relationship.

The bed was neatly made, king-sized and covered with a huge old shoofly quilt. He carefully peeled it back until the bottom sheet was exposed, then went over the quilt looking for more dark pubic hairs. And found none.

He saved the office for last. The centerpiece was an ancient oak desk, fully eight feet long and four feet across, the old wood polished to a high sheen, with ranks of drawers on both sides of the kneehole. The desk had been carefully updated with a keyboard where there'd once been a center drawer, with a rank of electric sockets installed along the back edge of the desktop. There was an empty spot there where a computer had been, its Canon printer still sitting to one side, its computer hookup cable curled next to it. Trane had taken the computer to research emails.

A bookshelf was stacked with academic journals, several medical books, and more academic detritus, all of it printed, none of it annotated, nothing that would help with a murder. There was another stereo, with two bookshelf speakers. Virgil noticed an LED light on a CD player, opened it, and found an unmarked disc sitting in the tray. He took it out: no markings whatever. He put it back, pressed the play button, and a minute later an unfamiliar singer pushed the uncomplicated lyrics of "Home on the Range" through his nose through the speakers.

He turned the CD player off with an involuntary shudder. He sorta lived on the range, but that didn't mean the song didn't suck.

The bookshelves also contained a collection of antique wooden boxes, and inside them he found important but routine papers—a checkbook, check stubs from his university paycheck, investment reports from U.S. Bank and Wells Fargo, tax records, insurance policies, titles to automobiles, a stack of last year's Christmas cards. He spent a half hour going through the papers and journals on the desk and on two side filing cabinets, looking for anything handwritten, anything out of place. He found nothing that looked important.

Virgil was lying under the desk, in the kneehole, when Trane asked, unexpectedly, "What are you doing?"

Virgil, startled, jerked half upright and banged his head against the bottom of the keyboard drawer. He dropped back on his elbows and saw Trane's shoes and cuffs of her pants. "Ouch. Jesus Christ, give me a little warning, will you?"

"Sorry. What are you doing?" She stooped and peered under the desk.

"My grandpa had a desk like this. Smaller, but old like this one, with a million drawers," Virgil said. He was digging around in a narrow space behind the drawers. "Pull the top left drawer out, would you?"

She pulled the drawer out, and Virgil asked, "Anything interesting?"

"Not that we haven't looked at . . ."

"Can you pull the drawer all the way out? So it comes loose?" Virgil asked.

She tried. "No. It's not made to come out. I can feel it hit some stops."

Virgil said, "Hmm." And, "Get anything good at the library?"

"Everybody agrees it's a pubic hair. Actually, three pubic hairs; you missed some. I was at the autopsy and I can tell you they're not Quill's. He was a real blond."

"Three pubic hairs . . . Unless the owner was shedding, they might have used it more than once."

Virgil crawled out of the kneehole and stood up.

"What are you looking for?" Trane asked.

"The case housing the drawer is about eight or ten inches deeper than the drawer itself. No good reason for it, but it's entirely enclosed," he said.

"Maybe if we pushed the desk away from the wall, we could look in from the back?"

"No. If there's a space there, you'd want to be able to access it without taking the room apart. My grandpa's . . ."

Virgil pushed down on the left edge of the top: nothing.

He pulled up: nothing. Looked under the edge, couldn't see anything except a scratch.

"There's a scratch . . ." he said, going down to his knees.

"So what?"

"Well, it'd be a hard place to scratch," Virgil said. "There's, ah, a hole here . . . by the scratch . . . That'll be it."

"For a secret door? You gotta be joking," Trane said.

"Everybody knew about my grandpa's hidey-hole, including me," Virgil said. "Wasn't a secret. A lot of these old desks had them. They weren't safes. You might put confidential stuff in there, maybe tax stuff and so on, but not money. Like I said, the drawers weren't all that secret at the time."

He stood up again, opened the top right drawer. A plastic tray held pencils, ballpoint pens, paper clips, fingernail clippers, scissors . . . and a single, right-angled Allen wrench. He took it out, carried it around to the side of the desk, fit it in the hole, and pushed.

A side panel clicked loose and out, then folded down. Inside was a vertical stack of small drawers, almost like trays.

"Agatha Fuckin' Christie," Trane said, amazed. "Open the drawers."

Virgil did. They were all empty. He crawled around to the other side of the desk, found an identical hole, popped the side panel, revealing another stack of drawers. He pulled open the top drawer, and they both peered inside.

Trane said, "Oh, no. Nope. Nope. Nope. Shut the drawer, I don't want to see that."

"Could be laundry detergent," Virgil said. "You know, like Tide? I could snort a little to see if it is."

"How much you think?"

"I never worked dope," Virgil said. "But I've seen cocaine, and that's cocaine. Not much, but we don't know what he started with."

"Our murdered boy's got cocaine stashed in a secret cubbyhole? That's the cherry on the cake, you know? That's just fuckin' perfect. I hope the television people find out about it so they can go berserk."

"Could be Tide . . ."

They called the narcs and continued to probe the office, although Trane had already done that. She took each of the antique boxes down, looking for false bottoms or secret drawers. They didn't have any. A Narcotics cop named Bill Offers showed up, said that the baggie had contained a standard eight ball, an eighth of an ounce of cocaine. "Good stuff, not been stepped on much . . . Originally, he probably paid a couple hundred bucks for it, depending on his connection."

"Then he could have gotten it from anybody outside the back door of a bar," Trane said.

"Yeah, like that. Might want to talk to his wife about it," Offers said.

"I will," Trane said. "Tonight."

"I was planning to call her," Virgil said. "Mind if I tag along?"

"Suit yourself," Trane said.

Not exactly a heartwarming welcome from Trane, but maybe a little progress, Virgil thought. Offers had a scale in his car. They weighed the coke, with the baggie, and Virgil and Trane signed it over to Narcotics for safekeeping.

"You said you were at the Graduate Hotel?" Trane asked Virgil, as they finished the paperwork.

"Yeah. All checked in."

"Nancy Quill doesn't live far from there, she's over by the Witch Hat," Trane said. "You could follow me over."

The Witch Hat referred to the Prospect Park neighborhood that had an old water tower perched on the second-highest piece of land in Minneapolis. Visible for miles, the tower was topped with what looked like a green witch's hat. Quill didn't live in Prospect Park itself but in an adjacent neighborhood, in a neat, yellow-brick condo. Trane called ahead, and Quill buzzed them through the door to the elevators.

On the way up, Trane asked, "Do you know anybody in the media? Here in the Cities?"

"Couple people," Virgil said. "Why?"

"It would be nice if word leaked out that we're actually making progress without it coming from me or anyone in Homicide. I don't want to get anyone in trouble," Trane said.

"Davenport is tight with a lot of TV people. He even has a daughter with one of them, at Channel Three. She's an executive now, used to be a reporter. I could ask him to leak it. He'd do it.

And if somebody smart tried to backtrack it, it'd come to me. And I don't care if it does."

"If you could make the call, it might take some of the heat off," Trane said.

"Soon as we leave here," Virgil said.

Nancy Quill was a tall, severe-looking blonde who spoke in short, precise sentences that were delivered in paragraphs.

"I never saw Barth use any drug. Not even aspirin. He didn't care for wine, although he took a glass from time to time. That was his effort to be social. He didn't use hard alcohol, with one exception. He did spend some money on tequila. He'd sip a glass of it at night, before bed, by himself. Cocaine seems unlikely. But, if he were to have a drug of choice, and I were asked to guess what it was, I would guess cocaine or one of the amphetamines. He would look for a drug that would intensify focus, not blur it."

"You never saw any hint that he used cocaine?" Trane asked.

"Never. He made it clear, though, that I wasn't welcome in his office," Quill said. "It looks messy in there, but actually everything had its place and everything was put in its place. I had my own office, in a spare bedroom. I moved my effects here when I left him. I have no idea what the signs of cocaine abuse might be, other than having seen some actor inhale some white powder in some movie."

Virgil asked, "Did he have any friends or associates that you saw who seemed, mmm, to strike a false note? Somebody who might have supplied him with the cocaine or might have been a connection to that world?"

"Barth didn't have close male friends, people he would confide in. He married three times, of course, so it seemed that he should like women, although I'm not sure he did. He needed us for sexual release, to be frank about it. I'm not sure he wanted us around for anything else."

"A misogynist, then?" Trane asked.

"Oh, I wouldn't use that word," Quill said. "A misogynist is someone who thinks of women as inferior. He didn't. He quite respected a number of women in his own field, for their work. He regularly corresponded with them. You have his home and office computers. I believe if you closely examine his emails, you'll find their names."

Trane said to Virgil, "We've done that. There were female academics among the people he wrote to, but I didn't see anything there that struck me as personal rather than professional."

Virgil to Quill: "To get back to my original question: what about false notes?"

"I've been thinking about that. Actually, there is someone. A lawyer, John Combes. Everybody calls him Jack. He and Barth had a regular weekly handball game over at the RecWell. Their relationship was . . . not exactly a friendship. They never socialized other than on the court and once a year at the Combeses' Christmas party. Jack always struck me as a bit sleazy—a criminal law attorney and not wildly successful. He does come from a prominent family. Perhaps their relationship went back to childhood, to school, I don't know. I do know that he's an excellent handball player."

That was all they got from Quill. If her husband had been using cocaine, she never saw any signs of euphoria or withdrawal. "Barth was incredibly even-tempered. With his job, I'm sure he must have felt stress, disappointment, anger, but he never showed it."

As they were leaving, Virgil asked Quill, "Did your husband like cowboy music?"

"What?"

"You know, cowboy music."

"I doubt that he ever listened to a cowboy song in his entire life. He liked Bartók."

"Jimmy Ray Bartók?"

"No, Béla . . . Oh, you were joking." She looked disappointed in him.

In the elevators on the way back down, Trane said, "Jack Combes might be something. I know who he is, but he's a small-timer in the legal world. Never handled a homicide, as far as I know. Or, if he did, not a big one. I wouldn't be at all surprised if he got a lot of work through court appointments for drug defendants. That would be about his speed."

"You want to do him or do you want me to?"

She thought for a moment, then said, "Why don't you take him? He sounds like a jock, and you're obviously a jock. Maybe you'll bond. I want to ride herd on our pubic hair. It could be critical."

"You gonna do DNA on all three of them?" Virgil asked.

"Think we should?"

"Yeah. They're probably all from the same person, but it would be very interesting if they weren't. If you've got a guy who takes a personal interest in women only because he wants the sex, as Nancy Quill says he did, and if he has a logical mind, like most scientists, then . . . why not a hooker? Or two or three? Be a lot cheaper than two-year marriages followed by divorces."

"As you would know as well as anybody," Trane said.

"Right. Thanks for mentioning it. Another thing: hotels have eyes for hookers and that might be a reason he'd take one to the library. And where you find hookers, you're gonna find drugs. And you might even find blackmail. You might find all kinds of things. Like motive."

"Good point," Trane said. "We'll do the DNA on all the hair."

"I'll find this Combes guy tomorrow," Virgil said. He looked down at his shoes for a moment, ruminating.

"What?"

"'Home on the Range.' He has 'Home on the Range' on his stereo. It sorta convinced me that the guy was deranged."

"That's almost a pun."

"I didn't mean it that way," Virgil said.

Outside, Trane looked at her watch. "I'm going home. You'll find Combes tomorrow morning?"

"Yeah. I'd like to solve this by tomorrow night. You know, so I wouldn't have to spend Sunday worrying about it."

"I'm all for that," Trane said. She offered him a tiny smile, the first he'd seen from her. "But it won't happen. I have to say, though, that you did good stuff today, Virgil. I didn't have anything to work on. Now I do."

"I'll call you after I talk to Combes."

"And talk to Davenport about leaking to the TV people."

On his way back to the hotel, Virgil called Davenport, who agreed to leak a progress report. And Davenport also knew Combes. "Combes is smart enough, but lazy. He *is* a jock—golf, tennis, basketball. Handball doesn't surprise me. I've played some basketball with him and he can shoot. But, you know, he comes from one of those old, rich mill families, and I don't think he ever needed to work," Davenport said. "Loafed his way through law school, managed to pass the bar exam, worked for the public defender for a couple of years, does some pro bono now. And, yeah, I think he could probably hook you up with a dealer."

At the hotel, Virgil got a steak, then wandered over to the beer joint for a brew. The place was busy, but he grabbed the last stool at the bar, next to an older, white-haired, red-faced man in a blue linen sport coat and white shirt; he smelled like a cheeseburger, but not offensively so.

The Latina-looking barmaid came along, and Virgil asked if they had Bud Light. She winced, said, "Um, no."

"Then give me whatever is most like Bud Light," Virgil said.

The white-haired man laughed, and said, "The boy's determined to drink cow piss, Alice. I wouldn't stand in his way. He could be armed and dangerous."

He turned and looked at Virgil, checked the shirt, and said, "You're in a band?"

"No . . . But I like band shirts."

"So do I, but they look stupid on you when you're as old and fat as I am. You got the hair and stomach for it."

"Thank you."

The barmaid came back with a glass of beer, pushed it across the bar to Virgil, and said, "Best we could do." She was a pretty woman, round-faced, brown-skinned, dark-eyed, with a flashing smile.

Virgil took a sip, and said, "Okay. PBR? Miller Lite?"

"Got it in two," she said. "Miller."

"Well, you got what you wanted, what was most like that other shit," the white-haired man said. And, "My name's Harry."

"I'm Virgil."

"Let me guess . . ." He gave Virgil a look, with Alice, the barmaid, getting interested, her arms on the bar, looking back and forth between them, and then Harry said, "You're reppin' for somebody. Something technical, a computer company maybe . . ." He stopped, examined Virgil even more closely, and then said, "No. Bless my soul, you're a cop. Some kind of cop."

Virgil laughed, shook his head.

Alice asked, "Is he right? Are you a cop?"

"Yeah, I guess," Virgil said. "No, actually, I'm sure I am."

"Who you coppin' for?" Harry asked.

"Minnesota BCA. Bureau of Criminal Apprehension."

"That's pretty amazing," Alice said to Harry. And again to Harry: "Another one?"

"Might as well," Harry said, pushing his empty glass across the bar to her. To Virgil: "You workin' on a case?"

"Yeah, I'm taking a look at the professor who got killed over at the university."

"Hey, I read about that," Harry said. "You gettin' anywhere?"

"We're early in the game," Virgil said.

"Bullshit. I read about it two weeks ago. If you don't have the killer by now, you're in big trouble."

"Nah, we're breaking it down," Virgil said.

"You don't mind talking about it?"

"Oh . . . no . . . I guess not." Virgil didn't mind talking. His attitude was, the killer knew everything about the case; and the cops knew some of it. Not talking about it didn't keep information from anyone but the taxpaying citizens. He gave Harry a one-minute summary, and Harry took it all in.

Alice the barmaid came back with Harry's beer, said, "On the house because of the cop guess," and Harry said, "Virgil's investigating a murder."

"What murder?" she asked.

"Professor over at the university," Harry said.

She shook a finger at Virgil. "I heard about that. The one at the library. You catch the killer?"

"We're working on it," Virgil said.

"Let me tell you something," Harry said. "I own three McDonalds, but I don't know the first thing about murder investigations except what I've seen on *NCIS*. You know that show?"

"Sure. Gibbs and those guys. I've gotten a few tips there," Virgil lied.

"Mark Harmon, hell of a football player. You're not nearly old enough to appreciate this, but Harmon was a quarterback at UCLA, and they kicked Nebraska's ass back sometime in the seventies. Huge deal. Nebraska was the defending national champ at the time."

"Didn't know that," Virgil said.

Harry leaned closer, breathing beer breath on Virgil. "That's because you're not old enough. I'm seventy and I remember it like it was yesterday. I wish it was yesterday. I remember when Joe Namath and the Jets upset the Colts."

"I know about that, though I wasn't born yet," Virgil said. "My dad was a jock; he told me about it maybe, mmm, two hundred times."

"You a jock?" Harry asked.

"I guess. Baseball, mostly. Here at the U. Couldn't see a college fastball that well."

"Played golf myself, at Michigan," Harry said. "I once shot a 66 against the Badgers over in Madison. Best I ever did."

They talked about sports for a few more minutes, and Virgil had a second beer, and then Harry said, "Let me tell you something about your case."

"Go ahead."

"A young person did it," Harry said. "I don't know if it was a male or a female, but it was a young person."

"Why is that?"

Harry held up a heavy index finger. "I started running my first McDonald's when I was twenty-seven years old. I've got three now. Most of my life is hiring young people to work in them, though we've got a few senior citizens. I've hired hundreds of young people. And fired quite a few, too. Here's the thing about young people now: a lot of them are no goddamn good. Mean little fuckin' wolverines."

"I don't want to say that's bigoted . . ." Virgil said.

"Not bigoted," Harry said. "I know bigoted. I was playing in an NCAA regional when I was in college, and we had this black kid on the team. The country club—this was down in Kansas City— got all out of joint because they didn't know there was a black man in the field. Didn't allow black guys on the course unless they had a rake in their hands. Seen a lot of that shit over the years; half my McDonald's kids are black and they tell me about it."

"But young people—they seem to me like anybody else, sort of all over the place," Virgil said.

Harry nodded. "Some of them are. Maybe most of them, I

don't know. But I get three types at my McDonalds. I got kids who want to make money for a whole lot of reasons, and they're serious about it. They want to buy a car or go to college, or whatever. They hang in there, and they're determined and they'll work hard until they get what they want. Or a better job. Good kids. Hate to see them go, but they always do. Then I got the kids who don't have any choice. Maybe they've got to work to eat, maybe they're bright enough to work at McDonald's but don't have a lot more going for themselves. I like those kids because I've had some of them stay with me for twenty years. But the third type: they're no goddamn good."

"How's that different than it's always been?" Virgil asked.

"It is, believe me. There have always been kids who were no damn good, but now it's everywhere. *Everywhere*. It's kids who know they're not going to be millionaires or billionaires or movie stars or famous singers or in the NBA, and it's all they want. They can't see past that. It's like they're not alive if they're not on TV. They don't want to be doctors or dentists or lawyers or businessmen, they want to be rich and famous right now. They don't want to work. All they want is to be a celebrity. Then at some point they realize it ain't gonna happen. They're not talented enough or smart enough, and they sure as shit don't want to work at getting to be famous. When they figure that out, that it ain't gonna happen, they turn mean."

"Mean?" Virgil said.

"That's right, mean," Harry said. "You get kids who'll kill you for no reason. To feel important. What's more important than killing somebody? You say, you'll go to prison. They don't care. They don't even care if they die. They'll tell you that. 'Go ahead and kill me, I got no life.'"

"You believe that?"

Harry drank half his beer down. "Virgil, I once got all pissed off at one of these school shootings, one of these massacres. I told one of my girls, one of my employees, that when they convict the guy, they ought to haul his ass out of the courthouse, make him kneel down on the steps, and then shoot him in the back of the head. You know what she said?"

"That you're nuts?"

Harry laughed. "No. What she said was, 'If you did that, the guy would be on TV. He'd be happy. He'd be famous. He was on TV.' Being on fuckin' TV. Being on the internet. She's right. I know some of those kids."

Virgil finished his beer, said, "On that cheerful note, I'm going to bed."

"I'm here most every night," Harry said. "Let me know how you're doing. And Virgil—it's a young person."

Virgil spent the rest of the evening watching a ball game from the West Coast and went to bed at ten o'clock, like a farmer. At ten minutes after ten, his cell phone rang.

It was Trane. "You awake?" she asked.

"Yeah. Barely."

"We need to go back to the Quill house," Trane said. "I thought of a reason he might have been listening to 'Home on the Range.' I'll meet you there at eight."

"Well, tell me," Virgil said.

She did, and Virgil said, "I believe that, Margaret. I mean, maybe you're wrong, but I believe it right now."

"Eight o'clock," she said.

Virgil turned off the lights again, dropped his head back on the pillow. Was she right? Or was it a silly fantasy? Why hadn't he thought of it when he was standing right there?

And then he worried a little about Harry.

CHAPTER

SIX

Katherine Green was sitting in the coffee shop in the Coffman Memorial Union when she saw one of her students going through the line.

He'd gone to India with her on a summer research trip with six other students. He was older than the others, more her age, she thought. She'd been tempted at the time to give him a mild hit, to see what happened. He was nice-looking: square shoulders, square jaw, neatly trimmed hair, crisp shirt, carefully ironed chinos. He was quiet, soft-spoken, often with a touch of humor.

One of her better students, even though she sensed an underlying skepticism about Cultural Science.

When he finished the line, he looked around for a seat. He saw Green, and she pointed at the chair opposite her. He smiled and came over and sat down.

"Professor Green . . ."

"How's the paper going?" she asked.

"Well enough, I guess. I've only taken the beginning course in stats. I need to do more, maybe go back and hit the algebra again. I'm struggling with the math."

"No matter what you wind up doing, stats is critical," she agreed. "You can look at something that seems so right, and a good analysis of the statistics will tell you there's nothing there."

"I've noticed that," he said. "In the media."

"Nobody should be allowed in the professional media without at least a year of statistics," she said, sipping her coffee. "The bullshit you see on TV and in the newspapers is beyond stupid. The phony research . . ."

"Maybe they know better but go with the clickbait."

They talked for a few minutes, mostly about the man's research and statistics, then he asked, "Anything new on the Barth Quill front? More cops coming around?"

Green hunched her shoulders and leaned into the table. "No. They don't seem to be getting anywhere, the police. They're spinning their wheels. It's awful."

"It *is* bad," the man said. "People have said the department . . . I mean, after the hassle at Quill's lecture . . ."

Green nodded, now grim. "I know. It's ridiculous. I've been reading about motives in violent crime ever since Quill got killed—murder never involves something like that. Quill was killed by somebody who hated him for personal reasons. Or by a crazy man. An academic feud isn't enough . ." She took a few more sips of coffee, then said, "Remember the reading I assigned on the causes of the Civil War? Did you get that?"

"Yeah, I read it," he said. He then used her favorite word. "Interesting."

"The authors make the point that there were serious economic stresses between the different sections of the country, but the spark that set it off was slavery. Without the emotional trigger of slavery, there would have been no war," she said. "This murder is analogous—it takes a specific, dynamic, emotional spark to murder, even with crazy people. The anger between members of our department and his was on an entirely different level."

"Suppose we have somebody in the department who's a little crazy who has some kind of hidden emotional situation."

"Like what?" Green demanded.

"Okay. This is hypothetical. Say they have an emotional attachment to you. They see you attacked, they see you called names that carry an emotional load—"

"Like 'twat'?"

"Exactly. They decide to attack your attacker."

"That's nonsense," she said. "There's nobody that attached to me, I promise you. Not enough to kill. I would feel it."

"We have at least two Ph.D. candidates who are close to getting their degrees. If something happened—"

"Oh, c'mon," she said. "It could be a setback. But a reason for murder? No."

"I'd disagree with you," the man said, "except that I know the two people and they didn't kill anybody."

"Have you talked to them?"

"Chatting. You know, bull sessions." He smiled. "As soon as I told them my alibi, they told me theirs. Theirs were better."

"Alibis . . . If you were planning to kill Quill, you'd figure out an alibi. A good one, unless you were an idiot. If you weren't planning to kill him and it was a random act, and the police didn't catch you in the first few hours, and you didn't leave behind specific kinds of incriminating evidence, then you won't need an alibi because they'll never identify you and won't be asking for one.

In fact, you could probably tell the police that you didn't know where you were that night. Who remembers where they were on a Friday night two weeks ago? You could say you were at home, in bed, reading a book. How do they break that?"

"You don't think they'll get the guy?"

"I have my doubts. I even have my doubts about it being a guy." She looked at him for a moment, then lowered her voice. "I don't want you talking to anyone about this conversation."

"I won't. Scout's Honor." He held up the three fingers in the Boy Scout salute.

She smiled at that, then said, "You know what I think? I think he was in the library with a woman. Maybe a paid woman, for sex. And she killed him. Maybe not even on purpose. He did something she didn't like and she struck out at him."

"A prostitute?" His eyebrows went up. "That would explain a few things. Like why he snuck into the library after hours."

"A man like that wouldn't want a prostitute in his house," Green said. "He probably wouldn't want her to know where he lives . . . or even his real name."

"I don't think . . ."

"Where else could he go where he could be sure he wouldn't be seen?" Green asked. "Not a hotel, not around here. His face was too well known. He was hidden there in the library—they didn't even find him after he was murdered, not for days."

"A prostitute. An interesting idea," the man said. "I wonder if the police are looking into it? Maybe you should be a cop."

She pointed a finger at him. "It occurred to me once that Cultural Science would be an excellent background for a police officer. The life experience, the research we do . . . You begin to understand the fabric of a culture."

———

Clete May was sitting barefoot on his couch watching a snooker tournament from England, swilling Dr Pepper and eating Fritos, when the doorbell rang. "Ah, shit," he muttered, and got to his feet and opened the door.

The guy there said, "Hey, man. You busy?"

"Watching a snooker tournament. If I only understood it, it'd probably be entertaining. What's up?"

"I was walking by and wondered if you'd heard anything new about the Quill thing?"

"Come on in." The guy stepped inside, and May led him to the couch facing the TV. They sat down, and May said, "Everybody's still talking. That detective chick—uh, Trane—is flying around like a rabid bat. I don't think she's getting anywhere . . . Want some Fritos?"

"Yeah, thanks." The guy took a half handful, crunched them. "Anybody got any new ideas?"

"Not that I've heard. I did hear that Trane told somebody that Quill hadn't been in a fight, looked like he was jumped by surprise."

"Huh."

May turned toward him, hands cupped, intent. "Listen. I'm thinking Quill had that computer up there. The big one. I'm wondering if it was hooked into his lab? Maybe somebody was going up there, in the middle of the night, and using it to get into the lab's files and download his research. That medical research can be worth a bundle. Or it could be the Russians or Chinese. Quill figures it out, see, and maybe, just maybe, there are logs, and he sees that library computer coming online and knows it's his, but he wasn't doing it. He sneaks into the library to see who's doing it, but the guy gets the jump on him somehow and kills him and then has to take the computer to hide what was going on."

"International spies. Russian or Chinese."

"I know it sounds wild," May said. "We know the Russians and Chinese do that stuff, though, steal tech, and they sure as shit wouldn't want to be caught at it again."

"You talk to the cops about this?"

"No, but I will if anybody asks me. Like I said, it sounds wild at first, but when you think it over . . ."

Carol Ann Soboda was walking back to her table at Stub & Herb's bar, after a visit to the restroom, and nearly bounced off a guy with a beer in his hand. The guy said, "Oops," caught her arm, got her right again, and she smiled at him, and he said, "Hey . . . Aren't you one of the people who worked with Dr. Quill?"

"I did, yeah. I don't remember you . . ."

"Ah, I was sorta on the other side . . . I was with Dr. Green at Fight Night. I didn't get involved, I thought the whole thing was crazy, but I saw you there."

The guy was good-looking and friendly, and Soboda was flattered that he remembered her. She was between relationships—*way* between relationships—so she let herself talk, what could it hurt? "Yeah, I was there. Who was that crazy guy with the chair?"

They spent ten minutes leaning on the bar, and the man, who said his name was Terry, said he'd read about the murder and wondered what was going on with Quill and his secret carrel in the library.

"Nobody knows," Soboda said. "My girlfriend thinks he was

looking at child porn or going out looking for hookups, but I don't think so. That computer was, like, a workstation. You can look at porn or find hookups on your iPhone."

"Maybe he was doing secret research? Maybe he needed a good computer for that. And maybe he was in the library because he was away from everything and liked a quiet space to think."

"He had all kinds of quiet places to think. I tell you, it's a mystery. We talk about it every day at the lab and we can't figure it out."

"What happens with the lab? You out of a job?"

"Nobody knows what's going to happen yet," Soboda said. "Our lab manager is looking around to see if he can merge us with somebody doing the same kind of research, but we're pretty far out there"

"Okay, how about this?" Terry said. "Your guy was spying on other labs doing the same kind of research, trying to get a leg up."

She thought about that, then said, "Wouldn't you have to be a hacker to do that? Barth wasn't a computer person. I mean, he could use our software, but that's like using a toaster. You don't have to be a programmer, and he wasn't one."

"Huh. Well, it's a mystery. So what are you up to? You come here often?"

"Not too often . . ."

Like that.

Megan Quill was standing outside a SuperAmerica store on Grand Avenue, where she'd tapped a Wells Fargo ATM and used a few bucks to buy Nestlé Drumsticks for herself and her friends Jerry and Brett.

On a hot day, the cones had a propensity to drip on your clothing if you weren't careful, so they stood in a tight huddle, bent toward one another, licking the cones, dripping on the sidewalk, and mumbling a few words like "Okay" and "Not bad" and "Watch the drip, Brett."

Megan was dressed in fashionable black, something like a sexy tennis dress, and it worked for her. Jerry was dressed in unfashionable black: a sloppy black T-shirt to cover up his overstuffed body, sloppy black cargo shorts, sloppy black cross-trainers with short black socks. Brett, the nonconformist, was wearing a plain white T-shirt and red running shorts and flip-flops. He was bobbing up and down to some music that only he could hear and that ran through his brain like the sound track to his life.

They all saw the guy coming: blue golf shirt, tan slacks, blue sneaks. He was older than they were—late twenties or early thirties, Quill thought—trim and square-jawed in a way that you didn't see that much. He had blue eyes and a nice smile. He slowed as he came up, and then asked, "Are you Megan Quill? Professor Quill's daughter?"

Quill stopped licking her cone, staring hard at him. "Yes. Who are you?"

"I'm a grad student over at the U. Jeez, I was sorry to hear about what happened."

Quill said, "Yeah . . ." She licked a couple of times, self-consciously now, with this good-looking guy watching her. "It was pretty awful."

"Any signs that they're going to catch whoever did it?"

"The cops don't have a fuckin' clue," Jerry said. He laughed. "They oughta make them all wear clown shoes so we'll know what we're dealing with. Bunch of fuckin' maroons."

"Harsh, man," Brett said. "They'll catch him. Trane's smart."

"Not a chance," Quill said. She asked the man in the slacks, "Do you work in medicine or something? Did you know my father?"

"No, I was sort of on the other side of the big feud," he said. "I'm in Anthropology, and I know Dr. Green. Or, at least, I see her around the building. She can be a little . . . out there . . . at times. Lot of people over at the U wonder if somebody in Cultural Science had something to do with it—the murder—but she doesn't seem worried. I see her laughing with her friends at lunch . . . Are you at the U? Or here?"

St. Thomas was across the street. "I'm here. I kinda wish I was at the U, but my mom thought there'd be better discipline here and that I needed that."

The man said, "At least you weren't right there . . . when it happened. I mean, if you'd gone to the library with him . . ."

Megan faked a shudder. "Yeah. Never thought of that." *Lick.*

"Actually, that might have been interesting. See a real guy killed," Jerry said. "I've seen about a million people killed in this goddamn game, but never . . ." He was poking at the surface of his cell phone, and Brett said, "Jerry's a game freak. He can't even stop to eat a freakin' ice cream cone."

"Some people think that shooter games desensitize game freaks and makes it easier for them to kill real people," Quill said. "What do you think, Jer? You kill my daddy?"

Jerry's finger poking never slowed. "You know what I think? He wasn't interesting enough to kill. If I was gonna kill somebody, it'd be somebody with a big payoff. Change the fate of the nation."

"Then you'd have to change the fate of your underwear. They'd be all brown instead of those white tighty-whities," Quill said.

"Fuck you." Jerry did something with his thumb, then looked up from the phone. "Can I look at your pussy when we get back?"

She glanced at the good-looking man, with maybe a little blush high on her cheeks, and said, "Ignore him. He tries to shock . . . older people. He usually fails."

"You know what?" Brett asked. "I don't think anybody in the feud had anything to do with it. I think there were people already in the library for something that didn't have anything to do with Professor Quill. Something illegal. He caught them and they killed him. You know, that's a big place. If you were up there late in the day, you could hide out, get yourself locked in, sleep there, probably go down in the basement—they've got a coffee place down there—get something to eat. A street guy, in there to steal stuff, or even some student who ran out of money . . ."

"What could you steal in the library?" the man asked. "Books? Who wants books?"

Brett shrugged. "There's all kinds of stuff laying around. You don't think about it, but people leave stuff in their offices—cameras, office equipment, tools. If you were strong, you could get out of there with a printer, or something, sell it at one of those used-computer places. Good money, if you're on the street."

Quill snorted. "You've thought about it."

Brett: "Well, yeah. I had to drop out the first semester of my third year. I went to Spain that summer using my school money, and the folks wouldn't give me any more. Said I had to make it up."

"Fascists," Jerry said. He was back poking at his cell phone.

"Ah, they're good folks," Brett said. "Anyway, seeing all the shit people leave around in university buildings, it was sort of tempting to pick some up."

Quill: "You do it? Go outlaw?"

Brett shook his head. "Nah, I chickened out. Got a job pushing a broom over at the HarMar Mall." He did a comic head turn, checking the street with narrowed eyes as if a cop might be listening. "I'll tell you what. There was this storage area over at the mall, stuff they used in the restrooms. Toilet paper, paper towels, cleaning stuff. They'd order like six months' supply at a time, in these big cardboard boxes. I'd push it a couple feet forward from the back wall—you couldn't tell—and I'd sleep back there. I had a foam mattress and a sleeping bag. I'd get off at two in the morning, shave and take a sponge bath in the restroom, and bag out. Get up at eleven, brush my teeth, hang out until it was time to go to work. My own little apartment."

"Cool," Megan said.

Jerry shook his head. "Pathetic."

The unknown man said, "I admire that. You gotta do what you gotta do. Did you go back to school?"

Brett flashed his smile. "Yeah. I graduate this winter."

"Great." He turned back to Megan as he started to step away. "Like I said, I'm sorry about what happened."

She said, "Yeah, thanks. It's all a mystery."

He ambled away, and Brett, looking after him, said, "That was sort of weird. Guy on the street like that coming up to you."

The guy got in a car fifty yards away, did an illegal U-turn, went past them, holding up a hand to wave. Megan nodded, and said, "I'd fuck him."

"Fuck me," Jerry said.

"No way. Why don't you fuck Elaine? She'd do it, if you'd tell her where the sniper's nest is."

"Fuck that. She'll never get past it," Jerry said. "She's hung up."

"And you won't get laid. She'll probably figure it out, sooner or later, so you might as well make it sooner and get laid."

"Good point." Jerry was looking at the man in the car, who'd stopped at the light down the street. He said nothing about Elaine, but he did say to Brett, "You're right. That was weird." He lifted his cell phone and took a shot of the car.

"You don't think . . ." Quill turned and watched as the car accelerated through the now green light and went on down Cleveland Avenue.

Brett: "What?"

"That he might have done it? That he was checking us out to see what we knew?"

"Oh, fuck no," Brett said. "Did he seem like a killer to you? He didn't to me."

"You can never tell," Quill said. "The killer could be anybody."

That night, at dark, the man was waiting outside Nancy Quill's condo when the Jaguar pulled into a visitor's parking slot. He knew the Jag, and the man who got out of it, and Quill as well, who waited for the driver to walk around and open the passenger door. He did, and they went up. The man looked at his watch. It was eight-twenty; her date had picked her up at six o'clock, they'd gone to a restaurant in downtown Minneapolis, and now they were back.

The man said, "C'mon, nail her. Give me something. Give me something."

But at eight twenty-five, the visitor walked out the condo's door, climbed in the Jag, and drove away.

The man shook his head, turned on the radio, and headed for home.

The man lived in an older area of St. Paul called Frogtown. The access to his rented house lay down a narrow unpaved alley. He turned in, followed his lights to the garage, which wasn't rented with the house—the owner used it to store lumber for his wood-working hobby—and parked beside it.

He got out of the car, looked up at the stars as he walked past the garage, and because he was looking up, instead of down, he caught the rush coming in from the side. He never actually saw much but felt that rush and put up his right arm and caught the club on his forearm, which broke, and he went down, screaming, and the attacker was all over him, a stout man in a black coat and a ski mask, nothing of his face visible. The club came down again, a flash of yellow wood, maybe a two-by-two, and the man put up his broken arm and caught another blow, which broke another bone, and he rolled, shrieking with pain, and the attacker was still there, swinging again, and the man put up his other arm, caught the blow, and his left arm broke, and the attacker cursed, and the man couldn't make out the words but it definitely sounded like a curse, and he rolled twice more, bellowing.

The attacker tried to hit the man's head and managed to scrape the side of his skull and rip his ear. And then somebody else was shouting, and the attacker swung once more, catching the man on the left side of his rib cage, cracking ribs, and then the attacker ran away . . .

Another man stood over him, and said, "Oh, man . . . Oh, man, are you okay? . . . Are you . . . I'm calling the cops . . . I'm calling an ambulance . . . Lay still . . ."

And the man heard the second man shouting into his cell phone, and, a little while later, a cop came, the man registering the flashing lights, which seemed to add to the pain in his arms and rib cage and the fire in his scalp, then an ambulance was there, and they picked him up and took him away, and the cool pillow felt good behind his head . . .

CHAPTER

SEVEN

Trane met Virgil at Quill's house the next morning at eight o'clock. She was looking fashionable in a dark blue blouse and black slacks, with low-heeled black boots. Virgil was wearing the same thing he'd worn the day before, except that he'd changed to a "Lamb Chop" T-shirt.

Trane was unlocking the door as Virgil walked up, and she said, "My rational side says there's not a chance in hell. My gut thinks I'm onto something. After you were talking about it last night, I had that damn song stuck in my head until I went to sleep, and this idea popped up. The song didn't go away, though. Probably going to be with me all day. 'Home, home on the range / Where the deer and the antelope play . . .'"

"Stop, please," Virgil said. And, "You know how to destroy any earworm?"

"Tell me."

"You hum that Walt Disney thing, 'It's a Small World.' It'll kill anything, but it's such a miserable song, such complete shit, it won't stay stuck in your head on its own," Virgil said, as they climbed the stairs to Quill's office. "It'll kill, but it won't hang out."

"Like whoever murdered Quill," she said.

"Over in that direction," Virgil agreed.

In the office, they turned on the CD player and, a minute later, were listening to "Home on the Range." Virgil picked up a remote and skipped to the next track, and "Git Along, Little Dogies" came up.

"This is awful," he said, and he pushed the skip button again.

A man's voice. "Man, you can't go ahead with this. It's unethical at best, it's dangerous at worse. You could kill him . . ."

Trane said, "Oh my God," just like a Valley girl.

A second man on the recording, maybe Quill: "He's going to die. And soon. Maybe he's got a month. Probably less. Right now, he's willing himself to die. He's given permission—"

Third man: "His permission is worthless. The only time he can give permission is when he's in extreme pain and he'll do anything to stop it. If he gives you permission, he gets opiates. If he doesn't give permission, you'll argue some more, and that delays the dope. You can't do that. You were essentially torturing him to get what you want."

The second man again: "You guys have to sign off on this. There's a good possibility that we'll never encounter this situation again. If this works as it should, it'll be a major breakthrough. We're talking about tens of thousands of lives around the world."

First man: "That you might not even be able to write about, to publish, because the ethical problems are so clear."

Second man: "We can have that fight later. After it's done. Maybe we could . . . obfuscate the precise circumstances to some degree."

Third man: "Oh, bullshit. The committee's not going to sign off on this. You go strutting in there like a peacock and expect them to fall over?"

Second man: "They'll fall over if you recommend we go ahead. Listen, they'll go ahead if your . . . if your, I have to say, inaccurate suggestion about his state of mind isn't mentioned—"

The recording cut out. Trane looked at Virgil, and said, "This can't be an original recording. Not on a CD."

Virgil nodded. "You're right. It's a rerecording. But why? Blackmail? They were talking about human experimentation. If it's blackmail, why hide it behind a couple of cowboy songs?"

"I don't know about that part," Trane said. "I've got a doctor I could talk to about the experimentation, see if he can clarify the situation."

"He might not want to. He might even have to report it to somebody, and we wouldn't want that to happen until we're ready for it," Virgil said.

"He won't report it."

"You're sure?"

"I'm sure, and I can get it done in a hurry," Trane said. "The fact is, I'm sleeping with him."

"That's more information than I needed," Virgil said. "And that doesn't guarantee—"

"The other thing is, he's my husband," Trane said.

"Ah. Then we're okay. I was wondering where those Louboutin boots came from on a cop's salary. I saw the red soles when you were walking up the steps outside."

Fists on hips. "You're were thinking I was crooked?"

"I was thinking you were looking good," Virgil said.

"You *do* know how to dodge a bullet," Trane said, with another of her uncommon smiles.

Trane wanted to talk to her husband, who was planning to spend the afternoon with his sketching group but would still be at home. "After I talk to him, I'm going back to wife number three. Maybe she knows exactly what situation they were talking about—who they were going to experiment on."

"I'll see if I can find Combes," Virgil said. And, "Hey, Trane, you did good. I wouldn't have thought of the CD in a hundred years."

"That makes us even," Trane said. "I never would have seen the tricky desk."

Virgil called Davenport about Combes. Davenport went away for a minute, then came back and gave him a phone number for a lawyer named Carleton Lange, who referred him to a lawyer named Shelly Carter, who gave him Combes's personal cell phone number, and said, "Don't tell him I sold him out to a cop."

Combes was on the sixteenth green at his golf club about to putt, he told Virgil, but would be done in half an hour or so. "Come to the clubhouse, I'll meet you in the grill. You can grill me."

Combes lived in the prosperous St. Paul suburb of North Oaks, which was north of St. Paul and had a lot of oaks and, from what Virgil had been told, had a decent, private golf course set among architecturally challenged McMansions. He'd never been on the course, which wasn't disappointing since he ranked golf only slightly above thumb wrestling and joggling as a sport. He suspected the members wouldn't let him on the greens anyway.

Saturday traffic slowed him down, and though North Oaks was only ten miles or so from Quill's house, it took a half hour to make the trip. Combes had just come off the course when Virgil walked in from the parking lot. He was a beefy, sun-reddened, square-jawed guy with square white teeth, his brown hair going a little gray at the temples, maybe looking like a high school tight end gone slightly to seed. He had on a red golf shirt like Tiger Woods wore—and maybe still did—and plaid golf shorts.

He was sitting with three other men when he was pointed out to Virgil. As Virgil walked over, he stood up to shake hands, and said to his friends, "Gotta talk to this guy. Be right back." They got a table away from other patrons, and Combes asked, "What's up? This is about Barth? . . . Wanna beer?"

"No, thanks, I'm working. I'd take a Diet Coke."

When Virgil had his Coke, he said, "We're talking to a lot of Barth's friends . . ."

"I hear you're dead in the water. If you're talking to me, you must be deader than I heard."

"We've started to make progress in the last few days," Virgil said.

"How you'd get my cell phone?"

Virgil lied. "I don't know. I'm friends with Lucas Davenport, who you know, and I asked him to make some calls. He did and got me the number."

"Huh. I'll tell you something about Davenport and basketball: you don't want to be standing in the paint when he's coming through," Combes said. "He'll lay that hockey defenseman shit on your ass and you'll wind up in the bleachers."

"He said you can shoot," Virgil said.

Jock bonding. Combes was pleased. "I do have my moments." Then, "So . . ."

"Yeah. How close were you and Dr. Quill?"

"Hell, not real close—we didn't go out drinking or anything. He came to my Christmas party most years; he kinda liked my old lady. We did play handball most Friday afternoons when we both were in town."

Virgil dropped his voice. "Here's the thing, Jack. I mean, you've done criminal law, you know what we do. We're looking for people who Dr. Quill might have been involved with, and who might have a propensity to violence."

Combes: "That's not me."

Virgil took a nip of his Diet Coke, and said, "That's not where I was going. We pretty much tore apart his house and we found the remnants of an eight ball of cocaine hidden in a desk drawer. You've dealt with druggies. Did you ever see any sign that Dr. Quill was using cocaine? Did you ever see him with anybody who might have been dealing it to him?"

Combes was already shaking his head. "You gotta know that I've defended a lot of these guys, court-appointed deals. Sure, I know the signs. All of them. I can look at two guys and tell you which one is a coke freak and which one is a methhead. I'll tell you this: Barth Quill never in his life used cocaine. He didn't know any coke dealers. The whole idea is laughable."

"But—"

Combes shook off the interruption. "No buts. Look. What you

really want to know is if I might have slipped him a little coke. If I might have introduced him to one of my clients. The answer is no. If I'd even suggested that he might like a little chemical fun, he would have crossed me off his list of friends. You know the phrase 'rectally challenged'?"

"I'm not—"

"That's the lawyer version of 'He's got a corncob stuck up his ass.'"

"I know that one," Virgil said.

"Well, that was Barth. He was a guy who'd get out of the shower to pee. A good guy, but stiff. *Way* stiff. You'd say something a little off-color and it would take him five seconds to decide to laugh, and you knew he didn't approve."

"Then why was he a good guy?"

Combes shrugged. "He just was. My wife went into the university hospitals to get her tits done up and she was in there three days. He stopped in twice a day, brought her flowers, chatted with her. Talked to her surgeon, explained some technical stuff to her. That was Barth. He had his own street guy, this beggar, who'd wait for him outside the hospital buildings every morning, and Barth would give him ten bucks. Every day. Told me that with ten bucks you could get enough calories at a Burger King to survive. Probably kept the guy alive. Because he thought he should. He didn't want anyone to thank him, either. It wasn't charity. It was his duty."

"His wives didn't like him much," Virgil said.

"'Cause he was stiff, and he could have a mean mouth. He didn't want to be that way, but he couldn't help it. He could dance, by the way. He was a hell of a dancer. Ask his wives about that."

"But no cocaine."

"No coke."

Virgil kicked back in his chair, looking at Combes. He knew the kind of guy Combes was. He might have tasted a little cocaine from time to time, probably drank a little too much, probably was okay to his wife, probably had a couple of kids—and they were probably pretty good kids—probably liked to watch a ball game in the evenings—any kind of ball you could name— probably knew his way around a fishing boat but wasn't a fanatic about it, probably slapped backs. Lots of probablys, but Virgil thought he was probably right.

And, Virgil thought, he was telling the truth. That was always disturbing in a source.

Virgil sighed, stood up, stuck out his hand. "Jack, I appreciate it. I probably won't need to, but if I do, I might call you again."

"Anytime," Combes said.

Combes went back to his friends, and Virgil walked out to the parking lot. As he was pulling out, Combes came out of the clubhouse and waved him down. Virgil pulled up next to him and dropped his side window. Combes said, "Had a thought. Maybe talk to Barth's daughter. She's a college kid, kinda out there. I was thinking about the coke. He mentioned one time that she was having some problems, hanging out with the wrong people. I don't know exactly what that meant. Could have meant, like, slackers. In Barth's eyes, that'd be as bad as dopers. He might have meant something rougher, though. I don't know. But he was bothered."

"I thought he didn't have much to do with his daughter," Virgil said.

"He didn't until she started going to college and messing up. Then they talked. At least occasionally. He mentioned once that she'd been over the night before. It might have been about money—probably was, to some extent. And I might not know what I'm talking about. She might be a real princess."

"I'll check," Virgil said. "Thank you."

Virgil drove out to the street, pulled over, and called Trane. Trane was in her car. "I talked to my husband. He's an internist, not a research scientist, but he knows some things. Basically, he said that the university would have a committee that would have to approve human experimentation. With what was on the CD, there's no way they would give it. He also thought that there was no way that Quill could have avoided getting it, either—no way around the rules. As it turns out, that doesn't mean anything for us."

"It doesn't? There could be a motive . . ."

"I talked to Nancy Quill. She listened to the recording and the first thing she said was, 'That's not Barth. None of them is Barth.'"

Virgil thought about it, silently, until she said, "Hello? You still there?"

"Then why would he have the recording? After he got it, why would he keep it? Why would he have been listening to it just before he died? I can't believe that CD was in the player for very long—he obviously listened to a lot of music and he had about a thousand CDs in there."

"I don't know the answers to any of that," Trane said. "Was he doing something with the computer, in the library, he didn't want anyone to know about and somehow tied into the CD? Maybe he reviewed the CD before he met somebody over there to talk about it?"

"How about this? Quill was given the CD by one of those

guys arguing against human experimentation. Something bad happened—like the experiment went bad and the patient died," Virgil said. "Quill did know who it was on the CD. He planned on giving it to the committee, or maybe even the cops, but he wanted to check it out first to make sure he wasn't being played."

"And somebody on the CD killed him to keep the secret safe. Because if the secret wasn't kept, some big shot doctors could be looking at murder charges."

"Yes."

"I like that," Trane said. "I like that a lot. But who are the other people?"

"Doctors."

"What doctors? And when?"

"I don't know. What do you think?"

"Maybe talk to some of his medical associates, the guys who actually do the surgeries for him. Find out what they think."

"You gotta be careful, Margaret. You don't want to play that CD for the wrong guy even if he's wearing a white doctor's coat."

"Not to worry. I've got a big gun, and I'm nervous. Now, what are you doing?"

He told her about his interview with Combes. "I believe him."

"Only one problem with all that," Trane said. "We know that Quill had cocaine and that somebody had used some of it. Maybe not Quill; maybe he provided it to the hypothetical hookers you were talking about. You say that the drawers in that desk weren't all that secret because your grandfather had one like that. Well, guess what? My grandfather didn't, and I'd be willing to bet that ninety-nine-point-nine percent of the people out there didn't have grandfathers who did. Those drawers were secret for normal people. I never would have found that coke in fifty years, and the

Crime Scene guys didn't, either. That toot was put in the desk by Quill."

"You're saying I'm not normal?"

"I thought there was substantial agreement on that."

Virgil told Trane that he wanted to make a run at Quill's daughter.

"You know I got nothing useful from her, but go ahead," Trane said. "Maybe if a cowboy blows softly in her ear, she'll cough something up."

"You think she's . . . needy . . . ?"

"That's a kind way of putting it, but yes," Trane said. "She's a sad sack. She wants somebody to love her, and she's nice-enough-looking, but she's annoying. She winds up sleeping with people who want the sex but not the woman. You'll see."

"Where am I going to find her?"

"You know, it's Saturday, so she'll probably still be asleep, if she's home. She's over in St. Paul. Let me give you the address."

CHAPTER

EIGHT

Megan Quill lived in the upstairs apartment of a tree-shaded private home off Selby Avenue, three blocks from the University of St. Thomas. The home was older, pre–World War II, two stories with an attic under the roof, with white clapboard siding and a stingy front porch. Virgil was familiar with Selby from his days as a St. Paul cop—he'd taken any number of calls on the street, including a murder, but miles farther east. He parked under a maple tree and walked up to the front door, which had three mailboxes to one side.

Access to the second-floor apartment was up an interior staircase.

Virgil rang the doorbell, and, a moment later, an elderly lady shuffled up to the door, opened it three or four inches, and asked through the crack, "Can I help you?"

Virgil identified himself, and asked about Quill.

"Well, she's up. I heard her flush the toilet," the old woman said, opening the door all the way. She was chewing something and smelled of masticated bread. "You can go on up, she's in number one. There's another ringer by her door, push the button. She has friends over."

The house smelled of musty wallpaper and bug spray, and the narrow, dark wooden stairs creaked as Virgil went up. A short hallway apparently led to a bathroom at the back of the house with a door that had a silver 2 next to it. Virgil went back the other way, to the front of the house, to a door with a 1. He pushed the button to the side of the door, and, from inside the room, a woman shouted, "What?"

Virgil didn't want to shout an answer, so he pushed the button again.

"For Christ's sakes, who is it? I'm not up," the woman said. "Is that you, Walt?"

Virgil said, as quietly as he could and still be heard on the other side of the door, "Bureau of Criminal Apprehension."

After a moment of silence, he heard voices, then footsteps coming to the door, which flew open. Megan Quill, standing there barefoot in a cranberry-colored terry-cloth robe, was a fleshy young woman. She was pretty, medium blond, with a narrow nose and thin lips much like her father's, and hazy blue eyes. Under her left eye, she had a bruise the size of a half-dollar, now going yellow.

At the same time that she opened the door, the door opened on apartment 2, and a white man with the North Korean dictator's haircut stuck his head out. Quill shouted, her voice shrill as a stepped-on cat's, "Go back inside, Dick. This is none of your goddamn business."

The man's head disappeared and the door slammed. Quill said to Virgil, "I already talked to the police. Like, three times."

"I know, but I'm new on the case and wanted to chat," Virgil said. "What happened to your eye?"

"Well, I wasn't beat up or anything," she said. "I got all these games stacked up in my closet. Some asshole in high school gave me a wooden chessboard, and when I tried to pull another game out, the chessboard flew off the top and hit me in the fuckin' eye. I mean, like, Jesus Christ, I thought I was blinded. It only weighed about fifty pounds."

"Can I come in?"

She walked away from the open door, and Virgil followed, pushing the door shut. Quill had two rooms—a living room, with a bed that folded out from a couch, and a kitchen/dining area. A fat kid, wearing a T-shirt that said "Waterboard Warehouse—America's Waterboard Super Store," sat at the kitchen table, cursing at an Apple laptop; and a tall, long-haired blond dude with an earring and wearing a knee-to-neck cook's apron, but nothing else, was scrambling eggs at the stove. Both the men appeared to be in their early twenties.

A side door led to a compact bathroom that once had been a large closet. Virgil could see a sink, with a medicine cabinet above it, the edge of a toilet, and a handle to a door that probably opened on a shower. There was a fourth door, closed but with no lock, so it was probably a closet.

Quill said to the two guys, "The cops are here."

The guy at the computer said, "Eh, what's up, doc?" in a perfect imitation of Bugs Bunny. The dude said, "I was offered some, but I didn't inhale," and, "You want some scrambled eggs? They're really good: I use paprika."

Virgil shook his head, said, "No, thanks," then said to Quill, "I need to ask you some questions. If you'd prefer to do it in private, you could ask your friends to take a walk around the block. The dude might want to put on some pants."

"No way," she said. "I want witnesses."

Quill dropped onto the bed, her robe parting as she did it, exposing her legs to a soft, unblemished mid-thigh. She said to Virgil, "There's a folding chair in the closet. Or you can sit on the corner of the bed."

Virgil wanted to look in the closet anyway, so he opened the door without a lock, found four metal folding chairs under a hanger bar that was loaded with jeans and blouses. He pulled out one of the chairs, unfolded it, and sat down.

The computer kid said, "If you lean forward just right, I bet you could see her pussy."

"Shut up, Jerry," Quill said, rolling her eyes. She picked up a ceramic ashtray from off the floor, groped in her robe, produced a pack of Camels and a yellow plastic lighter, and fired up a cigarette. She didn't blow smoke at Virgil, but she didn't try to blow it away, either.

She said, "Jerry's obsessed with my pussy. I let him see it, but I don't let him touch it. Brett can touch it anytime he wants."

"I appreciate the privilege," said the dude. Virgil was watching the bare-assed dude: he seemed to be too much in touch with the eggs he was stirring. He was coming down from a high, but from what Virgil didn't know. "I still vote to let Jerry watch."

Jerry said, "Props," and went back to his laptop.

Quill said, "We can talk about it when the cop is gone."

Virgil exhaled impatiently, as Quill blew another cloud of smoke through her Cheshire cat grin, and said, "I thought you kids vaped."

"A, I'm not a 'kid,'" she said. "B, I need the nicotine right now, and I get it from Camels. Like, instantly. And, C, it pissed off my father—he of the dented head."

"That's a little crude," Virgil said.

"Live with it," she said. "What do you want to know?"

"Eggs are ready," said the dude.

"Give her a plate," Virgil told him. "We can talk over it.

"One of the things we try to do is connect a murdered person with anyone who might have a tendency to be violent," Virgil told Quill. "Not saying you're lying, but I'd like to see that chessboard."

She stared at him for a second, the Camel hanging from her lower lip, then said, "Sure. It's at the top of the pile in the closet. Help yourself."

Virgil went back to the closet and opened the door. Above the hanger bar, a shelf was piled with old-fashioned board games in tattered cardboard boxes, as though they'd been inherited. Risk, Stratego, Scrabble, Clue, Monopoly.

Quill said, "The chessboard's up on top. On top of the Monopoly."

Monopoly was in its thick blue box, and Virgil reached up, grabbed it, pulled it forward, and the chessboard on top of it flew off and nearly clipped his forehead. It clattered to the floor, and Quill started laughing and simultaneously choking on the smoke from her Camel. "Told'ja," she said. "That motherfucker almost scalped you."

The fat kid and the dude were grinning at him. The kid said, moving to an Elmer Fudd voice, "You cwazy wabbit."

"I can see how it could happen," Virgil said. He picked up the heavy board, four inches thick, with internal drawers for the pieces, shook it once, then propped it against the wall of the closet.

"You guys play a lot of games?" Virgil asked.

"Jerry does. He's a fuckin' psycho, never stops," Quill said. "Brett and I play when we're not touching each other."

"True, dat," Brett said. "I spent three hours dreaming about that yesterday afternoon. The most beautiful dreams."

"All right," Virgil said to Quill. "Now let's talk about your father."

He went back to his chair, watching Quill as she switched one leg over the other, sliding the gown another two inches higher. Trane had called Quill a sad sack, but she hadn't come off that way to Virgil—if anything, she seemed manic.

"Tell me about your history with your father."

"I hardly knew him," she said.

"He was a fascist asshole," Jerry said.

"Jerry speaks the truth," said Brett. "It's possible that his death was karmic payback."

Virgil: "For what? Because he worked hard and didn't smoke weed?"

Brett: "No. Because he gave the orders about how everybody should conduct their lives and he expected everyone to follow his orders. And if you didn't spend your life studying medicine, you weren't worth talking to. You were basically something stuck to the bottom of his shoe."

"I know a lawyer he spent time with, played handball—they seemed to get along fine."

"Law, medicine, all the same thing," Jerry sneered. "You go to college for a hundred years, then work for rich people."

Her parents had been divorced when she was two years old because, Quill said, her father was never home, he was always pursuing his career. "He didn't care about Mom. At all. Especially not after I was born. His spermies had done their thing."

"He always supported you and your mother," Virgil said.

"That was the least he could do. He was rich and we weren't. Mom was working on her Ph.D. when they met, and he took her away from it and she never got it. She's been teaching at a community college ever since, over by White Bear Lake," Quill said. "Getting the money was better than nothing, but money isn't the same as having an actual, you know, father."

Brett was walking around the kitchen area, eating eggs off the cast-iron skillet, and he said, "An actual father gives solid structure to your life."

Virgil ignored him, and said to Quill, "Sergeant Trane told me that you'd been seeing more of him lately."

"Only so he could get on my case about schoolwork," Quill said. "He wanted to see if his investment in me was paying off. When he thought it wasn't, he'd get pissed off."

"Not so upset that he didn't give you that trust fund."

"Once again, the least he could do," she said.

"And when he was killed, you got a payday that stretches out for another eleven years."

"No. That comes from the trust. I would have gotten it anyway. I *am* getting it anyway." She snubbed out the cigarette. "Give me a fuckin' break, huh? I didn't kill him. I didn't even know how to find him if he wasn't home. Never even been up to his lab. As far as I know, he could be making a new Frankenstein up there."

"How often were you going over to his house?"

"Maybe every week or two. I'd go over to get money from him. I'd say, 'Let's talk about, uh, psychology, should I switch my major to psychology?' We'd talk about it, and before I left I'd say, 'Could I get some pizza money?' and he'd throw me a hundred or a couple hundred. That's a lot to me, but not to him. I don't even think he noticed what he was giving me."

"Doesn't exactly make the case that he was an asshole," Virgil said.

"Throwing your daughter a few bucks doesn't cure you of being an asshole," Jerry said.

Brett: "He was a global asshole, but he could be okay on the specifics."

Virgil asked Quill what she knew about her father's second and third wives. The answer was straightforward: nothing. "Never met either one of them."

"So you had no idea about any stress, or conflicts, he might be going through?"

"Well, his fight with that lady professor is pretty famous. Made the TV news. They even argue about it over here at St. Thomas. I'd look at her, if I were you."

"Or his girlfriend," Jerry said.

Virgil's eyebrows went up. "His girlfriend. I didn't know he had one."

"He did. I believe she was married—she was wearing a ring. I gotta wonder if his wife knew about her. Megan said when he died, the wife got in line for a bundle. If he doesn't die—and there must be a prenup—she wouldn't get much, and there's already a girlfriend set to scoop him up. Of course, maybe the girlfriend's husband got overheated and took him out. Or maybe the girlfriend didn't want her husband to find out she'd been fuckin' Barth and she did him in. Lots of possibilities there."

Virgil to Quill: "Sergeant Trane didn't say you mentioned a girlfriend."

She shrugged. "Jerry hadn't told me about her when Trane talked to me."

Back to Jerry: "You don't know her name? Anything about her?"

"Nope. What happened was, I walked into a Starbucks and saw Barth talking to this good-looking woman. Maybe forty. Reddish hair, cut short, like Olympic ice-skaters used to have. Looked rich: she was wearing clothes like she was going out horseback riding. You know, tall leather boots, tight-ass pants, the whole Brit horsey thing. Like she walked out of a castle to hunt a fuckin' fox. And that wedding ring. The two were laughing, and I thought, Hmm, because you never saw Barth laughing that much. But then I forgot about it."

"What made you think they might be close?"

"A week after that, I was over at the U, and I'm pretty sure I saw him walking along with a black German shepherd on a leash. That was a surprise. As far as I knew, he didn't have a dog."

Quill shook her head. "Never."

Jerry: "Then, let me see . . . Saturday? . . . No, Sunday morning . . . I saw the woman again and she was walking a

German shepherd, and it looked like the exact same dog. She went past me, six feet away; she called the dog Blackie, which was pretty clever since he was black."

"You're sure it was him you saw with the dog? You said 'pretty sure.'"

"That's what I was. Pretty sure. Not positive."

Virgil: "No idea where we could find the woman?"

"No . . . she was just a woman," Jerry said. "I can't even promise there was anything going on there. But . . . I think there was. Why would he be walking that dog when he didn't even like dogs? That was in the morning, early, like the dog had been with him the night before."

Quill, Jerry, and Brett all hung out in Dinkytown, a business/residential area adjacent to the University of Minnesota that catered to students, because there was more going on in Dinkytown than around St. Thomas. Quill and Brett both knew this because they had high school friends going to school there.

"I've got a guy over there in Dinkytown," Quill said. "About a month ago, I spent the night—you know, fuckin' and suckin'—"

"Don't tell me that," Jerry said. "I'm getting nothing—"

Virgil held up a finger. "Something for all three of you? In June, I busted a young woman down in Worthington, for murder. She was a couple of years younger than you guys, seventeen. She got drunk and wasted on methamphetamine. She was on the bed naked with her boyfriend and his other girlfriend, taking turns with each other, and she freaked out and started brawling with her boyfriend and the other girl. She wound up stabbing the boyfriend to death with a kitchen knife. Stuck it right in his neck, severed his carotid artery, and he spewed blood all over the trailer, coming out like a fire hose. The other girl was trying to help him, but then this first girl, the killer, went after her, too, and cut up the other girl's face and hands and breasts. When I saw her, the other girl looked like she'd been shoved through a wood-chipper. So neither your language nor your sex life is gonna shock me. The language is just sort of . . . tiresome. It makes me tired to hear it. If you wouldn't mind, knock it the fuck off. I'm trying to stay alert. I don't need to be dozing off."

Brett laughed, a soft, rolling laugh that made Virgil again think he might be coming down off a high, but Quill snapped, "Tough shit . . . Fuck you."

Virgil made a rolling motion with his index finger. "The friend. You spent the night with a friend . . ."

"Yeah. Suckin' and fuckin'," she said defiantly. She shook an-other cigarette out and twiddled it. "This was a month ago. About one o'clock in the morning we went out to see if we could get a slice at this bar, and I saw Barth go by in his sports car. This silver Bimmer with its top down, supposed to be some kind of rare ride. I thought he was cruising. You know, for women. I thought the car might be bait."

"Was he with a woman?"

She shook her head. "No. Passenger seat was empty. He was crawling along at ten miles an hour like he was looking for peo-ple coming out of bars."

"Young pussy," Jerry said. "Can't hold that against him."

Quill had no more information about that, and Virgil moved along to other topics. She said that she and her father didn't have many issues, except that he thought she was lazy and she thought he was a rigid asshole, and he'd smelled some weed on her one morning and had given her a hard time. She didn't use any other dope, she said, and could hardly wait until Minnesota legalized marijuana.

"Did your father use any drugs that you're aware of? Illegal drugs?"

Her eyes narrowed, and she took a moment to light the cigarette. "Interesting you should ask," she said. "I don't do cocaine myself—can't afford to—but it occurred to me once that he reminded me of a cokehead I used to know. This older real estate guy from Apple Valley who hung out at the bars by the U, trying to pick up the younger chicks. Talked about his deals and his coke, like anyone might give a . . . might care. I was at Barth's house a couple of times, and he made me think of that. But I don't know that he used anything. Like coke."

She had little more. The night or morning that her father had been killed, she'd been there, in her apartment, with a half dozen friends coming and going, eating pizza and drinking beer and playing the old games in the closet, and Twister—the Twister, she implied, was played totally ironically.

"Not by me," Jerry said. "I got in a couple of good gropes."

The friends had started coming over about eight o'clock, and all but one had left around four o'clock in the morning. Another young woman, who lived at home in White Bear Lake, hadn't wanted to drive all the way back and had stayed over. They'd both slept in until noon and then had gone out for bagels and coffee. The other girl hadn't left her apartment until almost two o'clock in the afternoon.

Virgil asked if she knew anything else he ought to know about. She didn't. Then, unexpectedly, she added, "You know, I didn't hate Dad. Toward the end, I even started to like him a little bit. But he was so hard-assed, and he never let up." She seemed about to tear up.

Virgil nodded, and told her he might be back. "I can't ever tell in advance what might be relevant, when I talk to people."

"Anytime . . . But call ahead. I'll want to get my story straight," Quill said, back to the sarcasm.

Brett said, "Hey. Tell him about that weird guy we met. On the sidewalk."

Quill frowned, and said, "Oh, yeah."

"What weird guy?" Virgil asked.

They told him about the neatly dressed man who they'd encountered on the street who'd asked questions about the investigation. They had no information about him other than a description, which Virgil took down in his notebook. "I thought afterward that he might be a cop, but he said he was a student. He was too old to be a student, though," Quill said.

"He didn't give you a name? Nothing at all?"

"No. We were standing there eating ice cream, and he started talking to us. Then he got in his car and drove off."

Brett said, "He knows that Green person, the professor. He said he was in Anthropology and saw her around the building. I guess they're in the same building."

"Huh." Virgil didn't know exactly what to think about that. "I'll ask around."

As he turned to leave, Brett said, "Have a good day, man," and he sounded sincere.

Jerry slapped his laptop, and said, "What a piece of shit. It's like somebody's gotta carry every fuckin' byte up the fuckin' stairs."

Quill asked him, "Want a pussy shot to keep your blood pressure up?"

"Absolutely."

Quill turned her back on Virgil and pulled the robe wide. Jerry said, "Oh my God . . ."

Virgil left, muttering, "Jesus."

"Fuck you!" Quill shouted after him.

Virgil had a text from Trane that said she'd be in the office. Virgil drove back across the river and found her eating lunch at her computer. When he walked in, she turned, and said, "Interesting interview with one of the lab technicians. Remember that I mentioned that Quill was involved in a lawsuit?"

"Yeah, I saw that in your notes."

"I talked to the university's lawyer, who'll be defending the case if it goes to court, but I didn't pay a lot of attention to it—I couldn't see a connection. Now the lab guy tells me that a year or so ago a quadriplegic named Frank McDonald had nerve rerouting surgery that was planned and directed by Quill. Another surgeon, a microsurgeon, did the actual procedure. Beforehand, McDonald had some small amount of movement in his arm and fingers; afterward, he got more movement, but supposedly he also had a lot of pain. He had a month of physical therapy after the surgery, but when he returned home that care was reduced to three hours a day, in the morning, early afternoon, and evening.

The first day the reduced care started, after his wife went out to a supermarket, the guy used his new mobility to swallow a whole tube of painkillers. He was dead when the wife got back."

"Whoa!"

"Yeah. His wife is suing the hospital and the doctors involved, saying they should have understood that McDonald needed intensive psychotherapy as well as physical therapy to deal with his new condition. Her main target was Quill, who she said talked McDonald into the surgery."

"You think she might have gone after him?"

"We should talk to her anyway. The lab tech said Quill described her as a greedy nutjob who was living high on her husband's insurance payments."

"You know, it sounds like the tape—talking somebody into surgery," Virgil said.

"It does."

"It seems unlikely that'd kill him, though," Virgil said. "If she has a lawsuit going, it seems like she's found an outlet for her anger . . . And how would she get up in the library in the middle of the night? And why would she be up there?"

"Don't go dissing my lead. She was up there to grab the computer to see what Quill was saying about the operation . . ."

Virgil said nothing, but he raised his eyebrows.

"All right, all right," Trane said. "You get anything from Megan?"

"She thinks it's possible that Quill used cocaine. And a friend of hers said he had a girlfriend."

"What!"

She got up, rocking back and forth on her feet, listening, as Virgil told her about the possible girlfriend. When he finished,

Trane said, "A redheaded married woman in English riding outfit who has a German shepherd and goes to the Starbucks. Shouldn't be impossible to find her."

Virgil: "The question is, why didn't anyone else know about her? Why didn't she come forward? She's gotta know that Quill was murdered. And, given that description, that we'd eventually hear about her."

"Unless it really is all disconnected—that she and Quill brushed by each other at Starbucks and exchanged a couple of words, the German shepherd being off the wall, coming from somebody entirely different."

"Or maybe it wasn't actually Quill that this guy saw walking the dog. He wasn't positive," Virgil said. "He was pretty sure."

"Look, if he had a girlfriend, we're starting to develop a picture of a guy who actually did talk to people. That cocaine could have belonged to a friend," Trane said.

"Jack Combes seemed to think that if you even mentioned it to him, he might cross you off his list of friends."

"Unless he needed something from the cokehead. Like sex."

Virgil agreed. "Okay."

She looked at her watch. "The early shift at Starbucks will be getting off. If we ran over there right now . . ."

Trane drove. As she did, Virgil said, "Things are starting to pile up. There's a computer and a phone and keys out there somewhere. If we could find any of them, that'd be big. Quill was fighting with Green, and Green supposedly has at least a couple of students who are capable of violence. He has an estranged wife who would greatly profit from his death. He might or might not use cocaine, so he might or might not know drug dealers. He might or might not have a girlfriend with a dog who hasn't made herself known, which is interesting. He was probably killed by somebody he somewhat trusted, since he was turned away from them in the carrel. He was selfish about giving his employees scientific credit. And Quill might have been involved—somehow—in an illegal medical procedure. The killer's probably male, or a strong female, to be able to hit him with a heavy laptop. Anything else?"

"I'll think of something else later. Right now, that seems to be the list. I don't see any connections."

"Neither do I. Maybe we'll get some from the horsewoman."

"There's a word you don't often hear: 'horsewoman.'"

"But you hear it more often than you do 'horseman,'" Virgil said.

They spoke to the staff at Starbucks. Nobody could remember seeing a redheaded horsewoman. They had a number of redheads, though, and a horsewoman in English riding gear who was a frequent customer, but the woman was black. Another frequent customer came in with a German shepherd guide dog, but was seeing-impaired and male, and the dog was mostly tan with some black markings.

Several members of the weekday staff weren't working. Trane got a Venti cappuccino, and Virgil a hot chocolate, and they walked back to her car. "I'll check with the staff on Monday. You're going home tonight?" she asked.

"Yeah. I'll take a printout of your files with me, read them again," Virgil said. "The rest of the day, I got the names of these two Green grad students who she thought might be capable of violence. I'll look them up before I leave town. I'll call if that turns into anything."

"I'm interested in this girlfriend. I'll check everybody on that, and I'll see if I can wake up a narc and ask about dealers who sell coke to faculty over here . . . if they know anybody like that."

"One hand on your gun if you find the dealer."

"Always."

CHAPTER

NINE

Virgil had gotten two names from Katherine Green, the Cultural Science professor. They were Clete May, the man who might have macho problems but was useful for carrying heavy stuff; and Terry Foster, an Army veteran who'd apparently fought in Iraq or Syria.

May lived in Dinkytown, which was closest, so Virgil went there first. He always preferred not to call ahead, when he could avoid it, but to surprise the subject. May's address turned out to be an old, blue two story clapboard house, cut up into four apartments, much like the house Megan Quill lived in.

May lived in apartment A, at the front of the house on the first floor. When Virgil rang the bell, he heard footfalls, and then a barefoot young woman with dark brown hair and dark brown eyes, carrying a bagel with cream cheese, opened the door, and asked, "Yes? Who are you?"

Virgil identified himself, showed his ID, and asked for May.

The woman said, "He's around the side of the house, shooting his bow."

"He won't shoot me, will he?"

"Not on purpose. But he's not very good with it yet, so I can't make any promises. You know, like, ricochets." She smiled and pointed him around to the side of the house, and he walked back outside and around and found May lying on his back on the concrete driveway, shooting extraordinarily long wooden arrows from an extraordinarily long wooden bow at a straw target the size of a dinner plate backed with a sheet of plywood.

As Virgil watched, May released an arrow, which missed the target but hit the plywood sheet and bounced off. Two other arrows were already sticking out of the target, and two more lay in front of the backing.

When the arrow bounced, Virgil asked, "What happens if you miss the plywood?"

May craned his neck around, took in Virgil, and said, "I don't do that anymore. When I did do it, they'd skid down the driveway until they stopped. It's not a heavy bow; they don't go far. Fucks up the arrow feathers, though."

Virgil identified himself again, and May stood up. He was an inch taller than Virgil, a bit overweight but with solid biceps and triceps, and he appeared to be in his mid-twenties. He had black hair that fell over his brown eyes, a scruffy beard, and a fleshy nose. He said, "I already talked to the lady detective. Who sicced you on me?"

"She did. She thought maybe you'd figured something out since she talked to you. And she told me about you being arrested for hitting a guy with a chair."

"I pled not guilty. The other guy was a serious asswipe," May said. "The county attorney is already talking to my dad—my dad's a lawyer—about me taking a plea on a lesser charge, but we declined. I didn't hit the guy with the chair, I defended myself with it. The video proves it. I was keeping him off me."

Virgil bobbed his head, but said, "That's not quite the reputation you have around Cultural Science. They say you can be a little overaggressive. Into martial arts and so on."

"Well, that's true," May said. "But I didn't kill Quill. I wasn't even pissed off at him. I sorta like Cultural Science because you don't have to work too hard at it, and if you've got the cash, you can make interesting trips to places you don't usually see. I've been to Egypt, Madagascar, Japan, made a couple trips to India. I'll get my Ph.D. and go teach someplace that's got a ski mountain and no restrictions on screwing your students. Utah, Colorado, Vermont. Like that."

"Did you know Quill?"

"Not really. I mean, he showed up at Katherine's lecture with a bunch of his apostles and started screaming at her," May said. "Called her a twat. If you didn't take it too seriously, it was pretty funny."

"Until you hit the guy with the chair," Virgil said.

"Like I said, that asswipe came for me," May said. "I didn't hurt him or anything; he had a bruise on his arm, the little fuckin' snowflake."

"But then you invaded their territory . . ."

"Yeah. Katherine asked me to go along. She likes to stir up shit, but she also likes to have me between her and the shit she's stirred up."

"You're a bodyguard."

"Sorta. I mean, we went to India, and she was talking women's rights to these unemployed guys who looked like they'd carve out your kidneys for two dollars and a bottle of beer," May said. "Stirring up some serious shit."

"If she's always stirring stuff up, why do you . . . go along with it?"

"Makes the Ph.D. easier. I'm good with Spanish, but my French sorta sucks," May said. "Japanese? Forget about it. The other thing is, after I get my degree, I'd like to turn her upside down, if you know what I mean. Have you seen her?"

"Yes, but . . ." He looked back at the house. "Aren't you married or something?"

"No, no, not me. That's a friend in there," May said. "I'm not even romantic with her. Not yet anyway. She comes over to watch my TV and wash her clothes. I have a washer and dryer in there. They're kind of a chick magnet. Better than a dog."

"Then you've got a few bucks . . . nice apartment, washer-dryer."

"My old man does. Has a few bucks. He's a good guy. With me he's hoping for the best, you know? Get a credential, get a job. Willing to pay for school."

May was beginning to seem unlikely as a suspect. Virgil couldn't even think of a reason why Quill would be in a carrel with him, and, if he was, why Quill would turn his back on him. And May seemed to be considerably less than the Cultural Science warrior Virgil had imagined, more interested in getting into the professor's shorts than actually becoming a cultural scientist.

Which Virgil could understand.

He asked May about the bow.

"Japanese," May said. "I like it because it's hard and weird."

"I read a Zen archery book when I was going to school . . ."

"*Zen in the Art of Archery*. Eugen Herrigel. You must have been a hippie—all the hippies read that. It's mostly bullshit," May said. "This Japanese guy told me that Herrigel didn't know enough Japanese to understand what his teacher was talking about, and his teacher wasn't a Zen guy anyway. In fact, he was sort of a crank. This archery I'm doing isn't *kyūdō*—that's what Herrigel was writing about. Mine is the Japanese combat form, *kyūjutsu*."

"You're teaching yourself to kill people?"

May snorted. "If I was gonna kill somebody, I'd use a fuckin' gun. If I had a gun."

"Okay. I'm told you study Zen."

"I do. That's another thing women kinda like, you know? Seems all mystical and so on, like you're spiritual. What I picked up in Japan was, Zen is about as mystical as dirt. But, it's still cool."

"'Girls only want boyfriends who have great skills,'" Virgil said, quoting *Napoleon Dynamite*.

"That movie was about my life: guys with skills," May said. "I got skills, but no girls—not right now anyway."

"How about ever?" Virgil asked.

May scratched his neck. "Oh, yeah. They come, but then they go. Know what I mean? One day they're sitting on your couch, the next day the couch is empty."

He made Virgil laugh.

Virgil asked May if he might have any idea of who had killed Quill. He didn't, and he didn't think it would be anyone in

Cultural Science. "The people in the department would talk about it for eight years before they could do anything like that. They're not people who act on impulse. If they saw somebody coming after them with an ax, they'd try to get the guy to discuss it rationally instead of running away."

He didn't have a suspect, but he did have a thought.

"It was a big deal when Quill got killed, even around Cultural Science," May said. "We wondered if the cops would come after us. A couple days later, Sergeant Trane showed up. After she talked to me, I got to thinking. Why did Quill have a carrel at the Wilson Library, on the west bank, and why did he keep a huge, heavy computer there?"

"I'm listening," Virgil said. "Why did he?"

May said, "I don't know, but it might help if you figured it out. Listen, he's a medical guy. We have a medical library here on the east bank. As far as I know, there are no medical books in the Wilson Library. He supposedly did some engineering work, too, in robotics, and the engineering library is over here. The university hospitals are here on the east bank, and he probably had an office there. I'm sure he had a private office at his lab—all those guys do. I understand his house is on the east bank. He has all kinds of private places and study possibilities over here, why did he go over there? You ever walk across the Mississippi footbridge in the winter? You can freeze your nuts off. Why did he have a little tiny carrel?"

"I don't know, but I'll think about it."

"Here's what I'm thinking. He went there because it was quiet and he was away from everybody else. Like, you know, where you want to think. This little Zen space is not your house. It's not your lab, you don't need to talk to anybody, you've got no TV to interrupt you. You want a clear, calm mind to digest it all. Then somebody . . . I'm thinking Russians or Chinese . . . Could be a big American corporation . . ."

Virgil: "Russians? Or Chinese?"

"Sure. You must have read about it. They've got all these guys out there stealing American technology, and what's more high-tech than medicine? Especially the kind that Quill was doing? Quill's over there generating ideas, and tech, and somebody finds out about it, Russians or Chinese, computer experts. They start going over there to monitor that computer—maybe they have the computer secretly spooling up all of Quill's input. Now he finds out that somebody is messing with his computer and knows they do it late at night because they need to do it when nobody's there. He thinks it's somebody from his lab, or a student, and he goes over to surprise the guy. And he gets the surprise instead."

"That does sort of hold together," Virgil admitted.

"Yeah, it does," May said. "It has the massive disadvantage of being too complicated. It fucks over Occam and his razor. It's possible that Quill was doing something online that he didn't want to risk any chance of being traced to him. You know, watching porn and yanking the crank. Maybe buying dope on the dark net. Here's a big question: was the guy who killed him in on whatever he was doing?"

They spent a couple of minutes speculating, came up with nothing solid. Virgil thanked him, gave him a card, walked back to his car, and then called Trane to tell her about May's thought—not about the Russians and Chinese, or Quill yanking his crank, but the question of why he'd even have an office at the Wilson Library.

"A good question," she conceded. "I wondered about that, too, but he was such a hotshot that I figured he could get an office anywhere he wanted one. So he got one there, maybe on a whim. Maybe his work took him across the river sometimes and he wanted a private place to rest his feet. I dunno."

Virgil rang off and went to find Terry Foster, the military veteran. Foster lived across the city line in St. Paul.

As he drove, he thought about what both May and Trane had said and decided that Trane's assumption was weak. If it was simply the casual exercise of academic power by Quill to get an extra office, what about the fact he probably had a library key? That would have taken more than clout: he'd have to have an illegal source for it. He'd probably have to evade janitors and other night workers if he didn't want to be seen. There was more to the carrel than met the eye . . .

But Russians and Chinese? Unlikely.

Terry Foster lived in a tiny, stuccoed rental house in the area of St. Paul called Frogtown. A couple of aging birch trees shaded the neatly kept front yard, where a sidewalk of cracked concrete blocks led to an enclosed front porch. Virgil parked, knocked on the front door. There was no reaction from inside, but, as he was standing there, a man came out on the porch of the house next door, and said, "There's nobody home."

"Do you know when Mr. Foster will be back?"

The man said, "No. He's in the hospital."

Virgil walked over—a matter of twenty feet—identified himself, and asked, "He's sick?"

"He got mugged, right in our own alley," the man said. "Somebody beat the sweet livin' bejesus out of him the night before last."

According to the neighbor, Foster's house had a single-car garage in the back, which wasn't part of his rental deal. He had, instead, a parking space in the yard next to the garage. "When he got out of his car, some guy was waiting for him. Jumped out from behind the garage and beat him up. Terry was yelling for help, and the neighbor in back, Joe Lee, heard him and ran out and started yelling at the guy, who run off. Joe run out there and found Terry and called the cops. I didn't hear him yelling, but I heard the ambulance, and I run out there and saw them put him in the ambulance. And he was a mess. He looked like he'd been blown up."

"How do you know that part about the guy jumping out from behind the garage?"

"It was in the *Pioneer Press*. I guess they got it from the cops," the man said.

Foster had been taken to Regions Hospital, the neighbor said. When Virgil asked, he said that Foster lived alone, as far as he knew. "He did drink a little. There's a street guy who goes around and takes aluminum cans out of the garbage and he told me once that Terry's was good for thirty or forty cans. I guess he was drinking a six-pack a day."

When the neighbor ran out of information, Virgil walked around behind the house to look at the garage. The thing had probably been designed and built before World War II and would be a tight fit for any modern car. There was an overhead door facing the alley and a door on the end closest to the house for access, with a graveled parking spot to one side. Two tall, aging arborvitae stood on either side of the access door, a good spot to hide if you were planning to ambush whoever parked on the graveled spot.

But no self-respecting mugger would have done that. If you got behind or between the arborvitae, you wouldn't be seen from anywhere but the back window of the house. But if anyone saw you sneak in there, there'd be no excuse, either. And if they called the cops, you'd never see them coming.

As Virgil was walking around the garage, a man came out on the back porch of the house across the alley, and called, "Who are you?"

Virgil called back, "State Bureau of Criminal Apprehension. Are you Joe Lee?"

"That's me." Lee came down from his porch and across the alley. "Have you found out anything?"

Virgil shook his head. "I haven't started looking yet. It's a St. Paul case, I'm looking to see if it ties into something else I'm investigating."

"Really." Lee was a brawny, sunburned man who might have been a heavy-equipment operator, probably in his late fifties or early sixties. "I figured there had to be something else going on. The guy had him on the ground, never did try for his billfold. He just kept pounding him—Terry."

"You ever see anyone who looked like they were scouting the alley? Somebody who shouldn't have been here?"

"No . . . nobody but Terry's girlfriend. I saw her a couple times, in the mornings—I guess she stayed over."

Virgil thought: Katherine Green? He asked, "What'd the girl-friend look like?"

"Like, I don't know, a woodpecker."

"A woodpecker?"

"Tall, thin, red hair—she wore it up in a thing, a peak, on top of her head. Like a pileated woodpecker."

"Good description," Virgil said. It couldn't be Green. "The attack . . . You don't have any idea of what that might have been about?"

"Nope. I talked to Terry once in a while, when we were taking out the garbage at the same time. Seemed like a nice enough guy. I didn't really know him, though."

Lee had nothing more to say, and Virgil walked back around the house. The next-door neighbor was still standing there, keeping an eye out for Virgil. He asked, "Do I have to worry about it?"

Virgil said, "I don't think so. Looks to me like whoever did it was targeting Mr. Foster."

Virgil gave the neighbor a card and drove five minutes over to Regions Hospital, where he'd spent a few hundred hours as a St. Paul cop, both as an investigator and as a patient.

When he asked at the emergency room desk, he was told that Foster had been moved to a regular room; he was conscious and expected to recover. Virgil got the room number, and as he went up in the elevator, it occurred to him to wonder why neither Katherine Green nor Clete May had mentioned the attack on Foster.

The easy answer was: they didn't know about it. But he'd ask.

Foster was a mess.

He might have been a good-looking guy, perhaps an inch under six feet tall and in good shape, but now he had bandages wrapped around his head, completely covering one eye and one ear, and what Virgil could see of his face, as he lay propped up in the hospital bed, was heavily bruised and abraded; he also had a plastic brace covering his nose. Both of his arms, which were in casts that left nothing exposed except his fingertips, were tethered to an overhead rack and suspended.

The one eye that was visible turned toward Virgil, and Foster croaked, "Who are you?"

Virgil told him, and then said, "I was looking for you over at your house. I wanted to talk to you about the Quill murder. Now I'm wondering if what happened to you had anything to do with that?"

"Don't know," Foster croaked. "Could you hold that water bottle so I could get a drink?"

There was a plastic cup on the bed tray with a bent plastic straw sticking out of it, and Virgil held it while Foster drank. When he'd had enough, his tongue flicked out to wet his lips, and he said, "Thanks. Least that asshole didn't bust my teeth . . . I don't know why this happened. I did three tours in Iraq and Syria, I even got wounded, but I wasn't hurt this bad."

All he knew about his attacker was that he was a white man— he'd seen his forearms—and that he was about average height and a little heavy. "The police are calling it a mugging, but I'll tell you what: he was trying to kill me. That's how my arms got broken. I kept putting them up so he couldn't hit me in the head. He had a club—like a nightstick or something, like a police baton. He never tried to get my wallet, but that was maybe because I was screaming my head off, and then Joe Lee was yelling at him and he took off."

They talked about it for a while, and Foster was insistent that there was no major drama in his life. He didn't have a full-time girlfriend, he said, but he wasn't gay, either, nor was he Jewish or Islamic, and the attack was white on white, so it wasn't a random hate crime. He'd gone to the Green lecture, where the fight started, but said he'd tried to break it up and hadn't hit anyone. "It's all on that video they got, you can see for yourself."

"You say you don't have a girlfriend. When I was over at your house, a neighbor mentioned a girl. Had you recently broken up with someone?"

Foster said, "No . . . I don't . . . Oh, somebody must have seen Sandy. She's not a girlfriend, she's just a friend from the U. She's stayed over a couple of times, but we're not dating. We're both up front about that."

"Women are sometimes less up front than men are. I mean, you think everything is up front but—"

Foster waved him off. "No, no. She drinks a little too much, I drink a little too much, and sometimes when we've both drunk a little too much and we're both feeling a little horny, she'll stay over. When we're both sober, then we're not attached."

"There's not another boyfriend who'd be unhappy about those sleepovers?"

"No. She says not, and she's telling the truth." And he asked, "Why are you talking to me anyway? Did somebody say something?"

Virgil said, "Because you're a military vet, which means that you're familiar with violence. You might even have done some."

"Well, Jesus, man, I was in the Army," Foster said.

"So was I," Virgil said, "I was an MP captain, and I did some violence myself. And I have as a cop. I don't think your history is a big deal, but when you're trying to figure out who might have done some violence, you gotta ask around about who might be capable of it."

Foster thought about that for a moment, then said, "Yeah, I guess."

A nurse stuck her head in, glanced at Virgil, then asked Foster, "Do you need the bathroom?"

"Not now," he said. "Ask me in an hour. My arms are starting to ache again."

"I'll talk to you in an hour."

When she was gone, Foster said, "They don't like to give me painkillers because they think I'll become a raging junkie. They can't see the pain, so they ignore it."

He had not killed Quill, he said, had never seen Quill at the library, and hadn't known what he looked like until the confrontation at Green's lecture.

He was a Cultural Science major, he said, because when he got out of the Army and started at the university, he hadn't yet figured out exactly what he wanted to do. "I took a whole bunch of classes, a bunch of hours, scattered over a bunch of subjects, and what I found out was that a lot of them were acceptable in Cultural Science. I signed up for Cultural Science because I could use credits I'd already piled up toward a degree. To tell the truth, a lot of Cultural Science is like a magic show. I don't understand how anybody could believe the shit some of those professors tell you. Even professor Green, she's sorta out there. But, she's got some nice . . . Well, hell . . ."

Virgil nodded. "I noticed that. You got something going there?"

Foster gave his head a half shake. "You know, she's only, like, thirty-four. Same age as I am. I screwed around for a couple years after school, and then I went down to the recruiting office and signed up. I was in for eight, thinking I might go lifer, but after that last tour in Syria I bailed."

"Hit hard?"

"Not so bad. Got shot in the thigh. Didn't do a lot of damage, through and through, but made me think I might want to do something safer, especially since they keep sending you back and back and back," Foster said. "I'm still in the reserve. If the college thing doesn't work out, the Army would let me back in, at the same rank and with credit for time served. What I'm saying is, I wound up in Cultural Science, and Katherine's got that hot bod and she's my age and not hooked up with anybody. I went to India with her last year, and there were a couple of times when I got the feeling that she liked my looks. You know, Dr. Foster's female cure."

"Nothing happened?"

"I'm sorta retarded that way," Foster said. He tried to smile but winced instead. "I got a girl knocked up in high school, she had an abortion, and everybody was yelling at me. I've been pretty wary about commitments ever since. But I had the feeling a couple times, in India, that if I reached out and patted her on the ass, she wouldn't have complained. I've got that feeling right now, though this whole mugging thing didn't do much for my looks. Goddamn near ripped off one of my ears. When I get out of here, I might have a talk with her . . . about things. I'm thirty-four, time's a-wastin'."

"I talked to Dr. Green yesterday. She didn't mention anything about you being attacked."

Foster tried to shrug, mostly failed, winced again. "I didn't tell anybody except my folks, and they live up in Black Duck. Nobody to tell her about it."

Foster said he had no idea of who might have killed Quill.

"There was a lot of hostility between him and the people in Cultural Science, and there are some goofy people in the department, but I can't say that any of them seem like killers."

"I talked to Clete May. He thinks Dr. Green is pretty attractive. You don't think he'd consider you a rival?"

Foster tried to shake his head and mostly failed again. "Wasn't Clete. We do that bumping-chests thing when we finish bad jobs for Dr. Green. Like setting up a hundred big old Army surplus tents. Or at the lunch table when we were in India. Shit like that. Anyway, he's lots bigger than me. The guy who jumped me was my size or shorter. Stocky. Maybe fat, but hard to tell in that situation."

They talked for a while, and Virgil thought he recognized the type. Some guys joined the military for the adventure and the idea that they might turn out to be Rambo. Others joined because they didn't know what else to do; they weren't qualified for any particular civilian job and thought they might try the Army.

Foster seemed to fall in the second group: not particularly aggressive, not angry with the world, just a guy struggling with what to do with his life that might have some significance.

He didn't see anything in Foster that suggested a murderer. He simply wasn't angry enough.

Back outside, he called Trane.

"There's an ex–Army guy named Terry Foster, one of the students in Cultural Science."

"I saw the name, didn't interview him. We need to look at him?"

"I already did. Somebody tried to beat him to death a couple of days ago, over in St. Paul. He's hurt bad and he's still at Regions. I don't think he had anything to do with Quill's murder, but it's a curious coincidence."

"When you say tried to beat him to death . . ."

"Attacked him with a club of some kind, broke both his arms when he tried to cover his head, broke his nose; he's got some scalp trauma . . . He said if a neighbor hadn't seen what was happening and started yelling at the attacker, he would have been killed."

"That worries me," Trane said. "I'll get with St. Paul, see what they have to say. Push them."

"Good idea. Right now, I'm told they're treating it as a mugging. Let me ask you something else: did you do any background on Katherine Green? Check out her love life?"

"No. Should I have?"

"Foster said that Green might have eyes for him, he felt some interest. I'm wondering if the attack on Foster might be a red herring—that it doesn't have anything to do with the Quill murder but is somebody who's interested in Green who might be taking out the competition. After talking to Foster, I got the feeling he was targeted. That the attack wasn't random. That it was an ambush."

"Well, poop," Trane said. "I guess I work tomorrow . . . Are you on your way home?"

"I'm meeting my girlfriend and one of her kids over at Davenport's place and then going home after that. When I found out what happened, I came over here to Regions. Now I'm thinking I should find out where Green is and talk to her about it."

"She's over in St. Paul, too. I went to her house. Let me get you that address."

Virgil considered calling Green to make sure she was around, but after getting her address from Trane, on Mount Curve Boulevard, he realized she must live within a few blocks of Davenport. The interview probably wasn't critical. And if she wasn't home, he'd try again on Monday.

She was home.

Green lived in a white clapboard house set high on a bank above the street, with a tucked-under garage and a big deck over it. Virgil pulled into the short driveway, climbed the stairs to the front door, and knocked. Green peeked out through a corner of the drape-covered picture window next to the porch, and Virgil twiddled his fingers at her. The door popped open a moment later, and she said, "Officer . . . ?" the question mark in her tone indicating she'd forgotten his name.

"Virgil Flowers," Virgil said. "We've had an . . . event . . . that I'd like to get your reaction to."

She pushed open the screen door. "Come in. What happened?"

The door gave onto the living room, which was filled with beige furniture and two side-by-side bookcases filled with texts; an archway to the right led to a generous kitchen with a table and four chairs. Virgil went left, perched on a couch, and she sat on a chair facing him.

"You told me that Terry Foster might have a predilection, or at least a familiarity with, violence, since he was in combat in the Army. Somebody attacked him the night before last, outside his house, and hurt him. Bad."

"Oh my God! Is he? I mean . . ." Her reaction seemed genuinely spontaneous. She hadn't known about Foster.

"He's not going to die, but his arms are broken, and he's sustained some head injuries," Virgil said. "The question is, is this related to the Quill murder? I need to talk to you about that."

"Why would it be?" she asked, frowning. "Wouldn't it more likely be a robbery? A mugging?"

"There are some unusual aspects to it." He explained about the ambush, about how the attacker apparently lay in waiting for Foster. "Most muggers want your money and don't want to kill anybody because then it becomes a big deal. Muggings are usually crimes of opportunity, a random meeting on the street. This guy never demanded anything. He hid, he waited, he attacked."

"What would I know about that?"

"Uh, don't take this the wrong way," Virgil said, "but are you currently involved in a personal relationship?"

She flushed, and a spark of anger flashed in her eyes. "I . . . What . . . How would that . . . ?"

"Foster is about your age, and he finds you attractive. He told me so. I was wondering if there was somebody else in your life who'd know about Foster's feelings, who would try to discourage him."

"Death would be discouraging," Green said, maybe with a hint of humor in her voice. She went serious again. "No. I don't have a personal relationship with anyone at the moment. Terry is not unattractive, but there are some . . . barriers . . . when it comes to relationships between professors and students. The university doesn't forbid them, but it does discourage them. If a relationship becomes a problem, it's the professor who loses. Always."

"He's not a kid."

"That does make a difference. A forty-five-year-old male Art professor having an affair with an eighteen-year-old freshman is in deep trouble. And if he doesn't already have tenure, he won't get it. A thirty-four-year-old female Cultural Science professor sleeping with a thirty-four-year-old Army combat veteran won't attract so much attention because the power differentials in the two situations are quite distinct," Green said. "What attention it did attract, though, wouldn't be good, especially for the professor. This is all theoretical, of course. I have no physical relationship with Terry and never have had."

"Might somebody think you do?"

She shook her head. "If somebody does, it's a fantasy. I had a pleasant relationship with a nice man, a Realtor, that ended two years ago. He wanted a comfortable home, two or three kids and a couple of dogs, a supportive wife to make sure the dishwasher didn't overheat. That wasn't me. We both eventually recognized that and we broke up. I haven't been on a date since then. Too busy. To say nothing of the whole male privilege thing, which I'm pretty tired of. You know, the little woman to bring his slippers and pipe after a hard day slaving over the listings."

"I thought it was the dog that brought the slippers and the pipe," Virgil said.

"The job descriptions are similar," she said.

Virgil peered at her, and said, "Huh."

"What?"

He slapped his thighs, stood up. "That doesn't get me anywhere. I was hoping you had a jealous boyfriend with a collection of baseball bats. That'd be simple. Now I have to go back to wondering if there's a connection to the Quill murder. Of if it was just a mugging gone wrong."

"I don't see how it could be connected to Quill. As far as I know, Terry had nothing to do with him," Green said.

"That's what Terry told me. But suppose somebody from Cultural Science did kill Quill because he was obsessed with the idea of protecting you. And maybe had reason to think that Terry could figure that out."

"That sounds like a TV cop show," Green said.

"Yeah." Virgil pushed hair out of his eyes. "That's always a bad sign. Whatever it is, it's never like TV."

CHAPTER

TEN

Virgil drove over to Davenport's after leaving Green's house, and, as he'd thought, it was only about four blocks and a half million dollars away. Davenport was a U.S. Marshal and had been shot in Los Angeles the previous spring by federal fugitives. The fugitives had been a colorful bunch, and had included a cannibal. When Davenport recovered from the shooting, he had gone back after them, with a couple of other marshals and an FBI man, and now most of the fugitives were dead.

When Virgil pulled into his driveway, Davenport was shooting baskets at a hoop hung over his garage door. He looked too thin, thinner than Virgil had ever seen him, and there was an underlying grayness to his face.

"Big guy," Davenport said, passing the ball to Virgil as he got out of his truck. Virgil banged the ball off the rim, and Davenport said, "Brick," and, "The ball's supposed to arc, Virgil. Arc, like a rainbow. You're not throwing a runner out at first."

"I know the theory," Virgil said. He'd been a college third

baseman but had played basketball in high school, without much enthusiasm. "It's hard to give a shit about basketball. If the hoop were at sixteen feet, and they let women play, it'd be different . . . How are you feeling?"

"Okay. I look bad, but I'm okay. Where's Frankie?"

"She's on her way up, with our Sam. She should be here pretty soon."

Davenport's wife, Weather, showed up a few minutes later with a sack of raw steaks, and they all went in the house, and Davenport's two kids still living at home went into the back to do whatever kids do when they get bored with their parents, and Virgil and Davenport drank beers and talked with Weather as she unpacked the steaks, after which Davenport started chopping up vegetables for a salad.

The talk drifted to Virgil's case. Margaret Trane, Davenport said, was maybe the best investigator in the Minneapolis Police Department. "When she called me about you, she said she was stuck."

"Things have loosened up," Virgil said. He outlined the past two days in Minneapolis, and Davenport frowned, and said, "That sounds like you've got a ton of stuff to work with. You oughta be making good progress. Instead, you're talking like you're seriously screwed."

"I don't feel screwed, but something unusual is going on," Virgil said. "I haven't put my finger on it. I got a lot of clues but no clue. While a lot of people didn't like Quill, it doesn't seem like they disliked him enough to kill him."

"You don't understand campus politics, Virgil," Weather said. "There's no meaner group of people in the world than academics when they get stirred up. I've heard a lot about this feud between Quill and Green. Believe me, something like that could lead to murder. But you know what your real problem is?"

"You're about to tell me," Virgil said.

"Yes. Your real problem is, all the people you're dealing with are really, really smart," Weather said. She was a plastic and microsurgeon and on staff at the University of Minnesota hospitals, among others. "If this wasn't a spontaneous murder, if the killer planned it, then you're going to have a hard time catching him, and an even harder time convicting him. I bet he's set himself up with an alibi, and it'll be hard to break. Maybe impossible."

Virgil said, "There's no prints, no DNA, no nothing. You're right about the killer being smart. It doesn't feel planned, though."

"The only thing harder than knocking down a well-planned murder is knocking down one that wasn't planned at all. If it's totally unplanned and the killer gets past that first day, then it gets tough. For example, I can't see Virgil's guy planning to use a laptop as a murder weapon," Davenport said. "That sounds spontaneous."

"Not entirely sure that he was hit by the laptop," Virgil said. "The head wound suggests it could have been—it's a good fit— but it wouldn't have to be. I could find ten things in our barn that could have made the same wound."

Davenport's son, Sam, dashed up to the kitchen door and shouted, "They're here."

"Well, go open the door," Weather said.

He dashed away, and, a minute later, Frankie tottered through the kitchen door, and said to Virgil, "You criminal. You did this to me."

Davenport went over to kiss her, and said, "Did what? You look terrific."

"You are such a charmer . . . If Weather hadn't married you, I would have."

"Hey, what about me?" Virgil asked.

"You could marry Letty," Frankie said.

"We all know that ain't gonna happen," Davenport said. "I'm gonna go fire up the grill."

When he'd gone, Frankie leaned toward Weather, and asked, quietly, "He still looks pretty rough. Are you sure you want him to keep working?"

"No. But Lucas is gonna do what Lucas is gonna do. It's always been that way. I can slow him down most of the time, when he's planning to do something crazy, but not all the time. This time, I can't."

"Can't what?" Davenport asked, returning to the kitchen, looking for a can of briquette starter.

"Can't wait for the babies to show up," Weather said. "I want to see what that fuckin' Flowers does with his dadhood."

They didn't talk about Davenport anymore or about the shootings in LA and Vegas. Davenport did mention that he'd stopped to talk to his adopted daughter, Letty, at Stanford before he went on to Los Angeles. She was about to graduate and was deciding between a hot job offer and an economics scholarship at Yale.

Virgil: "Did she ask about me? If she does, you could tell her I'm taken. For the time being anyway."

"Don't start," Davenport said.

They ate steaks, and Davenport's son Sam and Frankie's son, also a Sam, roughhoused around the yard and shouted a few off-color words and were corrected in a desultory way. The adults talked about everything but crime, and toward the end of the evening a U.S. senator called Davenport to say that he was needed for a confidential job in Washington.

The senator gave Virgil a hard time for a few minutes—while governor, he'd been involved with Virgil when Virgil purchased his boat—then signed off after Davenport promised to call him the next day. At ten o'clock, Frankie followed Virgil and Sam out of Davenport's driveway. Frankie and Virgil both had hands-free phone links in their vehicles and they raked over the details of Virgil's case as they drove, finally giving up as they pulled into the barnyard.

Sam got out of the truck, and Honus the Yellow Dog, who'd been sleeping on the porch, ambled over in the dark to meet him.

"Don't be going online," Frankie said to her son.

"I'm too sleepy anyway," Sam said, and Virgil rubbed his head.

Virgil woke up Sunday morning in his own bed, with gray clouds outside and a stiff wind blowing through the leaves of a sugar maple that grew in the side yard. He yawned, stretched, got up, and looked out the window. The hayfield was as slick as a Marine recruit's haircut, not a single bale waiting to be thrown. He smiled to himself, stretched again, and went to get cleaned up.

Frankie was having a second cup of coffee when he made it down to the kitchen, and she said, "Virgie, we gotta talk."

Virgil said, "Oh, shit. Listen, I didn't have any choice about going up there. If I hadn't been ordered to go, I would have thrown that hay. Really, I would have."

"No, no, I'm not talking about hay. I want to tell you I enjoyed myself last night, but I'm getting pretty lumpy. We might have to, mmm, go easy on the more vigorous sex until the kids get here."

"Oh, Jesus! Why didn't you say something?" Virgil asked. "I'd never hurt you. I—"

"We're not quite there yet. You didn't hurt me, and I enjoyed the heck out of myself," she said. "I'm not saying that the sex has to stop. We'll have to go to, you know, alternatives."

"I'm up for that," Virgil said. "Anytime, anyplace. Well, almost anyplace. The roof of the barn wouldn't be good. You'd probably roll off."

"Thanks. Anyway, I figured you'd be cooperative."

"Gotcha. We can start working on alternatives tonight," Virgil said. "Or this afternoon . . . if I don't have to do something with hay."

"Barn's full of hay. There won't be any hay next year, so you're in the clear. We're four years into the alfalfa now, we need to kill it off. Rolf wants to rotate in some corn."

She went on like that for a while, and Virgil heard "four years," "Rolf," as well as "alfalfa," "corn," and a couple other agricultural words, and when he realized she'd finished talking, he said, "You know what you're doing, I can't advise you. Except—"

"You going to advise me now," she said.

"Yeah. I'll advise you that next spring you're going to have two new kids and not a hell of a lot of time to do farmwork or architectural salvage. I've got to keep working to bring in the cash. Maybe it's time to ease off on the farming. And the salvage. Take a break. Or make a deal with Rolf: he does it all, he gets it all. He could use the money. That'd keep the company going."

"I hate it when you talk sense."

"I'm not often accused of doing that," Virgil said. "Anyway, what are we doing today?"

"We could start by going down to Fleet Farm. I need two fence posts and some reflector buttons."

They spent the late morning rolling around Mankato, running errands, stopped at a Pagliai's Pizza for lunch, at the riverfront Hy-Vee's, where they spent a hundred bucks on food that would hold them for maybe three days. Frankie talked about getting a couple of quarter horses so the kids would grow up with horses, in addition to Honus the Yellow Dog and the chicken.

"If we got horses, we'd have to build a stable," Virgil said.

"I've got the materials from the salvage operation. Rolf says he can get Lonnie Marks to pour the foundation at cost, and then you two could build it. Easy: post and beam. I'm thinking six stalls, a tack room, storage for concentrates, a loft for the hay. I'm not thinking we do it in the next fifteen minutes. Maybe start it next spring, finish it a year later. The only thing that would be expensive are the rubber mats I'd want to put down on the concrete."

"Who shovels the horseshit?" Virgil asked.

"Well, I mean, you know . . ."

"That's what I thought," Virgil said. But he liked the idea of horses. The image of himself galloping across the prairie. "We can talk about it."

On the way home, they were silent, preoccupied by different thoughts. For the first time in his life, Virgil had responsibilities that he couldn't walk away from—two kids on the way, a woman he wanted to marry and eventually, he thought, surely would.

That was not exactly what he'd seen coming. When he was in

the Army, in the Balkans, he'd taken a couple of leaves in Europe. He'd somehow imagined a writing life, on one of the coasts, with frequent visits to Paris, his favorite big city.

Not happening. He was a cop living on a Midwestern farm well outside a small city.

Still, he thought, he had the writing. He was doing a dozen articles a year for a variety of magazines, had been published in *Vanity Fair* and *The New York Times Magazine*.

And was edging into something new. He hadn't talked to Frankie about it, but he had three chapters of a novel in his writing drawer and was working on it regularly, so much so that he'd begged off a musky fishing trip to Canada with his old friend Johnson Johnson to keep it going.

That afternoon, Virgil did chores, including pulling out two old, rusting posts at the driveway entrance, then replacing them with two new wooden posts and mounting reflectors on them. That done, he spent three hours at his writing desk, sending out query letters to magazines about article assignments and working on the novel.

That evening, they caught a movie beamed down from the satellite, then, just before dark, went for a walk.

The night was quiet, except for the random cricket. The sky had cleared out in the afternoon, and the wind had dropped to nothing. Virgil could smell the hayfield, and, overhead, the stars were so close they could almost be touched.

"Is there anywhere better than Minnesota in the summer?" Virgil asked.

"There's isn't," Frankie said. "Unless you're dead in the library."

ELEVEN

Monday.

Virgil got an early start and was halfway to Minneapolis when Trane called. "Where are you?"

"Coming up to Shakopee. Did something happen?"

"Listen to this. I'm going to hold my phone close so you can hear it."

". . . Please leave a message. *Beep!*"

A man's voice, but pitched high, maybe faked: "Uh, this is a message for Detective Trane about Dr. Quill. I know a woman named China White who told me that she was afraid she killed him. She hit him with a laptop. He was talking on his telephone in his study room but left his computer out on a library table, and there was nobody around, so she picked up the computer and hit him with it. She hit him two times. This wasn't at night. The newspaper said it was at night, but she said this was in the daytime, right before the library closed. She took his cell phone, shut the door and locked it with his key, then took his computer and threw it in the river along with his car keys. She forgot about the cell until the next day. There should be video of her going out of the library. She did it because she was selling cocaine to Dr. Quill and he said there was something wrong with it and he wasn't going to pay her. She said there was nothing wrong with it and got angry and hit him. She sometimes goes to the Territorial Lounge. Thank you for listening."

Trane came back. "That's it."

Virgil said, "Damn."

"Thank you. That's the kind of insight I was hoping for."

"Well, give me a goddamn minute to think, will you?" Virgil snapped. "You've had it for a while. What do you think?"

"I've had it for, like, five minutes," she snapped back. "I don't know what to think."

"If you took all the different factual parts—that the caller knew to call you, that the laptop, phone, keys were missing, that he was hit twice—how much of that is public?"

"One way or another, all of it," Trane said. "The newspapers and television knew everything except the fact he was hit twice, but that was mentioned in the autopsy report, and his wife and daughter had access to it. Who knows who they might have told? The keys, laptop, and phone—all those details were leaked during the first week of the investigation, but at different times. Would a scammer have seen all those mentions on TV and in the papers? I mean, 'CCO had the missing keys and phone, but the *Star Tribune* got the computer."

Virgil said, "Have you talked to your Narcotics guys? You know what China White is?"

"Yeah, but we're not talking about China White, we're talking about coke . . . At least, I think that's what we're talking about. I'm trying to find somebody who knows about this Territorial Lounge."

"I got a guy at the BCA who might be able to help," Virgil said.

Virgil thought about the tip and China White as he continued into the Cities and across the Mississippi to the university. There were, in his experience, a whole bunch of reasons that somebody could wind up violently and illegally dead. There were a whole bunch more that somebody could wind up violently but legally dead, but those didn't apply in the Quill case.

In his territory, in the southern third of Minnesota, the most common murders were domestic conflicts. Domestics were followed in frequency by alcohol- or drug-inspired mayhem. Psychological upsets counted for a few, and the rest were for a variety of reasons: money, sex, revenge, immaturity—the ten-year-old who shoots his mother for taking away his cell phone—and ideology. Virgil had never seen a purely ideological murder, Republicans being too cautious, Democrats generally being bad shots.

Mostly it was domestics and booze.

Where would the Quill murder land in that matrix? Wasn't a domestic, and there was no reason to think alcohol was involved. Not ideology. Unlikely money, since he had an elaborate will that would be hard to break; people would get what he left them, no more, no less. All of the people who seemed possible suspects were mature adults except his daughter, who didn't have any reason to kill him except general disdain, which wasn't usually enough. So a maturity problem didn't seem likely.

Could be anger or revenge, if Green were involved, or somebody in Quill's lab, if the killer was an employee unhappy about not receiving credit for scientific work or a low salary or had other job tensions. Was somebody about to be fired?

Could be sex, if Quill were having an illicit relationship or if he were inviting hookers up to the carrel late at night.

Virgil thought about that for a moment. If the library was empty, and if he didn't want to take a chance of inviting a prostitute into his home, that would explain the pubic hairs on the yoga mat. The ex-wives did say Quill liked sex, and with the breakup with his third wife, he wasn't getting any. But a hooker? A hooker wouldn't likely forget a wallet, and Quill had seven hundred dollars in his and it was still in his back pocket when he was found.

Then, finally, drugs, and the tip on an unknown dealer called China White. Drugs could explain a lot. If the cocaine found in the old desk was Quill's, and if he were involved with a dealer, it would explain surreptitious meetings late at night. And if he was getting drugs from a prostitute, which was not unheard of, it'd be an even more credible explanation.

It would also mean that the attack on Terry Foster was almost certainly not related to the Quill murder. Maybe Foster was the victim of a random act, a coincidence.

He called Trane, who picked up instantly. "What?"

"I wanted to mention a couple of things that we should keep in mind. If the Terry Foster attack is related to the Quill murder, then we're dealing with a planner, not an impulse killer. If Foster is related, then the killer is male, not a female named China White. Foster was sure of that."

"That's all true, but only if Foster is related to Quill."

"You were planning to talk to the St. Paul cops yesterday. Did you get that done?"

"Nope. Do you know Roger Bryan?"

"Yes. He caught it?" When Virgil was a St. Paul cop, he'd worked with Bryan, then a new detective. Virgil considered him competent, and maybe better than that.

"Yeah. He was doing one of those low-rent Ironman things yesterday—bike fifty K, swim Lake St. Croix, run ten K. He was gone all day. He's working today, we're meeting up this afternoon."

"I'd like to sit in on that."

"You're invited," Trane said. "You still headed for the lab?"

"I'm there now," Virgil said. "Looking for a place to park where I won't get towed."

Virgil had taken a couple of required chemistry courses when he was at the university and had scored solid B's, which might have been C's if he hadn't impressed the chemistry professor with his formula for what the professor called, with a complete lack of cultural sensitivity, the "Yellow Peril." That is, a cheap and semi-lethal concoction of ethanol, orange juice, and pineapple nectar, which the professor served at departmental parties.

All Virgil remembered of his legitimate chemical efforts was measuring the density of Pepsi Cola and the confusing mass of glassware in the lab. He expected something similar when he followed a harried-looking woman through the door of Quill's laboratory but found, instead, something that more closely resembled a sophisticated computer lab. The room was the size of a high school classroom, with several doors down its interior length leading to other rooms.

The woman, turning to Virgil, asked, "Can I help you?"

Virgil identified himself.

"Barth's death was a complete shock," she said. "I can't help you with anything. You probably want to talk to Carl."

"Carl?"

"Anderson. He's the lab director, if we still have a lab. His office is back that way."

She pointed, and Virgil followed the direction of her finger, around a corner and into a second, larger room, where he found his forest of glassware and another woman who was using a multichannel pipette to transfer a liquid that looked like watery blood into multiwell microtiter plates. She looked up, and Virgil said, "Carl Anderson's office?"

She said, "Keep going. I'm not sure if he's still here."

The glassware room was the same size as the computer area, rows of easy-clean gray cabinets topped with a black rubberized work surface with shelves above. The shelves held bottles and hardware and boxes of vinyl gloves. A computer-linked sound system pumped quiet Adult Alternative music into the room, tempting Virgil to pluck out his earballs.

But he kept going and found a chubby, balding man sitting in an office with an identifying plaque beside the door that said "Carl Anderson, Staff Director." He was working at a computer on a separate table that right-angled his desk.

The door was open, and Virgil stuck his head in. "Mr. Anderson?"

Anderson, startled, jumped, turned, and asked, "Who are you?"

Virgil identified himself and his mission, and Anderson swiveled to his desk and pointed Virgil at a visitor's chair. "What a fucking mess," he said, running both hands through his nonexistent hair, leaving behind white lines on his sunburnt scalp. "You have any news?"

"No, not really. A few things have popped up—I can't talk about them—but there's nothing solid."

"How is it possible, in this day and age, that somebody could commit a murder, a beating murder, that didn't leave behind DNA? I'd think that would be almost impossible."

"There usually is a little DNA around, when you have a body," Virgil said. "In this case, there was apparently no physical contact between Dr. Quill and the killer."

Anderson wiped a hand across his mouth, said, "Unbelievable."

Virgil asked Anderson a half dozen questions, including about his alibi, which turned out to be the typical mishmash of times, places, and people that made it believable but not perfect.

"If you want my best reason for not killing the man, it's this: I'm making a hundred and fifty thousand dollars a year and now I might be out of work. I have a master's degree in organic chemistry, but I'm basically a bureaucrat. I do paperwork, I supervise grant applications, I make sure everybody gets paid, and I decide who gets routine raises and who doesn't. I tried to keep Barth inside his budget and that wasn't easy. Every big shot scientist has somebody like me, but there aren't a hell of a lot of openings. I may be comprehensively fucked."

He didn't know Katherine Green, Clete May, or Terry Foster. "I wasn't involved in that whole pissing match between us and Cultural Science. Seemed a little dumb, though Barth wasn't dumb. Those people should be ignored. Flame wars encourage them, because that's about all they got going for themselves."

"It was only a pissing match?"

"Academic feuds are endemic but don't usually end in murder. Honestly? I don't think those people are involved. I mean, they're crazy but not insane, if you see what I mean," Anderson said. "I'd be willing to bet that somebody was inside the library when they shouldn't have been. A street guy, looking for something to steal. He bumps into Barth and panics and grabs the computer and *Bang!* Barth's dead."

"You knew we were looking at the computer as the murder weapon?"

"Yeah. Sergeant Trane asked me about it, why he'd have it, what he was doing with it. I didn't know, but I asked her what the big deal was, we're not doing anything secret here. She said it was possible that the laptop was the murder weapon."

"Can you think of anything somebody could do with that computer, something that he might have on it, that would get him killed?" Virgil asked. "I understand it was a heavy-duty machine."

"Sergeant Trane asked me the same question. I couldn't think of anything. But I'm not sure the power of the computer was significant. Barth was a gear freak. If he bought a set of golf clubs, he'd get the best ones anybody ever heard of; if he bought a shotgun, it'd be a great shotgun—y'know, from Italy or something. If he bought a laptop, he'd get the fastest, most powerful he could find. He was rich. When it came to gear, he routinely bought the best. He had a Leica camera and a bunch of lenses he used for snapshots, the same stuff the rest of us use our iPhones for."

Quill wasn't sleeping with anybody in the lab, Anderson said, and none of the women there seemed like they'd be much interested in him. He had that three-wife history and was curt, at best, with all the lab people, even those he liked.

"Any possibility that he might get together with women on-line?" Virgil asked.

Anderson thought for a moment, then said, "I don't know. Frankly, it wouldn't astonish me. The efficiency of it would appeal to him. Sex on demand, without commitment. I understand that there's often a money exchange involved in the hookups."

"So, women might be another form of gear," Virgil suggested. "Get what you want, pay your money, and be done with it."

"That's about it," Anderson said.

Anderson walked through the lab and into the computer space with Virgil as Virgil was leaving but stopped to talk to the woman Virgil had followed into the lab. Anderson said to him, "This is Julie Payne. She knows everything." Then to Payne: "Was Barth interested in any of the women in the lab?"

She cracked a smile, and said, "No."

"It was that clear?" Virgil asked.

"Yes. He wasn't interested in any of us."

Virgil: "Did he have a girlfriend?"

"That's harder. Some days he'd come in—this was after he'd left his wife—and he'd have that look that men get after a night of hot sex," Payne said. "The postcoital, empty prostate macho glow. Both relaxed and predatory, looking for a new target."

"I didn't know we got that look," Virgil said.

"Well, you do. I first spotted it in my ex-husband. First because of me, then later not so much," Payne said.

"Then you think a girlfriend is likely?"

"Sex seemed likely. I wouldn't go so far as to say he had a girl-friend. One time, this girl from the hospital came over with some images for Sally—Sally works here, she's a tech—and they were talking, and this girl said she might try Tinder. Dr. Quill was going by and heard that and said something like, 'Real bad idea.' He didn't say anything else, just kept walking, but he obviously knew what Tinder was."

"Tinder is pay-to-play?"

"Not supposed to be but sometimes is," Payne said. "Not all full-time hookers. Sometimes, it's just a girl who needs a quick couple of thousand so she can go to Mardi Gras or something. The Virgin Islands or Cabo in February."

"Would Dr. Quill take that risk? A hookup for money?"

She shrugged. "Don't know. If he did, it would be calculated and probably not much of a risk."

"How would I find one of these women?"

"Stroke to the right, big guy," Payne said. And then she had to explain what that meant.

Something to think about. Pubic hairs, a yoga mat, an empty prostate macho glow. Why would a hooker kill him and why would she leave behind his wallet, with its unidentifiable currency? Everything she did take—the computer, the keys, the phone—would be evidence against her. And only the computer could be fenced, and not for much, no matter what it originally cost.

Virgil had some time to kill before the meeting with Trane and the cop, so he stopped off in St. Paul for a Butter Flake Roll at Breadsmith, went next door for a Strawberry Surf Rider Smoothie from Jamba Juice, then idled around the corner and looked in a bookstore window until he finished eating and drinking his smoothie, then went inside and bought the latest Dave Robicheaux novel by James Lee Burke.

He made it to St. Paul police headquarters fifteen minutes ahead of time and sat and read the novel until he saw Trane coming down the street.

"Get anything from the lab?" she asked.

"One of his lab employees thinks Quill was having a sexual relationship with somebody. She said he'd sometimes come in with—and I quote—'the postcoital, empty prostate macho glow.' And she said he was familiar with Tinder."

"Ah, the well-known postcoital, empty prostate macho glow. I'm *very* familiar with it," Trane said. "Maybe a hooker emptied it for him?"

"That we don't know. Yet. But I'm leaning in that direction. If I have time, I'm going to figure out how Tinder works, then I'm going to go sit by his house and stroke to the right. See who pops up."

"You're expecting something to pop up? I'm told you're expecting children."

"You have a dirty mind, Trane. I'm as faithful as the day is long."

"Winter or summer?"

The desk cop walked Trane and Virgil back to Roger Bryan's desk. Bryan was on the phone and waved them into chairs, ended the call, stuck out a hand to shake with Virgil, and said, "Virgil Fuckin' Flowers, as I live and breathe. And how are you, Maggie? I haven't seen you since when? Last summer on the jumper?"

"Yup. Poor kid." She turned to Virgil, and said, "Kid jumped off the Lake Street Bridge because everybody at school unfriended him."

"I read about it," Virgil said. "I never know what to think when something like that happens."

"The school held a memorial service for him, and they brought in a busload of shrinks to shrink the kids," Bryan said. "What they should have done is taken the little assholes out to the soccer field, lined them up, and then beat the crap out of them one at a time."

"I've always thought of you as the Gandhi type," Virgil said.

"What's going on with Terry Foster?" Bryan asked. "He's hooked up with the Quill murder? Is that right?"

"We don't know. We need to know about what happened to Foster. He's part of that clusterfuck going on at the U, between Quill and Katherine Green."

"I know, the culture professor. We asked him about that and came up empty," Bryan said. "Right now, we're treating it as a strong arm robbery attempt, but there are some problems."

"Like what?"

"Probably nothing you haven't thought of. Ambush in a remote spot in a well-lit neighborhood. Unless he was scouting Foster, the asshole could have stood behind the garage all night and not seen anyone go by. And he was serious about this thing. If the guy in the backyard hadn't yelled at him, I think Foster might be dead. But, you get all sorts. We pushed Foster on who might have it in for him. He couldn't think of anyone, and he looked to me like he was telling the truth. Said there was no reason any of Professor Quill's people would come after him, none he could think of. That's the only recent hassle he'd been involved in, and he wasn't much involved."

"Drugs?"

"They did the whole bloodwork drill at the hospital and he was absolutely clean."

"Women?"

"He says no. An on-and-off thing, nothing serious."

"Money? Gambling?"

Bryan was shaking his head. "None of that—at least, not that he'd admit to. We talked to friends of his and they said he's a quiet, routine guy. Likes a beer or two, or three, but doesn't need it. Not yet anyway. That's why we still have it as a strong-arm job—there doesn't seem to be any other motive. We even asked if it might go back to his military service, but he doesn't think so. He was an intelligence officer, got shot once, but he wasn't a guy ordering anyone into combat or kicking anyone's ass. He spent most of his time in an office. He got wounded sitting in a truck."

Virgil said, "Wait a minute . . . He was an intelligence officer? I got the impression that he was an enlisted man . . . a sergeant or something."

"Nope. He was a captain. You think that might be important?"

"I don't know," Virgil said. "Odd that he didn't say something. I was a captain myself, and I mentioned that when I talked to him. That'll usually bring on a few minutes of Old Home Week. You know, where were you, what'd you do, who'd you know, all of that."

"He's a quiet guy," Bryan said. "He was over there for a quite a while . . . Maybe a little PTSD? Doesn't like to talk about it?"

Trane asked, "That aside, you got anything?"

"We got zip," Bryan said.

"Exactly what we got on the Quill case," Trane said. "There's an uninteresting coincidence."

Outside again, Trane said, "I don't know what to do."

"I'm gonna go poke around Foster again," Virgil said. "There's something there. Best case, I find out who killed Quill. Average case, I catch a mugger. Worst case, I get what Bryan got."

"Which is zip."

Trane was parked in a no-parking zone a block in front of Virgil. Virgil got to his car before Trane got to hers and he watched her walking away, down the street, now talking on her cell phone, her free arm waving over her head. She was arguing with someone, and the argument looked hot. He started his car, rolled up the street, and Trane turned, saw him, and flagged him down. A moment later, she was off her phone and had walked back to him. Virgil rolled down his window.

"You won't believe what just happened," she said.

"Green confessed?"

"Worse. Fifty-four days ago I busted a guy for ag assault for a fight, the details not being important because we had him, cold, with a bar full of witnesses. Guess how I know it was exactly fifty-four days ago?"

"Ah, maybe because of the sixty-day speedy trial law?"

"You got it. He filed for a speedy trial the day we arrested him, and the paperwork got lost. Somebody finally woke up in the county attorney's office and asked what happened with the Logan trial," she said. "After some major clusterfuckery, they managed to schedule a trial on day fifty-nine out of sixty, royally pissing off the judge, but I've had no prep at all. I didn't even know about the speedy trial request. Anyway, I'm getting prepped for the next couple days, and then I've got to be there for the trial."

"You're telling me that I'm on my own," Virgil said.

Trane tipped back her head and closed her eyes. "Yeah, god-damnit. You could probably ask for more help, but you're doing pretty good, and you know the Cities. Keep your nose to the grindstone and your feet on the fence and your ears to the ground. I'll be back in a couple of days. Maybe three. Or four."

"That's so—" Virgil said.

"What can I tell you?"

"You'd think—"

"Yeah. You would," Trane said. "Anyway . . ."

"I'll try to make you proud."

"Do that, cowboy."

CHAPTER

TWELVE

Virgil sat in his truck and watched Trane drive away; she was still fuming about the trial, muttering to herself. After a moment, he called Katherine Green, but she didn't pick up. He called her again, still no answer. Finally he called Clete May, the guy with the Japanese bow. May picked up, and Virgil asked, "Do you know a woman in Cultural Science whose name is Sandy and looks like a pileated woodpecker?"

"Sure, Sandy Thomas. Personally, I wouldn't describe her that way. She's been studying jujitsu since she was nine years old and would kick your ass if she heard you call her that."

"Then I'll ask for your discretion on the woodpecker thing, if you run into her. So she's in Cultural Science?"

"Yes. Well, sometimes. She's twenty-six or twenty-seven and has had five or six majors, I think. Never graduated. But, right now, she's in Cultural Science."

"You know where she lives?"

"No, not really," May said. "If you're looking for her, she

teaches a jujitsu class about now. Over at the RecWell. I've been invited, but I've always had other commitments. Like, to my personal well-being."

"She's rough?"

"Rough and tough. My martial arts experience has been considerably more relaxed than hers. I'm not saying she's a fanatic, but she's a fanatic."

There was no Recreation and Wellness Center when Virgil attended the university; at the time, even the word "wellness" probably hadn't been invented, so he would go to "the gym." Still, he knew where the RecWell was located because he'd driven by it a number of times.

He went there, was astonished at what he found—a fitness center that was a monument to wretched excess. He showed his badge at the front desk, was told that he was a half hour early for Thomas's class. A female student aide, who looked like she could crack English walnuts between the cheeks of her ass, led him to a women's locker room, left him outside, and a minute later returned with a slender, muscular woman whose red hair did indeed give her the aspect of a pileated woodpecker. She was wearing a two-piece yoga outfit in red and black that ended just below her knee. Also, below her knee, Virgil spotted an impact hematoma. As she walked up to Virgil, she crossed her arms over her chest, showing off solid biceps—both had dime-sized bruises, as though she been poked by fingertips or sticks—and asked, "What's up?"

Virgil showed her his ID, and asked, "Have you talked to Terry Foster in the past couple of days?"

She frowned. "Well, no . . ."

"Terry was mugged—or beaten anyway—out behind his house," Virgil said. "He's over at Regions Hospital in St. Paul. He's in pretty rough shape."

She touched her lips with her fingers, and said, "Oh my God, he's not going to—"

"He's not going to die, but he's pretty busted up and not in much condition to talk," Virgil lied. "I'd like to ask you a few questions that might help us out."

"Sure. Let's go out in the hall, there are benches . . . When did this happen?" she asked.

"A couple of nights ago," Virgil said.

"Okay, I haven't seen him in a week. I'll go over there tonight if they'll let me see him."

"Tomorrow might be better," Virgil said. He didn't want her getting there before he did. "Like I said, he's hurting and a little drugged up."

"I wonder why he didn't call me?"

Virgil said, "For one thing, he can't use a telephone—both of his arms are broken and in casts."

"Oh, jeez."

They found a bench under a big red "M," and Virgil said, "Everybody says Terry's a quiet guy and friendly. Would you know of anything at all that might have led to his being attacked? No matter how unlikely it might be?"

She looked at him for a long time, and Virgil thought, Ah— she does, and then she said, "Terry is a nice guy, and I wouldn't want to get him in trouble."

"Are you saying there is something?"

She looked down at her shoes for a moment, then said, "You

know that there was a professor who was murdered here a couple of weeks ago? Over in the Wilson Library?"

Virgil tap-danced. "Oh, yeah. That doctor, right?"

She nodded. "Dr. Quill. Terry's in the Cultural Science Department—so am I, that's how we met—and we've had this feud with Dr. Quill's department. Dr. Quill and Dr. Green—she's the head of our department—were feuding. Last time I was over at Terry's, he told me he was going to look into it. The murder. He wanted to see if he could clear the department."

"Look into it? How was he going to do that?" Virgil asked.

"He said . . . Well, he said he was going to check some people out. I asked him how, and he said on the internet. He knows a lot of computer stuff from when he was in the Army. He was an intelligence officer."

"You wouldn't know any names of who he was checking on?"

"No, but I was curious and might have nagged him a little. He said he'd gotten all the names of the people involved from the newspapers and from talking to people around Cultural Science. He said he'd run them through the mill—through the net. Including Dr. Green," Thomas said. Then, "Oh, wait! I do know one other person. He was going to check Dr. Quill's daughter because people were wondering if she was going to be the big financial winner from Dr. Quill being murdered. The newspapers said he was rich."

That was all she had, but Virgil had now connected Foster to the Quill murder. There could be two reasons for Foster's investigation: he was trying to clear Green and her department or he was monitoring the investigation to see if the cops were getting close to somebody. Or both.

———

One way to find out.

Fifteen minutes after he left Thomas, Virgil pulled into the parking lot at Regions Hospital and took the elevator up to Foster's floor, walking through a hospital smell that might be alcohol that was the same in every hospital. When he looked into Foster's room, he found a nurse hand-feeding him. Foster said, "You're back . . . I'll be a couple more minutes here . . ."

"Take your time," Virgil said. He asked the nurse, "What causes the hospital smell? That makes all hospitals smell alike?"

"They don't all smell like that anymore. It was caused by disinfectants, maybe urine. A combination. I don't even smell it anymore."

"Huh."

When Foster had finished the last of the lime Jell-O and the nurse had gone, Foster said, "Thanks for the visit. It's nice of you, but it's not necessary."

"This is not exactly a social visit."

"I figured that out about three seconds after you came through the door, the look on your face," Foster said. "What happened?"

"One of my sources told me that you're conducting your own private investigation into the Quill murder," Virgil said. "Since you got jumped, you might have touched a live wire. I want to know what it is. I'd like to know why you didn't mention this the first time I was here."

Foster closed his eyes and blew out air. Then, "That fuckin' Sandy. I told her not to talk to anyone about it. I wouldn't have talked to her, except I had one beer too many. I gotta quit drinking."

"Not a bad idea, but Sandy who?"

"Don't bullshit me, Virgil. I know and you know that Sandy and I are in bed sometimes, and you already talked to her," Foster said. "She's the only one who knew about me poking around."

"I can't—"

"I'm sore enough without getting a headache because you're bullshitting me," Foster said. "Anyway, I've been thinking about it since I got beat up and I don't know what live wire I might have touched. I really don't."

"Who all did you talk to?"

"A few people in Cultural Science, the ones who seemed most outraged by the feud. Also, Megan Quill, because I thought she had the most to gain," Foster said. "Her father had a house that's got to be worth a million, plus a family fortune that's worth way more than the house. After I talked to Megan, I, mmm, saw a copy of Quill's will and according to its terms Megan gets exactly what she's already getting, for the same amount of time. In other words, her trust fund continues until she's thirty, and that's it. She gets it whether or not Quill lives or dies."

"I knew that. What else?"

"I was doing, uh, some research into his wife, who would have gotten hurt if the divorce had gone through. There was a tough prenup. His wife would get a hundred thousand dollars for each year they were married. There were smaller amounts for his first and second wives, and all the rest would have gone to a Quill Foundation, which would provide grants for medical research. Now with him dead while they were still married, the wife will most likely get half. I'm not exactly sure how much that would be, but I'd guess between fifteen and twenty million."

"How were you doing this research? On the wife?" Virgil asked.

"On the internet. I'm not going to say any more about that," Foster said. "I'd need to talk to a lawyer, and probably I'd need both federal and state immunity from prosecution."

"You hacked somebody," Virgil said. "Tell me this: does the information you hacked about his wife seem to suggest any level of guilt for the murder?"

"No. It doesn't, other than the fact that she'd benefit," Foster said.

"Hmm. I'll have to take your word for it, and I will, unless I find something that tells me you're lying. If that happens, you won't like what follows."

"Thanks a lot, pal. Look, I'm not even sure I broke any laws, but I'm not taking a chance," Foster said. "Anyway, you should be thinking about what facts I found, not about what methods I used. I'll tell you everything about what I uncovered but not how."

"What else did you do?"

"I followed the wife around for a couple of days. I wanted to see if she had a relationship—because if she did and it was serious, then that guy might be looking at a major payday."

"What came out of that?"

"She wasn't exactly dating, but she went to dinner with a guy, a lawyer named Jared Miles, a couple of times. And twice to lunch," Foster said. "They seemed friendly, but he never stayed overnight. And it's possible that they were talking about the will. But he *was* age-appropriate, and they were . . . friendly."

"Interesting. How'd you get his name?"

Foster thought for a moment, then said, "Miles picked her up at her house."

Virgil added another moment of thought, then said, "Ah . . . You got his license tag and hacked into the DMV for his ID."

"Virgil . . . I've got no comment about that."

———

Virgil rubbed his face, his eyes wandering around the hospital room, with its tubes, its stainless steel, its electronics, its video screens. He turned back to Foster, and asked, "Do you think that whatever you stumbled over, if that's what happened, was so serious that the guy who attacked you might come back?"

"How would I know that? If there's a connection to the Quill murder, and I heard or saw something that I don't understand, maybe he will," Foster said. "If it was a mugging, probably not. I talked to Megan Quill and a couple of her friends and didn't see anything but nerdy college kids. I got no hint that any of the people at Cultural Science might have killed Quill, and I don't feel any threat from them. They were mostly shocked. The only thing that jumped out at me was the difference between what Mrs. Quill would get before a divorce and what she would get after. It's pretty dramatic."

"I've talked to her," Virgil said. "She was in Cleveland." And, "Why did you do all this? You must've known that the cops would be pissed off if they found you messing around with a murder investigation."

Foster turned away for a moment, then turned back, and said, "Honestly—and don't take this the wrong way because later on I realized how wrong I was—but at first I was worried that Sandy might be involved. She idolizes Katherine and hated Quill for what he did, and she's, you know, a martial artist. Then I started getting some details from the papers, and she was over at my house until two o'clock the night that the murder probably happened. I'm not bragging, but she left in a very good mood. Not in a mood to kill someone."

"Sandy didn't have a boyfriend who might be jealous?" Virgil asked. "Maybe one of those stick fighter martial arts guys? And met you in the alley?"

"No. Not that I know of. It's an interesting thought, though. I'll ask her about that."

"Let me know what she says," Virgil said.

"It sounds like it comes down to a Quill connection or a mugging. Either one. Don't tell Sandy that I checked her out. Please."

"I won't, if I can avoid it," Virgil said. "Do you have any idea when you're getting out of here?"

"It'll be a few more days anyway. When they found out I had student health insurance, with no deductible, they jumped on me like a duck on a june bug. They're not all that anxious to cure me."

"Let me know before you leave," Virgil said. They talked a few more minutes about Foster's military career. He'd been an intelligence officer, had a degree from the University of Minnesota/ Duluth, and was now a grad student. "If I get a Ph.D., I could go back into the Army as a regular officer and be almost guaranteed to wind up as a full colonel or better. The Army's big on advanced degrees right now."

"You didn't do cop stuff?"

"No. I ran some agents, and when I was thinking about Quill, I was thinking I was kinda cop-like. I found out I wasn't. I'm now embarrassed about messing with your investigation," Foster said. "I consider myself warned off."

Virgil shrugged and stood up. "I'm not warning you off. You want to look some more, fine with me, call if you get anything. But don't blame me if somebody beats you to death. If somebody does, try to scratch him before you die so we can get the DNA from your fingernails."

"Look for blood on the casts," Foster said. "Right now, I couldn't scratch my own balls. Which I desperately need to do."

"Can't help you there," Virgil said.

Virgil got a lap desk out of the back of the Tahoe, sat in the passenger seat, and made notes on his conversation with Foster.

He didn't know it but he'd missed something.

THIRTEEN

When Virgil finished making his notes on Foster, he sat in the truck for a few minutes, thinking about the case, decided he didn't think that well in an upright position, and turned back to the hotel.

In his room, he took off his boots and emptied his pockets, plugged his laptop into the WiFi, dialed up the Lucinda Williams station on Pandora, put on his headphones, lay on the bed with his notebook on his chest, closed his eyes, and thought about it some more.

An hour later, he was back on his feet, with a short list in his notebook:

- The doctor's conspiracy as recorded on the western music CD.
- The map thief.
- Did Quill have an illicit relationship, possibly with a prostitute?

- Did Quill buy drugs from somebody called China White, at a bar called the Territorial Lounge?
- What was happening with the supposed malpractice lawsuit against Quill and the U?

All of the items on the list suggested motives for the murder—a wide variety of motives. Some seemed fairly simple to eliminate, and he decided to start there. After brushing his teeth, he got on the phone to Trane.

"You have a minute?"

"Sure. I'm sitting here in the county attorney's office like a dummy. Want to know something? Alternative newspapers suck. Especially after you've read them the third time."

"Yeah, but they're free."

"True . . . What's up?"

"Did you ever talk to the woman who might be a suspect in those map thefts?"

"I never got to her," Trane said. "That didn't seem like a major priority."

"I agree. But . . ." He told her about the list and his idea of knocking down the items one at a time. "I thought I might be able to take care of her with one stop. Then I got a guy from the BCA I want to bring in on the China White thing."

They discussed tactics for a few minutes. Trane gave him the suspected thief's address, and said, "She works from seven to three—she should be headed home." They ended the call after a few more words. Virgil put on his boots and got back on the phone to a BCA agent named Del Capslock.

"How you doin', Virgie?" Capslock asked when he picked up. "I heard you're on the Quill thing."

"Yeah. Listen, Del, you know a place called the Territorial Lounge? Or where I might find a woman named China White?"

"The Territorial's over by KSTP," Capslock said. "Stay away from the Philly cheesesteak unless you want to spend the rest of the week on the can."

Virgil told him about the China White tip. "If you have any sources in the area . . ."

"Let me call around," Capslock said. "You know what China White is, of course."

"Of course."

"Seems like a strange name for a dealer," Capslock said. "It's like having a sign on your chest that says 'Buy Your Smack Here.' It sounds made up by somebody who looked up 'heroin' in the dictionary."

"I know, but it is what it is."

"Long as you know," Capslock said. "I'll get back to you."

The suspected map thief, Genevieve O'Hara, lived in the small town of Lauderdale, not far from the university, in what looked like a postwar GI house, painted a faded yellow with white trim. An aging Nissan was parked in the badly cracked driveway, with cantaloupe-sized dents on both ends of the back bumper.

Virgil walked up to the front door and knocked. A moment later, a woman, perhaps sixty, wearing narrow rectangular glasses, opened the door and peeked out. Virgil identified himself and showed her his ID, and she asked, "Is this about the maps?"

"Not directly," Virgil said. "I'm investigating the death of Professor Quill."

"Oh . . ." She had been willing to attack, he thought, in her robin-like way, but now she deflated. "You better come in. The campus police asked me about the maps, and I had nothing to do with all of that. I don't work at the Andersen anymore, and I didn't steal a key. I turned them all in when I transferred to the Wilson. Every last one of them. The very idea!"

"Do you know how many maps they're missing?"

"According to rumors from friends, at this point, sixteen. But they never keep a good inventory over there—it could be sixteen maps over ten years, even twenty. And some might be misfiled. So, who knows?"

Virgil stepped inside the house and was hit by the smell of death. His nose wrinkled involuntarily, and O'Hara spotted it.

"My mother's dying in the back bedroom," she said. "Pancreatic cancer finally got her . . . It's been four years, and she has no more than a few days left, if that. God bless her, I hope she goes sooner. Now she's still with us, I roll her and wash her, I give her morphine under the tongue once every two hours, she no longer has control of her bowels. I have to buy diapers for her. She hates being alive."

"Do you have help?"

She snorted. "Barely. You know how much that costs? Mother had no home care insurance. I pay a service when I'm working; a nurse comes every two hours to check on her. Sticks her nose in the door and that's about it. A neighbor keeps an eye out her window in case the house catches fire while I'm gone. It's a disaster."

She pointed Virgil to a chair in the living room, and said, "Now, about Dr. Quill . . ."

She had seen Quill in the library from time to time, she said, usually working on his laptop in the carrel or reading. "He brought in his own chair, an expensive one, leather and all that."

He was not there often. "A lot of people want those carrels, and I don't think he was using his even once a week. It was a shame. But I never said anything to him about it."

She'd never witnessed any arguments, any conflicts, involving Quill. "He came and he went. By himself. I can't remember seeing him talk to anybody."

O'Hara's living room was tiny, perhaps twelve by twelve, smelled lightly of pasta, and had two walls taken up by floor-to-ceiling bookshelves. The shelves were packed. When O'Hara's cell phone chirped, she said, "Time for the morphine, back in a minute," pushed herself out of her chair, and disappeared into the back of the house. Virgil stood to take a look at the books. Mostly novels, and mostly seventeenth- and eighteenth-century British.

O'Hara came back, and Virgil reached to the highest shelf and took down a thick, battered copy of *The New Shorter Oxford English Dictionary* and handed it to her. "Lift this over your head and swing it at my face."

She tried and failed. She got the book up above her hair, but that was it, and then fumbled it. Virgil grabbed the dictionary, said, "Thanks," and put it back on the shelf.

"That was a test," she said. "Of what?"

"We think Professor Quill was killed when somebody lifted his laptop overhead and hit the back of his skull, then his neck, and hard. Anyway, the laptop was high-tech, expensive, and heavy—more than twelve pounds. That dictionary probably didn't weight more than seven or eight."

"Then you know—"

"Yes. You didn't kill Quill."

"Of course I didn't," she said. "The very thought is absurd."

Virgil smiled. "How about the maps?"

She looked at him, her face grave, and said, "I had nothing to do with the maps. I work and I take care of mother, and that's all I do. If I stole those maps, they'd fire me and I'd lose my pension. Thirty-five years and I'd lose my pension. The medical care in this country . . . Mother couldn't afford extended care, she just couldn't . . ."

Tears poked out at the corners of her eyes and ran down her cheeks, and she wiped them away with the backs of her hands. Virgil said, "I believe you. I'd bet those maps are lost somewhere in the library."

"Exactly," she said with a hint of defiance.

Virgil gave her his card, said good-bye, and left. As he was walking away, he knew for certain that O'Hara, by her telltale eyes and body language giveaways, had stolen the maps and that she'd done it to finance her mother's health care.

Basically, he thought, fuck a bunch of maps.

He called Trane. After the phone rang five times, she finally answered, and said, "You got me out of a conference. Thank you."

"O'Hara didn't kill Quill. She couldn't lift a seven-pound dictionary more than a couple inches over her head, and then it almost pulled her over backwards. She's about five-two."

"Okay. I didn't think there was anything there. Did you ask her about the maps?"

"Yeah. She says she didn't do it. I'm willing to let it go. I'm not interested in the maps."

"I'm with you. What's next?"

"Where's the CD with the cowboy songs?"

"In the evidence locker. You need it?"

"If it's not too much trouble."

"I made a recording of it. If you tell me where you're at, we've got a gofer, I can send him there with the recorder and some headphones," Trane said.

"I'm going over to Quill's lab. I'll meet him on the front steps in half an hour."

Virgil stopped at a Holiday store for gas and a Diet Coke, made it to Moos Tower a few minutes later. A cop car was sitting out front, its blinkers flashing out into the afternoon. Virgil knocked on the passenger-side window, and when the window dropped, the cop asked, "You Flowers?"

"Yes."

He handed over a compact recorder with two microphones shaped like extra-large thimbles—or extra-short condoms—and a pair of microphones. He said, "To play it, just push the green button. To rewind, push the rewind button. If you push the red button for any reason, you'll record over it. That's what Trane said."

"How come you didn't ask for ID?" Virgil said, as he took the recorder.

"Trane told me about the shirt. And the boots. I figured there couldn't be two of you."

"Well, you're right. But pop the door, I need to sit down for a minute."

In the cop car, Virgil played the recording once to get a feel for the machine, then rewound the tape, recorded its message to his iPhone, and gave the recorder back to the cop.

At Quill's lab, the same woman who'd directed him back to the lab manager's office on his first visit was sitting at her countertop inside the door, poking at a laptop. She looked up when Virgil walked in, and said, "You're back."

"Yes. I want you to listen—"

She interrupted. "You know they call you 'that fuckin' Flowers'? It's on the internet."

"What? The internet?"

"Yes. After you were here, we looked you up. There was a story in a Rochester newspaper that said you were widely known as 'that fuckin' Flowers,' but they put in asterisks in the 'fuckin'.'"

"I get tired of it," Virgil said. "It started in St. Paul, when I was a cop over there, followed me over to the BCA, and it got out of hand."

"Actually, the story was complimentary. You recovered some precious artifact from Israel."

"A complete nightmare, believe me," Virgil said. "My garage almost got burned down with my boat inside of it."

"Your boat? The horror!"

"I detected a tiny bit of sarcasm there," Virgil said. "Anyway, I want you to listen to a recording and tell me if you recognize any voices."

"Hit me," she said.

Virgil played the recording. She listened, gaped at Virgil, and said, "Let me hear it again."

Virgil played it again, and when it was done she said, "Holy . . . shit . . ."

"Recognize anybody?"

"Only Dr. Quill. I don't recognize the others," she said.

"That's Quill? Which one exactly?"

"The one that was pushing for the op. Man, that freaks me out. If they went ahead and did it, that'd be worth killing to cover up. I don't care who they were, how big a shots. If they did it and that recording gets played, their careers are over."

"If it doesn't get out?"

"Well, then, nothing happened . . . And Dr. Quill is dead," she said. "Has anybody else heard it?"

"Actually, we think it must be a rerecording. This could be a third- or fourth-generation recording."

"Blackmail," she said. "You know what? That could be years old. There's no way to know what they're talking about"—she looked over her shoulder as if she were frightened—"but if that recording gets out and it's about something recent, the university will go through this lab with a flamethrower. There won't be anybody left. I gotta get out of here. Before it's too late."

"Really?"

"Really. That's some bad juju, fuckin' Flowers. That's a fuckin' A-bomb."

Virgil left the lab, walked down the hall to the elevators, took one down to the street, went outside, called Trane again. When she answered her phone, he said, "We got a problem."

"Uh-oh. Did you screw something up?"

"Not exactly. I talked to one of the women in the lab about the recording. It scared her. She said that the bad guy was definitely Quill, which is too bad because I was beginning to like him. She seemed sure of it, but Nancy Quill said it wasn't him."

"Goddamnit. They've been rehearsing me all afternoon, treating me like a moron, and I was so frustrated and pissed that I was going to go home and eat an entire pie, but now I have to meet up with you and push Nancy Quill up against a wall."

"You wanna be the bad cop?"

"If she lied to me, I'll be the bad cop whether I want to be or not because I'll be mondo pisso," Trane said. "I'll meet you there. Like, right now."

Virgil found his way back to Nancy Quill's condo, spotted Trane parked on the street in a no-parking zone. Virgil rolled up behind her, put his BCA sign in the window, and got out.

"One good thing about this: if she lied, we might be onto something," Virgil said, as Trane got out of her car.

"I realized that on the way over," Trane said. "It eased the pain. But I'm still going to eat that pie."

"What kind?"

"Apple. I'll warm it up."

"Vanilla ice cream?"

"It ain't warm apple pie if there's no vanilla ice cream."

Quill buzzed them through the entry door. They took the elevator up and found Quill waiting in the hall outside her condo.

"What's going on?" Quill asked. "Did you get him?"

"No," Trane said. "Let's sit down."

"What?" Quill asked, as she backed into her front room. Virgil pulled the door closed, and they sat in separate easy chairs facing one another.

Trane said, "Agent Flowers believes there's a problem with the statement you gave to me about the recording I played for you."

Quill had been lying all right, Virgil thought. When Trane made the comment, he could see the pupils of Quill's eyes contract, the way they do when somebody's lying to your face. Trane saw it, too.

Virgil said, "Several people who knew your husband quite well said there's no doubt that it's his voice on the recording. We're wondering why you said it wasn't."

Quill recoiled, said, "I did not—"

Trane said, "Nancy, you can tell us you want a lawyer and kick us out or you can tell us the truth, but you can't lie to us without serious consequences. You're about to lie to us. Don't lie. We can both see it because you're no good at it."

After a moment, and with considerable frost in her voice, Quill said, "I have to make a phone call."

Virgil: "Go ahead."

Quill went back to a bedroom and shut the door. After a moment of silence, Trane said, "If we hear a gunshot, I'm making a run for it."

"You know her better than I do. She's smart, right?"

"Yes. She's an associate professor of linguistics."

"When you played the recording for her, I'll bet it meant something more than Barth Quill's voice. Either she knew the other people on the recording or she knows the case they were talking about . . . or . . . something else that I can't think of."

They speculated for a few minutes, then Quill reappeared, and said, "I talked to my attorney. He said I shouldn't talk to you without him present, but he can't come here tonight. He said we could talk tomorrow."

"What time?" Trane asked.

"Ten o'clock, at his office in Minneapolis."

Trane looked at Virgil. "Can you make that?"

"Sure. Will you be there?"

"If I can. But this trial . . . I might not be able to make it."

Back outside, Trane asked, "You okay with handling this?"

"I'm fine. And I've got some other running around I want to do."

"I was mostly interested in seeing Nancy's first reaction," Trane said. "We know she lied to me, but we don't know why. If her attorney shuts her down tomorrow without any explanation, then we'll have something to work with. Something on the Quill murder. On the other hand, maybe it's just something embarrassing . . . Something sleazy."

"You could be right," Virgil said. "I'll push her about the recording. I'd like to know how old it is, who else is on it, if she has any idea about who they're talking about, the guy Quill wanted to operate on. I'll try to open her up. The woman I talked to in the lab said the recording would be important enough to kill for, if it's recent. Although . . ."

"What?"

"If the recording was important enough to kill for, wouldn't it be Quill who would have done the killing? Killing a blackmailer? The other guys on the recording were trying to talk him out of what he wanted to do."

"We don't know what we're talking about, Virgil. If the other men talked him out of the operation, refused to go along, then the recording's not so important," Trane said. "But if they did do it and the patient died, that's something entirely different. You could argue that it was murder. The fact that Quill had apparently listened to the recording recently, or maybe even had just gotten it in the mail or something, suggests that the threat was active. Was real. Right now."

FOURTEEN

Virgil went back to the hotel, hit Applebee's—Bourbon Street Steak, fries, lemonade—got a brew at the beer joint, where he found Harry sitting on a barstool talking to Alice, the barmaid.

Virgil climbed up on the next stool, said, "Harry, Alice."

Harry said, "Another bottle of cow piss?"

Virgil said, "Yep," and Alice went away to get it.

"Catch the kid yet?" Harry asked.

"I investigated every one of them that I know about and they're all clearly innocent," Virgil lied. "Your theory sucks a hot desert wind."

"Haven't found the right kid yet, that's all," Harry said. "Let me make another observation—also from the files of *NCIS*."

"Feel free," Virgil said, as Alice delivered the Miller Lite.

"Here's the thing, Virgil: you've already met the killer."

"I've met the killer?"

"Sure. Gibbs always meets the killer early in the show when

he doesn't know the other guy is the killer. Every single time," Harry said.

Virgil said, "Huh. Harry, I suspect that might have more to do with the story structure of the show. They can't have Gibbs going along investigating and investigating, getting nowhere, and then pull the killer out of his butt at the last minute. If they did that, how would the audience even know that the bad guy was all that bad?"

Harry shrugged. "All right, don't believe me, but you'll see. A murder investigation, as far as I can tell, is exactly like you see on a TV show."

"I told somebody a couple of days ago that a murder investigation is never like TV," Virgil said.

"Well, you're wrong. You've got your cast of characters, and you know, going in, that one of them did it. If you've been investigating for weeks, you've already met the whole cast."

"We're going to have to agree to disagree," Virgil said.

Alice had been listening in and she said to Virgil, "Okay, so I ask you this, Virgil. Did you ever investigate, like, a real mystery? Not somebody holding up a gas station or a liquor store? A real mystery?"

"A few times," Virgil said.

"In any of those times," she asked, "did you ever not meet *el villano, el malo*, before you know that he was *el villano*?"

Virgil had to think a minute, then said, "You know, I guess I haven't. I'm sure I will, but so far—"

"Ha," Harry said. "Now that you know that you've met the killer, you can probably figure this out before morning. For that, you owe me a beer."

Virgil looked at Alice, and asked, "Where is he on the beer total?"

"Only two. After four, he recites this poem. That is not a good time to be here."

"That hurts, honey. Greatest poem ever written," Harry said. He looked at Virgil. "'The Cremation of Sam McGee.'"

Virgil: "No."

"All of it," Alicia said. "Unless the bouncer throws him out in the street."

"When I'm drinking wine, I can do all of 'Gunga Din,'" Harry said. After a moment, he added, "And that's about it. 'The Cremation of Sam McGee' and 'Gunga Din.'"

Virgil took a swallow of beer, leaned back in his chair, burped, and recited,

> *"There are strange things done in the midnight sun*
> *By the men who moil for gold;*
> *The Arctic trails have their secret tales*
> *That would make your blood run cold;*
> *The Northern Lights have seen queer sights,*
> *But the queerest they ever did see*
> *Was that night on the marge of Lake Lebarge*
> *I cremated Sam McGee . . ."*

Alice crossed herself, and Harry gawked at him. "You know it all?"

"Maybe after four beers. I memorized the whole thing for tenth-grade English," Virgil said.

Virgil wound up drinking three beers, one over his limit, and was a little tipsy when he decided to head up to his room. As he got off his stool, Harry clapped him on the back, and said, "You're all right, Virgie. But you gotta remember that one thing."

"What's that?" Virgil asked.

"You've met the killer. Who's a kid."

Virgil took a hot shower, read the James Lee Burke book until one o'clock in the morning, and bagged out.

He slept in the next morning, and when he did get up, he put on a fresh Cage the Elephant T-shirt, got out of the hotel at nine o'clock. He walked across the street for a bagel and a cup of coffee, taking a half hour with it; truth be told, he was loitering, checking out the coeds in their summer dresses—and a fine, sturdy bunch they were, in his opinion.

At nine forty-five, he dumped the truck in a downtown Minneapolis parking structure and walked through the warm morning to the offices of DC&H, Jared Miles's law firm.

He was five minutes early for the appointment. The reception- ist asked him if he wanted a cup of coffee or tea, but he declined, and the receptionist said, "I saw Cage the Elephant last year . . . in London."

"Must have been great."

"It was great . . . And we saw a bunch of shows. I'd like to go back, but it's so expensive. British hotels."

And so on until her phone beeped and she picked it up, listened for three seconds, put it down, and said, "They're ready for you."

She led the way to a conference room. Nancy Quill sat on the far side of a dark wooden table from the door, while Jared Miles sat at the end of the table, looking at a pad of yellow legal paper with a few notes scrawled on it.

He stood when Virgil stepped in; he was on the short side, and slightly balding, his remaining light brown hair showing touches of gray. He was about fifty, Virgil thought, and well dressed in a navy blue suit, white shirt, and maroon tie. He smiled as they shook hands. "I've read a couple of your fishing stories in *Gray's*. And the funny one about equipment. You should quit being a cop and write full-time."

"I've thought about it," Virgil said. He liked the guy already. "The gear story . . . I mean, a nine-thousand-dollar fly rod? For what?"

"You don't want to insult the trout," Miles said, laughing. He added, "Sit down. I think we can be done with this in five minutes."

Quill hadn't said anything. When Virgil said, "Morning, Nancy," she nodded, then looked at Miles.

Miles huffed once, shuffled the legal pad, and said, "Nancy may have, hmm, been misunderstood when she was interviewed by Officer Trane. She didn't flatly deny that her late husband was on the recording; she was uncertain about the voices."

Virgil could feel the story coming, and he said, "Okay."

Miles continued. "You see, the situation is, she didn't want to be on the record saying that the voice she heard was her late husband. If she agreed that it was, without the advice of counsel, that could have ramifications further downstream."

Virgil looked at Quill, and asked, "Like what?"

Quill looked at Miles, then said, "I am not especially affluent. When Barth and I began discussing divorce, he held our prenuptial agreement over my head and essentially told me I would get nothing from him if I insisted on taking it to court. Rather than go through a public divorce, he wanted a private settlement—a small one."

"A very small one," Miles said. "One might say miserly. Cheese-paring, even. Tight-assed."

"I pushed back, but I didn't have much to push with, given the prenuptial agreement," Quill said. "Then he was killed and that changed everything. Frankly, I began to think of myself as wealthy."

"Or at least rich," Miles chipped in. "The will hasn't been thoroughly worked through as of yet, but Nancy appears to be in line for something approaching fifteen million dollars, and possibly more, depending on some real estate valuations."

"I also knew I was a suspect in the murder," Quill said. "Margaret Trane made that abundantly clear. When she played the recording for me, two things immediately popped into my head. First, that she might think that I was the one who sent the recording to Barth, as leverage in the divorce."

"She didn't do that," Miles said. "She'd never heard, or heard of, the recording before Trane played it for her."

Quill continued. "Second, if this recording referred to an actual event, and if that actual event took place— an unethical operation with a poor or even bad result—the whole estate could be in jeopardy and might not be settled for years and years. If the patient's family sued the estate . . . You see what I mean."

"I do," Virgil said. "All of this occurred to you in a few seconds that Officer Trane was interviewing you?"

"Absolutely," she said. "If Officer Trane were here, I would tell her I absolutely did not lie to her, although I might have been somewhat equivocal in my answers to her questions. I did not kill my husband. I have no idea who did it or why. I was astounded when I heard, and even more astonished when I learned of the circumstances: beaten to death in the library. I mean, if he'd been walking down the street and somebody had tried to rob him or something, that can happen to anyone. But these circumstances . . ."

They all sat and looked at one another for a few seconds.

Virgil believed her. It was exactly the kind of unhelpful outcome he'd feared: a dead end.

He continued to stare at Quill for a couple of beats, then asked, "You told Margaret that you're not involved in a personal relationship at this time—or any time—since you and Mr. Quill started talking divorce."

Quill's eyes flicked toward Miles and then back, the round-trip taking only a microsecond. "That's correct. I was quite clear with her. I understood what she was asking—whether a friend might have killed Barth, hoping to benefit himself. There was no one."

Virgil asked about the other voices on the recording, but those, she said, she absolutely did not recognize.

"It's obvious where they come from, though—they must be other doctors. Barth only worked out of the university hospitals, so it must be somebody over there. If it actually was Barth, I'm still not sure of that. I'm not equivocating, I'm just not positive. There's something not right about the recording."

"What's not right?" Virgil asked.

"All those voices. They all sound different, but then they all sound the same." After a bit more thought, she added, "Of course, they'll all doctors, all working in the same place. Maybe it's a cultural similarity."

After a few more unproductive questions, Virgil was stuck. Miles said, "Are we done?"

"At least for the time being," Virgil said.

"All of this will be held in strictest confidence?"

"As far as I'm concerned," Virgil said. "I'll talk to Margaret, who's leading the investigation. We will have to see if we can find the other people on the recording. What happens then?" He shrugged.

"Oh, God, it's going to get out," Quill said to Miles.

"Not if the police handle it with even a little bit of restraint," Miles said. He smiled at Virgil. "I'm sure they will—for legal reasons, if nothing else."

Virgil smiled back. There was a threat in that comment, but it was nicely put. "Of course we will," he said.

"Something else," Miles said. "I can't tell you how to do your job, but isn't it obvious that the attack on Dr. Quill had nothing to do with this recording?"

"Explain how it's obvious," Virgil said.

Miles threw his hands up. "Think about it. Officer Trane described to Nancy what Dr. Quill was doing the night before he was killed. Apparently, he drove over to a commercial neighborhood and left his car and then wandered around aimlessly, going to the library maybe once, maybe twice. If these people who were talking to him on the recording actually agreed to this unethical operation—they must have been doctors—why would they link up with Dr. Quill at the library in the middle of the night? Why not in one of their offices during the day? Why not at one of their homes, if they wanted more privacy? I don't see it, Virgil. What happened in the library happened because of something Dr. Quill was doing in the library. Not because of something that happened in a surgical suite. If it happened at all."

"You have a point," Virgil said. "But doesn't it still come back to his professional life? Maybe there was something on that computer that would have caused somebody a large problem. Maybe that person knew about the computer, went there to steal it, and was surprised by Dr. Quill. What could it be? Could it be related to the recording? We know the recording was actually in Dr. Quill's CD player, so he must have been listening to it recently."

"That's a pretty thin connection," Miles said.

"No, it's not thin. The CD one day, the murder the next. There must be a connection. If I could figure out what it is, I could catch the killer."

Miles shook his head. "Good luck with that. I still don't see it."

When Virgil left Miles's office, he called Trane, who didn't answer the phone. Could be in court, Virgil thought. Disturbed by what Miles said, he decided to attempt to track down the other people on the recording. The best shot, he figured, was Carl Anderson, Quill's lab director. He called ahead to make sure Anderson was in the office. He was, and he said he would be there for a while. Virgil drove back across the river and went up to the lab.

Anderson was waiting, offered Virgil a cup of coffee, which Virgil declined, and they went back to his office, and Virgil shut the door. "I want to play a recording for you. I would have played it before, but I didn't. Anyway, listen to this."

Virgil played the recording, and Anderson frowned. "That's appalling. And it sounds like Barth."

"You're not sure?"

"Well, it sounds like Barth, but, no, I'm not sure."

"His wife thinks it's probably him," Virgil said. "Another member of the lab staff is sure it is."

"Okay, it probably is," Anderson said, frowning, bewildered. "Who are the other people?"

"That's what I was going to ask you," Virgil said.

"I have no idea. I know all the people who are closely involved with Barth's work and I didn't recognize any of their voices. You could ask some of them. The way they were talking, they must have been close to Barth."

"Give me some names."

Anderson said, "These guys would be over at university hospitals . . . Let me see, I'll give you four guys . . . No, five guys . . ." He wrote the names on a scratch pad, checked a computer contact list, added their cell phone numbers, and pushed the paper across the desk to Virgil.

"You don't think these guys were the ones talking to Dr. Quill?" Virgil asked.

"No. But maybe they'd have some ideas who they might be. If they're real."

"If they're real? They sound pretty real to me."

Anderson shook his head. "Listen, Virgil, I need to explain something to you. Okay? Listen carefully."

"I'm listening carefully," Virgil said.

Anderson leaned back in his desk chair, looked briefly at the ceiling as he gathered his thoughts. "What we do here uses multiple disciplines—chemistry, biology, mechanical engineering, brain science, surgery—and we pull in all kinds of scientists and doctors. What that recording refers to, apparently, was a proposed unethical operation on somebody suffering from a spinal injury. That's not something you pull out of your butt. That's not something you can hide. When we do an op, there are usually a couple of dozen people directly involved, everybody from scientists and surgeons to accountants. The surgical team alone would probably have a lead surgeon plus one or two assistant surgeons. Even the assistants would be big shots on their own. Barth would be in the room probably with one of our techs, or even two. There might be residents coming and going, and for sure several nurses, surgical techs, anesthesiologists and nurse anesthetists, imaging people, radiologists, and maybe some specialists in other fields—engineering, for instance. There's no *Weird Science* stuff going on, surgeries in the middle of the night by a couple of guys using lightning bolts for power. If a little cabal of doctors tried to pull off an unethical operation in Barth's field, they'd be immediately ratted out and challenged and hanged by their nuts the next day."

"Then what the hell is happening there?" Virgil demanded.

"I don't know. That sounded like Barth on the recording, but I don't know. I mean, it's like movie dialogue where they have to make things simple. The reality isn't simple. In Barth's field, it takes weeks or months to get an op together. Hours of talk and work. Whole seminars. It's all very public."

Virgil: "What if they had a guy they hadn't started on yet, all very preliminary, even before the guy was in your system? Quill knew he couldn't get past these other people without talking to them. I mean, they hadn't even talked to the human experimentation committee—or whatever it's called—yet."

Anderson chewed on his lip for a few seconds, then looked up. "Yeah. It could work that way. In fact, that's about the only way it makes sense."

Down in his truck again, Virgil sat and rubbed his eyes, then got on the phone to Trane.

"Where are you?"

"Courthouse," Trane said. "Might not be able to talk. They could call me this morning. On the other hand, they might not. There're rumors that the defendant's attorneys might make a bunch of motions about evidentiary custody this afternoon."

"I talked to Anderson, Quill's lab manager."

"What'd he say?"

Virgil told her about the conversation and Anderson's conclusion. "He thinks it's possible that this was a preliminary, very secret talk, so it's possible. Barely possible. He thinks it was Quill on the recording, but he's not absolutely sure."

Silence. Then, "You need to jack up some doctors."

"I got a list of names from Anderson, people who worked with Quill. He thinks that if the recording is real, some of them might be able to tell us who the other voices belong to. He doesn't think they belong to any of them."

"We need to jump all over that, get those guys on the list, see what they think. We need to follow through. Nancy now says it was Quill?"

"Sorta. But she's like Anderson: she says she can't swear to it," Virgil said. "She thinks the people on the tape sound odd. She might have a point."

"Listen, you've got that list of doctors. There's a decent chance that those guys know the people on the recording. And maybe even the killer," Trane said. "Why in the hell am I sitting here on my ass? I need to be out there. You, go jack up those doctors."

Because it was summer and the new semester was barely underway, two of the five doctors were out of town at their northern Minnesota fishing cabins. The other three, though, were in town, just scattered around. Because he wanted to talk to them face-to-face, it took Virgil the rest of the day to track them down.

Robert Harris, a microsurgeon and the last of the three that Virgil interviewed, said the same things the other two did. "I don't know those voices, I really don't. Not except for Barth's, of course—if that is Barth. Must have been a long time ago or very recent, nothing in the middle. We've got a solid team, and have had for five or six years now. Nobody wants to leave. We get our names in the journals, we make the big bucks. Barth could be a prick, but he was our prick. And, frankly, pricks are not unknown among the surgical fraternity. Not only can we handle it, it's a fact of life."

"If it's recent—and I have to think it's recent—he was listening to the recording shortly before he was killed," Virgil said.

"How shortly?"

"We don't know," Virgil conceded. "Anyway, is it possible that he was putting together another team that might not be so reluctant to go for the Hail Mary operation? The rest of you guys—the current team—could push back, right? What if he had a bunch of, say, younger, more obscure guys?"

"Nope. Agent Flowers, this is not work you'd do with a bunch of residents," Harris said. "I spent four years in med school and then eight years doing plastic and microsurgery residencies before I felt I could lead a complicated operation. Even then, I had to be careful. I mean, I was thirty-seven or thirty-eight before I felt I was hitting it out of the park. He wouldn't do something like nerve splicing with a pickup team."

"You're sure about that."

"I am. Listen, Flowers. Barth was a concepts guy, an intellectual. The way the thinking goes in medicine, you've got your really, really smart guys like Barth who think up all kinds of things, who know all kinds of stuff, but can't do anything. They're lab

people. Chin-scratchers. Thumb-suckers. Then you've got surgeons, who are looked on as the dumb guys in the profession but
dumb guys who'll try just about anything. 'We wanna cut. We
like it. Get in there and fix it. If the patient dies, we did our best.'
If anything, that recording is backwards: Barth was the conservative guy. The 'Let's do it' guys would be the surgeons. If that's
who he was talking to."

"Damnit," Virgil said.

FIFTEEN

Virgil called Trane and told her what he'd found.

"Virgil, this recording is tied into the murder. I don't care what these doctors are telling you. It's tied."

"Figure it out tomorrow. Where are you on the trial?"

"I'll be going on the stand tomorrow afternoon. The judge is going to make a bunch of rulings in the morning, but he's told the jury they have to be back at one o'clock."

"There won't be something weird, like a mistrial? And you'll have to do it all over?"

"No, no. The lead defense attorney is, like, about fourteen. I think he got out of law school on Monday morning, and he's filed so many motions that they contradict each other. I think it's possible that he's looking to wear down the prosecution and get a deal. Because his motherfucker is a guilty motherfucker."

"All right. I may stop by tomorrow to watch you do your act. Maybe we can have a séance after you're done."

"Talk to ya."

Virgil was headed back to the hotel when Del Capslock, the BCA agent, called. "You free?"

"Yup. As the breeze."

"Meet me over at the Territorial," Capslock said. "I'm there now, back by the foosball table."

"The sun's not down yet."

"Fuck the sun. The place opened at six. Don't see any sun in here."

Virgil got directions; the bar was ten minutes away. He found a spot on the street, walked a half block to the theater-type marquee that said "Drinks." And, under that, "Ladies Nite E ery Nite." Virgil spent the next few seconds of his life wondering if the "v" had fallen off, been stolen for some reason, or was simply a scarce letter that the bar hadn't happened to have on hand.

Calling the bar shabby was an insult to the word. Some dive bars had peanut shells on the floor; the Territorial made do with ordinary dirt, apparently ground in over several decades of near failure. Virgil made his way past the long, shabby bar, and its equally shabby bartender, to the broken foosball machine, and Capslock, who was sitting in a booth and facing a thin, shabby criminal whose narrow face was framed by brown, greasy hair pulled back in a pigtail.

Virgil flicked his fingers at Capslock, gesturing him to move over—he wasn't going to sit next to Pigtail—and Capslock slid over, and asked, "You want a beer?"

"No, I'm on duty."

Capslock laughed, finished his PBR, and waved at the bartender. "Hey, Rick, two more."

He turned back to Virgil, and said, "This is Long Wayne Gibbs, aka Long Doyle Gill, aka Long Bob Greer. Part of him used to make pornos."

Virgil said to the criminal, "Should I just call you Long for short?"

"Call him Wayne. That might be his real name," Capslock said.

Reacting to Virgil's "Long/short" comment, Wayne was giving him his version of the prison death stare, which was interrupted by the arrival of two more PBRs. When the bartender had gone, Capslock said, "Wayne, tell Virgil about China White."

"There isn't one," Wayne grunted.

Capslock said to Virgil, "There you go . . ."

"You mean, no one anywhere?" Virgil asked.

"Maybe in California—I wouldn't know about that—but not in Minneapolis or St. Paul. Nobody would call themselves that. It's too stupid."

"I'm not sure how many bright drug dealers I've known," Virgil said. "I could probably count them on the fingers of one finger."

"Still too stupid," Wayne said. "Even a dumb guy wouldn't call himself that."

"Or woman."

That caused Wayne to pause halfway through a swallow of beer, his Adam's apple stuck briefly under his chin. When he took the bottle down, he said, "You know, China White would be a good name for a porn star. One of them chink half-breeds, looks kinda white but with slanty eyes?"

Virgil: "So, you know any porn stars named China White?"

"Not yet," Wayne said.

Capslock: "Wayne's getting out of the art side of porn, going into production work."

Wayne: "That's where the money is."

Virgil said to Capslock, "Well, I appreciate meeting this gentleman. Now, I think I'll head over to my hotel—"

"Virgil, Virgil. Listen to the man," Capslock said.

"He said there's no China White."

"But that's not the only question you're asking, is it? Wayne's connections in the sex business are extensive . . . You tell him, Wayne."

Wayne leaned forward, dropped his voice: just us boys here. "I was, uh, auditioning this chick for a role in one of my upcoming productions, and we got to talking and she mentioned that this girl she knew was fucking a famous professor."

Virgil looked at him for a moment, then asked, "Why are you telling me this?"

"As a favor to Del," Wayne said.

"Wayne was supplying medical marijuana to some needy people—"

"Injured veterans," Wayne said

"—and was found to have twenty kilos of primo Mexican weed in the back of his Camaro," Capslock said.

"The whole thing was a total misunderstanding," Wayne said. "One of my friends put it there. I didn't even know about it."

"What happened to his friend?" Virgil asked Capslock.

"He returned to his residence in Juárez. He refuses to come back and testify on Wayne's behalf," Capslock said. "A group of us law enforcement officers pointed out to the county attorney that Wayne has insights into several local criminal enterprises. An arrangement was made."

"I gotta do two thousand hours of community service," Wayne said. "Two thousand hours. Jesus Christ and all the fuckin' Apostles didn't do that many."

"Careful," Capslock said. "Virgil's the son of a preacher."

"Well, then, I apologize to you, your dad, Jesus Christ, and all the fuckin' Apostles—the whole fuckin' bunch of you."

Virgil: "I'm losing track of the conversation. You have a friend who knows somebody who was fucking a famous professor?"

"Yeah. At the U."

"What's your friend's name? Not China White?"

"Paisley."

"Paisley what?"

"Just Paisley. Some of the guys call her Paisley Tied because, you know . . ."

"Yeah," Virgil said. "Like a necktie."

Wayne glanced at Capslock, then looked back at Virgil. "Necktie? What the fuck are you talking about?"

Virgil said, "What?"

Wayne said, "No neckties. She's called that because you can tie her up. Or she can tie you up. Strictly voluntary. Costs extra, of course."

Capslock laughed, and asked the world, "We're talking about a classy chick, are we not?"

"Where can I find her?" Virgil asked. "Paisley?"

"You gotta call her and she'll meet you. I got her number. Tell her that she was recommended by Richard. Ask her what facilities she offers," Wayne said. "That way, she'll know you know about the tie thing."

"I'll do that," Virgil said. "And Wayne? If word leaks back to her before I get there, you'll be doing six thousand hours."

Wayne looked at Capslock. "This guy's an asshole, Del. You said he was okay."

Capslock shrugged, and said, "Wayne, we can all be assholes. Isn't that the way of the world? Assholes everywhere. You're an asshole, I'm an asshole . . ."

Wayne took a swig of beer, tipped the bottle at Virgil. "And this guy's an asshole. You're right, Del. Assholes everywhere. Six thousand hours, shit snackin' crackers."

Virgil thought to go somewhere with Capslock to make the call to Paisley, but Capslock said, "Why not now?"

"You mean here?"

"Yeah. Here. I mean, we're already sitting down."

"Tell her you met Richard here, at the Territorial," Wayne said.

Virgil laid his phone faceup on the table so everybody in the booth could hear and he called. A man answered. "Who's this?"

Virgil: "Could I speak to, uh, Paisley?"

"She ain't here. Who are you?"

"Bob."

"Why do you want Paisley, Bob?"

"My friend Richard recommended that I take her out, you know, on a date."

"Richard, huh? Tall black dude with this bald spot?"

Wayne was shaking a finger, and mouthed, Short . . . white . . .

Virgil said, "Well, uh, this guy was a sort of short white guy. I met him down at the Territorial."

After a moment of silence, the man said, "Wait one. Paisley walked in."

A woman came on a minute later, and asked, "What'd Richard say about me?"

"He said to ask what facilities you offer."

"Well, Bob, what exactly do you need?"

"He said some people call you Paisley Tied. And, you know . . ."

"Are you here in town, Bob?"

"I'm from Mankato. I'm staying at the Graduate tonight."

"Huh. Nice place. Okay, it's a date. I'll meet you at the Applebee's. How will I recognize you?"

"I'm wearing an old Led Zeppelin T-shirt that just says 'Zep' and a sport coat, and I have blond hair down over my ears."

"Ooo, sounds handsome. Half hour from now?"

"See you then," Virgil said.

Virgil and Capslock said good-bye to Wayne as they all walked out to the street, and just before they parted, Wayne said, "Del, for extra credit . . ."

"Like what?"

"If you could put me down for like a hundred hours picking up trash on St. Dennis Road?"

"That's a lot of trash," Capslock said. "What do you have?"

"A warning?"

"Let's hear it."

Wayne said to Virgil, "That guy you talked to? That's Paisley's brother. The word is, he flunked out of the Vikings offensive line for being too mean. I swear to God, the guy could pull the arms off a gorilla."

Virgil went with that. "Okay."

Wayne turned to Capslock and lifted his eyebrows.

"I'll think about it," Capslock said.

A half hour later, Virgil was in a booth at the Applebee's, looking at a cheeseburger and a Diet Coke, and Capslock was across the room, talking to a waitress about her impending motherhood. Paisley walked in, but nobody turned to look. She was a nondescript, slender, dark-haired woman with a soft face, a mole under one eye, and dark eyebrows that nearly met in the middle. She was carrying an oversized leather purse. She was alone.

She spotted Virgil, took in the Zep T-shirt, and slid into the booth across from him. She said, "Give me your hand, Bob," and Virgil put his hand on the table. She gripped it, and said, "I can do about anything you want, but I don't allow myself to get hurt. When we go outside, you'll see my assistant. He's the guy who looks like an old telephone booth. And, I promise you, he could yank off your head and shove it up your ass. That's not a threat. I'm saying he's my protection. Do you understand?"

Virgil bobbed his head dumbly, and she went on with her price list. Virgil nodded in Capslock's direction, who broke away from the waitress, walked over to the booth in four long strides, and slid in beside Paisley, trapping her and pushing her to the wall.

Capslock smiled, and said, "I'm Del Capslock, Minnesota Bureau of Criminal Apprehension. This hippie gentleman is Virgil Flowers, also an agent with the BCA. We're cops, but this is not necessarily a bust."

She looked from Virgil to Capslock, and then snarled, "If it's not a bust, then what is it?"

"A good-natured search for information," Virgil said. "I taped your offers and your price list, so you're out of luck, Paisley. But,

I have very little interest in your moneymaking activities. I need to know something from you."

"What?"

"The name of a friend of yours who was having a sexual relationship with a university professor. Don't lie to us—we're investigating a murder, and if you lie to us, you'll be an accessory to murder. That's a whole different thing than a prostitution arrest."

She didn't argue but frowned at Virgil, and asked, "How'd you hear about my friend?"

Virgil said, "There's word going around on the street. It got back to us as a tip. A bad guy got a get-out-of-jail-free card."

Capslock was looking over Virgil's shoulder, and said, quietly, "A very large personage just walked in."

Virgil said to Paisley, "If that's your brother, wave him off."

"What happens if I don't?" she asked.

Capslock said, "Paisley, for Christ's sakes, we're cops. We've got guns. He starts on us, and I'll shoot him three times in the fuckin' heart and I won't lose ten seconds of sleep over it. Wave him the fuck off."

Paisley raised her eyes, looked over Virgil's shoulder, and shook her head no.

"That was a wise move for all of us," Capslock said, settling back into the booth. "Now, what's your friend's name?"

"Lilith."

Virgil said, "Lilith? I mean, does she read the Bible or something?"

"What?"

"Never mind," Capslock said. "Lilith. You have a number for her?"

"Yes. We sometimes party together." She looked at Virgil.

"We would have partied with you, if you weren't a fuckin' cop. You missed the best sex of your life."

"I'll live with it somehow," Virgil said. "Gimme the number. And let me make a few threats before you go. If the lunch box, or the phone booth, or whatever the fuck he is, tries to molest us in the parking lot, we'll shoot him. If he calls Lilith, you'll both get free five-year housing courtesy of the state government. Like I said, this is a murder case."

She said, "Okay."

They got Lilith's real name, which was Abigail Cohen, and which led Virgil to think that perhaps she did read the Bible, or at least had heard some Jewish folktales. They said good-bye to Paisley, who didn't exactly trot out the door. Still sitting in the booth, still working on cheeseburgers, they ran Cohen's name through the DMV and got her birth date and an address, and then through the NCIC database, which showed three arrests, but no convictions, two for soliciting and one for a small amount of marijuana.

"Must have a good lawyer," Capslock said.

"Or the courts just don't give a shit about sex and weed anymore," Virgil said.

"That could be," Capslock said.

Virgil called Jon Duncan, his nominal supervisor at the BCA, who called another agent, who got in touch with Verizon and AT&T. An AT&T billing address confirmed the driver's license address, and since hookers relied on cell phones at least as much as dope dealers, it was probably good. Virgil finished his third Diet Coke, then asked Capslock if he'd like to come along to Cohen's address.

"Why not? Might as well go fuck with a criminal in the dark. It's been a while since I got shot."

Cohen lived in a newer apartment complex in Dinkytown, where Quill had been wandering the night he went missing. The building was done in clapboard and stone with rows of windows that, in the back, looked out over railroad tracks. Virgil thought it had been designed for the richer class of students. With lots of moving in and moving out, and people coming and going, it was ideal for a woman with frequent male visitors. The front door was locked, but a resident manager let them in, and asked, anxiously, "Is Abby in trouble? She seems so nice."

"No, she's not," Virgil said. "Not at all. We're running down a list of people who knew a man who died, trying to find some relatives."

The manager might have been skeptical but shrugged, and said, "Up the stairs and to the left. Or up the elevator and to the right," and walked away.

At Cohen's apartment, Capslock said, "Watch the master and learn." He knocked rapidly, but not loudly, on the door, and said, in an anxious whisper, "Abby! Abby! Are you in there? Abby!"

A moment later, a woman's hushed voice: "Who is it?"

"Abby! It's me. Jesus Christ, Abby, we got to get out of here . . ."

The door opened a crack—a chain showed across the gap—and a woman peered out, and Capslock showed his ID, and said, "Police. Open the door, Miz Cohen."

"Fuck that," she said, and tried to slam the door, but Capslock had his steel-toed boot in the crack.

Capslock said, "If you don't open it, we kick it in. If you break one of my toes, I'll charge you with aggravated assault on a police officer."

"I'm calling my lawyer," Cohen said.

"We'll let you do that," Virgil said.

"What do you want?" she asked.

"We need to know what you saw in the library the night Barth Quill got killed."

"I didn't see anything," she squealed. "I got scared and ran away."

Virgil tipped his head back, and said, aloud, 'Thank you, God."

Capslock pushed on the door. "Open the door. You can call your attorney, but we want to make sure you don't run away again."

Silence. Then: "You promise?"

"I swear," Capslock said. "We'll sit on your couch, and you can call."

More silence, then she popped the chain, backed past a short hallway, which led to a compact kitchen, and into the living room. She was wearing a mid-thigh green satin dressing gown that showed off her slender legs, her best feature.

Otherwise, Cohen, like Paisley, was an average-looking woman, long-faced, thin-lipped, a chiseled nose, with auburn hair tied back in a ponytail. Harder-edged than Paisley, as though she might work out on a daily basis. She did smell good, like vanilla.

She backed up until she got to a couch, sat down, and attempted to tug down the hem of her gown. Virgil and Capslock took two easy chairs that faced the couch over a glass table. A second hallway led out of the living room deeper into the apartment but only showed three closed doors.

"Call your attorney," Virgil said. He got on his own phone and called Trane.

Virgil: "Where are you?"

"At home," Trane said. "About to eat another pie."

"We found the woman who was in the library with Quill when he was killed."

"Holy cow! Uh, who's 'we'?"

"Do you know Del Capslock?" Virgil asked.

"Del? He's there with you?"

"Yeah."

"I'm coming. Give me the address."

Virgil gave her the address and Cohen's name. "She's calling her attorney. We could be a while."

"I'm running."

Cohen was on the phone to her attorney. "I don't give a shit if you're at dinner, I got a big problem here, Larry. I got two cops sitting in my living room like a couple of tombstones and they think they got something big on me."

Pause to listen.

"I know she'll be disappointed," Cohen replied, "but think how disappointed she'll be if the details of our relationship come out."

Pause.

Then: "I don't know. They think I was a witness to whoever killed that professor."

Pause.

"Do you want me to answer that with them sitting here?"
Pause.

"Okay. You know where I'm at," Cohen said.

She hung up, and said, "He'll be here in twenty minutes."

Capslock said, "I gotta pee. Where's the bathroom?"

Without thinking, Cohen said, "Down the hall."

Virgil quickly grabbed her attention. "Why can't you tell us about Professor Quill right now? We know you had a relationship . . ."

"I really gotta . . ." Capslock was moving down the hall, and when Cohen saw him pass the first door on the right, she called out, "Hey, not that one . . ."

But Capslock had popped the farthest of the three doors, and now he stepped back, looked at Virgil, and said, "Oh my God. This is awful."

"Get out of there," Cohen screamed.

"I can't just leave—the poor guy might be in desperate trouble here," Capslock said. And, "Virgil, do you have a pocketknife? We have to free the victim."

"He's not a victim," Cohen shouted. "This is adult consensual sex."

Virgil walked down the hall, Cohen tagging anxiously behind him, and looked in the bedroom door: a large man—a fat man—pink in color, with fine skin resembling a baby's, was on the bed, nude, gagged, trussed up like an Easter ham, ropes to all four corners of the bed to hold him in place with his ass up in the air. A box of battery-powered sex toys sat on the bed beside him.

Virgil said, "Excuse me, Del, but I can't look at this."

"I don't want to, but we can't let the guy die," Capslock said.

To the man on the bed he said, "If you're okay, wiggle your fingers."

The man wiggled his fingers.

"All right, then. We'll leave the door open. You develop a problem, just yell."

"He's gagged, Del," Virgil said. "He can't yell."

Capslock turned back to the man. "If you get in trouble, make some of those strangle sounds. We'll hear you."

They all went back to the living room, and Cohen dropped onto the couch, her arms crossed over her chest, the classic female defensive position.

"You gotta admit, that's not something you see every day," Capslock said to Virgil.

"I had a case down in Trippton, a motorcycle guy hiring himself out to whip naked women. He had a pretty good client list," Virgil said. "One of the women told me that it was therapeutic."

"It certainly can be," Cohen snapped. "It probably helped her with all kinds of repressive neuroses, both known and unknown."

"I'm pretty sure it didn't," Virgil said.

"Oh, you're a shrink now?" she sneered.

"No, but another guy shot her in the head. That was the end of her psychological problems. As far as we know."

They all stared at each other for a moment, and then Capslock said, "Well, that was a conversation killer."

Virgil pecked away with questions about Quill, but Cohen kept her arms crossed and simply shook her head and sometimes grunted. Fifteen minutes later, there was a knock at the door.

Virgil answered it, and Trane said, "Got here as fast as I could." She looked at Cohen, and asked, "Is this the lady?"

"This is her," Virgil said. "We can't beat her up because her attorney is coming, and there's a witness down the hall in the bedroom. You might want to introduce yourself."

"Oh, fuck all of you," Cohen said.

Trane went down the hall, looked in the bedroom, showed no reaction at all, came back and sat down with a straight face, then looked at Virgil, and asked, "What?"

Virgil shrugged, and said, "I dunno, I thought you'd . . . I dunno . . ."

"Are you trying to tell me you've never done that?" Trane asked. To Cohen she said, "He's so straight he gives me a headache."

"He's an asshole," Cohen said.

Virgil: "That's the second or third time I've been called that in the last hour. I'm tired of it."

"Then why don't you leave?" Cohen said.

"Because he's a dedicated law enforcement officer," Trane said. To Capslock: "How are your hips, Del?"

"Still hurt when I get up in the morning, but Cheryl's got me doing yoga stretches. That helps."

To Cohen, Trane said, "Del got shot by some old people down on the Mexican border. Almost got killed."

Cohen said, "Good."

Time dragged. A half hour after Cohen called, her attorney showed up, was introduced as Larry Hardy, also known as "Call me Lare" on his ubiquitous billboards.

"I thought you did personal injury," Trane said.

"I do a little of everything," Hardy said. "Gotta make the monthly nut."

"Speaking of nuts, you might want to take a look in that last bedroom down there," Trane said.

Cohen: "Fuck all of you. Again."

Hardy went to look, came back, and asked, "Is this a great country or what?" and then added, "Are you charging my client?"

"She's going to be charged with something," Trane said. "She left the scene of a crime, for one thing. A murder. If Piggy down there chokes on his gag, we'll probably add manslaughter."

Hardy said to Cohen, "Maybe you should cut him loose. Just to be kind."

Cohen nodded, went down to the bedroom, and came back three minutes later. "I need to talk to my attorney privately," she said to Virgil.

"We'll wait in the hallway," Virgil said. To Hardy: "If she drops out the window, you go to jail. For a long time."

Hardy, exasperated: "She's not going anywhere, Virgil. Jesus. Give us twenty minutes. We'll get this all straightened out, and then we can all go home and go to bed."

"She's already admitted to two of us that she was there," Virgil said. "Keep that in mind when you try to find a way to weasel out of this."

Virgil, Capslock, and Trane stood in the hallway for ten minutes, then, by mutual consent, sat in the hallway with their backs against the wall opposite Cohen's door. Virgil told Trane how they'd gotten to Cohen's place, beginning with the Paisley interview. A woman carrying a pizza went by, asked, "Are you locked out?" and they all said, "No," as one, and the woman said, "Whatever," and went down the hall with her pizza.

"Smelled like pepperoni," Capslock said, looking after her. "I could use a slice."

Five more minutes, and the fat man stepped through the door. He was wearing a blue-striped seersucker suit and a red tie. Trane said, "We need to talk."

"Completely voluntary," the man said. "A once-in-a-lifetime experiment. Can I catch a break here?"

"Let's go down the hall where we can talk privately away from these two," Trane said to him. "They're not sensitive to this kind of adult behavior."

She led him away, turning only to say, "Call me when they're done in there."

When they were out of earshot, Virgil said, "Tell you what, Del. Trane is sort of freaking me out here. That guy—"

"She's fuckin' with you, Virgil," Capslock said. "I know her. This is what her sense of humor runs like. She's laughin' up her sleeve."

"You think?"

"I know." He laughed. "She's fuckin' with you the same way you fuck with Davenport. About his daughter."

A few minutes later, Cohen's apartment door popped open and Hardy stuck his head out. "Come on in."

Virgil called down the hall to Trane, who was still lecturing the man in the suit. She tapped him twice on the chest and then walked toward them, and Virgil and Capslock went to meet her, where Hardy couldn't hear them.

"Got his details," she said. "I'll look him up when we finish here. He admits he paid for the service. I told him that if Cohen wants to take it to trial, he might be called as a witness. But I also told him that I doubt she'll do that."

"He got a family?" Virgil asked.

"Divorced. He's a schmuck. But he agreed to appear if we need him. I'm going to bust Cohen on the prostitution charge so I can get her in an interview room and on a video."

Inside Cohen's apartment, they got chairs from the kitchen so everybody would have a place to sit, and Hardy said, "My client is happy to cooperate if we get some consideration on potential charges. She's willing to concede that she was with Professor Quill in the library when he was murdered but didn't know he'd been murdered. She doesn't watch local television news and doesn't read newspapers. When she heard the sounds of a struggle, she got frightened and ran away. She never saw the other person that Quill was struggling with."

The cops digested that for a moment, then Virgil said, "That's not much of a concession, Lare, since she already told Del and me that she was there. If she wants consideration, we'll need more than that."

Hardy cleared his throat. "Unfortunately—and I mean it, this is unfortunate—she didn't see anything. She can give you her history with Quill, but she can't help with the library situation. She's willing to make a formal statement about that."

"That's it?" Trane asked.

Hardy said, "Unfortunately, that's what we've got."

Trane said to Cohen, "I'm arresting you on a charge of prostitution. I'll drop you off at the jail, and we'll all meet down at my office tomorrow to figure out what to do. Is ten o'clock good for everybody?"

Hardy said, "Come on, Sergeant Trane. Arresting her won't do anything but piss everybody off."

Trane said, "I don't care if she's pissed off. I won't risk losing her."

Hardy: "You bust her on prostitution, we make bail, we don't cooperate. With anything."

Trane: "Then we will add a few charges, and some of those might take her down to Shakopee."

Cohen: "What's Shakopee?"

Virgil: "The women's prison. It's not nearly as unpleasant as you might think."

Cohen, wailing: "Larry . . ."

Hardy to Trane: "Okay, be a hard-ass. Ten o'clock tomorrow."

Trane to Cohen: "On your feet."

CHAPTER

SIXTEEN

Virgil should have woken the next morning with a feeling of accomplishment and well-being, but he didn't. Instead, he thought of Cohen sitting in jail overnight and the extortion that Trane was about to drop on her. All of it was part of a game that both sides played: we bust you for prostitution, but we're willing to let it go if you cooperate on something else.

He'd done it himself, but arrests for prostitution, where the woman was selling her services rather than having a pimp selling them for her and taking the big cut, had always seemed pointless. They weren't going to stop it. From a cop's perspective, the biggest problem with prostitution was the spin-off to other crime—drugs, blackmail, assault. And if a pimp were involved, sometimes the violence used to keep the women in line.

In a way it was like weed, he thought while he shaved. Weed was everywhere, and arresting people on charges that would be dropped or result in no jail time, even with a guilty plea, were pointless and a waste of police time and a lot of money.

A *lot* of money. On the other hand, weed was implicated in touching off schizophrenia in teenagers. One look at the weed-smoking, mental homeless problem would suggest exactly how not good it was.

He patted some bay rum aftershave on his face, smiled at himself, dragged his fingers through his hair, and went to get dressed. He selected a Larkin Poe shirt he'd been wearing a lot and that had developed a nice vintage look to it from being hung in the sun on an actual clothesline.

Cohen would be a dead end, he thought while pulling on his boots. She hadn't said much the night before, but she had said that she'd never seen the person who attacked Quill. The best that could be hoped for was that she'd solidly pinpoint the time of death, which might affect some alibis.

Trane would take care of all of that.

The question was, what would *he* take care of? He hadn't been able to find doctors involved in a conspiracy with Quill or even find anybody who believed that the cabal existed. Nobody believed in China White, though Quill's desk had held a squib of cocaine. The theft of the maps didn't relate to Quill.

Something was going on with the attack on Foster. He would think about that, but Foster wasn't any help. And there didn't seem to be any useful witnesses or entryways into the case. The St. Paul cops had come up dry.

There was also the matter of a malpractice suit against Quill and other doctors on Quill's team. After giving it some thought, he decided to check the lawsuit.

He called Trane to tell her that. "Listen, about that cocaine in Quill's desk: push Cohen on that, find out if she ever went to Quill's house. Maybe she's China White."

"I'll do that," Trane said. "I can only give it a couple of hours. I'm supposed to be at the courtroom at noon. I'm the first witness after the lunch break, and they want to do some last-minute prep before I go on."

"Good luck," Virgil said.

Trane had mentioned that she'd gotten a copy of the malpractice lawsuit from the attorneys who were on a retainer with the university. He checked his notes, got an address in downtown St. Paul, made a call, was told they'd make a copy of the document for him, and he drove over. The offices of John Brennan, LLC, were in a remodeled firehouse, and they had done a good job, Virgil thought, as he stepped through the palm forest on the first floor. A plaque on the wall listed seven attorneys as partners of the firm, and eight more associates, in addition to Brennan himself—a bigger organization than Virgil had expected.

A receptionist gave him a copy of the lawsuit in a yellow legal envelope, and said, "Mr. Brennan would like to speak to you for a moment."

"Sure. How soon? I could run across the street and get a Diet Coke if he's busy right now."

"He should be only a minute," the receptionist said. She made a call, and said, "Follow me."

Brennan's office was on the second floor. Virgil stepped out of the elevator into what would probably have been the firefighters' sleeping quarters when the house was active, with polished pine plank floors and exposed pine beams bigger around than Virgil's torso. Brennan used a rosewood table rather than a desk and had a row of matching rosewood file cabinets behind the table to hold whatever papers needed to be held. An oversized picture on a side wall showed a man in a University of Minnesota football uniform cradling a football to his gut and pretending to stiff-arm the photographer who took the picture.

"That was me in younger days," Brennan said.

Brennan stood behind the table, fussing with papers. He was a large man, with white hair, a fleshy nose and fleshy ears, and querulous green eyes that matched the green of his necktie. A white shirt and gray suit completed his ensemble. His face was finely hatched with burst capillaries, which could be a sign of too much golf, too much drink, or both.

As Virgil walked away from the elevator, Brennan came out from behind the table to shake hands, and asked, "Is Sergeant Trane still working this case?"

"Yes, but she's in court today," Virgil said. Brennan pointed at a chair, and Virgil took it. The receptionist came back unasked with a can of frosty-cold Diet Coke, a glass full of ice, and a napkin to protect the desk. Virgil thanked her, said, "I don't need the glass," and she took it and went away.

When she'd closed the door, Brennan said, "Sergeant Trane had concluded that our case didn't have much to do with the murder of Barth Quill."

"She's probably right," Virgil said. "I'm running out of leads and thought I should take a look. We've had a couple of minor breaks in the past couple of days, and maybe something in the suit will, mmm, mesh with those."

"I see . . . You haven't read the actual suit, though?"

"No, I read Margaret's summary of it. A short summary."

"All right. Let me give you a little more. It's basically a nuisance suit, and if we settle—and we just might—the biggest benefactor is going to be a sleazy fellow member of the bar named Robin Jones. He's an associate with the Larry Hardy firm over in Minneapolis. You know, 'Call Me Lare,' the billboards?"

"Wait a minute! Hardy's involved in this?"

Brennan's heavy white eyebrows arched. "Shouldn't he be?"

"I talked to him last night," Virgil said. "We—Sergeant Trane and I—arrested one of his clients on prostitution charges. She's directly connected to the Quill murder. A witness. We talked to them for half an hour, and Hardy never said a thing about this lawsuit."

Brennan leaned back in his chair, and said, "That is extremely interesting. Extremely. The suit was filed against the university and not Dr. Quill directly, but I've had some rumblings from Jones about amending the suit to go after Quill's estate. Which I understand is quite large."

"It is," Virgil said. "Many millions." He drew his hand down over his eyes, thinking, and finally added, "It's interesting, but I don't see how it would tie to the murder."

Brennan: "The plaintiff, in the original suit, made a series of statements about assurances she got from Quill before she and her husband agreed to the operation that led, indirectly, to her husband's death. With Quill dead, he's not available to counter those claims. Which is why I suspect that Jones is talking about amending the suit. It wasn't likely to be especially successful against the university, which also indemnified Dr. Quill on charges of malpractice. But now if the plaintiff should claim that Quill personally made fraudulent promises about the success of the operation, then they might be able to split the estate away from the university. A successful suit against Quill's estate could be lucrative."

"I don't know enough about the suit . . ."

"Then here it is in a nutshell," Brennan said, making a steeple with his fingers. "Carl McDonald was quadriplegic. He'd been an electrician with a company called The Brothers Electric. One day he fell off a ladder, landed on the back of his head, and pinched off the spinal cord at the neck. He still had some mobility in his left arm, hand, and fingers, but little control. And that was all he had. Quill agreed to take him as a patient, and after some time an operation was done by a team of surgeons under Quill's direction."

"I understand that Quill doesn't operate himself," Virgil said.

"That's correct. Anyway, after the operation, McDonald did in fact recover further use of his left arm, hand, and fingers. He went through a period of physical therapy in an effort to maximize the use of all three. He also used pills, administered by his wife, to control pain in his neck, as well as elsewhere—new pain, his wife says, the result of the operation. When he got home, after the main round of physical therapy, his wife left the pain pills on a bedside table, and, while she was out shopping for groceries, McDonald managed to get ahold of the bottle and remove the lid with his teeth. He swallowed all the pills and was dead by the time his wife got back."

Virgil stared for a minute. "He committed suicide? And Quill's team is being sued for malpractice?"

"Yes. McDonald's wife claims the operation was a failure and even created new pain—that's the malpractice part—and that Quill and his team should have known that McDonald would require extensive psychological counseling in the wake of the failure. She claims that Quill told them that McDonald would make a substantial recovery. When I asked him, Quill denied saying that, and his team backs him up: they say he never said such a thing."

"Then what's the problem?"

"The problem is, we have a bereaved wife suing a big, rich university and a big, rich doctor, and the decision will be made by a jury that—"

"Isn't big and rich. Got it," Virgil said. "You haven't said so, but the wife, and Hardy's firm, may stand to benefit from Quill's murder."

"I probably wouldn't actually say that out loud myself," Brennan said with a grin. "But if somebody else suggested that, I wouldn't object."

"I gotta talk to Margaret," Virgil said, looking at his watch, "right now. We don't want to make any deals with Hardy's client. Not yet."

"Feel free," Brennan said. He pointed to a door in the side wall. "If you would like some privacy, that goes into my personal bathroom."

Virgil stepped into the bathroom—a wood-lined cubicle that included a steam shower—wondered, in a brief fit of paranoia, if the room was bugged, and called Trane. She was in an interview room with Cohen and Hardy and stepped out to take his call. Virgil told her about his conversation with Brennan, that Hardy might benefit, possibly in a significant way, from Quill's murder.

"What are you telling me? You think Cohen might have done it?"

"I doubt that, but she could have told somebody about hooking up with Quill at midnight in the library," Virgil said. "I was told Nancy Quill could get fifteen million from the estate. Even if they peeled off only two or three, it'd certainly be worth doing."

"No kidding . . . Oh, God, I got no time. I gotta be in court. I gotta call off this negotiation and send Cohen back to jail. I gotta make sure we hold her for the full forty-eight before the bond hearing. I gotta lot of shit to do."

"You do that. And I'll go talk to McDonald's wife about the lawsuit."

"Stay in touch, Virgil. We're moving."

The Hennepin County Medical Examiner's Office was located in another fundamentally unimaginative, dirt-colored, ugly build-ing in downtown Minneapolis, which didn't bother Virgil be-cause he didn't have to look at it very often. He'd spoken to an assistant medical examiner on the ten-mile trip to Minneapolis from St. Paul, and the AME had promised to have the residue of the suicide ready to view.

The AME's name was Julia Parker, and she met him in her modest cubicle, dumped an evidence box on the desk. The evi-dence included an amber pill bottle that had once contained thirty oxycodones; the bottle's white plastic cap, which was well chewed; photos of the deathbed and the deceased in it; and au-topsy photos. Parker hadn't done the autopsy itself, which had been done by another AME who was now on a fishing trip in the Boundary Waters. "He told us if we had to reach him, we couldn't."

"How dead was he?" Virgil asked. "McDonald."

"Completely," Parker said with a hint of a smile. "The pre-scription had just been refilled, and they still had a few pills from the previous one. Mrs. McDonald said she'd consolidated them in the single bottle. As a matter of neatness, I guess."

"And he was full of this stuff?"

"Yup. At least twenty-eight or twenty-nine, maybe as many as thirty to thirty-two. That'll do it. Eighty milligrams can kill you, and he probably swallowed more than three hundred."

"Fingerprints on the pill bottle?"

"Only Mr. McDonald's. Frankly, if I was facing what he was facing, the inability to move anything but his head and with partial use of one arm, I'd do the same thing," Parker said. "I've got nothing but sympathy for the poor man."

Virgil picked up the autopsy photos. One of them showed McDonald's mouth stretched open, with a couple of tiny flecks of white plastic between his teeth.

"So he chewed through the bottle."

"Right. Mrs. McDonald had left it on a tray attached to the bed. She had no idea he could move his arm enough to reach the pills. But he did. We think he managed to bump the tray with his shoulder hard enough that the bottle fell over. Then he bumped the tray until the bottle fell off the tray and onto his arm. He grabbed it with the fingers of the other hand and pinned it to his chest, where he could reach it with his mouth. He still had good motion in his upper neck and head—he could turn it—and we think he managed to get the bottle in his mouth. He then chewed the cap until it came off, and, holding the bottle in his teeth, tipped his head back far enough to get the pills to fall into his mouth. Then he swallowed them. We also found fragments of the plastic cap in his gut."

Virgil had a lot of sympathy for McDonald, too, but the police world didn't run on sympathy, it ran on checks. He left the

Medical Examiner's Office and drove to a Walgreens drugstore, where he showed his ID to a pharmacist and was given four empty amber pill bottles with white plastic caps identical to the ones in the evidence box.

Then he sat in his truck and chewed one of them. And called Trane, who'd not yet gotten on the witness stand. "Complete clusterfuck in there," she said. "What happened with you?"

Virgil told her about his visit to the medical examiner and about the bits of white plastic in McDonald's mouth and stomach. "I went over to a Walgreens—that's where his prescription had been filled—and got some of those pill bottles and tried to chew one of them open. I stopped because I was afraid I'd break my teeth. I did get the cap ragged enough that I cut my lip twice, and probably jabbed it three or four more times, but I had a hell of a time chewing that cap without dropping it, which I did. I kept having to pick it up and put it back in my mouth, and McDonald couldn't do that."

"And . . ."

"As far as I could tell from the photos, McDonald hadn't done any damage at all to his lip. Pieces of plastic in his mouth, but no physical damage, and I don't see how that would be avoidable. Also, the bottle had only his fingerprints on it. It should have had a lot of Mrs. McDonald's prints because she was supposedly dispensing his medicine. It's almost like somebody wiped the bottle clean of hers and then printed it with his."

"Picture me weeping," Trane said. "Are you telling me that McDonald was murdered?"

"I think assisted suicide is a possibility."

"Connecting the dots, then, McDonald was either murdered by his wife or helped along to kill himself, and she then hired the

Hardy firm to represent her in a lawsuit, where they learn about Quill's financial status and realize that if he were killed and were then unable to defend himself—"

"They could make a lot of money," Virgil said. "A tub of money."

"To get him in a private place where they could do the deed, they got Hardy's other client, Cohen, to set him up. I talked to Cohen long enough to know that this was her third trip to the library. If she was familiar with the routine, she could probably have done something to the door to keep it open after Quill used his key."

"We should at least keep all that in mind," Virgil said.

"At least," Trane said. "What's your next step?"

"I'll talk to Mrs. McDonald. See if she's strong enough to lift a laptop over her head. If she killed once—"

"You, of course, see the fly in that particular ointment."

"Maybe not."

"The man who attacked your Mr. Foster: Foster says it definitely was a man, and a fairly large one. Not tall, but heavy."

"We'll call it a mugging," Virgil said.

"That's not what you were calling it before," Trane said.

"That's when I thought I had a lead," Virgil said. "Now things have gotten funkier. I will call you as soon as I know something."

"Wish I was there."

CHAPTER

SEVENTEEN

Trane had spoken to Brennan, the university's lawyer, about the lawsuit, but had never talked to McDonald. Virgil found McDonald's first name—Ruth—in the lawsuit, ran her full name through the DMV, found three Ruth McDonalds in Minneapolis and St. Paul, cross-referenced it with Frank McDonald, found three Franks, but only one common address among the six.

Virgil needed to get a sandwich before he went hunting for McDonald. He thought for a moment, then called BCA headquarters and asked for Jenkins or Shrake, the BCA's resident thugs. Shrake was there, picked up a phone, and asked, "What do you want? Wait. I know. You want me to drive to some godforsaken shithole on the edge of SoDak where somebody will shoot me in the eye with a BB gun—"

Virgil interrupted. "St. Louis Park."

"St. Louis Park?" He sounded nonplussed. St. Louis Park was an inner-ring suburb of Minneapolis. "What do I have to do?"

"Scare the shit out of a middle-class woman," Virgil said.

"Huh. Sounds like fun. What else do I get out of it?"

"I'm driving over to the Red Cow Uptown before I go find her," Virgil said. "I'll buy."

"See you there in twenty," Shrake said.

"Sounds unlikely, but I'll wait."

Virgil was sitting on the street down from the Red Cow Uptown, chatting with Frankie on his cell phone, when Shrake pulled up beside him, held up a wrist with a Rolex on it, tapped the watch face twice, and went up the street and around a corner. He was walking back a minute later, debonair in a summer-weight gray wool suit, white shirt, and shiny blue silk tie. Virgil caught him at the door of the Red Cow.

"I didn't understand the watch signal," Virgil said.

"Twenty minutes on the dot," Shrake explained. "I had to do a little shake 'n' bake on 94. There might be an eighteen-wheeler up in the weeds."

Shrake was a large man with a complicated nose set over too-white implanted teeth—replacements for teeth he'd broken or had knocked out over the years. The last time he'd worked a major case with Virgil, he'd been grazed with a broadhead arrow. The arrow left a foot-long scar between his shoulder blades that Shrake claimed had tightened up his golf swing and cut three strokes off his handicap.

"I made the mistake of saying that out loud," Shrake said, as they took a table. "If I'd kept my mouth shut, and my old handicap, I'd have made a thousand bucks by now."

"I feel sorry for you not being able to cheat," Virgil said. He handed Shrake a menu. "Get what you want, I'm going with the Double Barrel."

Virgil told him all about the Quill case—everything he had. Shrake had been following the story in the papers but hadn't heard anything else, other than that Margaret Trane was working the case. "Trane and I had a thing once, back when we were young."

"I'm not sure I want to hear this," Virgil said.

"I'm not going to tell you anything else . . . other than the fact that when you got out of Maggie Trane's bed, you definitely knew you'd been in bed with Maggie Trane. I lost about five pounds that first night."

"She's married now," Virgil said. "A doctor."

"I know. He's a fourteen handicap out at Edina."

"Jesus, Shrake, your mind is like a golf garbage dump."

"Golf is the only thing in there that's not garbage," Shrake said. "Tell me again about chewing up those pill bottle caps . . . You say McDonald had fragments in his mouth?"

"Fragments, but no cuts on his lip. Could be murder, could be assisted suicide, but I don't think he swallowed the pills on his own."

"Why didn't the medical examiner catch it?" Shrake asked.

"Probably because they didn't have anyone dumb enough to chew on a pill bottle," Virgil said. He pulled at his lower lip and it hurt. "I cut the heck out of myself and never even got the cap off."

"Poor baby."

As they were finishing lunch, Virgil got a call from an unknown number.

"Mr. Flowers?" A woman's voice, high and shaky. "Officer Flowers?"

"Yes?"

"This is Genevieve O'Hara. You interviewed me about Dr. Quill."

"Yes, of course," Virgil said.

"I wanted to tell you my mother died yesterday afternoon."

"I'm sorry. I hope she went peacefully," Virgil said.

"Well, of course she was heavily drugged, so I suppose it was peaceful as it could be. But that's neither here nor there. I was actually calling you about Dr. Quill."

"Yes?"

"After you were here . . . Well, not right after, I didn't think of it until the next day but didn't call because I've been so preoccupied with Mother . . . Well, this morning I saw your card and thought I'd better call . . . I didn't steal those maps, by the way," she said.

"I believe you," Virgil said, though he didn't. He was curious about where the conversation was going.

"Thank you. Last winter, Mother was still conscious and getting around, and I remember telling her about this . . . I was working up on the second floor at the Wilson, where Dr. Quill's carrel was, and I saw this man. He was looking at books in the stacks. You know how sometimes you can watch a child doing something and you know he's only pretending to do it? Like, he's pretending to look at your silverware but he's really thinking about stealing a cookie?"

"I do understand the concept," Virgil said. "A bad guy goes into a gas station to buy a candy bar, but he's looking at the cash register and counting the clerks."

"That's right," O'Hara said. "Like that. I got that feeling about this man. That he was not interested in the books, that he was up to something else. I would occasionally see it with a student who was planning to steal a book. I asked this man if I could help him, but he said no, and a couple of minutes later I saw him heading out the door. Then, a week later, I saw him near the carrels again. Have you been up there?"

"Yes."

"You know how the carrels are lined up along that outer wall? He was walking along there, slowly. I got the feeling he was up to something again. Both times, he was right by Dr. Quill's carrel."

O'Hara said the man was white, of medium height, balding but with reddish brown hair pulled back in a short, brushy pony- tail. "He wasn't fat, but I'd say he was a little porky. He had a porky face. A red face, like a drinker. Small eyes. He was a smoker, I could smell it on him. When he saw me the second time, he sped up and walked away and went down the stairs. I think he recog- nized me from the first time and wanted to get out of there."

"Miz O'Hara, thank you. This could be important. I will come by to interview you again. I'd like to record this."

"I'm afraid I won't be here for a while. I'm leaving in a few minutes for Eau Claire. Mother was registered ahead of time with the county medical examiner, so the body was taken di- rectly to the funeral home and is being transferred to Eau Claire this afternoon for burial. I have to be there to make arrange- ments."

"Okay. You said this was last winter when you saw him?"

"Or early spring—not later than March. I wasn't focused on it at the time. I will think about it some more to see if I can recall exactly when it was."

"Call me as soon as you get back from Eau Claire."

"I will."

"Something good?" Shrake asked.

"Could be," Virgil said. He slipped a couple of French fries off Shrake's plate. "Somebody seen hanging around Quill's carrel up at the library. But quite a while ago. Don't know if it's connected. Anyway, let's go talk to McDonald."

McDonald lived in a tree-shaded rambler in St. Louis Park, which was good because the day was both hot and humid. They'd driven over in their separate vehicles, left them at the curb, and as they walked up the driveway, Shrake asked, "If she's here, which I doubt, you wanna go in hard?"

"Semi-hard," Virgil said.

"Last time I heard that phrase, I was in bed with a woman from the county recorder's office," Shrake said.

"I didn't want to hear about Trane sex, and I don't want to hear about county recorder sex," Virgil said. "Push the fuckin' doorbell."

People were rarely home when the cops pushed their bells for the very good reason that they were at work, unless they were the kind that didn't work. McDonald, as it turned out, did work, but as a nurse on the three-to-eleven shift at the Hennepin County Medical Center.

She came to the door in her white nurse's uniform, wrinkles of concern across her otherwise smooth forehead. She was a bit overweight, with a round face, dark hair cut short, and dark brown eyes. Virgil held up his ID, and said, "Mrs. McDonald, we're agents of the Bureau of Criminal Apprehension and we're investigating the death of your husband, Frank. We have a few questions for you."

She looked from Virgil to Shrake and then back to Virgil. "But . . . that's all over with. Frank died almost a year ago."

"It's not quite over with," Virgil said. "May we come in?"

"Well . . . Could you wait here for a couple of moments while I make a phone call?"

Shrake said, "Don't run away, Ruth. Make your call."

"I'm not going to . . . Don't be stupid."

She closed the door, and Virgil said to Shrake, "Yeah, don't be stupid."

"Maybe I ought to watch the back door," Shrake said. Virgil gave him a look, and Shrake said, "Okay, maybe not."

Virgil said, "I'm going to stand in the shade."

"Good idea."

They were standing in the shade of McDonald's dwarf maple when a St. Louis Park cop car slid to the curb behind Virgil's Tahoe.

Shrake: "She called a fuckin' cop on us. Can you believe that?"

"On you," Virgil said. "Nobody calls the cops on me because I'm not that kind of guy."

The cop got out of his car, and Virgil walked over to him, holding his ID out in front of him.

"BCA. Did McDonald call you?"

The cop looked at Virgil's ID, then looked at Shrake, and asked Virgil, "Who's the mook?"

Shrake said, "Hey, I thought that was you. Still dating fourteen-year-olds?"

"She was twenty-three," the cop said. "What I didn't know was, she wasn't entirely divorced."

"So you guys know each other and we're good?" Virgil asked.

The cop waved at him. "Yeah, you're good. I'll call in and tell them to cancel the SWAT team."

Before he did, the cop knocked on McDonald's door, and, when she opened it, he told her that Virgil and Shrake were legit. "Catch you later," he said to Shrake.

When the cop was back in his car, Virgil said, "You never introduced us."

"Couldn't remember his name, but he claims he's a nine handicap," Shrake said. He showed his overly white teeth to McDonald. "We need to talk. Right now."

They sat in the living room, McDonald perched on a couch, Shrake in a La-Z-Boy, Virgil sitting on a kitchen chair. McDonald said, "Everything is settled, the estate—"

"We're looking at a murder—the murder of Professor Quill, whom you know, at the University of Minnesota, almost three weeks ago, now. That murder has some ties back to the death of your husband," Virgil told her.

"What!"

"When we looked at your husband's death," Shrake said, stopping momentarily to probe his teeth with a silver toothpick, which had both McDonald and Virgil leaning toward him, waiting, "we discovered some . . . unusual aspects . . . So, Mrs. McDonald, did you murder your husband?"

"What!"

"Did you—"

"No! Are you crazy? I loved Frank! I'm a nurse, I'd never . . ."

Virgil, quiet and gentle: "Did you help him with his pain pills?"

"Of course. Every four hours. I'm very professional . . ."

"Yeah, right," Shrake said. "Then how come there were none of your fingerprints on the bottle? It's like it was wiped clean before your husband supposedly picked it up."

She started to blubber, then stood up, her arms straight down at her sides, and said, "I'm calling my lawyer."

"Jones or Hardy?" Virgil asked.

"Mr. Jones. You two get out of here. Go back out. I want to talk to Mr. Jones in private."

"Don't run away," Shrake said, grinning at her, "'cause we'll getcha."

They went back to stand under the maple tree, and, five minutes later, McDonald came out of the house and trudged across the yard and handed her cell phone to Virgil. "Mr. Jones wants to talk to you."

Virgil took the cell, and said, "This is Virgil Flowers, Minnesota Bureau of Criminal Apprehension."

"What do you think you're doing, Flowers?" the attorney demanded. "The medical examiner's report found that Frank McDonald died by suicide. What the hell is going on over there?"

"The report was incomplete," Virgil said. "We're working to enhance it."

"Enhance it? What are you talking about? Who put you up to this?"

"Listen," Virgil said. "We're probably going to take Mrs. Mc-Donald over to the BCA to properly interview her. She'll want a lawyer with her. Would that be you?"

"Take her with you?" Jones was shouting now. "That's absurd. And abusive. I'll be filing a very serious complaint with—"

Virgil overrode him. "We need to ask her some questions about the murder of Barthelemy Quill. I believe your firm also represents the woman who was with Dr. Quill when he was murdered."

"What? What are you talking about?"

"Ask your boss."

Long silence, then: "Flowers? You stay right where you're at. I'm fifteen minutes away, and I'm coming. Let me talk to Ruth."

Virgil passed the phone back to McDonald, who listened for a moment, then clicked it off, and said to Virgil, "He says I shouldn't answer any questions until he gets here."

"How about one question?" Shrake said. "Can we go back inside? It's too hot to be standing out here. I'm afraid a robin is gonna shit in my hair."

She said, "No," and half jogged back to the house, arms stiff at her sides once again.

Virgil moved deeper into the shade, and said, "I'm glad I wasn't dumb enough to wear a suit and tie."

Shrake yawned.

Virgil: "Listen, You did okay with her, but now let's dial it back to a seven."

"That's where I was, a seven," Shrake said. "You ain't never seen my eleven."

"Okay, take it back to three. I don't want Internal Affairs taking up residence in my shorts."

A lawyer arrived, but it wasn't Jones, it was Hardy. He jumped out of his green Range Rover, looked at Virgil as though he couldn't believe his eyes, then strode across the lawn, and Virgil said, "Mr. Hardy," and Shrake said, "Watch your hair. There's a robin up in the tree that's been trying to shit in ours."

Hardy looked up in the tree for a second, wiped his hand across the top of his head, then turned back to Virgil, and asked, "What are you doing here?"

"Waiting for Mrs. McDonald's attorney of record. As a courtesy. Before we take her in."

"A courtesy? Take her in? For what? And, by the way, I'm one of her attorneys of record. In addition to Robin Jones."

"We find that interesting," Virgil said. "And that's what we want to talk to Mrs. McDonald about. You guys filed a nuisance suit against the university, which is prepared to take you on, with one of the smartest and most admired men in the Cities ready to testify that everything you claim is bullshit. Then it turns out that one of your clients lures—"

"She didn't lure anybody!" Hardy shouted. "They were lovers."

Shrake snorted. "A famous rich doctor is in love with a hooker when he could date any one of a thousand single women in the Twin Cities for free? Tell me another one."

Virgil rode over both of them. "Lures him into the library, where he's killed and therefore can no longer testify in your lawsuit, which Robin Jones has said he might split and sue Quill's estate separately? Did I get that right?"

"No. It's like you're taking crazy pills."

Another car arrived, a Mercedes SL550 with its hard top down, and Hardy said, "Here's Robin."

The top on the Mercedes started up, and Shrake said to Hardy, "You know those billboards of yours? 'Call me Lare'?"

"What?"

"You ought to call yourself Batman since your sidekick's named Robin. You could put—"

"You know how many times I've heard that joke?" Hardy asked. "About a million. You should be embarrassed."

Shrake shrugged, but in fact he was. Nothing like being the millionth guy to tell a bad joke.

Jones got out of the car and hurried over, a briefcase under his arm. Virgil pegged him to be in his early thirties, with a well-tailored light blue summer suit that was too expensive for his age. You tended to look at him, with his car and his suit, and think, Asshat. He nodded at Hardy, and said, "Glad you could make it. I wanted to talk to you before I file a criminal complaint against these two."

Shrake yawned again and scratched his ribs.

Jones to Virgil: "You're Flowers? That's the most disrespectful outfit I've ever seen on a cop. A poetry shirt? They'll be hearing about that, too."

Virgil looked down at his shirt; it took a minute, but then he tumbled: Poe. Jones must have thought that Edgar Allan's first name was Larkin. It made him smile.

"You wanna go inside?" Shrake asked. "I'm sweating like a blind lesbian in a sushi bar."

"Hey! I don't want to hear that misogynistic kinda talk. And before we go inside, I want to tell you you're not taking Mrs. McDonald anywhere," Jones said. "Not to the BCA, not to Hennepin . . ."

Virgil said to Hardy, "Robin's giving me a sharp pain in the ass."

"That's another count," Jones sputtered. "That's another—"

"Shut up, Robin," Hardy said.

They went inside and found Ruth McDonald in the La-Z-Boy with the leg support down; she was huddled in like it was a cave, protecting herself from the wildlife.

She raised her head, and said to Virgil, "I did not kill my husband."

Jones blanched. "What!" He turned to Virgil, "Did you accuse this woman—"

"Shut up, Robin," Virgil said. He turned back to McDonald, and said, "We want to hear your story before we decide what to do. I can tell you, my colleague and I have handled a lot of suspicious death cases, and this is one of them. I need to hear the sequence of events the day he died, and more about his physical condition. From what I've heard, it seems almost impossible that he could have done what you told the medical examiner."

"He did it because he was desperate," Jones said.

Virgil to Jones: "We're talking to Mrs. McDonald. You can say 'Answer that' or 'Don't answer that,' but nothing else. You can't answer for her."

"That's bullshit."

Virgil to Shrake: "You got your cuffs?"

"Sure do."

Hardy: "Whoa! Whoa! Whoa! . . . Robin, shut up. And stay shut up."

Virgil said, "Thank you. Now, it seems impossible—"

"It was because he was desperate. Robin is exactly right," McDonald said. "He was in pain. The drugs couldn't stop it without his mind getting all fogged up. Before the operation, he didn't have much pain."

"But he couldn't move at all, as I understand it," Virgil said.

"He could move a little. His thumb and forefinger, some muscles in his upper arm. After the operation, he could move more, but not enough to mean anything to him. And the pain was on top of the disappointment," McDonald said. "Then, when they could see the operation hadn't worked, Quill and his pals just let him go. 'Sorry, we've done everything we can, have a nice life.' The criminals."

She began to cry. Hardy moved over to her and patted her shoulder.

"Was there anybody around the house that day?" Virgil asked.

Hardy handed her a tissue from a pocket pack and she took it, wiped her eyes, blew her nose, and said, "No, nobody. Mr. Jones left, and I told Frank I was going to run to the store and I'd be right back."

Shrake: "Wait. Mr. Jones was here?"

They all looked at Jones. Jones shook his head, and said, "I left well before Mrs. McDonald left for the store."

"How do you know when she left for the store?" Virgil asked.

"Because we talked about it," Jones snapped.

"Did you have a key to the house?"

"No, of course not. I'm her lawyer, not a close personal friend. I didn't have any need for a key."

Virgil said, "Huh."

"What's that supposed to mean?"

"Well, it just keeps getting more interesting," Virgil said.

Shake said, "I'm with you, big boy. This is getting fascinating." To Jones: "Exactly what percentage do you get if you win this lawsuit? Thirty?"

"Completely irrelevant," Jones said.

Shrake asked Hardy, "What do you think? Was the question 'completely irrelevant'?"

Hardy's eyebrows went up, the corners of his mouth went down. "Maybe not completely irrelevant, but if you're suggesting that Robin came back here and . . . attacked . . . Mr. McDonald, then you're way out of line. The question may not have been irrelevant, but the answer is clear: he, or our firm, would get paid whether or not Frank died. Look, Frank could talk perfectly well. If we wanted to get a big award, we would want nothing more than to be able to wheel Frank into the courtroom to testify. To talk about his pain and the promises that Quill made. We certainly wouldn't want anything to happen to him. His death by suicide weakened our case, it didn't make it stronger."

"But the death of Dr. Quill did," Virgil said.

They argued about that for a few minutes, then Hardy said, "Believe what you want to believe, but I'll tell you—and this is the truth—I represent Abby Cohen and Mrs. McDonald, and they were both involved with Dr. Quill, in vastly different ways, in what is a gigantic, pluperfect coincidence."

"It never occurred to you last night?"

"Of course it did, but not before then," Hardy said. "Abby never told me that she'd been with Quill. I had no idea. Now things are fucked up. I dunno. I'd already decided I'd have to sign off as counsel to Abby. I was planning to talk to another guy this morning about taking over the case—not somebody at my firm—and I'm probably going to wind up paying him out of my own pocket."

———

When they finished working through it all, Virgil said to McDonald, "We're not going to take you in to question you. Somebody from the BCA or the St. Louis Park Police Department will want to have further conversations with you. Please don't leave town, go on vacation, without telling Agent Shrake. He will give you a business card—"

"I'm not going anyplace anytime soon," she said.

"Good. But should your plans change, notify Agent Shrake," Virgil said. "We'll leave it to you to further notify Mr. Hardy or Mr. Jones should we need to continue our interviews."

"I don't see," Jones began, "what you could possibly hope to achieve—"

"Shut up, Robin," Hardy said. And to Virgil: "We're good with that. Frank McDonald committed suicide. Remember this: there is a huge coincidence here and it's meaningless. If you want to find out who killed Quill, you'd do well to keep that in mind."

Virgil followed Shrake out the door but hesitated before closing it, and he heard Jones say to Hardy, "I resent that 'Shut up, Robin' shit, by the way."

Hardy said, "Something for you to think about, Robin. You're a civil lawyer, you're not a criminal lawyer. Those guys are cops. They know what they're doing and you don't. So please, shut the fuck up . . . Ruth, sorry about the language."

Virgil went on down the steps behind Shrake.

EIGHTEEN

Before they went to their separate vehicles, Shrake said, "I dunno, I might have taken her in, to ramp up the stress. To see what would come out of that."

"I thought about it, but the lawyers are all over us—they won't let her say a thing. And the chances of a conviction are zilch unless she admits it," Virgil said. "We'd be wasting our time. I'd like a good close look at Jones, though. I expect your thirty percent guess was close to the mark."

"Or more. This guy who attacked your Army guy, Foster . . . Would Jones fit?"

"Not real well. Foster's not tall, and he said the attacker was his height, but stocky," Virgil said. "Jones might be too tall, and he's not especially stocky."

"Okay. You want my opinion, I've got a couple," Shrake said.

"Shoot."

"I wouldn't be surprised if McDonald killed her husband, or at least helped him kill himself. In fact, I'd say it's likely. One thing

I've noticed about nurses is, they see so much death that it no longer affects them much. It's not that they're hard. It's that death comes to seem like an natural, ordinary thing. She could very well have thought that she was doing him a favor. A loving favor. No thought of money, which might have come later. But—and it's a big 'but'—I doubt that she would have anything to do with the murder of Quill. If Jones killed Quill, he never would have told McDonald what he was going to do. There wouldn't be a conspiracy that you could break down."

"I agree," Virgil said. "Next opinion."

"About Quill. If the killer was planning to murder Quill, why didn't he have a better weapon? You think he might have been hit with his own computer? Why? Why would anyone do that? It couldn't have been planned that way. So either he wasn't hit with a computer or the whole encounter was an accident. From what you told me, I think you have more to learn from the hooker. The small details. Like, the exact circumstances of the attack. Was Quill ambushed, was it planned? Or did he and the killer stumble onto each other? The killer couldn't have known about the hooker because he never looked for her."

"Anything else?"

"What do you think about Foster? Was it a mugging? Or was the attack involved with the Quill murder?"

"Don't think it was a mugging."

"If it wasn't a mugging, then either it was involved with the Quill murder or he's involved in something else dangerous that he's not telling you about. That seems unlikely, a grad student. Maybe you should check his Army record, see what kind of a discharge he got. But probably that attack is somehow related to Quill. In my humble opinion."

"I'll buy it all," Virgil said. "You're right about all of it. I need to talk to our hooker. I'll call Trane and see if we can get together."

Shrake headed back to St. Paul.

Virgil called Trane, filled her in on the McDonald interview, and asked about a new interview with Cohen. The trial that Trane was attending was right across the street from the jail where Cohen was being held.

"How long would you need to talk with her?" Trane asked.

"If she cooperates, ten minutes."

"I'll be out of here later this afternoon. I'm not sure about the time. What if we pick a time—like, five o'clock? I'll be out of here for sure by then. We'd have to call Hardy, tell him what we want to do," Trane said.

"I'm parked right behind him," Virgil said. "I'll grab him when he leaves McDonald's."

"Worth a try," Trane said. "I want to talk to her about the cocaine at Quill's house, too."

As she said that, Hardy and Jones walked out of McDonald's house and started down the front walk to their cars. Virgil said to Trane, "Here's Hardy. I'll call you back in five minutes."

He got Hardy and made the offer. "There's some possibility that Abby Cohen killed Quill, but I also have some reasons to think that she didn't. What we need from her is ten minutes of honesty. I don't care about the prostitution charge, and neither does Trane. If she cooperates, I can talk Trane, and whatever county attorney's involved, into cutting her loose. She might have to testify in a trial, but we wouldn't necessarily want to hit her with all the other stuff . . . If she cooperates."

"If you can do that, I'll recommend that she goes along," Hardy said. "How long before you know?"

"Trane would have to make some phone calls."

"We'd want some paper on it," Hardy said.

"That's why she'd make some phone calls. We'd like to get it done as soon as we can."

"I've got a thing I've got to do early this evening, I can't get out of it, but I'm good any time before six," Hardy said.

Virgil called Trane, and Trane said, "All right. Let's say we meet in my office at five o'clock and walk over to the jail."

Virgil passed the word to Hardy, who agreed to meet them at the Homicide office unless Virgil or Trane called it off.

Virgil had three hours before he had to be in Minneapolis, so he fought the afternoon traffic across the Cities to St. Paul, to Regions Hospital, where he found Terry Foster trying to read a newspaper.

"This is awful," Foster said from his bed. "I'm developing a deep sympathy for the physically handicapped." He dropped the paper, which landed out of reach on his stomach, and asked, "What's up?"

"Who in the hell beat you up?"

They spent forty-five minutes digging around the problem. Foster swore that he was not involved in anything that could get him attacked. "I have nothing to do here but think about it," he said. "I'm not dumb, but I can't get anywhere. You'd know better than me, but I'd think if somebody gets murdered, it has to be for some big, important reason, right?"

"Most of the time, yes. But, you know, you get these little

ratshit murders where somebody didn't respect somebody else or somebody tried to rip off somebody's else's weed," Virgil said. "Murders for a dollar forty-two."

"I didn't do any of that. The guy had to be after me, it wasn't random. I'm sure of that now after thinking about it for two hundred hours. He must've known where my parking place was . . . I keep thinking it had to be because I was poking around, but I've been over every possibility. Every word. I get nothing. Except . . ."

"What?"

"That computer. Somebody kills Barthelemy Quill, it's a big deal. I keep thinking about that computer. There had to be something on it. That was a thing in Iraq and Syria—you had guys running around with laptops, and some of them had really heavy shit on them. Top secret shit. Maybe that was the deal here. Maybe . . . Maybe if you went to his lab and looked at the computers there you could find some talk back and forth with the library computer that would give you a hint."

"Not bad," Virgil said. "The Minneapolis Crime Scene guys have his home computer. I'll spend some time with it."

"Gotta be the laptop. That's all I can see as a motive . . . This woman he was with, it couldn't be jealousy . . ."

Virgil shook his head. "She was for sale, and Quill knew it. It wasn't jealousy. We were thinking that maybe she let somebody in to take pictures for blackmail reasons . . . Or maybe a robbery . . . Except he had a lot of cash on him and it wasn't touched . . ."

"Well, why couldn't it still be that? Didn't mean to kill him but did, and ran in a panic?"

Virgil grimaced. "It could be. But it doesn't feel right . . . Just doesn't feel right . . ."

Before he left, Virgil picked up the newspaper lying on Foster's stomach and helped him pinch it between his suspended hands. "How much longer?"

"Don't know, exactly. Less than a week, I hope. They're telling me six to eight weeks before the bones completely knit . . . I'm a fuckin' mess," Foster said. "If that asshole comes back, if he gets in here, I'm helpless."

"You could call for help," Virgil said.

"Yeah, there's that," Foster said. "And I will. I do already."

Outside in the Tahoe, Virgil checked his watch: he still had almost two hours before the meeting at Trane's office and he was only fifteen or twenty minutes from the university. He could make a quick stop at Quill's lab to ask a couple of questions.

He left the Tahoe in a university parking structure and walked over to the lab; there were only three people inside: two women researchers and the lab director, Carl Anderson. He got them together, and said to Anderson, "The last time I talked to you, you convinced me that Quill couldn't be doing something on the sly because there are too many people involved."

"That's correct," Anderson said, and the two women nodded in agreement.

"But that's with the surgical procedures. Here's the thing: he was over at the library in a secret space that even the authorities— university authorities, cops, whoever—would have a hard time spotting. The library knew he was there, and some of you folks knew, but it was not obvious. If the FBI had raided him, they could miss it. Or if they found it, it might take a while. Everybody agree?"

They all agreed, and one of the women, whose name was Ann-something, said, "I work here, and I didn't know about it."

"Okay. What I'm asking is, what could he do with an extraordinarily fast laptop that he would want to keep in a secret place and that would have something on it that would be worth killing for? That has to do with his research?"

The three looked at one another and simultaneously shrugged.

Virgil: "Goddamnit, people, I'm asking for speculation here, not evidence, not proof."

The second woman, who was named Rosalind-something, said, "Okay. Suppose he detected something in our lab results that the rest of us haven't seen. We've been working on microinsertion of adipose-tissue-derived stem cells into traumatically damaged spinal cords. Now, if he spotted something significant, that could be valuable to a biology-based medical company."

Anderson said, "But then you have to ask, what would Barth have gotten out of it? A, money. But he already had more money that he needed and gave a lot of it away. B, anonymity for an important scientific discovery. But one thing Barth was known for, that pissed off a lot of people, was that he always wanted credit. He wanted the full credit for what came out of the lab. His name always came first on the papers."

Rosalind leaned back into the conversation. "How about this? What if he was using the machine to review the work of other teams and he didn't want anyone to know about it? He's always said there was a lot of bad science going on. What if he found a whopper in our area? A paper that got something wrong, maybe committed outright fraud, and he was using his machine to work through the numbers and demonstrate that? That might be worth killing for."

Ann nodded. "Never thought of that. You know, with these

new online papers, the open publication business, there's a lot of bad science. If he found something and was going back and forth with that person, you might have somebody who needed to both get rid of Dr. Quill and get ahold of the laptop."

"How would they even know about the laptop?" Virgil asked. "Or where it was?"

"We're not computer people, but I think a real hacker could do that," Ann said.

Rosalind said, "How about this? He found something bad and got some hacker at the university to access that lab's computer system. Once he knew how to get in, he could get in anytime. That's just typing. So he's sneaking around in there, pulling out stuff, and the other lab spots him and calls in some security service to find out who's hacking them. They find out where the computer is and go after it."

They all looked at one another, and then Ann said, "I see one big problem with that, from your perspective."

"Tell me," Virgil said.

"If the computer's in the river, and Dr. Quill is dead, and you don't have any other evidence, DNA, fingerprints—any of that— how would you ever find out what was going on and who was involved? I think you'd be, you know, screwed."

"Wish you hadn't said that," Virgil said. Then, "A woman who works in the library told me she'd seen a man hanging around Dr. Quill's carrel last winter. Had kind of brownish red hair, a little porky, a ponytail . . ."

Rosalind put her fingers to her lips, turned to Anderson, and said, "Boyd Nash."

Anderson leaned back in his chair as if slapped. "Oh . . . Let's . . . Ah, Jesus . . ."

Virgil registered the name but couldn't remember exactly where he'd seen it. "Who's Boyd Nash?"

"He's this guy. You know, those guys who drive around the country looking for antiques they can buy cheap? They're called pickers?"

"Antiques?" Virgil said. "I don't—"

"Nash is like a picker, but he doesn't pick antiques, he picks scientific ideas. He's a giant asshole."

"And a creep," Rosalind said. "He dyes his hair so it's auburn, but he's got all this furry white hair coming out of his ears."

Virgil: "Wait a minute. He does something with patents? Did you guys tell Sergeant Trane about him?"

"I might have mentioned him in passing," Anderson said. "I don't have any good reason to think he'd hurt Barth, but he's such a greedy, criminal pissant."

Rosalind: "He did patent trolling. The most unethical . . . I don't think he still does it, he got in some kind of trouble."

"Tell me about patent trolling. Sergeant Trane mentioned it, but I don't remember the details," Virgil said.

"Nash has some kind of technical or scientific background. He'd look for companies or labs that were doing research toward a certain product. Something that can be monetized. What he did was, he'd figure out what must be part of that product when it's finally produced."

"Give me an example," Virgil said.

Ann jumped in. "Supposed you knew Apple was doing research on cell phones, so you draw up plans for a tiny microphone, or speaker, because you know the phone will have to have those things. Then you say your tiny speakers are to be used in cell phones and you patent them without any research at all," she said. "When the iPhone comes out, you sue, claiming it infringes on your crappy patent. Usually, it's a bunch of unethical lawyers, and all they have going for themselves is the willingness to sue forever and be a nuisance until the company they're suing finally buys them off."

"Okay. Trane told me about this guy. But you don't think he's still doing that?"

Anderson said, "I heard—I don't know where—that he moved over to industrial spying. Instead of faking patents, he's looking for people willing to sell out original research. Real research. Go to Motorola and figure out what they were doing with phones and then try to peddle that information to Apple."

Ann said, "I heard—I don't know if it's true—that some witness got caught lying in court about one of his patent trolls, and it looked like he could be in serious trouble, and so could the law firm he was working with. Subornation of perjury or something."

"I heard that he and the law firm broke up, and that's when he went to industrial spying," Anderson added.

"And he might have approached somebody at this lab?"

"Not Barth, but a couple of surgeons over at the med school who worked with us. They told him to take a hike and reported Nash to the university," Anderson said. "The guy lives here in the Minneapolis area, and he's been known to snoop around Medtronic, Boston Scientific, 3M, St. Jude, and a whole bunch of hearing aid companies. Either Medtronic or Boston Scientific actually got a restraining order against him, is what I hear."

"Any hint that he might be violent?" Virgil asked.

"Yes!" Rosalind said. "He was arrested for assault after he was caught trespassing somewhere. I remember seeing it in the *Star*

Tribune. I don't remember where he was trespassing, but I remember the story."

"The problem with Nash is, he has an alibi," Virgil said. "If I'm remembering right, he was at a convention that night. There were several people who were willing to back him up on that."

"Then he probably did it for sure," Anderson said, leaning toward Virgil, a light in his eyes. "One thing I remember Barth telling me about him is that he always has an alibi. He never moves without an alibi. He's been arrested at least a couple of times, but always had a story. Wasn't there, didn't do it. Wasn't there when somebody talked directly to him. Barth and I were laughing about it. I was anyway."

"Interesting," Virgil said. "Boyd Nash."

"That's him," Rosalind said. "I got a little chill when I thought of him. I think he could be something."

Back across the river again in Minneapolis, Virgil found Trane, Cohen, Hardy, and a Hennepin County assistant attorney named Harmon Watts in an interview room at the jail. Virgil pulled Trane out—"We only need one minute"—and in the hallway told her about Boyd Nash.

"You think it could be something?"

"The lab people thought it was something," Virgil said. "I think we've got to take a serious look at him."

Back in the interview room, Watts asked, "What's the history here?"

Virgil said, "You guys have to handle the details, I'm here as

Maggie's assistant. But I proposed to Mr. Hardy that we weren't so much interested in the various possible charges against Miz Cohen as we are in getting complete cooperation from her."

"How will you know if you're getting complete cooperation?" Watts asked.

"Because if we don't think we're getting it, we walk away and refile," Trane said.

"I'm going to need a false arrest waiver," Watts said.

"We're okay with that," Hardy said.

Cohen said, "Wait. False arrest? Can we sue them for this?"

"Not really," Hardy said.

Watts: "If you don't sign the waiver, we don't drop the charges and you go to jail. 'Cause it wasn't a false arrest, but we don't want you coming back later saying that it was."

Hardy: "She'll sign."

And so on and so forth. Cohen signed, Watts picked up the paper, said, "Bless you all," and left.

Virgil and Trane started pushing Cohen. She and Quill had made three separate trips to the library, all in the middle of the night. "An adventure," she said, which Quill seemed to enjoy. "I wasn't all that big on it because that yoga mat wasn't thick enough and it hurt my back and ass," she added.

Quill paid her five hundred dollars per trip.

They'd met on Tinder, first hooking up in Dinkytown. She knew he was well-off because of the car, but she hadn't known his real name. She'd asked, and he told her it was Alex Nolan. She'd later tried to look him up on the internet, and while she'd found lots of Alex Nolans, none of them seemed to be the man she was having sex with. She hadn't learned his real name until she'd seen a TV news story about his murder.

"So you did know about it," Trane said. "In your apartment you told us—"

"She may have misspoken," Hardy said. "Hardly a major issue."

Cohen admitted that she knew that Quill must have been the man who'd taken her to the library, but said she was afraid to talk to the police. "I didn't see how anything good could come from that. I mean, I didn't know anything. And, you know, with my job and all, I'd be an easy one to pin it on."

They took her through a second-by-second recital of their approach to the library. They'd met at a bar in Dinkytown, had walked across the campus, then across the footbridge, past a couple of dormitories, scouting the Wilson Library for lights.

"We saw some kids outside the dorms, around the dorms, but there was never anybody around that library. I mean, this was midnight," she said. "The first two times, it was even later—like, one o'clock."

Quill had a key. They entered the library, listened for sounds, heard none, then Quill took her hand and led her up a flight of steps to the second floor. His carrel was behind some high book stacks, and as they got close, they saw a light.

"I think it was an iPhone light. Alex—I mean, Dr. Quill—was holding my hand going up the stairs, but then we saw the light."

Quill dropped her hand and whispered for her to stay where she was. She didn't. She hid behind one of the tall bookshelves on the other side of the aisle from the shelves near the carrel. She heard Quill say something but wasn't sure exactly what it was but thought he said he was calling the police. "I think I heard that word 'police.'"

"Do you think they just ran into each other? Or was the killer waiting for Dr. Quill?" Virgil asked.

"Oh, I don't know." She squinted at the ceiling. "You know, why would he have the light on if he was trying to sneak? I think maybe it *was* an accident, that they ran into each other."

Virgil: "Do you think the person, whoever it was, was already in the carrel when you got there?"

"Oh, yeah, I think so. Something else, you know, that I just thought of: I think Dr. Quill knew the person. Recognized him. I don't know what he said, but the tone of his voice, it was like he knew him."

"Maybe somebody from his lab?" Trane suggested.

"I don't know. I'm not even sure about it. But when I think back, I think he recognized him. Knew him."

She heard the struggle, heard the door close, thought she heard keys, but remained huddled behind the shelves where she thought she wasn't visible. When the light headed toward the stairs, she didn't look at it, or the man who carried it, because she was afraid he'd see her eyes. "I kept my head down. So I never saw this other person."

Virgil asked about drugs. "I'm not going to hassle you about it, but I need to know. Do you use coke?"

"I've tried it," she admitted. "The guy buys it and wants to party, you know? I don't buy it myself. It's nice, but it's expensive."

"Did you ever give any to Quill?"

"Oh, no. He never mentioned drugs to me. You know, he was intense about the sex. He even got me off once, which never happens, but he did it because he was so into it. But as far as I know, he wasn't into dope."

They went over the story twice more, but nothing changed.

Cohen had never been to Quill's house, didn't know he was a doctor. "I thought he was probably a finance guy. He acted like a finance guy. Except he didn't fuck like a finance guy. He knew how to get it on. If you know what I mean."

In the end, Trane said she'd go with Hardy to walk Cohen through the release procedures, which Watts had already approved. Virgil told Trane about talking to Foster and Foster's suggestion that there must be something important on the missing laptop.

"Foster's a smart guy, and he thinks the computer is the key, which would fit with this Boyd Nash character. When you think about it, if Nash is an industrial spy, it'd fit with the CD recording, too—an attempt at blackmail. Maybe he found out about the laptop but didn't know Quill was . . . comforting . . . Miz Cohen."

"'Comforting,'" Trane repeated. "Nice."

"You want to take Nash or should I?" Virgil asked.

"You found him, you take him. I'll take a look at Hardy's partner, this Jones guy. I'm interested in that whole sequence of events. Remember, Quill might not have practiced medicine, but he *was* an M.D. If he spotted that whole pill bottle problem—the one you spotted—and started mooting around the idea that Frank McDonald was murdered . . ."

Virgil concurred, and asked, "You want to look at my cut lip?"

"No, I believe you. But . . ."

"What?"

"Until you showed up, I was running a nice logical investigation. Somehow, Flowers, you got me up to my hips in weird shit. How'd you do that?"

NINETEEN

Virgil started his run at Boyd Nash by going back to Trane's desk at Minneapolis Homicide. He got Nash's records from the DMV. Both his past and current driver's licenses showed the same address. Virgil checked the address with the street view on Google Earth and found himself looking at a rambling ranch-style house, of white stone and natural wood, in the city of Edina, south of Minneapolis. A quick trip out to Zillow suggested the house would be worth something like a million and a half dollars.

If Nash was a thief, he was a good one.

Next he called up the files Trane had pulled from the National Crime Information Center. Boyd had been arrested twice for assault. First for going after a security guard at a Medtronic office in Fridley, a suburb of Minneapolis. That was a mistake: the security guard moonlighted as a bouncer at a biker bar and kicked Boyd's ass before he called the cops.

The charges had been dismissed.

Then he was charged with domestic assault by a woman named Jon-Ellen Nord.

Again, the charges were dismissed.

Fridley was in Anoka County and he couldn't raise anyone at the county attorney's office, but the second arrest was in Hennepin County—in the city of Bloomington—and he did get an assistant county attorney in Hennepin and she was willing to give a little after-hours help.

She walked away from the phone for a few minutes, came back, and said that the woman who was attacked had dropped the charges. When the county attorney had resisted that decision, Nord had said that she'd overstated the seriousness of the attack.

Virgil: "What do you think?"

"There's a totally improper note in the file," the assistant county attorney said. "It says 'The bitch was paid off.' Remember that because I'm now removing it."

"What do you think about that? The note?"

"I think the bitch was paid off," she said.

"You got an address for her?"

Jon-Ellen Nord lived in a snug green bungalow on Minnehaha Creek in south Minneapolis, a distinctly upscale neighborhood with lots of trees and the creek running through backyards. There was a light in the window, but no cars in sight; there was a detached two-car garage in back, so the cars could be there. Virgil cruised by the place a couple of times before he slowed and pulled into the driveway. He could see the flicker of a television screen as he walked to the front door and rang the bell.

Jon-Ellen Nord was a lanky, small-headed, dark-haired woman with suspicious dark eyes. She was probably around fifty years old, Virgil thought. Virgil identified himself and held up his ID so she could read it, and, after she had, she pushed open the door, and asked, "What's this about?"

"I'd like to talk to you about an acquaintance of yours, Boyd Nash."

"Haven't seen Boyd in a couple of years. What's he done now?"

"I don't know if he's done anything. We're looking at a serious crime, and his name came up. Could be nothing, but we have to check."

"How serious a crime?"

"Murder," Virgil said.

She pushed the door farther open, and said, "Come in."

He followed her inside; she left behind a light trace of floral perfume that reminded him of the scent of lilies of the valley. The house itself was snug: older, with smaller rooms, hardwood floors, a fieldstone fireplace, and built-in bookshelves. Nord had cats, three of them. Two were tabbies, one red and one gray. The third was black and white with a pink nose. The tabbies were shy and peeked around corners. The black-and-white cat came up and rubbed against Virgil's leg, and when Nord pointed Virgil at a chair, the cat made a move to jump on his lap. Nord grabbed it and deposited it on top of an upright piano. She took an over-stuffed chair facing Virgil, and said, "If Boyd killed somebody, it was either an accident or involved really big money. He wouldn't kill anybody unless there was a large payoff."

"You think he could kill somebody?"

"Oh, sure. He's a classic sociopath. Doesn't care about anyone but number one," she said. "He can be charming, if he tries, but it's always calculated. Taking care of number one would include staying out of jail. I'm sure you know he assaulted me, that's why you're here."

"I saw that in a case file," Virgil said. "Exactly what was the situation there?"

"He beat me up. We'd dated a couple of times—maybe three—and then I broke it off. He showed up at my door, right here, high as a kite and angry. I tried arguing with him through the screen door, and he grabbed the door handle and yanked the hook right out of the jamb," Nord said. Her voice was flat, unemotional, as though she were talking about something she'd read. "I tried to push him out, and he started slapping me, and then he hit me with his fists. I had bruises all over my face and my rib cage. I hurt for weeks. Lucky for me, a neighbor was passing by with his wife, and they witnessed it and called nine-one-one. Boyd ran for it, but the neighbors jotted down the license plate number and the make of his car, and the police caught him less than a mile from here. He had blood on his hands."

"But you dropped the charges."

"We . . . came to a private settlement."

"A large one?"

"I don't want to get into numbers. It was substantial. I was at a critical stage in my entrepreneurial career, and the money was welcome. I inherited this place from my mother and mortgaged it to start my business and didn't have enough money to expand when I needed to do that. Boyd, uh, filled the gap."

She owned three coffeehouses, she said, in different but trendy parts of the Twin Cities. Virgil had been in one and liked it: the coffee was good, all the local papers were free, and *The New York Times* and *Wall Street Journal* were sold over the counter.

"Who'd he kill?" she asked.

Virgil explained that he was investigating the death of Barthelemy Quill, a professor at the University of Minnesota. Nord's head started going up and down as soon as Virgil mentioned the name, said she'd read the news stories about the case.

"This all ties into his rather crappy career as a patent troll? Or his spying?"

"You knew about that?"

"Sure. He wasn't embarrassed about it. He was right up front, in fact. He said if a company didn't protect itself, it deserved what it got." She shook her head. "He crossed a lot of lines, though. He would actually spy on companies, I think. He got beat up once by a security guard. He could beat on a woman, I guess, but apparently wasn't real good against somebody who actually knew how to fight."

"I have a note about that," Virgil said. "He was charged in that case, too, and it was also dismissed."

"I don't know what happened there, but I knew about it," she said. "He was a slippery fuck, if you'll excuse the language. That was my final verdict."

"As far as you know, did Nash have a relationship with Dr. Quill?" Virgil asked.

"I don't know anything about that. I didn't know much about what Boyd did, the details. I picked up a little in conversation while we were going out, and of course I looked him up on the internet. I don't even know why I went out with him that third time. I didn't like him that much on the first date, but I guess I decided to give him a second chance, and then maybe I went out the third time because I was bored. I wasn't bored enough to go out a fourth time. Then he beat me up."

"You said he was high when he beat you. That doesn't sound like marijuana."

"Cocaine, his drug of choice. I doubt he ever tried marijuana. Or, if he did, not more than once. It was always cocaine."

They talked for another ten minutes, but she didn't have much to add. They'd never gotten to a sexual relationship—not even close.

Virgil asked about Nash's friends. "I don't think he had any real friends, but he did have, like, an acolyte. This guy who followed him around and did chores for him. His name was Dex—short for Dexter, I think. I don't know if I ever knew Dex's last name. He was a short, stumpy guy. Like one of the Seven Dwarfs, only two feet taller. Among other things, I think he got Boyd's dope for him. I'm not sure if Dex knew a dealer or was a dealer, but he held Boyd's coke."

"If you only went out three times, how did you get to know Dex?"

She smiled for the first time. "Because he sorta came on the date with us. All three times he was in the backseat when Boyd showed up, then Boyd would drop him off somewhere near the place we were going for dinner, he'd disappear, and I wouldn't see him again until the next date. He had a line of patter he'd keep going from the backseat: news stories, stuff about the city, about where we were going, about people he knew. It was weird. I actually sorta liked Dex better than Boyd, except he was funny-looking. A funny-looking guy. I think he was probably in his thirties maybe. But he looked old. He had a sixty-year-old face."

When Virgil ran out of questions, Nord said, "I hope you get him. I know I shouldn't have settled, but I really, really needed the money. And Virgil"—she reached across the gap between their chairs and touched his knee—"you be careful. I do think Boyd could kill somebody. Maybe he already has. He's a bullshitter, but there's a mean bastard under that fat face."

Virgil was on his way out the door when he was struck by a thought. He turned back, and asked, "You wouldn't have a picture of him, would you?"

Nord said, "Hmm, probably. I take pictures of everyone and never clean them out of my phone. Let me look."

She scanned photos for a moment, her thumbs and fingers moving as fast as a longtime typist's, and then: "Ah. Here we go. What's your number, I'll send it to you."

A moment later, it popped up on Virgil's phone: a smiling, overweight man with reddish brown hair pulled back in a ponytail.

Back in his car, he called O'Hara, the map thief. When she answered, he said he was going to send her a photo. "Could you take a moment to look at it?"

"Of course."

He sent the picture, and a moment later O'Hara said, "That's the man."

His next call went to Del Capslock, got his wife. He knew Cheryl, and they chatted about Frankie's pregnancy for a moment while Capslock got out of the bathroom. When he did, Cheryl handed him the phone. "What's up?"

"Did you ever know a guy named Dex, maybe Dexter, may or may not have dealt drugs, looks like a taller version of one of the Seven Dwarfs?"

"Sure. Dexter Hamm. He's a hangout guy, does this and that."

"Selling drugs?"

"Maybe, at one time or another, but not as a profession. He might have dealt to friends as a favor. Deals a little real estate, buys cars out at the auction, resells them. He puts this guy with that guy, and deals get done. He's been around forever, knows everybody. Like that."

"A street guy, then," Virgil said.

"Yeah, but not a bottom-feeder. He'll make a few bucks by the end of the year."

"Where would I find him?"

"Damned if I know," Capslock said. "He's more Minneapolis than St. Paul. I've never been to his place, but I wouldn't be surprised if he had a set address. Check the DMV."

"Thanks for that," Virgil said.

"Sure. Hamm—two 'm's. I get the feeling that I'm your new go-to guy for dirtbag contacts."

"Well, yeah."

According to the DMV, Hamm lived in a condo in what used to be the warehouse district adjacent to downtown Minneapolis. Though it was getting late, Virgil decided to take a shot at a contact and headed downtown.

Hamm's place was a brick-and-glass cube, a couple of decades old, with a keypad at street level to get into the lobby and a video camera that looked down at a brass plate with buttons for each individual apartment. Hamm was listed, and when Virgil pushed the button, he answered, "Do I know you?"

"No. I'm an agent with the Bureau of Criminal Apprehension," Virgil said. "I need to speak to you for a few minutes."

"About what?"

"Boyd Nash."

"We're no longer associated," Hamm said.

"I still need to speak to you. Push the button for the door or it'll get unnecessarily complicated."

After a moment of silence, the door buzzer sounded, and Virgil pushed inside. Hamm lived on the third floor, and Virgil took the stairs, both because he needed the exercise and because if Hamm ran for it he'd probably take the stairs.

Virgil met no one coming down, and when he emerged in a third floor lobby, he saw Hamm standing down the hall at an open door; he *did* look like a taller version of one of the Seven Dwarfs—Sneezy, Virgil thought.

On the other hand, his voice sounded like Waylon Jennings's. He said, "In here," and led the way into his apartment. "What's your name?"

"Virgil Flowers."

"Flowers? I used to know a Tommy Flowers, out of Chicago."

"No relation," Virgil said.

Hamm's apartment was like an unconscious man cave—not designed to be one, but it was—two brown corduroy-covered easy chairs, with a matching ottoman for each, facing an over-sized TV with five-foot-high speakers on either side of it tuned to an all-sports channel, the baked-in scent of cigars and micro-waved mac 'n' cheese, floor-to-ceiling windows looking out at the condo across the street.

Hamm pointed at one of the chairs, and said, "This has got to be way after duty hours. Want a beer?"

"Sure," Virgil said.

Hamm got two Dos Equis out of his refrigerator, popped off

their caps with a counter-mounted opener, handed one to Virgil, settled into the other brown chair, and asked, "What's that asshole up to now? Boyd."

"I was hoping you could tell me."

"We haven't been associated for more than a year," Hamm said. "I set up a deal on a nice piece of property off Lake Nokomis: little old lady died and left a teardown sitting on a gold mine. The relatives—the heirs—were out in Dayton, didn't know their ass from a hole in the ground. Nobody saw it but me. My piece would have been fifty K. And Boyd fucked me out of it."

"I've been told that he's ethically challenged," Virgil said.

Hamm snorted. "That's the kindest description you could put on him." He poured some beer down his throat, coughed, then asked, "What are you looking for?"

"I would fear for your future as a go-to guy if I told you and then you spread it around," Virgil said.

"Us go-to guys can keep our mouths shut when we need to," Hamm said. "That's part of our package."

Virgil nodded. "I'm investigating the murder of Barthelemy Quill, a professor over at the university. He was doing cutting-edge research on spinal cord repairs. You know, trying to repair nerve damage in quadriplegics and paraplegics."

"Okay, that sounds like something Boyd would try to steal. You think he killed Quill?"

"I don't know, but his name came up as somebody who'd spent time stalking Quill's lab," Virgil said. "You think he could kill?"

"Boyd? Sure, no problem. Well, small problem: he wouldn't want to get caught. He wouldn't kill unless he thought he was ninety-nine-point-nine percent likely to get away with it. If he planned to kill, he'd have a heavy-duty alibi."

"And you have no idea of what he's up to now?"

"I didn't say that," Hamm said. "I asked if you knew, to see if it was the same thing I know."

"I have no idea what he's doing," Virgil said. "I've never seen the guy or spoken to him. So, what do you know?"

"He won't hear it came from me? Because he could be a killer, and I know he holds a grudge," Hamm said.

"I'll keep it under my hat best I can," Virgil said.

Hamm took another swallow of beer, then said, "Have you ever heard of a company called Surface Research?"

"No."

"It's not huge," Hamm went on. "But, it's not small, either. The engineers who started it, they have a private jet, you know. A small jet, but they'd like to have a big one. What they do is, they develop paints for different kinds of difficult to cover surfaces. That's where their name comes from—they cover surfaces."

"Paint?"

"Yeah. Big money in it, you'd be surprised," Hamm said. "Stock tip: you can buy Surface Research for ten bucks a share right now, and it's going to fifty in two years, maybe more."

"Why would—"

"—Boyd be interested in paint? Because of the money involved," Hamm said. "What I hear is, Surface Research is developing a glass-and-metal-based paint for striping highways. It has to be certain specific colors—white and yellow, I guess—and, I'm told, also a clear paint, transparent. It has to be *way* durable and make it through all kinds of traffic and temperature extremes twenty-four hours a day."

"The road paint they've got now isn't good enough?" Virgil asked. "Seems like there might be a lot of competition."

"This paint is designed to get driverless vehicles down the road," Hamm said.

Virgil said, "Ah."

"Yeah. It has some built-in components that'll work with car sensors and even allow, you know, road painters—the state, I guess—to paint instructions on roads that people can't see but the cars can pick up to warn about hazards and so on. If this all works, Surface Research will go to a thousand bucks a share, and we'll all be billionaires. I've got a thousand shares myself, and I'm seriously thinking about mortgaging this place and buying another ten thousand."

"What's Nash doing?"

"Boyd's been scouting them for a while—even back when I was working with him. Lately, I've heard, he's gotten inside. He's got some kind of low-level connection inside the company, and he's been in there at night taking pictures."

"Pictures?"

"Yeah. You know, photographs. Get a computer up, start pulling files, taking photos of the screen. If they're getting close to a viable product, and he moves that stuff over to another paint company, could be a major score."

"He's still doing this?"

"That's what I've heard," Hamm said. "Friday, Saturday, Sunday nights, when the place is empty. I thought about calling the cops, but that could lead to some awkward questions."

"Like, how you know all this?"

"Exactly. Cops never leave well enough alone."

"How *do* you know all this?"

"That's hard to explain . . . to most cops," Hamm said. "I'm talking to you because you took a beer on duty. I knew about

Surface Research from back when I was working with Boyd. Then he screwed me on the real estate deal and I told him to go fuck himself. Still, I'm out there, looking for deals, and I hear shit from all kinds of people. That's what I do: I hear shit. People know I used to work with Boyd, so his name comes up. He's got another guy working with him now, and I think that guy might have talked to some people I know and the word starts leaking out."

"Okay. You think he might be working right now?"

Hamm shook his head. "Too early. This kind of thing, Boyd would be going in after midnight or later. Two in the morning, four—those are the dead times when nobody's around, except a few cop cars. He can get some serious quiet to work in."

Hamm finished his beer, and Virgil did, too. Hamm asked, "You want another?"

"No, I'm good," Virgil said.

"What are you going to do?"

"I'm investigating a murder, not a paint theft," Virgil said. "Still, this is interesting. Nash sounds like a possibility. You're the second person who's told me that he could kill."

"Wouldn't bother him a bit," Hamm said.

"I'm gonna look at him," Virgil said, standing up. He put his beer bottle on the kitchen counter, and said, "And you keep your mouth shut."

"Don't worry. I want you to do good. Get me some payback," Hamm said. "When it's done right, payback's a bitch, huh?"

Thursday night. If Hamm was right—and he did sound like he knew what he was talking about—Nash wouldn't be making another run at Surface Research for at least twenty-four hours.

He could wait. If Nash was actually doing industrial espionage, catching him in the act would generate a lot of leverage.

Virgil headed back to the hotel, had dinner, stuck his head in the bar. Harry wasn't there, but Alice was, and she asked about the case.

"I dunno. It seems to be drifting toward some kind of conclusion," Virgil said. "Keep your eye on the newspapers."

"I'm like everybody else," she said. "I don't read the papers."

CHAPTER

TWENTY

Virgil stayed up late to finish the James Lee Burke novel, slept late on Friday morning, then called Trane, who was immersed in a study of Robin Jones, the attorney representing Ruth McDonald in the malpractice case. "I've talked to a few people and I'm having some doubts," she said. "Turns out Jones is basically known as a chickenshit, both physically and otherwise. He would be unlikely to go after anyone physically, and I'm told he sure as hell wouldn't be breaking into a library. He wants to be a congressman, and breaking into anything would be the end of that."

"What are you going to do?"

"Keep looking. I'm not quite done with him yet," she said. "What about you?"

He told her all about Nash. "He's at least a solid suspect. I've been told that he's basically a careful criminal and knows about setting up alibis for himself. The medical convention down in Rochester sounds like an alibi to me. Goes around slapping backs, buying drinks—he's the life of the party. Disappears at ten o'clock, but at eight the next morning there he is again. What happened between ten and eight? Nobody knows."

"All right," Trane said. "I'm pulling for you."

Virgil went for a run around campus, browsed the bookstore in the basement of the student union, went back to the hotel, got on his computer and dug for everything he could find on Nash. Reviewed all the notes he'd taken in the past week and concluded that Nash was the best lead they'd come up with, assuming that Cohen hadn't killed Quill and was in the process of getting away with it. He went on Google Maps satellite, spotted Nash's house and the Surface Research factory, and the routes between them.

He talked to Frankie for an hour, about the condition of both the farm and her womb, was told that both seemed to be doing fine. Late in the afternoon, he took a nap because he suspected he'd be up all night. At six o'clock, he called Shrake, who claimed to have an absolutely critical, and possibly life-changing, date. "Jenkins wanted to go shoot some pool. That was an hour ago, so I know he's not doing anything. I think he's driving around town."

"I was hoping for a less visible car," Virgil said. Jenkins drove an aging Crown Vic. Even though cops no longer drove them because they were no longer made, the used versions still screamed "cop."

"We've got a late-model silver Camry at the office that's not doing anything but sitting in the parking lot. He could get in that and be practically invisible," Shrake said.

"Will Jenkins fit?"

"Maybe."

Virgil made the call, and Jenkins said, "You're saving my life. I'm so goddamn bored I was thinking about masturbating."

"How would that end your life?"

Puzzled silence, then, "Ah . . . No, see, the two things aren't connected: saving my life and masturbating. I was trying to make a point about . . . Oh, fuckin' forget it. I'll get the Camry and meet you. Hey, how about if I stop by Jimmy John's and get us some hoagies?"

"Sounds good. I'll be starving by the time it gets dark," Virgil said. "Maybe a couple of Diet Cokes."

As the sun reluctantly lowered itself below the horizon—it had been a boring day—Virgil drove south to Edina, spotted Nash's house from the street. The house showed lights all across what must have been a half dozen rooms. As he watched, one of the lights went out, so somebody was inside. He drove around the block, found a spot where he could sit and look through a couple of yards and see Nash's garage door.

Jenkins arrived twenty minutes later, parked behind Virgil's Tahoe. Like his partner, Shrake, he was a large man, dressed in jeans, a black golf shirt, a light cotton sport coat, and black Nike running shoes. He got out of his borrowed car, got into Virgil's passenger seat, and passed over a bag of hoagies and two Diet Cokes.

"Heard you'd been working with Shrake and Capslock."

"Yeah . . ."

Virgil explained the situation, as he chewed through his sandwich. Jenkins, looking out at the quiet suburban street, said, "You know, somebody's going to call the cops on us. We're gonna have a squad car with a bunch of flashing lights. We'll probably get shot."

"You think?"

"Yeah, I think." Jenkins got out his phone and called the duty officer at the BCA and asked him to call the Edina cops and tell them about the surveillance. The duty officer called back a moment later and said Edina had already had a call and a patrol car had been dispatched, but now had been recalled. "Told you," Jenkins said.

"You're *way* smarter than you look," Virgil said.

"Thank you . . . A hoagie? Don't mind if I do."

They ate for a while, then Virgil said, "I just had a thought."

"Don't be afraid," Jenkins said. "New experiences can be valuable teaching moments."

"Right. My thought is, if he actually does this and we think we know where he's going," Virgil said, "why should both of us follow him? I could run over to this paint place and already be there. That way, you could stay way back of him and wouldn't have to worry about losing him as long as it looked like he was coming to me."

"That is a valuable thought," Jenkins said. "Let me get my shit"—he meant the bag of food—"and get out of here. Stay in touch. If he moves, I'll call. And you say this guy could be a killer? So don't . . . Uh, don't get hurt. Or at least wait until I get there before you get hurt. That way, I can call the meat wagon for you."

Jenkins gathered up his food, and, as he backed out of the car, said, "Call the duty officer. Tell him you're moving and where you'll be at, that you'll call when you get there. You won't want those cops coming around, either."

The Surface Research headquarters and manufacturing facility was in a flat, rectangular steel-and-concrete-block building in an industrial zone south of Minneapolis–St. Paul International Airport, not far beneath the wheels of the jets landing there. Virgil crossed the Minnesota River on I-494, took a right on Pilot Knob Road, another left, and was there, in a zone of sodium-vapor lights, other flat buildings, and empty parking lots.

He spotted the Surface Research building, circled it slowly. The biggest parking lot was at the front of the building, outside three separate sets of doors: one, in the middle of the building, behind three silvery flagpoles, looked like it was the formal public entrance; the other two, on opposite sides of the public entrance and about a third of the length of the building away from it, appeared to be for employees. The parking lot was empty, with not a single vehicle in sight.

There was another entrance, up some steps on the back side of the building, along with four loading docks with overhead doors. An eighteen-wheeler was backed up to one of the docks; a dark-colored compact SUV sat one space over from it. If Nash were going into the building, Virgil thought, it'd be through the back. A lone car parked in front would advertise the presence of someone in the building. A car parked between the tractor-trailer and the SUV would be virtually unnoticed.

He called Jenkins. "Anything?"

"No, but his lights are still on. He's awake."

"All right. I'm there, looking for a spot."

He found his spot a block away, at a warehouse where a line of tractor-trailers was backed up to loading docks but there was no activity. He backed between two of the trucks, with nothing more than the nose of the Tahoe poking out. He got his iPad and binoculars from the back, and, after a moment's thought, his Glock, which he checked and then put on the passenger seat.

He called the duty officer, told him where he was at, asked him to check what city he was in and to call the police there to tell them what he was doing. The duty officer called back two minutes later, and said, "You're in Eagan. I don't know what you and Jenkins are up to, but you must look suspicious as hell. The cops there got called by a security guard at the Aerotop warehouse, asking them to check you out."

"I think I'm in their parking lot," Virgil said. "But I don't see a sign."

"Hiding behind some semis?"

"That's me."

"Well, smile, because you're on camera. I got the cop car turned around."

"Good. Now, I got one more thing for you," Virgil said. "I need a current phone number for a Stuart L. Booker, Jr. He's the president of a company called Surface Research. He lives here in the cities, but I don't know where."

"Gimme ten minutes."

He came back in ten with two cell phone numbers for Booker and one for Booker's wife, Andi. With that, Virgil settled down to watch the back of Surface Research while he used the iPad to check wildlife magazine websites for article ideas. Two kids coming, eighteen years to save for their college educations. With his luck, they were already thinking Yale *in utero*.

He was focused enough on the task that he nearly had a heart attack when a man rapped on the driver's-side window a few inches from his head. He jumped, looked, saw an elderly man in a gray security guard's uniform peering in at him.

He dropped the window, and said, "Jesus, you scared me."

"Sorry. I got a call from the Eagan police saying you were doing surveillance. If there's any way I could help . . ."

"Not really. I've got a partner already in place."

"Okay. I needed to tell you that there'll be a lot of trucks showing up here starting about five o'clock."

"I won't be here that long," Virgil said.

"Can I ask you what you're looking for?"

"Can't talk about that," Virgil said.

"But there won't be any . . . shooting . . . or anything like that."

"No, no. And it's not right here anyway. I'm looking up the block."

The guard looked up the block, where a half dozen buildings were partially visible in the orange lights, and said, "I've got a station, up those steps, right inside the double doors." He jerked a thumb back over his shoulder. "There's a candy machine and a pop machine and a restroom right inside. If you need something, need to pee, just knock on the door, I'll come let you in."

"You sound like an ex-cop," Virgil said.

"I was that, up north," the man said. "Turns out the retirement benefits weren't good enough to keep my head above water, so now I sit and watch TV pictures of empty parking lots. Shit job. Save your money, buddy."

He tapped the Tahoe's door panel a couple of times, then faded back toward the building, trailing fumes of disappointment and depression. Virgil went back to the iPad with renewed intensity, made notes for an article on possible ways to control the Canada geese population. He was thinking: weed whips.

Jenkins called a few minutes before two o'clock. "We've got movement. Looks like one guy, in a big, black Audi. He backed out of the garage, so I couldn't see if he was carrying anything."

"Where are you?"

"On the back side of the block, watching his taillights. Haven't even started the engine yet."

"Be cool."

"I'm cool. His taillights are really distinctive. I'll sit way back. I'll call you when I get an idea of where he's going. Right now, he looks like he's headed toward Highway 100."

"Call me."

Jenkins called again. "He's headed south on Highway 100. Not much traffic, but I'm way behind him. I gotta tell you, this Audi's made to be followed: there's a taillight on each side of the rear, with a bright red line across the whole back of the car that connects the two. You can see it for half a mile."

"Then you've got no excuse for losing him," Virgil said.

Jenkins called a third time. "East on 494. He's coming your way, big guy. Hot damn, this is better than sex. Your kind of missionary, son-of-a-preacher sex anyway."

_____

And again. "South on Pilot Knob."

"Okay, he's coming here," Virgil said. "Don't turn down Pilot Knob. I want his rearview mirror to be empty. There's hardly any traffic right now."

"I'll go on through and circle back. I'll come up behind your location and walk over to your truck."

Virgil called Jenkins ten minutes later. "He's not here yet. I wonder what the hell happened?"

"Maybe he *is* checking his rearview mirror before he comes in. Doing a random check. I better stay away for a few more minutes."

"Do that." As the words came out of Virgil's mouth, a pair of car lights turned onto the street that led down to the Surface Research building. "Wait a minute, I got lights. Hang on."

The car was moving slow, slowed even further, then made a decisive turn into the Surface Research parking lot and pulled in between the tractor-trailer and the SUV. The taillights were as distinctive as Jenkins had described them. Virgil said, "All right, that's him. He's here."

"I'll come in behind you. Give me five minutes."

As Virgil watched, a man got out of the car. He was dressed all in black and was carrying a black bag. He walked around the back of the SUV, climbed the steps to the entrance doors, one of which was pushed open as he approached. He went inside.

Virgil sat and waited until Jenkins walked up, patted the hood, and then climbed in the passenger side. "We going in?"

"Not yet," Virgil said. "Let him settle down to work."

He took out his cell phone and called the duty officer at the BCA and asked him to call Stuart Booker, the president of Surface Research. "My phone comes up as 'Caller Unknown,'" Virgil told the duty officer. "I wanted you to use the official line that identifies you as the BCA. When you get him, tell him to expect a call from me, Caller Unknown. Call me back after you get him . . . And if you don't get him, call his wife."

The duty officer called four or five minutes later. "They were sound asleep. They didn't believe me, so I had them look up the BCA number and call me. They did and now they believe me. They're waiting for you to call."

Virgil called Booker, who picked up immediately. Virgil identified himself, and said, "Sir, I'm working on a complicated case that has somewhat touched upon a man who does industrial espionage. He has just gone in the back of your building in Eagan."

"What!"

"I need your permission to go in there and hold him."

"I live in Sunfish Lake. I'm eight minutes from there. I can bring keys." Virgil heard him call to his wife: "Andi, get my pants and a shirt." He then came back to Virgil. "You have my permission to go in, but I can bring keys."

"Do you have keys for the back door, by the loading dock?"

"Yes!"

"Then let's do that," Virgil said. "You know where the Aerotop warehouse is? A block down from you and—"

"I know it."

"Come in from the back, park on the other side from your building so you're out of sight. We'll wait for you there."

"I'm coming. I got my pants on. I could bring my Ruger, I've got a carry permit—"

"No, no, no . . ."

Virgil sent Jenkins to sneak back around the Aerotop building to meet Booker; while Jenkins did that, Virgil called the duty officer at the Eagan Police Department and explained the situation. "We'll be going in the back. If you can do it, I'd like you to keep a car a few blocks away, not too close, and then when I say go, have them pull into the front parking lot with their flashers on to discourage runners. There are three doors, grab anybody coming out."

"We can do that. We got nothing going tonight."

Virgil waited, watching the back door of the Surface Research building with his binoculars; he saw no movement at all. Ten minutes after Jenkins left, he was back with a tall, thin man with curly black hair and a large, bony nose. The man got in the back of the Tahoe, and said, "I'm Stu Booker. How'd you find out about this? Do you know what he's doing in there?"

"We got it from one of our confidential informants, and I can't disclose the source quite yet," Virgil said. "Our source says this guy is accessing a computer to get all the information he can about paints that will be used to guide self-driving cars."

"Sonofabitch! Sonofabitch! I thought that had to be it," Booker said. "Jesus Christ, if that gets out of the building . . . We gotta stop this."

"We will. You should know that our source says he's already been in there several times."

"Oh my God!"

"Did you bring a key for the back door?"

"Yes." Booker fumbled in his jacket pocket and produced a key on a horsehair ring. "I go in the back myself sometimes. Listen, the guy must be in the engineering office."

Booker described a route through the production facility and up into the engineering, design, and administrative offices. "I'll come with you and point the way."

"Let's go," Virgil said.

They walked along the exterior wall of Aerotop, hidden by the trucks, then behind it, across the street, around another warehouse, and finally across the street again and up to the windowless side of Surface Research. From there, they walked to the corner of the building, a hundred feet or so from the back door.

They paused while Virgil called the Eagan police; the cars, two minutes out, would be rolling in seconds.

"Go," Virgil said to Jenkins, who had the key. "Quick, now."

Jenkins was a runner; he sprinted down the back of the building and up the stairs to the door next to the loading dock. Virgil and Booker arrived right behind Jenkins, who had already fit the key in the lock. He twisted it, pulled his pistol, and bumped the door open with his hip.

To an empty hallway.

"Straight ahead," Booker whispered.

Virgil led, Jenkins trailed, watching either side. Moving quickly, they crossed a pair of hallways that led into the production area of the building. Most of the lights were out, and Virgil could barely make out what looked like racks of machinery and barrels and, in the biggest open area, cone-shaped machines, twenty feet tall and fifteen feet across, like alien invaders from Mars.

He paused to look at them, and Booker, catching up, whispered, "Mixers."

Halfway through the plant, they crossed another hallway that led to offices to their right and a flight of stairs going up. They had not heard, let alone seen, a single living being.

Booker whispered, "Production offices down here. They'll be up in engineering. The night guard's name is Allen Young. He is armed. The stairs are metal, and they'll make noise if we're not careful."

"Eagan cops gonna be here soon," Jenkins whispered. "We gotta move before we get a parking lot full of flashers."

They tiptoed up the metal stairs, emerging in a hallway lined with offices. To his left, Virgil could see that the offices on that side looked over the production facility. To the right, they looked over the front parking lot.

They could see a dimly lighted window halfway down the hall in front of them. "Engineering," Booker whispered.

Virgil said, "Stay right here," and he and Jenkins walked down the hall toward the office. They were fifteen feet away when a man stepped into the hallway, saw them, shouted, "Hey!" and made a move for his hip.

Virgil shouted, "Police! Freeze!"

Jenkins yelled, "Freeze! Freeze! Put your hands up where we can see them. Hands up! Don't touch that gun."

Virgil shouted, "Allen, hands over your head or we will shoot . . ."

The man stopped moving, then slowly lifted his hands. Down the hall, another door burst open, and a man ran through it and away from them, and Virgil said to Jenkins, "Get him."

Jenkins took off, and Virgil shouted at the guard, "Don't move, man, or we'll shoot. We *will* shoot you."

Jenkins blew past the guard, and from behind Virgil Booker shouted to Jenkins, "There's another stairs . . ."

Virgil closed on the guard, his Glock up in the man's face. "Turn around, put your hands on the wall."

"I'm the security guard here," the man said, as he put his hands on the wall above his head.

"We know, Allen. I'm going to take your pistol. Keep your hands on the wall, I'm nervous here, and this trigger is pretty light. Take it easy, and we'll all be fine."

Jenkins piled down the second flight of metal stairs, thirty feet behind the runner. The two large men hit the treads hard, making a racket like somebody beating on an oil drum with a ball peen hammer. At the bottom of the stairs, the runner, who'd been carrying a black bag, dropped it. Jenkins vaulted over the bag and kept closing in on the man and caught him as they got to the back door. He pushed the man hard on the back of the neck and the man lost his balance and fell face forward, nearly colliding head-on with the door. Jenkins knelt on the man's back, wrenched one of his arms up and back, clicked on a cuff, said, "Gimme the other arm, Boyd. C'mon, don't make me dislocate your shoulder."

"How'd you know my name?"

"We know all," Jenkins said. Nash relaxed his other arm, and Jenkins snapped on the second cuff. "See, that was easy. Let's go back upstairs, see what's what."

On the way back up, Jenkins retrieved Nash's bag. When they got back to the engineering office, Young, the security guard, was sitting on an office chair, his hands cuffed behind him, while Booker was peering at a computer screen and chanting: "Those fuckers. Those fuckers. Those fuckers . . ."

Red lights flashed off the dim interior walls, and Jenkins said, "One runner, one bag, and the Eagan cops are here."

Virgil said, "Leave Mr. Nash. Run down there and tell the cops to come on up, we'll need them to transport these guys."

Jenkins pushed Nash into another office chair, as Young said, "Listen, I don't know what this is all about."

Nash said, "Shut up. Keep your mouth shut. We want an attorney. You don't want to say another fuckin' word, believe me. We can settle this."

Young dropped his head, and said, "Okay."

Booker, still peering at the computer: "If they were working through this file by file, they already got a lot. We need a major investigation here. We need to know what they've already taken out. We need to know who they were taking it out for."

"Attorney," Nash said.

"You'll get an attorney," Virgil said.

"You're gonna need more than an attorney," Booker shouted at Nash. "You're gonna need a fuckin' miracle. You're going to prison, you got that? So are the guys you're selling this to. You're all going to jail, you motherfucker!"

Virgil said, "Easy, there," and he squatted and looked in the black bag. A Sony video camera was sitting on top of some bubble wrap, a GoPro, and some other gear.

"That's private property," Nash said.

"It's burglary equipment," Virgil said. "But I'm not going to mess with it. Because, you know, your prints are all over it. I wouldn't want to smudge any of them."

"We need to know what's in the camera," Booker said.

"We will," Virgil said. "Not right now, though. We'll turn this stuff over to the Eagan cops, let them transport these two to the Dakota County Jail and get with the prosecutors tomorrow. We have a lot of business with Mr. Nash. We'll need you to come and look at the photos. I'll call you in the morning after we know what we're doing, let you know what time we can get together."

"My whole life is in that camera," Booker said. "These two need to go to prison. Forever."

Young whined, "Mr. Booker . . ."

"Shut up," Nash said.

Virgil smiled at Booker. "I even think we might have a cooperating witness." He slapped Young on the back. "We'll take care of you, Al. Don't pay any attention to Boyd. He can't help you. But we can."

The Eagan cops came up. The cop in charge, a sergeant, looked at the two cuffed men, and then Virgil, and said, "Tell me everything."

CHAPTER

TWENTY-ONE

When the Eagan cops had taken Nash and Young away, Virgil said to Jenkins, "We've got to go back to Nash's place. We need to see if there's anybody there. We need to grab his home computers and any paper we can find that might tie him to Quill. We'll probably have to sleep in the cars until we can get a search warrant."

Booker asked, "Who's Quill?"

"He might have been another one of Nash's targets," Virgil said.

"What about my place?"

"We'll look for that, too. We'll see if we can spot who the buyer was, if he already had one. If we see anything that looks right, we'll call you for identification," Virgil said. "What you should do now is go home and go back to bed."

"I won't sleep," Booker said. "You don't know how bad this is."

"Try to sleep. I'll set us up with the Dakota County Attorney's Office tomorrow morning. They'll want to talk to you and you'll want to be sharp," Virgil said. "Nash might be prepared for something like this, might have a lawyer ready to launch."

"I'll call my legal guys tonight, we'll all be there tomorrow," Booker said. "Anytime you say. I'll lock this place down before you leave. I'll call the security company and have them send some guys over here to patrol the parking lot."

As they were leaving, Virgil asked Booker, "How'd he get into your computers? Don't you have them protected?"

"That's one thing we need to find out right away," Booker said. "They all have passwords, of course, that are supposed to be restricted to the engineers. The one he was on wasn't assigned to one guy; it's used by people like me who come through here but don't actually work in this office. While we change the passwords every month, several people have the password for that particular computer."

"Then you might have another leak. Besides the guard."

Booker thought about that for a moment, then shook his head. "Probably not. If it was an engineer, he could have worked a little late—which is common enough—loaded all the information onto one flash drive, and carried it out. Since Nash had to be here, I suspect somebody like Allen was standing in the corner with his cell phone in his hand, set to video, recording keystrokes when somebody signed on to the computer."

"I will check with Allen," Virgil said. "About that thumb drive thing: that sounds a lot easier than taking pictures of a video screen with a camera. Why didn't Nash do that?"

"Because when you plug a thumb drive in, there's an on-screen prompt that asks for some ID information, which is different for each engineer. Couldn't make movies of that unless you were standing right behind the guy who was inputting."

_____

Virgil and Jenkins drove back to Nash's, parked in the driveway, leaned on the doorbell. No answer.

Virgil called the Edina police, asked for help. The duty officer said they could cruise the house every half hour or so, but they were working a bad pedestrian accident and didn't have a lot of flexibility. Virgil told them there'd be two cars in the driveway and maybe somebody asleep on the front porch.

"Who's going to sleep on the front porch?" Jenkins asked when Virgil was off the phone.

"One of us," Virgil said. "We can't let this get away. I'm going to slap crime scene tape on all the doors, then you can have a sleeping bag and air mattress and sleep on the porch or a yoga mat and Army blanket and sleep in the back of my truck. Your choice."

Jenkins took the sleeping bag and air mattress and porch. Virgil slapped crime scene tape on the doors and crawled into the back of the truck, got a solid four hours, before his phone/alarm rang at seven-thirty. He called Trane.

"Gimme a break, I don't wake up for a half hour," Trane said. Then: "Something happen?"

He told her about the arrest from the night before and that he'd been sleeping in the driveway at Nash's house. "We need a search warrant quick as we can get it, I mean, like, right now. You'd know better how to get one fast outta Hennepin County. I'll give you the details."

As he was doing that, Jenkins walked up, yawning, said, "I'm going to a Starbucks. Coffee?"

"Hot chocolate and a couple of bagels."

"My breath could slay a dragon," Jenkins said, as he wandered away to his car.

Virgil called the Dakota County Attorney's Office at eight o'clock, talked to the chief assistant county attorney, whose name was Don Wright, and explained the situation. "This sounds heavy," Wright said when Virgil had finished. "I'll call Mr. Booker now. Let's tentatively plan to meet at ten o'clock. This is the Stuart Booker from Sunfish Lake, right? Stuart and Andi?"

"Yes. You know them?"

"I know of them," Wright said. "The Bookers are well known in, uh, what you might call political donation circles."

"Sounds like Boyd Nash might have stepped in it," Virgil said.

"If he goes to trial anywhere in Minnesota, he has. In it up to his chin."

Jenkins came back with hot chocolate, bagels and cream cheese; he'd stopped at a drugstore, where he got two toothbrush-and-paste travel sets for three dollars each. They got water from an exterior faucet and brushed their teeth, and Jenkins said, "Now, if the cheeks of my ass weren't stuck together, I'd feel almost human."

They had the search warrant by a few minutes after eight-thirty, Trane and a computer tech from the Minneapolis crime lab turning up in separate cars, along with two cops who specialized in searches. Jenkins forced the front door, and, inside, they found three computers: a desktop and two laptops. Both the laptops were ThinkPads, nothing like the one stolen from Quill's carrel. All were password-protected. The technician took all three computers out to his car for transport back to Minneapolis.

"This is your first priority," Trane told the technician. "Don't let anyone bother you about other jobs. If they do, call me. Be best if you could crack these by, say, noon."

Nash also had three two-drawer file cabinets in his home office, filled with papers, apparently going back several years, in not very neat file folders, and envelopes. Among the files, Virgil found a bound copy of Nash's most recent income tax returns and, among them, 1099s from five separate companies, none of which Virgil had ever heard of.

He called Booker, who picked up instantly. "Virgil. We're meeting at ten."

"You sound a little wired," Virgil said.

"No, I'm a lot wired. I'm sitting here with my attorneys. We're going to nail this asshole to the cross."

Virgil said, "I'm going to read you five names . . ."

He did, and with the fourth Booker shouted, "Wait. Boardman? B-o-a-r-d-m-a-n?"

"Boardman Chemicals."

"That's the one, those fuckers," Booker shouted. "They're going down! They're going down!"

At nine o'clock, a young woman in a suit and carrying a briefcase turned up at the door. She represented Nash, she said. Trane gave her a copy of the search warrant, which the young woman said was illegally broad and not soundly based.

Trane smiled at her, and said, "Your client was caught red-handed inside the Surface Research building at two-thirty this morning accessing confidential files and photographing them. He's toast. If you would like to sit and watch the search, you're welcome to. But we're allowed to look anywhere there might be computer files hidden, and, as you know, they can be hidden on a thumb drive. We're going to take the house down to the studs."

At nine-thirty, Jenkins went home to sleep. And as the search continued, Trane took Virgil aside and told him that nothing she'd found in her further research into Robin Jones suggested that he might have killed Quill. "That's not going anywhere. I'd give you an in-depth explanation, if you want it, but it's not going anywhere. He didn't do it."

"Alibi?"

"Yeah, he's got an alibi, and a witness—a woman he's seeing. She spent the night. She's a law clerk, smart enough to know not to lie, at least for Jones's sake."

"All right. Let's keep him in mind, but . . . All right," Virgil said. "I'm telling you, we haven't seen one fuckin' thing here that points at Quill or the university. We know Nash made some moves, and was even in the library, but I can't find anything to back it up. No references to any medical companies, nothing on the tax returns."

"If he killed Quill, there's a good chance that he'd have wiped away any evidence of it. Stopped what he was doing and walked away," Trane said.

"True. Probably have to take a deeper look at his client list, see who he might have been talking to, who'd be interested in stuff coming out of Quill's lab." Virgil looked at his watch. "I've got to run down to Dakota County for this meeting. I'll see if I can get with Nash, see what he has to say for himself."

"He's pretty lawyered up . . ."

"He won't deal anyway," Virgil said. "Trying to get a break on Surface Research in exchange for taking the bullet for a murder? No way. I'll talk to him, see if we can eliminate him. Or not. Not would be interesting."

The meeting with the prosecutors didn't take long. Stuart Booker was treated with deference, but it stopped well short of actual slobbering. They knew who he was and who his friends were, but it wasn't that huge a deal, just huge enough to ensure that both Boyd Nash and Allen Young were denied immediate bail on grounds that they might destroy evidence in the computer files.

Virgil asked to interview Nash but Nash refused to budge, instead referring Virgil to his attorney, a man named George Wesley. Wesley, as it happened, had visited Nash in the fortress-like Dakota County Jail. He was on the way back to his office in the Twin Cities when Virgil called him with the interview request.

"I won't let him do it today, not until he's out on bail and back at his house," Wesley told Virgil. "If you want to submit written questions, I'll consider them."

"There's something going on here that you don't know about. What if I came by your office for an off-the-record chat?"

After a moment, Wesley, who was still in his car, said, "I could do that. You won't get much from me, but I could do that."

_____

Virgil said good-bye to Booker and headed back north to Edina, where Wesley had his office in a neatly kept brick building that was full of law offices. A secretary emailed Wesley that Virgil was in the office; Wesley, who was apparently no more than twenty feet away through a couple of walls, came out and waved Virgil into his office.

"I can't imagine why we need this conference," he said with a friendly smile as they shook hands, "since I'm not going to give you anything."

Virgil took a chair as Wesley, a thin, pale man with a shock of blond hair, sat behind his desk.

"Here's the thing. What your client was doing to Mr. Booker was rotten, and I don't care about it. Or I do a little bit, enough to send Mr. Nash to prison for a while. What I care about is another case I'm working on, the murder of professor Barthelemy Quill at the University of Minnesota."

Wesley sat back. "Wait a minute. You're saying that my client is a suspect in that case?"

"That's a little strong, but we know he made a couple of passes at Quill's lab and some of Quill's associates. Other physicians. We also know that he was actually in the Wilson Library, near Quill's carrel, sometime in the weeks before Quill's murder there. What we need to do is eliminate Nash as a suspect, if that can be done. If it can't, then we'll be considerably more interested in him."

Wesley thought about that for a moment, then said, "You want an alibi?"

"If he's got one. We'd look into it," Virgil said. "Otherwise, we'll start looking at him for the murder."

"Give me some details on the Quill case," Wesley said. "I'll talk to Boyd and get back to you. I'm not saying we'll provide an alibi, but I'll talk to him about whether we might be willing to cooperate at all."

"Fair enough," Virgil said. "If you want to make a couple of notes . . . Dr. Quill was killed three Fridays ago, very likely around midnight on Friday . . ."

After leaving Wesley's office, Virgil was feeling wonky from a lack of sleep and food, so he stopped at McDonald's for salt, grease, and carbohydrates, and then headed back to the hotel for a nap. He'd been in his room for five minutes when Wesley called back.

"Mr. Nash said that you have all the evidence you need to clear him. That's all he has to say."

"Huh. That could be taken in a couple of different ways."

"I'm sure you'll think of the relevant one," Wesley said.

Virgil called Trane. "What's happening with Nash's computers?"

"Don't know. I can check."

He told her about Wesley's statement, and said, "I think they're sending us a signal without admitting to anything. I think they're telling us that something in the files will indicate that Nash was down at Surface Research that Friday night. We'd been told he'd gone there several times, that he went on Friday, Saturday, and Sunday nights late, when nobody was working."

"We're going to provide him with an alibi?"

"I think that's what they're signaling," Virgil said.

"I'll get with the techs. What are you going to do?"

"I'm going to go take a nap, then pack up my dirty clothes and head home. I'll be back on Monday."

"Goddamnit, I feel like we've got all kinds of possibilities. But it's, like, trying to squeeze Jell-O, if you know what I mean."

"I do. Let's take a break and think about it."

They agreed to meet Monday morning in Trane's office.

Virgil shaved, showered, and dropped on the bed and was asleep in five minutes. He woke up groggy, looked at the clock: almost six. He was thinking about Frankie: he needed to call her. He was fishing around on the night stand for his phone when it rang. He picked it up and looked at the screen: no caller ID.

He answered with "Virgil Flowers . . ."

A woman screamed at him, "Brett's dead! He's dead. Right here."

After a moment of confusion, he thought: Megan Quill. Brett was the sleepy, bare-assed dude. "Easy," Virgil said. "How do you know he's dead?"

"Because I'm looking at him," Quill shouted into her phone. "And he's dead."

"You're looking . . . Did you call the cops?"

"You're a cop," she said. "I got your card."

"Yeah, but . . . Where are you?"

"In Brett's room."

"Do you have an address?"

He heard running footsteps, then heard her: "What's the address? What's the fuckin' address here? Hey, you . . ."

There was more shouting in the distance, and then she came back with a St. Paul address not far from the University of St. Thomas.

"Stay where are, don't touch a thing. And leave the room," Virgil said. "I'll call the St. Paul cops, they should be there in five minutes. I'll be there in ten. Stay right there."

"It looks like he . . . I think he OD'd. There's a syringe on the floor. He's all white-and-gray-looking."

"What—"

"Heroin. Sometimes he did heroin. He said it made him dreamy." She started to sob.

"Stay there," Virgil repeated.

"Jesus Christ, he's really dead!" she screamed.

Virgil again told her to leave the room, and she did, and he said, "Go someplace and sit down with your back against the wall. You don't want to faint and hurt yourself. Don't let anybody go in the room. Sit, and the cops will be there in a couple."

He clicked off, dialed 911, identified himself, explained the situation, gave the operator the address Megan Quill was calling from. "I'll be there myself in a few minutes. Tell the responding guys that this could be part of another murder investigation and to be careful with the scene. Tell them to freeze it, nothing more, and call Ryan at St. Paul Homicide."

When he got off the call to 911, he called Trane. "Megan Quill found her friend dead about two minutes ago," he said. "She thinks it might be an overdose. St. Paul cops are on the way. I'm going over."

"Give me an address. I'm sitting in my car at the office. I'll be right behind you."

TWENTY-TWO

As Virgil walked out of the elevator, he almost ran over Harry, who was headed for the bar.

Harry said, "You finally get a clue? You look like it."

"Maybe," Virgil said. "Can't talk."

"It's a kid, isn't it?" Harry called after him, as he went out the door.

A dead kid, Virgil thought, as he jogged out to his truck.

From the University of Minnesota to St. Thomas normally would have been a ten minute run, but Virgil had grille lights and a siren and he punched them up and made it in eight. He found two St. Paul cop cars at the curb outside an old, decrepit house.

Virgil talked to the first cop he came to, who said another cop was on the second-floor landing of the house with Megan Quill. "We stuck our head inside the room to see if the victim could be resuscitated, but he appears to have been dead for a while."

"Okay, I'm going up," Virgil said.

The cop touched his arm. "We didn't mess with the body, but we looked at it to make sure he was cold and not breathing. Check his stomach."

"What?"

"Check his stomach."

As Virgil walked toward the house, another car pulled to the curb down the street and honked once. He turned and saw Trane getting out.

Trane flashed her badge at the St. Paul cops and hurried up to Virgil.

"Have you been inside?"

"No. And the cops are being mysterious."

"What?"

"Let's go up. I've been told to look at the dead kid's stomach."

"What?"

They went up to the second floor of the house, where the other cop was standing next to Quill, who was sitting on the hallway floor.

Trane identified herself and Virgil to the second cop, said hello to Quill, who was stricken, red-faced and sporadically weeping, and the cop said, "We've got an investigator coming, he'll be here in a couple of minutes."

"The victim . . ." Virgil began.

"Has been dead for a while," the cop said. "He's on his back. We're seeing some rigor in the eyelids, and the blood's already settled in his back and legs. There was no hope of resuscitation."

Trane said, "Would you mind if we took the witness outside?

We know her, we've dealt with her, it might be better . . . We'll wait for your investigator by the front door."

The cop nodded. "Sure. She's shook up."

Virgil: "We need to take a quick look at the victim. Your partner outside . . ."

The cop nodded again. "Yeah. Take a look."

Quill said in a choked voice, "His name is Brett Renborne. Somebody's got to call his parents." And she began weeping again.

"Hate this shit, when it's a kid," Trane said, as they walked down the hall to the room—it was a single room, perhaps fifteen by twenty feet, walls painted a medium blue, with a bed, an Apple laptop on a small wooden desk with the printer on the floor next to the desk, a shelf with a microwave on it, and there was a closet. But no bathroom. Virgil asked, and the cop at the door said, "Down the hall."

Virgil led the way inside Renborne's apartment, both he and Trane stepping carefully. Virgil pointed silently at the syringe on the floor.

Renborne was sprawled on the bed, on top of a sheet, mostly on his right side, with his right arm extended out from beneath his body. He was wearing a white T-shirt, which was pulled up to expose most of his stomach, and a pair of Jockey briefs. The shorts were soiled, and there was the distinct odor of fecal matter in the air.

Virgil bent over the body to look at the stomach. "Oh, Jesus," he said.

"What?"

"Look."

Trane bent over the body. "Do you think . . . ?"

"Yeah, I do."

Seven words were scrawled in black ink in a wobbly hand on Renborne's stomach: "I did it. I can't stand it."

Virgil looked around, saw a black Sharpie pen poking out from under the other sheet. He pointed at it. "Pen."

"Let's get out of here," Trane said.

Back out in the hallway, Trane said to Quill, "Come on, honey," and held Quill's hand and led her down the stairs. Outside, a woman who lived on the lower floor brought a chair out, and Quill sat down.

"Tell us about your day," Trane said. "When did you last hear from your friend?"

"His name is Brett Renborne. I called him last night to see if he was going to be around this afternoon, but he said he had a class at one o'clock, and I had one from two to four, so I tried calling him after class."

"What time was that?"

"I don't know, but I . . . Wait a minute." She pulled a cell phone from her back pocket, clicked it on, thumbed it a couple of times, then said, "At four twenty-three and at four forty-one. I tried to call him twice. I don't live far from here. I checked my email, and after a while I decided to just walk over here and knock, to see if he was sleeping or something. His door was unlocked, and I peeked in and . . . I knew he was dead. He looked like a dead person in a movie. I went in. I couldn't believe it. I wanted to scream, or something, but couldn't. I had this police card from Mr. Virgil in my purse, so I called, And then I could scream . . ."

"Do you know what time that was? When you found him?"

"About one minute before I called Mr. Virgil . . . Wait. That's not right, is it, Mr. Virgil?"

"Close enough," Virgil said. He checked his phone. "Virgil's my first name . . . And you called me at five fifty-one."

"That's when I found him," she said.

She said that Renborne had experimented, in serial fashion rather than simultaneously, with marijuana, cocaine, LSD, and opium, because he said the drugs loosened up his mind. The heroin was more recent, Quill said. She'd argued against it, but he said that he wouldn't get addicted because he was careful and only did it once a week and would quit in a month or two.

"I believed him. He was good with drugs," Quill said. "He'd try them and then he'd quit. Except for weed. But, I mean, who doesn't do weed?"

A dingy-looking sedan pulled to the curb, and Roger Bryan got out, looked at them, and said, "Oh, shit."

Virgil said, "Hey, Rog. This is Megan Quill, Dr. Quill's daughter. She found the victim."

"Oh . . ."

"You don't have to repeat yourself," Trane said. "We've already said it a few times."

Another car pulled in, and a thin black woman got out, grabbed a briefcase. She looked past Bryan, and said, "Virgil Fuckin' Flowers. I'm living the nightmare."

"How are you, Honey?"

"Where've you been, man? Somebody said you went out for

coffee ten years ago and never came back." Honey Marshall was a longtime medical examiner's investigator who'd look at the body before it was moved. As she walked up, she eye-checked Bryan and Trane, and said, "What've we got here? Some kind of multi-agency cop convention?"

"It's complicated," Trane said. She tipped her head toward Quill. "This young lady is the daughter of Dr. Quill, the professor who was murdered at the university a couple of weeks ago. She found the body of a friend of hers. She thinks it might be an over-dose. And it might be . . . A deliberate overdose."

"What makes you think it was an overdose, Miz Quill?" Marshall asked.

"I knew he was messing around with heroin . . . And there's a syringe on the floor . . ."

"Ah. Well, let's go take a look."

Bryan said, "Let's go take a *careful* look. It could be a crime scene."

Marshall popped open her briefcase and took out a pack of plastic booties, handed pairs to Bryan, Trane, and Virgil, took a pair for herself. They filed up the stairs, and Bryan asked one of the cops to stay with Quill. "You don't want to go in there any-more anyway," Bryan told her.

She hugged herself and shook her head, said, "No."

Marshall and the three cops put on their booties and went into Renborne's room. Marshall scanned the body, bent over to look at Renborne's arms, said, "Huh." She read the message on the dead man's stomach, scanned the body again, spent some time looking at the area behind Renborne's left knee, stood up, and said, "Give me a minute."

She went to the door, stuck her head out, and called to Quill, who was waiting down the hallway. "Do you know if your friend was left- or right-handed?"

Quill called back, "Right-handed, I think. Yeah, right-handed."

"Thanks."

Marshall stepped back into the room, put her hands on her hips, gazing at the body, then turned to Bryan, and said, "You need to be careful here, Rog. He has what looks like a regular injection site behind his left knee, including a fresh one. He has another fresh one on the inside of his right elbow. But only one there, no signs of more on either arm."

"Why would he change regular injection sites?" Trane asked.

Marshall said, "That happens. Can't tell what junkies are going to do, especially if they're already high when they do that second hit. But, it's a little unusual to inject into your dominant arm. Most junkies inject into their nondominant one. Also, that injection in the left leg would be typical of a right-handed guy using that hand to hold the syringe. To inject his right arm, he would have had to use his left hand."

She went back to the door and called out to Quill. "Did your friend wear a lot of short-sleeved shirts?"

Quill called back, "Yes. All the time."

Marshall turned to Bryan, and said, "Which makes it even less likely that he'd inject in his arm, where it'd be visible. So, we gotta let the docs take a look at this. But I'm tentatively calling the manner of death undetermined. From the writing on his stomach, it was not an accident. Could be suicide, but it also could be that somebody murdered him. Gave him a hot shot while he was sleeping off the first injection. We'll have to wait for the autopsy to be sure, but I think the cause of death is clear enough."

Virgil said, "We need to talk with Megan."

Bryan: "I'm with you." Trane nodded, and Bryan added, "I'm bringing in Crime Scene."

Renborne had the only rented room in the house. The rest of it was occupied by the owner, an older woman, who agreed to let them use a bedroom down the hall from Renborne's to interview Quill.

As they took her in, she said, "I've never seen a dead person before. Not a real one. When my dad was killed, his wife had him cremated, so there was nothing at the funeral except this vase. But I knew Brett was dead when I went in and saw him."

"Did you touch the body?" Bryan asked. "We need to know if we wind up doing DNA tests."

She jerked her head up and down, sobbed again, caught herself, and said, "I touched his shoulder, his shirt. I kinda poked him. He was like wood. I knew he was dead."

"All right."

Virgil said, "Give me a minute. I need to look at something."

While Bryan was asking Quill about her time line that day— what she'd done, where she'd gone, who she'd seen, and when— Virgil left and walked down to the room where Marshall and the cop were waiting for a Crime Scene crew.

"I need to look at something: his desk."

He got a single bootie from Marshall, scanned the room carefully, then looked at the top of the desk, which held Renborne's laptop, a stack of spiral notebooks—all used—and a tall, gray marmalade jar that looked old, possibly a real antique, which held a variety of pens and pencils. He put the bootie on his right hand and used it to open the desk drawers. He looked inside, then closed the drawers, stepped back to the door, gave Marshall the bootie, and walked back to the bedroom where Quill was still talking about what she did that day.

When she finished, Virgil asked, "Where's your friend Jerry?"

"He went home to Faribault last night."

Byran: "Who's Jerry?"

Quill said, "Jerry Krause. He's a friend. He and another guy—Butch-something—went down to Faribault last night."

"Does he go down there a lot?" Virgil asked.

"When he starts running low on cash. He gets an allowance from his dad and sometimes he spends it too fast," Quill said. "His parents are divorced, and he goes down when he runs out of clothes and washes them all at his mom's house. She usually slips him some money. He's probably down there every three weeks or month."

Trane asked, "Was Brett unhappy about something? Depressed?"

She shook her head. "Not that I noticed. And I think I would have noticed. I didn't want him fuckin' around with those drugs, I kept telling him that. He was a happy guy, really. If he over-dosed, it was an accident."

"What about the message?" Bryan asked.

She shook her head again. "What message?"

"You didn't see the message?" Trane asked.

"No, no note. There's nothing."

Virgil: "There's a message written on his stomach." He turned to Trane and Bryan. "I'm pretty sure you guys spotted this detail, but the note was written so it could read right side up. But from his perspective, he'd have had to have written it upside down and backwards. Upside down and backwards, and he was stoned."

"I wondered about that," Trane said, and Bryan said, "Yeah."

"I looked around the room," Virgil said. "Unless there are some Sharpies under the bed, where I couldn't see them, or in the closet, there aren't any others. Only the one on the floor."

Bryan said, "That worries me."

Quill: "Somebody murdered him?"

"We have to think about it," Bryan said. "And the note . . . Let me ask you this: how well did Brett know your father?"

"I mean, he was with us a couple of times when we went over there. Dad didn't like him because he thought Brett was a slacker. And Brett couldn't help himself, he'd get sarcastic. But not mean sarcastic. He'd sort of tweak Dad. One time, he was looking around the music room—the Steinway and the stereos and all—and he said something like, 'Man, the shit you can get when you inherit money.' Dad got pissed, went on about hard work and millennials not knowing hard work if it bit them on the ass."

Bryan: "Do you think Brett could have killed him? Even if it was, you know, by accident?"

Quill: "My father wasn't killed by accident . . ."

"You know what he means," Trane said. "They don't like each other. They run into each other up there in the library. Your father thinks Brett is stealing something, like his computer, and Brett hits him with it. Doesn't mean to kill him, but there's a struggle."

"You told me there wasn't a struggle," Quill said to Trane.

"Well, a tussle. An argument. Your father turns away, and Brett hits him."

"I don't think so," she said. "Brett didn't want to have anything to do with violence."

Virgil: "You said he experimented with cocaine. When was that? How long ago?"

"A while ago. During the summer. I don't know exactly."

"Do you know where he got it?"

"No. I'm not up to date on coke dealers, but I don't think he had to go very far. He liked to go to clubs when he had the money. You can get coke if you go to the right clubs."

"Did he ever mention a dealer named China White?" Trane asked.

"No. He never mentioned any dealers." She put both hands on her forehead. "I can't believe he's dead. Right over there. He's dead. He was alive last night. Now he's dead."

Trane patted her on the shoulder. "Look. Let's go back outside, get some air . . . Virgil, we need to talk."

Outside, Bryan spent a few moments getting names from Quill: Renborne's parents, other friends. The landlady said she'd heard Renborne speaking on his cell phone early that morning, before she got up, when he was coming back from a late night out. "I heard him on the steps about, mmm, six o'clock."

"Was he usually up that early in the morning?"

"Not usually, but that boy would come and go at all times of day and night. Sometimes, he was just getting home at six. Sometimes, he'd be going out the door at six. I got so I didn't pay much attention."

"Did you hear him during the day? He had a class at one."

"No, I'm not here. I get up around seven, I go to work at eight-thirty, I get back at four-thirty or five, depending. Sometimes the other girls and I go out after work."

She worked as a secretary at the Minnesota Historical Society in St. Paul. She was divorced, and Renborne was the only other person who lived in the house. "My ex never lived here. We broke up, split the money, and I bought this place with my share."

"Are you sure it was Brett that you heard going up the steps this morning?" Virgil asked.

She shrugged. "Sounded like him. He wore running shoes, he was quiet."

Renborne, she said, was "a real nice boy. I had no idea he was fooling with drugs. I never saw him, you know, drugged up or anything."

Virgil and Trane drifted away. Trane asked, "Are you still going home?"

"I'd like to. This isn't our scene, and St. Paul will do the work. I'll be back on Monday morning. They should have some labs by then, an autopsy report. Not much for me to do on a Sunday."

"All right. How are we doing otherwise?"

"I can't . . . I don't see where we're going yet."

"Neither do I. By the way, your guy Nash . . . Our guys broke into some of the files on the computer. There are some other files there that are encrypted, we'll probably never get into those. But of the files we've seen, a couple of dozen of them were photographs transferred out of a program called Lightroom."

"I know it," Virgil said.

"Yeah, and it's got this metadata stuff. The photos apparently were taken the same night Quill was killed, unless they've been faked somehow."

"So we gave him his alibi."

"And solidified the charges of industrial espionage," Trane said. "Which doesn't solve my problem."

Virgil said, "I'm going to run down to Faribault, see if I can find this Jerry Krause kid. It's not exactly on my way, but it'll only add twenty minutes or so to my drive time. If he hasn't changed his driver's license, he should have a home address on it."

"Okay. You think he'll know anything?"

"Nah, not really. But the three of them were a gang, and not an entirely healthy one. I oughta check."

Virgil said good-bye to Quill and headed south on I-35. Faribault was a bit less than an hour straight south, and, on the way, he talked to the duty officer at the BCA and got Krause's home address. He got turned around once he was in town, but he found the house with help from his iPhone map app; it was an older but well-kept neighborhood whose maple trees were already showing a hint of autumn orange. An older woman came to the door, looking sleepy, said she was Jerry's mother. "He's not in trouble, is he?"

"No. A good friend of his has died, and it's possible that it's suicide. We're talking to his friends—"

"Oh, boy, not Brett?"

"I'm afraid so."

"Oh, boy. Oh, Jerry's going to be upset," she said. "Let me get my jacket. He just walked over to the Kwik Trip."

Virgil and Krause's mother, whose name was Connie, walked a zigzag course four blocks over to the Kwik Trip and saw Krause walking back toward them, eating an ice cream cone. "Always with the ice cream," his mother said.

Krause stopped eating the cone as they came up, and he said, "You're that Virgil officer."

"Yes. Have you heard from Brett recently? Talk to him at all this morning or last night?"

"No. Why? What happened?"

"I'm afraid he's dead," Virgil said.

Krause started, his hand tilted, and the top of his cone fell on the grass verge. He cried, "Shit," and kicked it into the street. "Oh my God!" Tears came to his eyes, and he asked, "Was it drugs?"

"It looks that way," Virgil said. "Did you know—"

"Does Megan know?"

"She found him."

"Oh my God! I gotta get up there. She's gonna be wrecked."

"Did you know he was using?"

"Yeah, I did," Krause said. "Megan and I—we tried to get him to stop. But he said it was just an experiment. He did all kinds of research on the internet, how much you could use, about addiction and all that. He used opium, is what he did. He said he got these great dreams, and he was going to write a book about it . . . Ah, God!"

"It wasn't opium," Virgil said. "It was probably heroin."

"Ah, yeah, it could have been, he was talking about that. He didn't tell me he'd started because I gave him so much shit about the other stuff."

Tears were streaming down his face, and his mother patted him on the shoulder. "I'll take you back up there," she said. And to Virgil, "Jerry doesn't have a car."

Virgil asked a few questions. Krause had seen Renborne the afternoon before, and they had talked a while at the student center. Then his ride had shown up, and he and another student, Butch Olsen, had driven down to Faribault.

"When I saw Brett, he was perfectly cheerful. He wasn't high.

He said he and Megan were going out that night, over to the U. I thought they'd probably spend the night at her place. They did that sometimes. I was invited, but I had to come back here: I was, like, wearing the same underwear for the third day running . . . Butch is going to pick me up tomorrow morning."

"I'll take you," his mother said again.

He'd spoken to Megan once, Jerry said, that morning, about nothing. "She just called me, said she was walking around, might go over to Grand Avenue, look at some jeans. That's all she really said. She was bored, and I think Brett was in class this afternoon."

"Do you have any idea where he got his dope?"

Krause looked up at the sky and blinked. "He told me he got it from a woman in some skanky club up by the university. Maybe her name was White? . . . Yes, I think it was White . . . I think she got all the other shit, too. He told me once that his connection was Vietnamese, but I'm not sure that was the same person. I think it was, I'm just not sure."

China White, Virgil thought. Vietnamese were nothing like Chinese, but if you were street scum in St. Paul, they probably didn't spend a lot of time parsing the difference.

Virgil asked a few more questions that didn't produce anything significant, and then they went back to the Krause place. "I may want to talk with you again," he told Jerry. "If you could check with Brett's friends, if they have any idea of where I could find his connection . . ."

"I will," Krause said. He pressed the heels of his hands in his eye sockets, and said, "Ah, Jesus. Ah, shit . . ."

TWENTY-THREE

Virgil cut cross-country to the farm.

He hadn't spent much time thinking about it because he hadn't had children, but now that Frankie had a couple of his buns in the oven, it occurred to him that there could be no lower point in life than losing a kid. And when you have a kid, you're putting a heavy mortgage on your future. Everybody dies eventually, but when you have a kid the best you can hope for is to die first. Preferably, in the distant future.

Brett Renborne hadn't seemed like a bad kid, no more lost than a lot of guys who later turn out to be good people. The drugs were a little extreme, but, in his heart, Virgil could understand the experimentation. A bit lost himself, he'd wandered out of college and into the military, looking for adventure and willing to risk his neck for it. Brett had done something analogous, in a way, and had gone down. If he had decent parents, they'd be hurt more deeply than Brett ever was. Even in death.

When he came up on the farm, he saw Sam, Frankie's youngest at eleven years old, rolling down the road on a fat-tire bike, Honus the Yellow Dog running along beside him in the weeds in the ditch. Sam looked back over his shoulder at Virgil's approaching truck and waved, and Virgil felt a sudden pang of fear: a mortgage on your future.

Like, if this ever ends, because somebody dies too early, my life will be over . . .

He parked by the barn, and Frankie came out of the house, and said, "Let's go eat in town. I'm starving and don't feel like cooking anything."

"Gimme kiss," Virgil said. She gave him a kiss, and he held on for a while, and when Sam came up, skidding in the gravel, he said, "Holy shit, you guys are goin' for it."

"You say 'shit' again and I'll kick your ass," Virgil said. "Or your mom will."

Frankie said to Sam, "It's all right to say 'shit' sometimes, but only when it's appropriate. You have to learn when it's appropriate and you haven't done that yet. I'm not sure I like that 'goin' for it,' either."

Sam rolled his eyes, and said to Virgil, "Throw me some passes."

"How about some grounders instead? You're never playing football, if I can help it, so there's no point in practicing."

"You played football."

"I was stupid," Virgil said.

And so on. The usual.

———

They went into town and got a pepperoni pizza, saving a slice for Honus, who was waiting impatiently in the back of the truck, knowing what was coming. They talked about this and that and a house that Frankie was bidding on, for demolition, and how she'd found online plans for a horse stable she thought might be right for the farm. "I took them up to Dave Jensen, and he's going to print them out on his architectural printer. He said he'd do it today and drop them off tomorrow morning on the way to church."

And they talked about Brett overdosing, if that's what had happened.

"It's very strange, especially the note on his stomach. 'I did it. I can't stand it.' He must've meant he killed Quill. But, jeez, he didn't seem like the type."

"You get in a jam and you react," Frankie said. "You don't think. If you could take it back, you would, but you can't. That's why you all think Quill was killed with a laptop—it was an impulse. You don't plan to kill somebody with a laptop."

"Yeah, I know. He didn't like Quill, he told me so himself," Virgil said. "Then there's the whole note thing, that it was written upside down from his perspective. How do you do that if you're stoned on heroin?"

"You don't know the sequence," Frankie pointed out. "Maybe he wrote the note sober and then got high later on, then went for the second injection. It's like that could be the same kind of almost accident as killing Quill. You get freaked out, you react, and then you can't take it back."

"I gotta think about it," Virgil said. "When he wrote the note, there were no practice strokes, no do-overs."

"I'll never use drugs," Sam said. "I plan on dying because I ate too much pepperoni."

"You could do that," Frankie said. "The way you pack it away, you could burn a hole right in the bottom of your stomach."

"Or, you could die because you decided to play football," Virgil said. "Have you even looked at the Benson boys? John Benson's your age and he's gotta weigh a hundred pounds. What are you, sixty? He'd rip your head off."

"I'm too fast for that. He'd be standing there, holding his dick, and I'd be gone," Sam said.

"You say 'dick' again—"

"I know, you'll kick my ass," Sam said. "Or Mom will."

"I don't know where a kid his age gets this stuff," Virgil said to Frankie. "Things have changed since I was in school."

Frankie was staring at him. "Virgil?"

"What?"

"He gets it from you. 'Standing there, holding his dick.' Or how about, last week, 'His motorcycle is about the size of my dick'? I don't even know if that's supposed to mean it's big or it's small."

"Small for a motorcycle, big for . . ." He looked at Sam. "Anyway, I'll start watching it. The language."

"Too late," Frankie said. "This little twerp knows every word there is."

"That's true," Sam said. To Virgil: "You gonna eat that pepperoni?"

"Fuckin' A." And to Frankie: "You said he knows all the words."

At the house, they had some cleaning and straightening to do, and Virgil's clothes to wash and dry, then they watched a movie and all went to bed. Virgil and Frankie fooled around for a while, after which the house was quiet.

The next morning, Dave Jensen dropped off the drawings for the stable, and they spent an hour going over them. Virgil agreed that his building skills were probably up to the task, with a bit of paid help. "I could do the inside electric, but I'd want help bringing it down from the pole."

"Help? We're gonna hire somebody to do the electric, period. I don't even want you in the vicinity."

"Wouldn't hurt to have another well, either," Virgil said. "Either that or get some work done on the one we've got. It's gotta be eighty years old."

Later in the day, they checked on Virgil's house, which he was still leasing until November, and made two trips between Virgil's and the farm, moving more of his belongings. He'd have to do some touch-up painting where Honus had scratched up the doors, but that could wait.

All minor stuff, but it sucked up most of the afternoon. After supper, Sam had to do homework, and Virgil and Frankie talked about a couple of possible wildlife articles that Virgil might do that would still keep him close to home.

And they talked about the case.

"You've been brooding about it all day," Frankie said.

He told her about Harry's theory that he knew the killer because that's the way it would work on a TV show.

"Okay, that's nuts," she said.

"He's right about one thing: I've had any number of people who could turn into suspects but haven't. Not yet anyway. I'm almost to the point where I think it's a stranger who did the killing. Somebody broke into the carrel—"

"He didn't break in," Frankie said.

"Right, didn't break in. Okay, that's a problem, because then there had to be a key."

"It's like this: there was somebody lurking in the library, looking for something to steal . . ."

"But, like you said, there's no sign of a break-in," Virgil said. "He would have had to hide himself in the library and then come out after everybody was gone. Why'd he wait so long? Why'd he wait until midnight if he could have done it at ten o'clock?"

"Too many people around," Frankie said. "You said there were dorms all around the library, and it was a Friday night."

Virgil nodded. "I'll give you that one. He didn't move until there was nobody to see him coming out. Seems weird. But, okay . . ."

"Did you check on janitors and maintenance guys? Maybe there's somebody around after closing who stays into the night."

"Trane did all of that and came up empty."

"Anyway, he was in there, hiding, when Quill came in. Quill opened the door, picked up his computer, and then saw the guy. There's some pushing but no injuries, and Quill says he's calling the cops, and the guy gets the computer away from him and hits him with it."

"Quill didn't open the door," Virgil said. "Our hooker said he saw the guy way before Quill got to the carrel and jumped him. Quill wouldn't have had time to use his key."

"But you think the key was used, that the door was opened, the computer was taken out and used as a weapon?"

"Maybe. Or maybe he was hit with something else, and the

killer used Quill's keys to open the door. Quill may have had them in his hand because he'd opened the outside library door with them and was planning to open the carrel's door. The killer needed to hide the body, so he opened the door—the carrel's—dragged the body inside, saw the computer, knew he could hock it for something, maybe a lot . . ."

They hashed that theory over for a while, came to no conclusions. Quill may have known the killer, but it could just as well have been a stranger.

"The other weird thing about the whole case is the number of possibilities that seem to pop up in our faces," Virgil said. "They keep coming in and they keep going nowhere."

Frankie lay back on the couch and slipped her toes under Virgil's thigh. "My toes are cold. So, like, what possibilities?"

"We had Quill and Katherine Green, the head of the Cultural Science Department, in a bitter feud that actually involved a little violence. An assault. We got a CD that looked like blackmail, but it never panned out. We found a twist of cocaine in Quill's desk and a note that said he bought it from a dealer named China White, but there apparently is no China White—not a person named that anyway, it's slang for 'heroin.' Quill might have had a girlfriend, but we couldn't find her; she supposedly wore English riding clothes, had a black German shepherd called Blackie, and hung out at Starbucks. We couldn't find her, but we were told that a black woman in English-style riding clothes hung out at that same Starbucks and that there was a handicapped guy with a German shepherd, but not a black one, just a regular one . . . It's all very weird . . . Then we have Terry Foster . . ."

Virgil went on for a while, and, when he was done, Frankie asked to hear his rerecording of the CD. He played it for her, from his cell phone, and she said, "It sounds like blackmail all right. If that was on a CD that he was listening to right before he was killed."

"It was. It was in his CD player, in his office."

They both thought about that for a while, and then Frankie said, "That CD was sure to be found with a detailed search."

"Not a sure thing," Virgil said.

"But it *was* found," she said. "Just like the cocaine."

"You think the recording was faked?"

"It is odd."

Virgil rubbed his chin, played the recording again. "It's even a little tortured. That line about Quill strutting around like a peacock."

Frankie yanked her toes out from under Virgil's leg and sat up. "Virgil! A woman in English riding clothes . . . a guy who's a peacock . . . a woman named Green . . . a person named China White   a dog named Blackie . . ." She was excited.

Virgil was puzzled. "Yeah?"

Frankie: "They're all names from the game of Clue. Green. White. Peacock. I'm pretty sure there's a Mr. Black who's the murdered guy. Wait, I've got Clue somewhere in the closet."

"I've never played it," Virgil said. She went to get the game, and Virgil called after her, "Megan Quill had Clue in her closet."

She came back, said, "We're missing some pieces, but here's the whole thing about 'Mr. Peacock killed him with a candlestick in the library.' You know that bit?"

"I've heard something like that."

She told him about the game, showed him the pieces, the clues, the rooms . . .

"So Mrs. Green killed Dr. Quill in the library with the computer."

Virgil lay back on the couch and closed his eyes. "Yeah. But it wasn't Mrs. Green." Then, after a moment, he said, "I gotta go online and look at Wikipedia. Back in a minute."

In a minute, he was back. "There's nobody named Black in the American version. Clue was originally called Cluedo and was invented by an English guy. The victim was named Black, but in the American version that was changed to Mr. Boddy."

"I knew about Boddy," Frankie said. "I thought that was pretty clever. *Not.*"

"All those clues," Virgil said. "From an Anglophile game freak who was dragging us all over the goddamn Cities with fake clues. From a freakin' board game."

Virgil called Trane. She answered with, "Flowers, you figured it out?"

"Yeah, we did, me and Frankie—mostly Frankie. I know who killed Quill and probably Brett Renborne."

Trane crunched on something, maybe an apple. She paused. "Okay. Well, don't keep me waiting. Who was it?"

"Jerry Krause. Who, twenty-four hours ago, was crying his lyin' eyes out about his dead buddy Brett."

CHAPTER

TWENTY-FOUR

Virgil met with Trane and Lieutenant Carl Knox in Knox's office the next morning so Virgil could lay out the argument for Knox. "It's gonna sound weird. It *is* weird. This whole case is weird," Virgil said.

He and Frankie had diagrammed the arguments on a yellow legal pad the night before with a variety of arrows demonstrating how one thought led to another and eventually to the conclusion about Jerry Krause. Knox took in the mess of notes—annotations in the margins, inserts, underlines, yet more arrows—and said, "Tell me one thing to start with. Why'd he do it? This Krause kid."

"It's so basic that we didn't see it. He simply wanted the computer," Virgil said. "He didn't want anything in the computer. He didn't want data or software or any of that. It had nothing to do with the feud between Cultural Science and the medical guys. He wanted the fuckin' computer because it was the fastest thing he'd ever seen and he's a crazy gamer. He's obsessed with games. I actually saw him slap his Mac laptop because it was too slow.

Slapped it. Called it a piece of shit. I'd bet my left nut that he's still got Quill's machine."

"With twins on the way, you probably don't need your left nut anymore, so that's not much of a bet," Trane said.

Knox waved her off. "Stay focused. What are all those scribbled notes?"

"We kept adding things that seemed relevant, stuff that we knew. First of all, from something she said, I'm almost certain that Megan Quill took her friends over to her father's house at one time or another. We can talk to Megan about that. Both Renborne and Krause knew him, they both disliked him, so there was some contact. I'd be willing to bet that's where Krause found out about the laptop in the library. Quill had three cars. He had a fob for each of them, with lots of keys on them—for his house, his lab, his various offices and the carrel, and probably for the library's outer doors. I wouldn't be surprised that if we looked at all three, we'd find that one of them is missing the library keys. Because Krause was inside the house, knew what they were, and he took them."

"How would he know which keys were which?"

Virgil shrugged. "I don't know. But if you're smart, you could find out. Like, if Quill had two similar keys and three different ones on each fob, then the two similar keys would be for the library."

"That's thin," Trane said.

"I know, but if I could figure it out, I think Krause could, too. I'd be interested to know if Megan had a key to her father's house and knew the security code. If she did, that would mean that she and her friends could have been in the house when Quill wasn't. Could have looked around."

Trane said, "I've been talking to the Ramsey medical examiner.

They say Renborne's death is suspicious. The cause of death is definitely an overdose. The manner of death they're going to list as undetermined—possibly accident, suicide, or homicide. The question is, why would Krause have killed him?"

"Because Renborne figured it out," Virgil said.

"Couldn't prove it now," Knox said. "Unless he told somebody else."

"Like Megan," Trane said.

"She could be in jeopardy herself if she's figured out who killed her father or who killed Renborne," Virgil said. "Krause wants to get in her pants. If he gets in and there's some pillow talk . . ."

"We need to talk to that girl," Trane said.

"Let's go with Virgil's line of thought here," Knox said, "the rest of your scribbles."

"Terry Foster got attacked," Virgil said. "He had talked to Megan Quill, Renborne, and Krause on the street, over by St. Thomas. I called him last night. He said he never identified himself, but when I pushed him, he said he drove his car past them. If Krause saw his license plate—he's a hacker—and if he looked at the DMV, he'd have Foster's home address. And Krause exactly fits Foster's description of his attacker."

"There's more?" Knox asked.

"All kinds of stuff," Virgil said. He was talking a hundred miles an hour. "When I was talking to Megan Quill the first time, Krause was there—that's when he slapped his laptop—and he did perfect imitations of Bugs Bunny and Elmer Fudd. We have people who say the person on the CD sounded like Barth Quill, but maybe not exactly like him. They're doubtful."

"So Krause can do voices—like the CD, and China White tip we got," Trane said.

"Yeah. And the rest of it: there's a Clue game in Megan Quill's closet, and he's a fanatic gamer. He's been toying with us, all those Clue names: Green, White, Peacock, Blackie, the dog. Here's another thing: he went to high school in England for eleventh grade, and Megan said he came back with an accent. He said Barth Quill's girlfriend was wearing English riding clothes and had a dog named Blackie. Well, in the English version Clue Mr. Black is the victim; in the American version, it's Mr. Boddy. Krause played the game in England . . . I don't believe there's actually a girlfriend; I think he made her up of composites of people he saw in that Starbucks—a woman in riding clothes, a guy with a dog."

Knox pressed his index finger to his lips, thinking, then said, "Okay. I'm buying it."

"So am I," Trane said. "Because I've got one more thing that Virgil doesn't."

Virgil: "What?"

"After you called last night, I got up early and got Krause's phone records," Trane told Virgil. "His phone was often blacked out, as if he'd pulled the battery."

"That little asshole has a Faraday bag," Virgil said. "He used it on Quill's telephone."

"That's what I think," Trane said.

Knox: "I'm buying it, but I don't think we're going to find a judge who'll issue us a search warrant on the basis of Krause playing Clue and the coincidence of those names."

"Not really a coincidence," Virgil said. "He knew the Green name, and he played on that with the others."

"Do you think we could get a warrant?" Knox asked.

"Maybe with the right judge."

"Not here in Hennepin. Maybe from one of those good ol'

boys down in Hogwash Corners, but not here," Knox said. "Maggie, what do you think?"

"I think you're right," she told Knox. "We're not there yet, on a warrant. I've talked to Megan Quill a couple of times. She felt bad about her father, even if they had a rough relationship. I know for sure she's freaked out about Renborne. I think we talk to her. I think we can set a trap, if she'll cooperate. Bug her room. Get Krause in there . . ."

"Could work," Knox said.

"Gotta be careful," Virgil said. "If he reacted like he did with Barth Quill, he could whack her with something before we could get in the room."

"We also have to be ready for an adamant and detailed denial of why he couldn't have done it," Knox said. "Get that on tape and it'd get a lot tougher in court later on; the jury would hear nothing but a denial."

"Let's work through all of that, do some brainstorming," Trane said. "Maybe we don't have to get Megan involved. If we do, we'll have to be careful."

"All we need is enough to get a warrant," Virgil said. "I'll bet you a zillion dollars that he's still got that computer. I'll bet he's hotter for that laptop than he is for Megan Quill."

Knox asked, "Which one of you is going to talk to Quill?"

Trane and Virgil glanced at each other and simultaneously said, "Both of us."

TWENTY-FIVE

Virgil and Trane drove over to Megan Quill's apartment, but she wasn't there. Virgil called her a half dozen times, walking up and down the sidewalk outside her apartment. Each time, the phone went to voice mail. But, in Virgil's experience, people Quill's age tended to walk around with their cell phone in their hands, and his persistence eventually paid off. On the sixth call, she answered, with a weak, tremulous, "Who is this?"

"Virgil Flowers. We need to talk to you. It's pretty urgent. Where are you?"

"Student center. What do you want to talk to me about?"

"Best to do it face-to-face," Virgil said. "We're at your apartment. Do you want us to come over there or do you want to come here?"

"I'm with a girlfriend."

"This talk has to be a private. So, whatever you think, but it has to be private."

After a moment, she said, "I'll walk home. It's five to ten minutes."

"We could pick you up."

"No, I'll walk."

She took longer than five to ten, long enough that Virgil started to worry, but Trane said, "Girls that age don't always have a tight grip on the passage of time. Give her a few more minutes."

And, a few minutes later, they saw her coming down the sidewalk, head down, hair loose and frizzy, carrying a backpack by a single strap over her shoulder.

Virgil said, "She looks like she's been hit hard."

Trane agreed. "She has been. Death of a lover, first dead man she's ever seen, and she found him. She'll remember this all of her days. She'll be sad all of her days."

When Quill came up, she raised her head and looked at them, and asked, "Is somebody else dead?"

"No, nothing like that," Virgil said.

Trane said, "Why don't we go up and talk in your room . . . Where it's cool."

In Quill's room, Virgil and Trane took the two kitchen table chairs, and Quill perched on the corner of the bed, which she hadn't folded back into a couch that morning. Quill put her backpack aside, and said, "What's up?"

Trane looked at Virgil, who said, "Megan, we think we figured out who may have killed your father."

She looked from Virgil to Trane and back to Virgil, and said, "Jerry."

Trane: "Why would you say that?"

"I'm triangulating. Dad's dead, Brett's dead, you're talking to me about figuring it out. The only other one you and I know who knew Dad and Brett is Jerry. Why do you think Jerry did it? Do you think he killed Brett, too?"

"We think it's a real possibility," Virgil said.

"Then it's my fault, isn't it?" She dropped her head again and looked down at the floor between her legs. "I led him on with all that pussy thing, letting him look but not touch, and sleeping with his best friend. He got back at me by killing my dad and his friend."

Trane said, "No. That's an amazing thought, but that's not it. We think he went to your father's library carrel at midnight and, purely by accident, bumped into your father."

Now Quill looked up with a sudden light in her eye. "That fuckin' computer . . ."

Virgil said, "Yes. We think he went there to steal the computer. One of the best gaming computers you could hope to get, and he ran into your father who was there for another reason. There may have been some pushing. And the woman who was there with your dad thought she heard him say something about calling the police. Jerry may have had the laptop in his hand and struck him with it."

Now Quill straightened, and said, "I totally believe that. Totally. I don't know why I didn't think of it."

Virgil and Trane laid out the other thoughts they had that pointed at Krause, and Quill confirmed that they'd been in her father's house several times when he was out of town. "We joked about stealing stuff that he wouldn't miss, but Brett wouldn't actually let us do that. We watched movies on Netflix. Dad left his Z8 in the garage, and we talked about driving around like Brett and me once saw in some old movie."

"*Ferris Bueller's Day Off*," Trane said, "Only, I think it was a Ferrari."

"That's the one," Quill said.

"You went in while he was gone . . . Did you ever run into a housekeeper or anyone?" It would be nice, Virgil thought, if a housekeeper had seen Krause.

"No, but Jen—she's the housekeeper—only comes in the mornings. We knew that. Brett and I would go up and fuck on Dad's bed. We made Jerry stay outside the bedroom but told him he could listen. We were such assholes."

Trane made the pitch. "We want you to help catch Jerry. We're not there yet."

She explained that the information they had wasn't enough for a search warrant and that the best confirming evidence they could possibly find would be the laptop. "We thought that if we could get Jerry up here—"

"He's coming over this afternoon," Quill said.

"Okay. We wanted to bring some technical people over here to put in some listening and recording equipment."

"Bug the apartment?"

"Yes. We'll be down the hall, in the next apartment—that's a fellow named Dick, correct?"

"Correct."

"We'd want you to ask Jerry if he had anything to do with Brett's death."

"He was down in Faribault."

"Somebody, we don't know who, walked up to Brett's room before six in the morning. Could have been Brett, but we think Brett may have been unconscious by then. We think Brett may have had a fairly late night, went back to his apartment with some heroin, shot up. We think he was probably asleep, dreaming, when Jerry arrived. He may even have told Jerry what he was planning to do."

"They *did* talk about it," Quill said.

"Faribault's less than an hour from here," Virgil said. "Jerry would have had access to his mother's car. He could have left there at five o'clock before she got up and been back before seven."

"What exactly would I say to him? Jerry. That's not something you'd blurt out: 'Did you kill Brett?'"

"I don't know, maybe you could," Virgil said. "What time is he coming over?"

"I told him I'm going home to White Bear tonight. We were going to go out for a pizza about five o'clock. My mom's picking me up right after the rush hour, probably about six."

"You don't have a car here?"

"No, I don't need one. I'm trying to save money. Tuition is forty thousand dollars a year, and that comes out of my trust fund. I get a scholarship, which saves some, but after rent and everything else there's not a lot left. I'd like to transfer to the U . . . Anyway, what should I say to Jerry? Exactly."

"We're coming to that," Trane said. "We wanted to get your okay for doing this. I'll suggest a few things, we'll rehearse. If we're going to do this, we need to get the technical people over here."

Quill nodded. She seemed to be coming alive. "I'll do it. Call them."

They had time to rehearse and set up the recording equipment and talk to Dick, the guy down the hall, who agreed, eventually, to go away between four and seven o'clock, not that he wanted to.

"I'd just watch," he told Virgil.

"Can't have outside witnesses," Virgil said. "All the local police forces would be very, very grateful if you'd go watch a movie or go on a date or something. I'll give you twenty bucks out of my own pocket to get a pizza."

Dick took the twenty, but grumbled about it.

At four forty-five, Virgil, Trane, and the tech services guy, whose name was Barry, were all in Dick's room listening to Quill playing a Chainsmokers album. Barry said "She's gotta turn that down."

"We told her, she'll kill it when Krause gets here," Virgil said. "Did you tell her to turn off her phone?"

"Yeah. That's all we'd need, a girlfriend call in the middle of a confession."

"She's played that goldarn song about thirty times since we started listening," Barry said.

Trane: "'Until You Were Gone,' with Emily Warren . . . Megan's boyfriend was killed a couple days ago."

"That song ain't gonna fix her head," the tech said.

"We don't know that," Trane said. "Anyway, it's nice. I think it's nice."

"Nice the first eight or ten times."

Krause had told Quill that he'd come get her at five o'clock. Virgil had talked to the phone tech guy at the BCA, had given him Krause's phone number, and they knew he was running late: his phone was still on the other side of the St. Thomas campus. They didn't want Krause out of the house with Quill, so they decided that Quill would order a pizza and have it show up about the same time Krause did. At ten after five, the pizza delivery truck showed up, but Krause was still on campus.

The phone tech called a minute later, and said, "Okay, he's headed your way."

Virgil had placed himself at the corner of Dick's only window, where he could watch the sidewalk, and at five-twenty he saw Krause hurrying toward the house.

Trane called Quill, and said, "He's here," and she asked, "You okay?"

"Actually, I'm fine," she said. "I'm putting the pizza in the microwave."

They heard the door downstairs bang shut when Krause came in, his footsteps on the stairs, and then the quick rap when he knocked on Quill's door.

She let him in, and said, "I can't go out. I'm sorry, I'm all fucked up. I ordered a pizza, I thought we could sit around and talk until Mom gets here." The volume of the music dropped to nothing.

"Okay with me," Krause said.

Trane: "So far, so good."

"We're ten seconds in," Virgil said.

"I can't believe it about Brett," Quill said, her voice wavering, climbing a half octave. "I still can't believe it."

Trane: "She's crying."

The tech: "Heck, she's good at this."

Virgil: "Shh. Shut up, everybody."

Krause said, "Nobody can believe it. I was talking to some guys today: nobody can believe he was involved with heroin. That's not . . . That's not what we do here."

There was a ding in the background, and Quill said, "I got hungry, the pizza was cold, so I stuck it in the microwave. Let me get it."

"Great. What're you doing with your mom?"

"Nothing. I wanted to get away from campus for a couple of

days. Hide out in White Bear. I'm going to meet a girlfriend up at the mall, I need some shoes and shit."

There were dishes banging around for a moment, the scrape of silverware, then Krause said, "You got that nightgown on. You got on anything underneath it?"

Five seconds later, he said; "Oh. My. God. C'mon, give me another shot. Oh. My. God."

Virgil: "Holy shit, she's taken off her clothes. She did that when I first talked to her; she was flashing Brett and Jerry."

Jerry: "You gonna let me touch?"

"Fuck no. That hasn't changed," Quill said. "Not yet anyway. I mean, Brett . . ." And now she sobbed.

More dishes, and, a moment later, Jerry said, "Good. Hot. What are the green things?"

"Spinach."

"Cool."

"Jerry, I need to ask you something . . ."

"Here we go," Virgil said.

"You didn't . . . I mean, don't take this wrong, okay? . . . You didn't have anything to do with . . . Dad?"

"What!"

"You know, that computer up there. I was thinking about it. It's, like, a hot gaming computer . . ."

Long silence.

Then, "Hey, fuck you, Megan! You think I . . . What the fuck are you taking about?"

"I don't know. Those cops were over here this morning asking me if I knew what Dad was doing with the laptop, they said it was really, really superhot and they wondered what he was running on it. After they left, I thought about it, and I wondered . . . I mean, what if it wasn't what he was running, what if it was just the laptop itself?"

"Oh, for Christ's sakes, Megan. I wouldn't hurt . . . Hey! If you think I killed your old man . . ." Krause was shouting.

"I didn't say that."

"Do you think I killed Brett? Is that what you're thinking?"

"No, no, I didn't think that, Jerry. Brett did it to himself. But I was wondering, you know? I remember when Dad bought that laptop, and you couldn't believe it, looking at the box and everything. Listen, forget I said it."

"I can't forget it. How can I? Fuck you and your pussy. And you can take this fuckin' pizza and stick it up your ass. I'm outta here."

"Jerry," Quill wailed. "C'mon, I didn't mean . . ."

The door slammed, and then they heard Krause banging down the stairs and out. Virgil stepped to the window and saw him stomping down the sidewalk, shoulders hunched. He looked back once, his face either angry or maybe frightened, then turned away and disappeared under the canopies of street-side maples.

Barry said, "Well, that didn't work out as well as it might have."

"Let's go talk with Megan," Trane said.

"Krause could come back," Virgil said. "I still think he's the guy and I don't want him to know this was a setup. Let me make sure we're still tracking the phone so that if he turns back, we'll get a call."

Virgil made the call to the BCA tech and then they went down to Quill's apartment and found her changed into jeans and a light pullover blouse. When she let them in, she walked away to the table, picked up a slice, and said, "Now I know for sure."

Trane: "Know what?"

"Jerry did it. Killed Dad. And probably Brett. I just . . ." She ran out of words.

Virgil: "How do you know?"

She swallowed pizza, and said, "I guess you had to be here. When I popped the question, he was quiet for a long time, and I could see him thinking about what to say. But I could see it on his face: he did it. I've known him for a long time and I could see it."

"That's probably not going to work in court," Trane said.

Barry, the tech, was stripping microphones from the apartment, then packed up the receiver and checked out. Quill said, "You had so many mics here, we could have made a record."

"Could have. Didn't," he said with a smile. "But don't give up. We can try again if we can get him back here."

"I could try to fuck him into saying it," Quill suggested.

"No, no," Trane said. "You saying that could probably get me thrown out of the police department. 'Yeah, Trane got a teenager to fuck the suspect into a confession.' Jesus. I get goose bumps thinking about it."

There were footsteps coming up the stairs as the tech was going down, and they heard him say, "Excuse me," and Quill looked out the door, and said, "Hi, Mom."

Out on the street, shadows cast by the setting sun spreading across the lawns, Virgil said to Trane, "I'm gonna get a steak. I'll see you tomorrow."

"My husband's at a doctors' party," she said, "talking about the lower intestinal tract. And maybe the upper intestinal tract. Telling proctologist jokes . . . Why don't you buy *me* a steak?"

"An Applebee's steak?"

"That's not as classy as it might be, but I'll take it."

They drove separately to the hotel, found a line at the Applebee's, went over to the beer joint—which actually had a name, The Beacon—ordered steaks, and beer for Virgil and wine for Trane while they waited, and talked about the case for a few minutes, what they considered a near miss with Krause. The steaks came, and they'd almost finished them when the BCA tech guy called.

When he identified himself, Virgil blurted, "Jeez, I'm sorry, I forgot—"

"Krause's phone just went dark," the tech guy broke in.

"What?"

"It disappeared."

"Where?"

"He was just turning south on Highway 61 up by White Bear."

"Oh, Jesus." He looked at Trane. "It's Krause. He's going after her."

Trane yanked her phone out of her purse and punched some buttons, and then said, "Ah, no. We told her to turn her phone off. We told her . . . She hasn't turned it back on."

"What's her mom's name?" Virgil asked.

"I . . . I don't know. I doubt it's Quill. I think she remarried . . ."

"We gotta go," Virgil said. "We gotta go."

CHAPTER

TWENTY-SIX

They went together in Virgil's truck, lights and siren. Virgil took three seconds to dig his Glock out of the backseat gun safe. "I might need this, God help me."

Trane was on her cell, trying to track down Quill's mother's name, without luck. Virgil was on his own hands-free phone, talking with the BCA tech guy.

"We might have a desperate situation here. If we can't track Krause, we've got to see if we can locate a Megan Quill. I have her phone number but I don't know which service."

"I'll find her."

"Gotta be fast. Gotta go, man."

"Where're you going, where're you going?" Trane snapped at Virgil, pulling her face away from her phone. "You're going the wrong way."

Virgil said, "I'm not taking city streets. Even with the lights, they'll be slower. I'm going over on 94 and then up 35E."

Trane said, "Okay, I see . . . Go! . . . Go! . . . I can't get anybody to tell me her mother's name. It must be somewhere."

"St. Thomas probably has it."

Virgil fought his way out to I-94 and sped east toward St. Paul as Trane, who tried to talk to somebody at St. Thomas, wound up shouting, "So I'll have the fuckin' nine-one-one operator call you. Jesus, this is . . ."

She hung up, called 911, identified herself, explained the situation, and gave the operator the number for the woman she had spoken to at St. Thomas. The operator said she'd call back after she talked with St. Thomas.

Virgil was trying to drive fast and thumb-dial his car phone, got it done, talked to the BCA duty officer. "Call the Faribault cops and have them check the house of one Connie Krause. If she's home, check to see if her son has her car and, if so, the make, model, and license. This is an emergency. We need the information as fast as we can get it."

Virgil got stuck behind a pair of cars pacing each other side by side at exactly fifty-five miles an hour. He got the truck's bumper a foot behind the Prius's in the fast lane and laid on the horn in case the idiot didn't hear the siren or see the flashing lights, and the Prius reluctantly sped up and moved over, and Virgil hammered on by, and Trane, clutching her phone, said, "I've never driven a hundred and ten down I-94 in the middle of the Cities . . . Kinda pretty, the way all the lights blur."

"Where in the hell is nine-one-one? Where in the hell . . ."

He blew past a five-liter Mustang.

Nothing but silence from their phones until Virgil's buzzed, as he turned north on I-35E in St. Paul, and the BCA phone came up, and the tech said, "I've got your girl, but she's not in White Bear Lake. She's moving, she's on Highway 61 going south from White Bear toward 694. She could be with Krause, but I think she's ahead of him."

"Stay on her. We're just north of 94, heading north on 35E, and we should run into her if she keeps coming south."

"Yeah, she's coming up to the intersection of 61 and 694. If she heads your way . . ." A minute later, the tech said, "No, she's turned east on 694. She's going away from you. She moving pretty fast . . . Got a heavy foot."

Trane's phone buzzed, and the 911 operator came up. "Quill's mother's name is Trixie Hahn. I have her home and cell phone numbers."

Trane called Hahn's cell phone. She answered after a few seconds, and Trane identified herself, and said, "We're trying to find Megan. We think she might be in danger. Do you know where she's going?"

Hahn, sounding frightened: "She's meeting a friend at the Maplewood Mall. What happened? Why—"

"We think a man who she believes is a friend might pose a danger. We're tracking her phone, though it's turned off. We can see her going east on 694."

"Yes! She's going to the mall. The Maplewood Mall. She's meeting Kaitlin Chambers there, Kaitlin's a friend from way back in kindergarten."

"She's driving your car?"

"Yes."

"Give me a description, please."

"It's a one-year-old green Subaru Forester, sort of a moss green . . . Wait a minute, I've got the insurance paper, I can get you a license number."

Hahn went away from the phone for a moment, and Virgil asked Trane, "I know where the mall is, but how far do you think we're behind her?"

"Six or eight minutes . . . We're probably ten minutes from the mall. Maybe. Shoot, I don't know, I've only been there, like, twice in my life."

Hahn came back with the license plate number, and Trane thanked her and told her that she'd call back later when she had more information. She punched off Hahn's call and dialed 911 again, and told the operator to contact the Maplewood police to find and stop the Subaru as it approached the mall or in the mall parking lot and to hold and secure Quill.

She called Hahn again. "Do you have a phone number for this Kaitlin, Megan's friend?"

"No, no, I don't."

"Okay . . . We'll check back."

A few minutes later, Virgil rocketed through the intersection of I-35E with I-694, heading east, and Trane, who was now doing something with her phone's map app, said, "We're maybe three or four miles out. Take the White Bear Avenue exit. The mall's right there."

There was traffic, and while it did move aside, they were slowed down anyway. The four miles seemed like they took forever, a bit less than three minutes, before they came off the entrance ramp and charged across the intersection into the mall parking lot. As they did, they got a call from the 911 operator. "We've got Maplewood calling back. They've located Quill's car in the west parking lot."

"We're coming into the west parking lot now," Trane said. "Tell them to turn on their flashers."

A few seconds later, the flashers popped on, and Virgil steered around the aisles of parking slots to the Maplewood police car, where a single cop was standing, and Virgil and Trane piled out of the truck.

Virgil: "Any sign of her?"

The cop shook his head. "No. I spotted the car pretty quick because the door was open. Her purse is inside."

Trane: "Purse?" She turned to Virgil. "He's got her. He grabbed her. He's going to kill her."

Virgil said, "He's probably got his mother's car. He doesn't have one of his own." To the cop, he said, "His mother is Connie, or maybe Constance, Krause, of Faribault."

The Maplewood cop slid back inside his car, and, a moment later, said, "Okay, I got her. I'll get the information out, we'll get all the local departments and the patrol looking for it . . . A 2017 silver Chrysler."

And as they stood there, Virgil took a call from the BCA duty officer, who said, "The Faribault cops checked with Mrs. Krause. Her car is parked outside her house."

Virgil: "Damn! Damn! Now what?"

Trane was inside Quill's car, backed out, and said, "Her phone is gone. She's still got it."

"What?" Virgil went back to the phone tech. "You still see Quill's phone?"

"Yeah. You're right on top of her. I mean, a few blocks. She's not moving now."

"Where? Where is she?"

"Go south on White Bear a couple blocks to Beam Avenue,

take a left. There's a park there. Let me see . . . Maplewood Heights Park—"

"We're right there," the Maplewood cop said. He hustled around his car, and shouted, "C'mon. Follow me!"

Jerry Krause backed the unfamiliar car out of the garage carefully, easing it into the street, watching the nearby houses for anything that looked like an alarm. He didn't see anything. He drove back to Megan Quill's apartment, planning to take her out—at knifepoint, if necessary. He got there just in time to see Quill get in the car with her mother.

He went after them.

He tracked them out to I-94, allowing them to get well ahead in the lane three lanes to his left. The ride to Quill's mother's house in White Bear Lake took half an hour. He'd been there twice. He watched as they left the car in the driveway. Quill had told him that she was meeting a girlfriend to go to the mall. He wasn't sure which mall that was, but he could wait.

The wait wasn't long. At a quarter to seven, Megan Quill walked out of the house and got in the car, backed out of the driveway, and drove past him out toward Highway 61. He followed, down 61, remembering then to cloak his phone with the Faraday bag, and onto I-694 East toward the Maplewood Mall. He'd been to the mall twice, both times with Quill: it was her go-to shopping destination. The possibilities played through his mind; his best bet, he decided, would be to take her in the parking lot.

He could probably kill her there, he thought, if there weren't too many people around. The sight lines at a mall were always broken up by the ranks of cars, especially the taller SUVs and pickups. Quill had to die, but her death wasn't the only thing he wanted.

Krause moved closer, as she got off the highway at White Bear Avenue and drove into the crowded parking lot. He took the X-Acto knife out of his pocket; it had a cylindrical cover on the blade, and he pulled it off and dropped it on the passenger seat.

Quill slowed to a creeping pace, looking down the rows of parked cars for an empty space. When she spotted one, she rolled down the aisle, with Krause thirty feet behind her. She pulled into the empty slot, with a pickup on the mall side and an SUV on the other, and Krause stopped behind her car, blocking the view of his driver's side with the SUV.

He picked up the X-Acto knife and popped his door, and when he saw the door of Quill's car opening, he rushed it. She was still turning out of the driver's seat and didn't see Krause until he grabbed her hair, yanked her out of the car. She screamed, but not loud enough to attract attention—they were, at best, a hundred yards from the mall's entrance—and he forced her to the ground and held the X-Acto knife in front of her eyes.

"We're going for a drive," he said. "If you scream or fight me, I swear to God I'll cut your fuckin' face off."

"Jerry—"

"Shut up!" He dragged her by the hair, and she half screamed again, and tried to scrabble along behind him. He turned the corner at the front of the SUV and pushed her into the driver's seat, then climbed in behind her and shoved her shoulders, forcing her over the center console, and said, "On the floor. On the fuckin' floor!"

She dropped to the floor. He let go of her hair long enough to switch the X-Acto knife to his right hand, now in front of her forehead where she could still see it, then quickly shifted the car into drive and started out of the parking lot.

"What are you doing?" Quill asked. She began to cry. "Why are you doing this?"

"You're gonna tell the cops that you think I killed Brett. I can't let you do that."

"Did you?"

"Yeah, but I can't let you tell."

"You killed Brett?"

"He came busting into my room and saw me with the laptop. Nothing I could do about it. I told him I took it from your dad's house when I heard he'd been killed. I said, 'Why shouldn't I get it if he's never going to use it again?' He said you told him the cops said the computer was stolen at the library and that the killer stole it. He said he'd talk to you in the morning. I couldn't let him do that. I knew he was going out for some heroin that night, and he always slept for a long time when he did that. I also knew he usually got two or three hits at the same time, so, if he died in his sleep, it's not like he couldn't have overdosed—"

"Jerry, you killed your best friend—"

"—who was going to turn me in to the cops," Krause said. "For murder. For an accident."

They were out of the parking lot and around the corner in the park. There were some dog people there with lights around their necks, and Jerry took the SUV up on the walking path and around the lake.

"You're going to kill me, aren't you?"

"Maybe, maybe not. One thing I'm going to do first is finally get in your pussy. And I'm gonna like it."

"I won't tell anybody."

"You might be lying."

"DNA."

"Got that covered."

He stopped the truck and grabbed her hair. "Come up out of there. Come across that console." He popped the truck door and began dragging her out, and she was crying and half screaming, and he wrestled her out of the car, and she flopped onto the ground.

"Please don't do this. Please!"

Virgil and Trane, in Virgil's truck, slewed out of the parking lot behind the Maplewood cop. They ran fast through traffic a couple blocks, cornered left around a Walgreens, went another block to a left turn into an empty parking next to a basketball court. Just off the court, a half dozen people were throwing Frisbees in the twilight, with a half dozen dogs running around them, both dogs and people with multicolored lights around their necks, chasing down lighted disks.

Virgil got back to the BCA phone guy, who said, "I still see her phone, on the north side of the park."

"No time to fuck around," Virgil said to Trane. He shouted at the Maplewood cop, "We're taking the trail. See if you can get more cops up here. Go around the other direction. Her phone is here in the park, but on the other side."

The cop yelled back, "The trail goes around a lake."

A hard-surfaced walking trail, wide enough for a car, went both left and right past the parking lot. Virgil went right, toward the people with the dogs. He stopped when he got to them. Trane rolled her window down, and shouted, "Did a car just take the trail?"

"Yeah, a black SUV," said a thin, bearded man. His dog woofed a couple of times as the man pointed farther to the right. "He went around the lake. We wondered—"

Virgil didn't wait to hear any more, instead hammered the accelerator, leaving the dog people looking after them. The trail was perhaps ten feet wide and circled to the left. Clumps of trees, half visible in the growing darkness, dotted the banks of the small lake, and they were halfway around when they saw a black SUV pulled into the trees along the north shore.

Virgil: "That's one of Quill's cars. He took the Mercedes."

Trane said, "Huh," pulled her pistol, and pointed with her free hand. "Put me there, right next to the car."

Virgil swerved off the trail onto the grass, aiming at the Mercedes. The car appeared to be empty, the offside door open, interior lights on, nobody on the close side. Trane popped her door, and when Virgil hit the brakes, she was out and running toward the black car. Virgil was out right behind her, running, and when Trane went left around the back of the truck, he went right.

Quill was on her back in the weeds, Krause standing over her with the X-Acto knife in his hand, when a truck came barreling around the lake and hit them with its headlights. Had to be cops, Krause thought. He was fucked.

He grabbed Quill by the hair and physically lifted her off the ground, Quill screaming and struggling to get away. A handful of hair ripped out, but he grabbed another handful, yanked open the car door, and backed up until his butt was pressing against the driver's seat. Margaret Trane rushed around one side of the Mercedes, gun in hand, and he jerked Quill's head back between Trane and himself, and shouted, "I got a razor. On her neck. I'll fuckin' slice her open."

Virgil Flowers came around the front of the truck, also with a gun, but he'd be shooting through the window, and he slid sideways until he could see enough to shoot around the edge of the door. Flowers shouted, "Give it up, Jerry. C'mon, man, you don't want to hurt her. She's your friend."

Quill shouted, "He killed Brett, he told me."

Krause shouted, "Shut up!" and sliced Quill's face from her hairline next to her ear down to her jawline. Blood poured out of the wound and down her neck, and she began screaming and frantically slapping at her face.

Trane shouted, "I'm taking the shot," and she edged in closer, gun up in a two-handed grip, but Krause, still holding Quill's hair, bent her head back far enough to cover himself, and shouted back, "I've got the razor on her artery. I'll cut her throat. Back up in one, two, three, or I'll cut her. And who gives a shit if you kill me? Nobody gives a shit about me anyway."

He had the X-Acto knife on Quill's throat to the left of center. He shouted, "One . . ."

Virgil backed away, "Okay, Jerry. Man, take it easy, we're backing up, we're backing up, let's talk it out. Nobody has to get hurt." He sounded a little stupid to himself, with the blood gushing out of Quill's face, but he shouted it again. "Nobody has to get hurt . . ."

"We're going in the car," Krause shouted. He boosted himself backwards into the car, onto the driver's seat, now his head was behind the B pillar, from Trane's perspective: she had no shot. Krause pulled Quill after him, the knife jabbing her in the throat, and he screamed, "Up, up, up," until she was on his lap, and he reached past her for the door handle and slammed the door. "Crawl," he shouted at Quill. "Get out of my way. Crawl, or I'll cut your fuckin' throat. Crawl. Get over there!"

She crawled over him, screaming, weeping, her face and neck and hands covered with the blood streaming from the cut on her face. Krause squeezed himself down in the car seat, pushed the starter button, put the truck in gear, and accelerated toward the walking track, then left, then out on an intersecting track to the north. The track eventually merged with an actual street that ran between suburban houses.

Virgil and Trane were a hundred feet behind, and Trane was on her phone to the Maplewood cops. More cops were coming in, but Krause drove out to the end of the street, took a hard left, and, seconds later, a hard right back onto White Bear Avenue. Virgil held close behind, focused on driving, as Trane shouted into her phone. Virgil hit his grille lights and the siren, as much to warn off other drivers as anything else, as Krause bulled his way through mall traffic and then past Mattress Firm and Verizon stores and, with a hard right, onto the I-694 eastbound ramp.

Trane said, "We got cops coming from everywhere. We've got a highway patrol trooper coming up behind us. I can see him. He's motoring—"

"If Krause jumps on the gas," Virgil said, "I can't stay with him. He's probably got an extra twenty miles an hour on me."

"The trooper can stay with them. The nine-one-one guy's got everybody up to date on the situation. Goddamnit, I should have taken the shot. I had an opening, but he was jerking her head around."

"You did right . . . You did right . . ."

Virgil saw the highway patrol car coming up behind him and he moved right to let it pass. The Tahoe was doing the best it could, but it topped out at a hundred and ten, and Krause was probably doing close to a hundred and twenty, weaving through the traffic.

"What's the trooper doing, do you think?"

"Dunno. But they're generally pretty crazy motherfuckers."

The trooper was probably moving five miles an hour faster than Krause. And Krause, who had the Mercedes in the right lane, saw him coming in the left wing mirror. He had the pedal to the floor, and the Mercedes had topped out, and then the trooper was even with him. Krause couldn't see the cop's face because he was sitting higher, and then the highway patrol car began edging right until the two speeding vehicles were only two or three inches apart, and Krause shouted, "Jesus," and the patrol car scraped the side of the Mercedes, pushing it toward the shallow ditch on the right side of the road.

Krause hit the brakes, but the patrolman had anticipated that and stayed with him, came back and bounced against him again, fender to fender. Quill had sunk down off the passenger seat, into the footwell again, holding her hands to her bloody face, sobbing in fear. When the cop hit the Mercedes the second time, Krause said, "Shit!" and the car's right wheels went off the main lane and began rattling over gravel and roadside debris. Then, with a third hit, the right-side wheels ran off the road entirely and began bouncing over the unpaved roadside rocks and dirt.

Krause hit the brakes again, bringing his speed down—sixty, fifty, forty—as he struggled for control. He yanked the wheel to the left, trying to knock the patrolman off, but the cop was ready for that and swerved left and came back and gave the Mercedes another whack.

Krause, who'd been holding the X-Acto knife in his right hand, dropped it and grabbed the steering wheel with both hands, struggling to hold the heavy SUV in a straight line. Quill saw the knife as it dropped, and, after a second, when Krause turned his head away from her and toward the highway patrol car, she groped for it on the floor, found the thin aluminum shaft, figured out which end held the blade, pushed herself up with her left hand and with the X-Acto in her right, stuck the blade deep into Krause's right eye.

Krause screamed and grabbed the shaft of the knife. Quill fell back, and the truck went right, Krause heavy on the brakes, down into the ditch, sideways for a few dozen yards, up the other side, where it crashed into a chain-link fence and stopped. When it hit the fence, the driver's side air bags blew into Krause's face, knocking him back.

Virgil had caught the Mercedes, as it had slowed in the chain of side-by-side collisions, and he pulled onto the shoulder of the highway, as the Mercedes went into the ditch, and braked hard. Then both he and Trane were out and running, Trane shouting into her cell phone, a gun in her free hand. Virgil got to the Mercedes first, the passenger side. He yanked open the door, saw Quill on the floor, and grabbed her by the shoulders, and pulled her out of the truck.

Trane ran around to the driver's side as Krause lurched out of the truck, clutching the X-Acto. Trane shouted, "Drop the knife, drop the knife," and Krause, bleeding heavily from his eye, took a step toward her, lifting the knife, and Trane shot him.

Virgil jumped at the gunshot, then shouted at Trane, "What happened?"

"Krause is down," she shouted back.

Virgil: "Megan's bleeding, I gotta get my kit . . ."

He ran up the bank, popped the door, and got his medical kit, pressure bandages, ran back down, ripping the covers off the bandages, knelt beside Quill, and pressed one of the bandages hard to her face. He said, "You're gonna be all right, honey."

The highway patrolman, who had stopped forty or fifty yards up the road, now ran down the bank, gun in hand, covering Krause, who lay on the far side of the Mercedes, weeping and bleeding. Trane had shot him in the hip.

The highway patrolman said, in a calm, conversational voice as he holstered his pistol, "Ambulances on the way. Have been for a while. I figured it'd end in a ditch."

Trane, out of breath, told herself to be cool. She began to slow down, watching over Krause, noticed only one queer thing about the scene that would stick in her mind forever: the highway patrolman was smiling, and, after a few seconds, began quietly laughing, then he turned away, seemingly unable to stop. She thought later it might have been stress, and even later, that he might have simply been happy.

Crazy motherfucker.

The first ambulance arrived three minutes later with the paramedics.

TWENTY-SEVEN

The ambulances took both of the wounded to Regions Hospital in St. Paul, not the closest facility but the closest Level 1 trauma center. Virgil and Trane followed, after Virgil called the BCA Crime Scene people and talked them through the three crime scenes that they knew about: the Maplewood Mall, the park, and the final crash. The Maplewood cops had frozen all three and would hold them tight for the Crime Scene crews.

By the time they got to the hospital, both Krause and Quill were in surgery. Krause was in the hospital's main trauma OR, suffering from the wound to his right eye—that would be permanently blinded, the eyeball having been destroyed by the X-Acto knife—and from the hip wound. Trane's bullet had destroyed the ball joint, and he would need hip replacement. He had taken two units of blood by the time Virgil and Trane arrived.

"I'm glad I didn't kill him," Trane said, as they drove into St. Paul. The paramedics had told her when they picked up Krause that'd he'd mostly likely survive. "I didn't even want to shoot, but he looked like a zombie and he had that knife, I simply reacted . . . I dunno . . ."

"No cop in the state of Minnesota would say you overreacted," Virgil said. "A guy *that* close to you, with a razor knife, who'd already slashed open another victim? No problem. I'm amazed that you didn't give him three Speer Gold Dots in the breadbasket, as another young woman suggested she'd do if attacked."

"I don't use Speer Gold Dots," Trane mumbled, looking out the window. "I hope I didn't hit him in the Oompa Loompas."

She hadn't, but she was still shocked by the shooting. When she was talking to one of the docs at Regions, Virgil called Minneapolis Homicide, got Trane's husband's cell phone number, then called him and explained the situation. "She's okay, but she might need a little tender loving care over the next few days," Virgil said.

"Thanks for calling . . . fuckin' Flowers."

Quill had been taken to another surgical suite, where a plastic surgeon spent three hours closing her wound, as her mother waited, often crying, outside. When the surgeon came out, she told Quill's mother that "this won't look good when you see it, it's still too raw. But the cut was very clean, even though it was fairly deep. In a couple of years, you won't be able to see the scar unless you stand right next to her and look for it. If she uses any makeup at all, it'll be invisible. It'll be no worse than the scars left by face-lifts."

Virgil called Frankie, and told her that he wouldn't be home that night and would probably have to work through Sunday.

"We've got him, but we've got a lot of details to lock down. A lot of details."

He told her about the chase and shooting.

"We're fine here," Frankie said. "I don't want you taking any more assignments up there, though. Those Cities are a dangerous place."

"Probably less dangerous than driving our tractor around," Virgil said. "I'll call you late tonight, and we'll talk."

Later that evening, Trane got a search warrant, and, with a Crime Scene crew, they broke into Krause's off-campus apartment, which was in an aging brick apartment building a mile or so from St. Thomas. They found Barth Quill's laptop computer hidden under a board in a closet with old shoes piled on top. One of the Crime Scene people looked at a sharp corner of the laptop with a Sherlock Holmes style magnifying glass, and said, "I don't think he got all the blood out of the seam."

They also found a box of blank CDs and a CD recorder that could be attached to Krause's Mac laptop. The blanks were identical to the one found in Barth Quill's CD player.

"We should have suspected that all those clues we were getting were phony," Virgil said. "Everybody said that Quill never used cocaine. He led us around by our noses. That China White bullshit, I'm sure he planted the CD. He took Quill's keys when he killed him. Probably threw the car's keys in the river but kept the house's. After that, he had access to this house."

In addition to the laptop, they found a coin collector's book filled with gold American coins going back to the nineteenth century. "Darian Seebold Quill" was written on the cover flap.

Trane called Nancy Quill, who said that Darian S. Quill was Barth's father. Krause had apparently stolen them from the house. Trane would have them evaluated the following week, and a Minneapolis coin dealer suggested they'd be worth around a hundred and fifty thousand dollars.

On Sunday, the day after the chase and arrest, Virgil stopped at Regions and visited both with Quill and Terry Foster. Quill was still in shock, her face heavily bandaged. The first thing she said when Virgil walked in was, "They say I'll be okay."

"That's what everybody tells me, too," Virgil said. "In a couple of years, there'll be no sign of a scar. You might have some scary psychological after-effects for a while, but, in my experience, those will fade away."

"That Jerry . . . I guess he's here in the hospital."

"Yes. He's hurt a lot worse than you are. And he'll be going away to prison for years. Jerry's psychotic."

"He's crazy."

"Yeah. I would have seen it sooner, if I'd been around him more," Virgil said. "I feel really stupid for not seeing the computer for what it was: a heavy-duty game machine. I kept thinking about what it might contain, the files, and about what your father might be doing on it."

"I already miss Dad," Quill said. She sniffed. "He was such a hard-ass. And our history . . . wasn't good . . ."

"A hard-ass, but not a bad guy," Virgil said. "A good guy, in fact."

"All he thought about was medicine," Quill said. "He was so into it. Now, I've been talking with the surgeon who put my face back together. It's interesting. *She's* interesting. She has some amazing stories."

Virgil nodded. "Think about all of that. You've lost a couple of friends, but maybe when you spend some time thinking about it, you'll find that they were less interesting than they seemed. You won't believe me, but you've still got a lot of kid stuff to get out of your head. Sex is everywhere—that's why there are seven billion people in the world. Sex isn't hard, fooling around isn't hard, experimenting with dope isn't hard. Medicine is hard."

"I will think about it," she said. "I don't have the grades for it right now, but I could get there. School isn't hard, but I have to get to it if I'm going to do it."

Virgil patted her foot. "Then get to it."

When he visited Foster, the ex-soldier said, "Professor Green dropped in. You missed her by ten minutes. She told me. You got the guy."

"He's the guy who jumped you," Virgil said. "A nutjob. He could come after you again, but you'll be at least sixty by then."

"Glad you got him," Foster said. "For the explanation, as much as anything."

Virgil asked, "What about you? You're lying here thinking all day. Are you going to try the Army again?"

"We'll see what happens. I'll be in school for another year at least, that'll get me to the all-but-the-thesis point with my Ph.D. I could finish it on active duty. But, uh, Katherine—Professor Green—gave me a little peck on the forehead when she left. She said she was looking forward to getting me back in class, volunteered to bring course work around to me as long as I'm in here."

"Hmm."

"You took the hmm right out of my mouth," Foster said.

Between chores, Virgil spoke with Genevieve O'Hara and told her about the Surface Research arrests and that the company's CEO might want to talk with her about seeing Boyd Nash in the library. "He's trying to nail down every aspect of the case. The idea that Nash may have been involved in other activities would help make that point. I'm sure he's going to be calling you."

"I'll still be there, in the library. And Virgil? Thank you."

"For what?"

"I think you know for what."

Virgil encountered Harry, the beer drinker, when he stayed over Saturday night. Virgil walked into the bar, and Harry asked, "You get him?"

"Yup."

"Hey, congratulations." He flagged down Alice, said, "Give him another bottle of cow piss. He got the killer." To Virgil: "He was a kid, right? I want to hear the whole story."

"No, he was a grown adult," Virgil said.

"The way you said that makes me suspicious," Harry said. "How old was he in years?"

"Not certain yet."

"Was he going to high school or college?"

"Maybe," Virgil said.

"Ha! He's a kid," Harry said to Alice. "I was right. Had you met him before?"

"Only briefly," Virgil said. "Not really long enough to make much of an impression."

"Ha! You *did* meet him. He was part of the cast, like I said," Harry crowed. "With that kind of insight, I should have been a cop. Or a psychiatrist. Anything but a McDonald's owner."

"Maybe a bartender," Virgil said. "You want another one? To celebrate your insight?"

"Sure."

"That'd be five," Alice said. "I dunno."

Harry shook a finger at her. "'There are strange things done in the midnight sun / By the men who moil for gold.'"

"Oh, no," she said.

Virgil: "Go for it, man."

The governor called Virgil early on Sunday morning. "I just heard from Bunny Quill, and she told me you got the killer. I wanted to thank you personally. I would even suggest you might apply for a spot on my personal protection detail."

"Ah, thank you, but no, I have a farm to tend, Governor, and I . . ." He was tap-dancing at a ferocious rate and managed to stave the man off.

Dipshit.

When he got off the phone with the governor, he called Davenport, who was still in bed, and asked him to tip off his media connections about the chase and the arrest. "Emphasize that Margaret Tranc shot Krause when he got out of the car with a knife and was about to attack her. Get some cameras over to her house."

"I can do that."

Trane called two hours later. "Did you have anything to do with the crowd of TV assholes that turned up on my lawn an hour ago?"

"Mmm, maybe."

"We had a nice talk," she said. "Virgil, thank you. I'd like to find a more substantial way to thank you."

"I'm open to that as long as it doesn't involve sex," Virgil said. "I'm already committed."

"You know, you're not always as funny as you think you are," Trane said.

Virgil said, "Okay. When I get my ass in trouble down south, I may give you a ring. Get some cow manure on your Louboutins."

"I'll look forward to it," she said.

Krause would get a public defender, who eventually suggested, after several long interviews, that his client would plead guilty to a second degree murder charge in the death of Quill. He said that Krause denied killing Brett Renborne and had an excellent alibi: he'd been in Faribault without a car.

Krause, he said, had been misunderstood by Megan Quill: he'd never told her that he'd killed Renborne, she had imagined it in her fear. The kidnapping, he said, had essentially been a domestic fight between friends.

None of it would wash, Trane told Virgil in a phone call, but he might evade doing a full thirty years in prison, without parole, the minimum sentence for a first degree murder charge in Minnesota. "If the state takes the second degree plea and kidnapping, served concurrently, he could get thirty years, but without doing the mandatory full term of a first degree conviction. He could be out in twenty or so."

"What's the county attorney thinking?"

"I think they're thinking they'll drag along for a while. After the press gets back to worrying about movie stars and their love lives, they'll try to sneak through the deal. His public defender is a good one: he knows every rope there is."

"Well, at least the asshole got shot and stabbed in the eye," Virgil said.

"There you are, brother."

Katherine Green called, and asked Virgil if he thought Trane might participate in a longitudinal study of policewomen who have shot criminal suspects. Virgil said he had no idea. "Give her a call. Who knows? Could be interesting."

"That's what I was thinking," Green said. "Interesting."

Virgil made it out of Minneapolis late Sunday night, arriving at the farm at eleven o'clock. Sam got out of bed to meet him, and Virgil and Sam and Frankie had warm rhubarb pie and vanilla ice cream in the kitchen.

When Sam was back in bed, and Virgil's clothes were in the wash, he and Frankie went up to the bedroom. They lay awake in the dark for a while, talking about the case, and then Frankie said, "So, I needed to get a yellow highlighter pen. I couldn't find one downstairs, but you've always got a bunch of them. I stuck my nose in your desk—honest, I was looking for a highlighter—and I found the novel."

Virgil didn't know exactly what to say. "An experiment," he said finally. "I don't know what I'm doing yet. I'm trying some things out."

"It's good," she said. "I'm not lying. It pulled me right in. Virgil, you've got to run with this. You've got to."

"You think so?"

She rolled over so she was hovering over his face. "It could be a whole new chapter, sweetie."

He nodded in the dark. "Okay, then. That's what I'll do, Frank. I'll run with it."

NEON PREY

At first, Clayton Deese seems like your run-of-the-mill
criminal – a gun for hire that keeps the boss from the cops.
But after he skips bail following a job gone wrong, the
U.S. Marshals see that he could be the key to
the whole operation's undoing.

As marshals begin the search of Deese's place, they find
something far darker than they ever expected. There are
countless graves lining the back of the house, trophies from a
score of killings. Deese may have seemed small-time but the
evidence says otherwise – they are dealing with a
frenzied and prolific serial killer.

Now Lucas Davenport must find him – after all, that's
what he does best. But Deese is ruthless, has an endless
network of allies and – as Davenport will come
to find – he is also full of surprises . . .

SIMON &
SCHUSTER

TWISTED PREY

Lucas Davenport had crossed paths with her before.
A rich psychopath, Taryn Grant had run successfully for
the U.S. Senate, where Lucas had predicted she'd fit right in.
He was also convinced that she'd been responsible for three
murders, though he'd never been able to prove it. Once
a psychopath had gotten that kind of rush, though,
he or she often needed another fix, so he figured
he might be seeing her again.

He was right. A federal marshal now, with a
very wide scope of investigation, he's heard rumours
that Grant has found her seat on the Senate intelligence
committee, and the contacts she's made from it, to be very
useful. Pinning those rumours down is likely to be just as
difficult as before, and considerably more dangerous.

But they have unfinished business, he and Grant. One way or
the other, he is going to see it through to the end.

SIMON &
SCHUSTER

HOLY GHOST

A Virgil Flowers thriller

Pinion, Minnesota: a huge city of all of seven hundred
folks who define the phrase 'small town'. Nothing has ever
happened in Pinion and nothing ever will . . . until the mayor
of sorts (campaign promise: 'I'll Do What I Can') comes
up with a scheme to put Pinion on the map.

He's heard of a place where a floating image of the
Virgin Mary turned the whole town into a shrine, attracting
thousands of curious people and making the townsfolk
rich overnight. Why not stage a prank in Pinion and do
the same? No one gets hurt and everyone gets rich.
What could go wrong?

And then a dead body shows up. It turns out
that lots can go wrong with a get-rich-quick
scheme like this one . . . and lots will.

It'll take everything Virgil Flowers has to put
things to rights – before someone else dies.

SIMON &
SCHUSTER

GOLDEN PREY

Lucas Davenport has a job with the U.S. Marshals Service – an unusual one. He gets to pick his own cases, whatever they are, and follow wherever they lead him.

And where they've led him this time is into real trouble. A house at the centre of a drug-smuggling ring is attacked and briefcases full of cash are stolen. But whoever took the money left something behind: five bodies, including that of a six-year-old girl. Davenport vows to track down the cash and find the killers. But he's not the only one on the hunt . . . the drug smugglers want their money back, and they've sent two assassins, including an infamous torturer known for her creative use of home-improvement tools, after Davenport.

It'll take every ounce of Davenport's predatory instinct to track down the killers and money before he becomes the prey.

SIMON &
SCHUSTER